THE CAMELOT
BETRAYAL

ALSO BY KIERSTEN WHITE

THE CAMELOT
BETRAYAL

A CAMELOT RISING NOVEL

KIERSTEN WHITE

EMBER

To eighteen-year-old me, for choosing right.
And to my husband, for letting me choose him.

Text copyright © 2020 by Kiersten Brazier
Cover art copyright © 2020 by Alex Dos Diaz

All rights reserved. Published in the United States by Ember, an imprint of Random House Children's Books, a division of Penguin Random House LLC, New York. Originally published in hardcover in the United States by Delacorte Press, an imprint of Random House Children's Books, a division of Penguin Random House LLC, New York, in 2020.

Ember and the E colophon are registered trademarks of Penguin Random House LLC.

GetUnderlined.com

Educators and librarians, for a variety of teaching tools, visit us at RHTeachersLibrarians.com

The Library of Congress has cataloged the hardcover edition of this work as follows:
Names: White, Kiersten, author.
Title: The Guinevere deception / Kiersten White.
Description: New York : Delacorte Press, [2019] | Summary: Sent by a banished Merlin to protect King Arthur, a sixteen-year-old impersonating the deceased Guinevere struggles to fit in at Camelot where the magic she practices is banished.
Identifiers: LCCN 2018041028 (print) | LCCN 2018047967 (ebook) | ISBN 978-0-525-58169-7 (ebook) | ISBN 978-0-525-58167-3 (hc : alk. paper) | ISBN 978-0-525-58168-0 (glb : alk. paper)
Subjects: | CYAC: Characters in literature—Fiction. | Guinevere, Queen (Legendary character)—Fiction. | Magic—Fiction. | Impersonation—Fiction. | Arthur, King—Fiction. | Knights and knighthood—Fiction. | Camelot (Legendary place)—Fiction. | Fantasy.
Classification: LCC PZ7.W583764 (ebook) | LCC PZ7.W583764 Gui 2019 (print) |

DDC [Fic]—dc23

ISBN 978-0-525-58174-1 (pbk.)

Printed in the United States of America
10 9 8 7 6 5 4 3 2 1
First Ember Edition 2021

CHAPTER ONE

Guinevere's room was dark, night more a cloak than the bed curtains she never drew. The dream clung like smoke, so real that she expected to find the surrounding stone newly carved and running with water.

She put a trembling hand to the wall behind her, fingers curled by dread that she would find the carvings there, fresh and recognizable. But they were only hints of memories beneath her fingers. The castle was as it had been since she arrived: ancient and worn with the passage of unknowable time.

Yet she could not escape the feel of that fall, air rushing around her, knowing what would meet her at the bottom. She climbed out of bed and pulled on her robe. Brangien shifted softly in the corner, lost in her own dreams with her beloved Isolde. Listening to her, Guinevere realized a horrible truth.

She should not be able to dream at all.

She had used knot magic to give all her dreams to Brangien for weeks now. Ever since her captivity at the hands of Maleagant, ever since Merlin had pushed her out of the dreamspace that connected them, ever since she was tricked by Mordred into giving the fairy Dark Queen physical form once more, ever since she chose to return to Camelot instead of escaping—no, not escaping, *running away*— with Mordred, she had had no desire to dream. Which meant that whatever dream she just had . . . it was not her own.

As she hurried through the night-black secret passage against the mountain that connected her room to Arthur's, she folded her arms around herself, unwilling to touch the stone again. Distrustful of it. She was awake enough now to check that every knot she was connected to was still in place. The knot on the door to the secret tunnel entrance into Camelot that only she, Arthur, and Mordred knew about. The knot on her own door, her own windows, every way that the fairy queen—or her grandson, Mordred—might access Guinevere.

Nothing. Everything was as she had left it, all protections in place. Which terrified her even more.

She opened the door to Arthur's room and drew aside the tapestry. She half expected him to be sitting at his table, writing letters or reading them, his candle merely a pool of wax and a flickering wick. That was how she found him most nights. But his room was dark.

"Arthur?" she whispered, moving toward his bed. There was a rustle of blankets, and then quick movements and the telltale hiss of a sword being unsheathed—along with the swirling sickness and overwhelming dread that hit her whenever she was near Excalibur.

"Put it away!" she gasped.

"Guinevere?"

She could not hear over the pounding in her ears, but she could *feel* as soon as Excalibur was once again in its sheath. She tripped against the bed and turned to sit on it. The shaking was coming, violent trembling that no amount of heat could warm away.

"Sorry." Arthur pulled her next to him. He tucked the blankets over them both, holding her close as though he could stop her shaking by his strength alone. "I was not awake. It is always my first response these days, ever since . . ."

He did not finish. Neither of them needed him to. They had both watched the Dark Queen emerge, a creeping nightmare made real with the flesh of a thousand beetles, twisting roots, and Guinevere's own blood. She did not question why Arthur's reaction to being startled awake would be to seize their one true defense against that abomination.

"What did you need?" He brushed her hair from the pillow so that he could lie as close to her as possible.

"I had a dream," she whispered to the darkness. It felt further away, less important now that he was holding her.

"A bad dream?"

"I should not have dreams at all. I knotted them away." She had not told him about what she was doing for Brangien, or why. That was Brangien's secret to keep or to reveal, not Guinevere's. And with magic banned in Camelot, she would not risk her friend's safety.

Arthur *hmm*ed thoughtfully. They were so close that she could feel the vibrations in his chest. "Perhaps the knot came undone? Maybe you did not do the magic right?"

"Maybe." Guinevere wanted to agree. It would be easier, safer, simpler if that were the case. But she did not think it was. There had been something so visceral about the dream. It was a dream with purpose, a dream with intent. And it had not been her own dream, of that she was certain. But . . . *could* she be certain? Her mind had been tampered with—holes created and holes filled by Merlin, whether or not he meant to. How could she say what her mind would dream?

"Do you ever feel like you do not know yourself?" she whispered.

Arthur was quiet for a long time. Finally, he answered, his voice gentle. "No. Though there are parts of myself I wish I did not have to know. Why? Do you feel that way?"

"All the time."

Arthur settled, one arm around her, his hand next to her head, stroking her hair. The fight had left his body and she could feel him moving back toward sleep. Arthur was ready at a moment's notice to face any threat, but he was also very good at accepting a threat was not there and releasing whatever was coiled to strike. She envied that ability. She had constant tension from her magic knotted into the rooms and surrounding city, and even if that had not been the case, she found herself perpetually mulling over the figurative knots of her life and her choices, checking for weaknesses, for where she could have done better.

"This is a problem I can help with," Arthur said. "I know you very well. You are kind. You are clever. You have far more a sense of humor than any princess could."

"But I am not a princess."

"No, but you are a queen." She could hear his smile. His arm around her was comfortingly heavy, her trembling almost past. "You are strong. You are brave. You are quite short."

She laughed, poking him in the side. "That is not a character trait."

"No? Hmm."

She felt him drifting further away, back to sleep.

"You are Guinevere," he murmured, and then his breathing went soft and even.

She wished with a ferocious longing that any of it were true.

CHAPTER TWO

It had been a long summer, and autumn was only beginning to appear with a hint of chill in the evenings and the promise of work to come. Guinevere understood things like harvests now, how much went into them, how vital they were. A good harvest was the difference between a comfortable winter and a deadly one. With a city as large as Camelot, already they were preparing. As queen, she had taken over Mordred's role in keeping track of supplies and making certain everything was ready. And riding all over the countryside taking stock of the harvest and speaking with farmers gave her an excuse to search for evidence of the Dark Queen's seeping reach.

Guinevere had wards set in Camelot; she would know if a threat arrived on their shores. But she wanted to know long before then. She would not be caught off guard. No one would trick her, ever again.

"Should we check the perimeter of the forest?" Lancelot asked. They had just finished with one of the farthest tracts of land. Guinevere was hot and itchy in her dress, layers of bold blue and red. She envied Brangien her simpler clothing. But Guinevere was out here as the queen, and she had to look the part. Lancelot, too, looked the part. Her armor was no longer patchwork. She wore uniform leather with metal plates over chain mail and a tunic with Arthur's sigil on it. Guinevere missed Lancelot's old armor, though she was glad Lancelot no longer had to wear a mask.

Brangien looked longingly over her shoulder in the direction of Camelot, but offered no complaint. Only Brangien, Lancelot, and Sir Tristan could accompany Guinevere on these trips. They alone knew that she wielded magic. If word reached anyone else, everything would be at risk.

Arthur rode with them when he could, but it was not often. Guinevere preferred it that way. Though normally she longed for more time with him, the Dark Queen was her fault. Her responsibility.

"Yes." Guinevere guided her horse toward the dark smudge of trees waiting meekly on the edge of the tamed land. Elsewhere the forests loomed and lurked, dominating the countryside. But in Camelot's boundaries the trees had been felled, and where not felled, tamed. They were gentler forests, there to serve man.

Guinevere's sleeves rubbed at her wrists, where she bore thin white tracings of scars from trees that were old and hungry and angry.

"Did you sleep well?" Brangien asked, riding at her side. Her tone was so deliberately even and pleasant that Guinevere immediately knew she was fishing for information. Brangien was never pleasant without a reason. Guinevere had not slept in her own bed, and her friend and maid wanted to know about it.

Alas. As always, sleeping in Arthur's bed had simply been sleeping. Guinevere had awoken to find herself alone. She always woke alone. Sometimes she wondered what would happen if he stayed. If, warm and muddled with sleep, he reached for her in something other than companionship. If they shared a kiss as fierce as the one Mordred had stolen the night Lancelot won her tournament.

"Is that a blush I detect?" Brangien teased.

Guinevere yanked her mind back from where it had wandered. That was the treacherous path that had led her to the fairy queen's meadow. A path with clever smiles and eyes like the pools of green shadow beneath a tree. Mordred had not been the one to abduct her, but he had used her to hurt Arthur. And he had hurt her, too. Guinevere would not forget it. "I will let you know when there is something to blush about," she told Brangien.

Brangien frowned at Guinevere's curt tone, but Guinevere could not explain. "Did you dream with Isolde last night?" she asked instead, remembering her own disturbing dream and Arthur's suggestion that her knot magic giving away her own dreams had failed.

"Yes." This time Brangien blushed, a dreamy smile on her face.

That was not good news. It made Guinevere's odd dream even more puzzling and worrisome. It would need to be addressed, and she hated anticipating how Brangien would take the news. So much of magic was about taking—power, control, even memories—but with Brangien and the dreams Guinevere had been able to *give*.

Guinevere hurried toward the trees, pulling away from her companions. It was a problem for tonight. She did not have to think about it now, not while she was out here. She wanted to reclaim the sense of peace she found in wild lands. Though Camelot was home now, she had grown up in a forest.

Once again her mind halted. *Had* she grown up in a forest? She had mere handfuls of memories, and if her last visit to Merlin was any indication, they were not accurate. The cottage she remembered sweeping was a ruin, uninhabited for decades. How could she have lived in a place that was unlivable?

Lancelot had caught up to her. She was subtle about it, but Guinevere's knight never let her too far out of reach.

"How much do you remember of your childhood?" Guinevere asked.

"My childhood?"

"Your teeth."

"My *teeth*?"

There had been a conversation at a market with Brangien and Mordred. They seemed confused that Guinevere did not remember losing her first teeth to make way for her second teeth. She repressed a shudder at having to once again acknowledge the fact that all children with their tiny pearls of teeth had other, bigger teeth, lurking beneath the surface, waiting to burst free. "When did you lose them?"

Lancelot had a hint of laugh in her voice. "I would imagine at the normal times? My first was before my mother—" Lancelot broke off. Her father had been killed serving Uther Pendragon, Arthur's tyrant father. And while she had never specified how her mother had died, it had driven her to pursue vengeance and then knighthood with singular intensity. "My two front teeth I bashed out falling from a tree. It took quite a while for them to grow in. I had a lisp."

"Were you teased?"

"Never more than once." Lancelot smiled at the memory.

Guinevere envied her both the ability to defend herself even as a child and the memories of those events. She was hungry for a past, for some way to fill the emptiness she found when she tried to excavate her own history from memories. In the magical dream where she had connected herself to Merlin to look for him, walking back through her life, she had hit a certain point and found . . . nothing.

A void. Wiped clean. It did not feel clean, though. It felt like a violation, and filled her with shame. She cleared her throat and continued, wanting Lancelot to talk. To distract her. "Where did you go after you lost your parents? You have never told me much about that."

Lancelot's smile faded and something closed in her face. Lancelot was never dishonest, but there was a hint of evasiveness in the way she changed the subject. "We should focus. What are we looking for in the trees?"

Guinevere pulled her horse to an abrupt stop, dread and an odd sense of triumph warring in her breast as she looked at what should have been an orderly line of trees and found a riot of enormous, twisted oaks, draped with vines that rustled and reached in the dead, windless air. "That," she whispered.

"We should wait for the king." Lancelot eyed the trees warily, sword drawn and held ready. Guinevere did not know whether Lancelot could feel it the way she could—the way the air felt like a breath being held, the sense that if she whipped around fast enough, she would catch the trees moving—but it was clear Lancelot could feel the threat.

They had left their horses outside the forest with Brangien while Sir Tristan dashed madly for Camelot and Arthur.

"I came back to help Arthur in the fight against the Dark Queen. This is that fight." Guinevere crouched, resting a hand against the dirt beneath them. Her fingers dug in. The soil was hard and unbroken, and it compacted beneath her fingernails. A worm wriggled by and brushed her skin.

Not a worm.

Guinevere pressed her searching fingers against a root snaking through the soil—years of growth in mere seconds. At this rate, the forest would overtake the farmland, destroy their crops, and ruin their harvest within days. Maybe even less. If she had not been riding here, who could say how long it would have taken word to reach Camelot?

And the trees could destroy more than just fields. She had left the horses outside of the forest for a reason. She could still hear the screams of Mordred's horse as the roots dragged it beneath the soil of the Dark Queen's meadow.

The screams of the men, too. Though that had been her own work, which made it far worse to remember.

"She is here." Guinevere pulled her hand free of the soil and stood, hoping she had not given herself away. She stared into the depths of the trees, pierced by only the sharpest shafts of light, going on for what could be half a league or two dozen. The growth was so thick it was impossible to tell.

"The Dark Queen is here?"

Guinevere shook her head. She could not know for sure. "Her magic is." She tore her eyes from the impenetrable doom of the forest, resisting the impulse to push in as far and deep as she could. To find that heart of chaos, that heart that her own blood had given shape to.

"Come on." Guinevere turned toward their horses. Lancelot followed. There was no sense of relief as they emerged from the tree line.

Brangien stood, a few body-lengths away, her eyes wide. When they had entered mere minutes ago, she had been at least twice as far from the edge of the trees.

"Did you move?" Guinevere shouted. Brangien shook her head.

Guinevere wasted no time. She reached into the pouch on her belt and pulled out a coiled line of iron thread. It was heavy and cold in her hand, unpleasant to the touch. She could bind the trees, but

they were individual trees. She would have to go down the entire
line, and it stretched on and on. The leaves rustled. The branches
and trunks groaned.

It had to be iron, though. She would not try to influence the trees
directly again. She would bear the scars of their indifference to her
demands for the rest of her days.

But there simply was not enough time to bind iron knots to each
tree. If she was going to bind something, it would have to be—

"The soil," she said to herself, triumphant. She could not stop
every tree from moving, but she could stop what they were moving
through. She dropped to her knees and clawed at the earth, dredging
up the dark loam beneath the fallen leaves and small rocks of the
topsoil. Brangien, braving the proximity to the trees, joined her as
Lancelot stood guard, sword at the ready.

"How deep?" Brangien asked.

"A few more inches. There, that should be good." Guinevere un-
spooled the thread, tying it in a complex knot of binding. It was not
unlike the knots she had attached to every exterior of the castle.
Nothing fueled by magic could pass those barriers. Her idea now
was that by plunging the iron knot into the soil, it would infect the
rest of the soil, making it inhospitable to magic.

That was the hope. She had never tried it before. Pulling out her
iron dagger, an impossibly low note hurting her ears and setting her
teeth on edge as always when she handled it, she cut her bottom lip.

Lancelot let out a hiss of anger. "Let me do it!"

"It has to be my blood." Guinevere pressed the elaborate rings
of the iron knot to her lip, whispering her intent, binding it to the
iron through the iron in her blood. Then she pushed the knot into
the earth and leaned over it, letting the blood from her lip drip down
into the hole, watering the seed of her anti-magic and hoping it
would spread.

Brangien held out a handkerchief and Guinevere took it, holding it to her lip and standing. She could feel the dirt beneath her fingernails, but she could not feel the magic she had performed. Iron took all and gave nothing back. It was an ending. Poison to the natural magic and chaos of the fairy realm, and poison to the Dark Queen.

The trees shuddered, dropping leaves. There was a creaking and groaning noise, as though a terrible wind raced through the woods, threatening to uproot them. But there was no wind. Their branches strained, clawing the sky, and then stopped.

"Is it over? Did we win?" Brangien eyed the trees dubiously. They were no longer advancing, but they were still there.

Guinevere dabbed at her lip, frowning. "We bought time to consider the problem."

"Then can we please move farther away?" Brangien shuddered as she turned her back on the trees and stalked toward the horses. Guinevere did not join her.

"What are you thinking?" Lancelot asked.

"I am thinking about how much land we would have lost if we had not caught this. And wondering how much land we did lose. I am not familiar with this area. For all we know, yesterday it was rolling fields as far as the eye could see."

"I am thinking I should also bring an ax with me on our rides, not just a sword."

Guinevere laughed, reopening the cut on her lip. She pressed the handkerchief to it again. "I wonder how far the binding spread. I connected it to the soil, but what is the reach?" She gazed up and down the line of trees. "We should explore."

"We are not going back in there."

"The perimeter. Not the woods themselves." Though Guinevere had to admit she wanted to do that, too. Iron dagger in hand, stalking the queen that threatened her king. Stalking the queen who had taken Mordred from them, who would take everything if she could.

Guinevere began to inspect the edge of the forest. Several smooth white stones were nestled in her bag—it was not a light bag—and she dropped them every few feet so they could be certain the trees were not advancing. But before they got far, the sound of thundering hooves approached. Guinevere turned, squinting against the sun.

Sir Tristan had found Arthur. He was galloping toward them, flanked by five knights and at least twenty soldiers. Guinevere hastily dropped the stone she was holding and used her handkerchief to wipe the dirt from her hands.

Arthur closed the distance between them in a mad gallop, leaping from his horse almost before it had finished moving. "Are you safe?"

Guinevere nodded. "I stopped the advance. The trees are halted, but I have not decided how to finish it."

Arthur squeezed the pommel of Excalibur, fingers twitching in protest at not being allowed to draw it. "I can take care of it. But not with you here."

Guinevere had seen Excalibur drain the life from a tree possessed by magic. In a way that she could not explain, it made her almost as sad as remembering the horse that had been devoured. And Arthur was right: she could not stay once he began to wield the sword. "I can help. We will go in opposite directions."

"I will not have you wandering in a Dark Queen–infested forest alone. We know she is interested in you."

"I can defend myself."

Lancelot shifted uncomfortably. Guinevere shot her a look, but Lancelot did not meet her eyes. Her chin was lifted, her body at rigid attention as her king spoke.

"I know you can." Arthur put a finger against Guinevere's cut lip, troubled. "But in this case, you do not have to. You found this threat, and you warned us. I am here now."

"How are you going to finish it?" It would take weeks to cut back the trees that had moved forward, and she did not like the idea of Arthur riding into the woods, searching for the Dark Queen. Excalibur or not, he would be vulnerable and she would not be at his side. "How will you find her, if she is here?"

"Simple. We will burn the forest."

"Burn it?" Guinevere spun toward the trees. "But that will ruin the whole forest! These trees did not ask to be possessed by dark magic."

Arthur gave her a puzzled look. "They are trees. They do not ask for anything."

"There has to be another solution. Burning everything seems excessive. Can we not just find the Dark Queen, or the source of her infection here, and get rid of that?"

"It would be like cutting off the shoots of a weed. The roots are still there, and the weed will come back in the same spot, or in a new, unexpected one. We have to remove everything. She is in there or she is not, but her magic cannot linger in trees that are burned."

"I can go in. I can trace the lines of the magic, find—"

From deep within the trees, a lonely howl drifted on the air. Guinevere felt it on her skin and shuddered in spite of herself. She had faced wolves in a wood before. They nearly got her, and they almost killed Sir Tristan, as well. She was afraid, and she hated the fear more than anything else the Dark Queen had done here this day.

Arthur and Lancelot shared a look heavy with unspoken agreement. Guinevere's fear transformed into nagging worry at what she would do if Arthur commanded her to leave. If Lancelot followed his command and forced her to.

She did not want Arthur to make her leave, and she did not know what Lancelot would do if placed between her queen and her king. And she did not want to find out.

"Very well. I will be nearby, if you need me." Guinevere trudged toward where Brangien waited a safe distance away with their horses.

She did not want to be safe. She wanted to be useful. And she hated that the best thing she could do to defeat this threat was to get out of Excalibur's way.

CHAPTER THREE

Guinevere watched as the forest burned.

Lancelot was equally agitated and anxious, stalking in a tight prowl back and forth, her eyes on the line of bright flame and dark smoke billowing up into the unassuming afternoon sky.

"You can join them," Guinevere said. Excalibur would not make Lancelot sick, and Guinevere was perfectly safe in this tamed, lifeless field.

"No. My place is here." Lancelot stopped, but it seemed to require some effort. Her gaze kept drifting to the blazing destruction the other knights were overseeing. Brangien had returned to Camelot. Guinevere wanted to stay in case she was needed.

A knight broke free from the line of men controlling the flames and rode toward them. Sir Tristan was squinting, a strip of cloth around his mouth and nose as protection against the smoke. He pulled it down when he reached them, bowing his head to Guinevere.

"My queen, King Arthur sent me to tell you that he has this under control and wishes you to go back to Camelot."

Guinevere twitched against the command. She was the one who

had found this. It was her job to fight magical threats. But if Arthur felt like this situation was under control, she had to trust him. At least in Camelot she could check her wards and make certain no additional threat had crept in while they were occupied here. It made sense.

It did not make her resent being sent home any less.

Without a word, Guinevere went to her horse. Lancelot helped her mount, and then they rode back toward the city, equally silent, equally determined not to look over their shoulders at the fight they should be part of. The ride was insultingly dull, the afternoon sullen with heat that plagued them until they reached the lake.

Guinevere wanted another chance to prove herself against the Dark Queen. But last time her presence had not only brought the fairy menace back but also prevented Arthur from wielding Excalibur to end the fight once and for all. She was angry and she was humiliated and she was on yet another ferry across the abominable stretch of water that separated her from the castle.

It might have been preferable to take her chances with Excalibur over this trip across the cold depths of the lake. The ferry dipped and she grabbed Lancelot's arm, squeezing. "Tell me something," she whispered, shutting her eyes.

"What should I tell you?"

"Anything."

"It is more valuable to anticipate a blow than to avoid it. If I know which direction a blow is coming from, I can move with it instead of against it. I use their momentum against them, because they will be focused on following through with their strike while I am already moving into position with my next one. So by taking a blow, I can often end a fight sooner than if I expended as much energy and thought on avoiding being hit."

Guinevere frowned, leaning her head against Lancelot's shoulder. Lancelot was so steady. "Why are you thinking about that right now?"

"When I do not want to think about something that is bothering me, I replay sparring matches and fights in my memory, going over the movements, what I could have done better, what my opponent did well."

"Which fight are you replaying?"

Lancelot paused so long Guinevere thought she would not answer, but when she did, Guinevere regretted having asked. "Mordred. Always Mordred. No matter how I go through it, he wins. He always wins."

Guinevere wanted to redirect the topic. "So momentum is the key in fighting? I would have thought strength."

"It does not hurt." Lancelot smiled gently at Guinevere's obvious topic change. "Momentum is also critical to climbing. People think climbing is also about strength, and it is, to a certain extent, but so much of it is confidence and movement. If you freeze, you use up precious energy that might be the difference between reaching the top and falling."

Guinevere had seen Lancelot scale walls and cliffs she would have thought impossible. "Could you teach me? Not climbing. But fighting."

Lancelot patted Guinevere's hand. "Some basics. Self-defense. If you ever need more than that, I have failed at my job. But I have not failed at this one."

"What one?"

"Distraction." The ferry bumped against the dock. Lancelot escorted Guinevere off, and Guinevere took a moment to gather herself, to reclaim who she was when she was in Camelot. That cursed lake. It made her life so much more difficult. Being plunged into mortal terror every time she left or returned to the city was not good for maintaining a queenly presence.

Knowing that Merlin had placed the fear there to protect her from the vengeful Lady of the Lake made the fear less shameful, but no less terrifying. Wretched wizard. Wretched lake.

"My queen?" a young, eager voice asked.

Wretched Sir Gawain. Guinevere forced a pleasant expression, repenting of her mean thought. Sir Gawain was one of the youngest knights, her age—sixteen—but eager and accomplished with a sword. Unlike the older knights who kept with current styles, he wore his hair as short as he could to imitate Arthur. Combined with his round face, it made him look even younger than he was. According to Lancelot, all his spare time was spent in the chapel, praying or helping. He had taken to Christianity with the same fervor he had taken to Arthur.

Sir Gawain was tasked with helping Guinevere oversee the granaries within the city, which he also took to with extreme fervor. Guinevere had forgotten they were supposed to check one earlier this afternoon.

"Sir Gawain. My apologies. Our time afield took longer than expected."

"No apologies required, my queen. I am ready to go now."

The scent of smoke lingered in Guinevere's hair. She wanted to shed her cloak and peel off her dress, to rest in her dim bedroom and confer with Brangien about her troubling dream. "Excellent," she said, following Sir Gawain.

The lowest granary, in the southeast sector of the city, was a huge circular building. It had not always been a granary, but what its original purpose was, no one could say. The only opening was a hole at the very top, at least twenty feet up. Arthur's masons had created a door, as well as several openings at various levels. When all the grain was harvested, the doors would be sealed and the grain poured in through the opening, which would then be covered against the weather.

The granary smelled musty and warm, the floor dusted with the memory of harvest seasons past. It held the promise of safety. The promise of a winter made as easy as possible.

Guinevere did not know what she was supposed to be doing. She walked the circumference, making a show of checking it. "Good. See that this is swept out more thoroughly and look for holes along the perimeter that vermin might get in." It was not really necessary. This was one of the original buildings of Camelot, which meant that it had no seams, no visible cracks or places where it had been formed. The only flaws were the ones they had made to use it.

She should have been glad, but with last night's dream tugging at her, Guinevere found the building unnerving. "Do we have anything else to check today?" she asked.

Sir Gawain shook his head. "No, my queen. The others are being prepared and we can look at them tomorrow." The older knights mostly ignored Guinevere, but Sir Gawain always seemed a little flushed and wide-eyed when he spoke with her. Guinevere did not assume it was herself that created that effect, but rather her proximity to Arthur, whom Sir Gawain outright worshiped.

"Very good. You have done excellent work. I think we can expect a comfortable winter. I will tell King Arthur."

He bowed, his ruddy skin even redder with pleasure at the compliment.

Guinevere exited the dim space back into the late shafts of golden sun piercing the street. Brangien was waiting for her. "I heard you had come back," Brangien said. "Did everything go well?"

"It is in progress and under control." Guinevere tried to sound clinical, not petulant. The important thing was that the threat was neutralized. It did not have to be her doing the fighting. Even if her pride wanted it to be.

"Good. We have so much to do." Brangien took Guinevere's arm and marched uphill toward the castle. "Dindrane has requested I come to her dress fitting, and if I have to go, you do, too, since it is your kindness that has created this waking nightmare for me."

Guinevere laughed. "I thought you liked Dindrane."

"I do not *like* her. She is my friend. One must no more like their friends than they must like their family. They are simply part of your life, and you tolerate them as best you can."

Guinevere put a hand over her heart. "Brangien, are you saying you do not like me?"

Brangien wrinkled her nose impatiently. "I love you. You know that. And I often like you. But I do not like you today, because I have to sit through Dindrane's infinite picking about her wedding ward-robe, as well as answer every single question about what you will be wearing so she can match."

"She wants to match me? At her own wedding? I should wear something that does not draw attention."

"Oh, no. Dindrane *wants* you to draw attention. She wants everyone at her father's estate to see that the queen of Camelot is her closest friend and that you and she are basically the same, right down to your colors."

The fact that Dindrane accompanied her brother, Sir Percival, to a new land rather than staying on her own estate with her father spoke to an unhappy arrangement. Camelot was a land of hopeful newcomers, though. Under Uther Pendragon there had been suf-fering and oppression, but under Arthur Camelot was growing every day. People were drawn to him and the kingdom he had cut free on the edge of Excalibur.

It felt odd, talking about granaries and weddings and dresses while somewhere Arthur was eradicating a fairy assault, perhaps even facing off against the Dark Queen herself. The constant disso-nance of being both queen and witch, Guinevere and not-Guinevere, was disorienting. It would be so much simpler to be just one thing. But she was inside Camelot now, and when she was here, she was Queen Guinevere. She tried to focus.

Brangien was not finished complaining. "And why do we have to travel to her father's lands for the wedding? Dindrane lives in Camelot. Sir Bors lives in Camelot. Most importantly, I live in Camelot and do not want to leave."

"You are going to be even more cross with me." Guinevere drew Brangien closer so they were side by side and she did not have to see the impending rage on her friend's face. "That was my idea."

"*Your* idea. Your idea that means not only do I have to prepare a queen for a week of festivities but I also have to figure out how to pack that week of festivities for a five-day journey?"

"Dindrane's father is a southern lord. His lands are to the east, as well, which means he has increasing numbers of Saxon settlers around him. Arthur is wary of the Saxons marrying into these families and creating alliances that he has no knowledge of or connection to. I have learned about strategic social visits from you, so I suggested he go honor Dindrane's father to make certain that bond is firm. And it will give him the chance to meet and speak with several other important men of that region, all without looking aggressive. He will be there for a celebration, not for a negotiation." The southern part of the island was riddled with lords and kings, everyone staking out their claim to rulership. The east was being settled by Saxons who thought nothing of pushing out whoever initially lived there, and, when that failed, married into the families and took over that way. And the north was ruled by the Picts, with whom Arthur had an uneasy alliance. Guinevere had met them and their glowering bulk of a king, Nechtan. It had been a marginally pleasant dinner until Maleagant had shown up and complicated things. But the Picts and

Arthur had settled into peace. They needed to turn their eyes to the south and the east.

Brangien huffed. "That was very clever of you. But I am still angry."

"I understand. You are welcome to be angry for as much time as you need to be. As long as you still love me and occasionally like me."

Brangien's soft tone surprised Guinevere. "You are doing a good job."

"Of having you love me?"

"Of being queen."

One of the invisible knots in Guinevere's chest—not a magic knot, but a worry knot—loosened ever so slightly. "Am I?"

"You are. I have always been proud to serve our king, and I am just as proud to serve you. He is lucky to have you. After all, think of the alternative. Dindrane could be our queen." Brangien shuddered exaggeratedly.

Guinevere laughed. They turned a corner and Guinevere noticed a wall where the carvings were not quite as worn as they were elsewhere, sheltered against wind and rain by the angle of the street. It punctured the busy distraction she had allowed herself. She was back in the dream, rushing up these same streets.

"Brangien, we need to talk about the dream magic."

Brangien's hand drifted to the back of her hair, where a lock of Isolde's copper hair was woven in with her own, allowing them to dream together. Every night Brangien was reunited with her lost love. "What about it?"

"It was probably nothing." It was not nothing, but she could not tell Brangien the full truth about anything. Brangien knew that Guinevere did magic, and she knew that the Dark Queen had re-emerged thanks to Mordred's betrayal. But she did not know the truth: that Guinevere had been sent here by Merlin for her own protection against the Lady of the Lake, that Guinevere was the reason the Dark Queen was able to come back, and that Guinevere was not Guinevere at all, but a changeling.

Guinevere remembered Mordred's confident assertion that Merlin was not her father. But if Merlin was not her father, who was? She shook it off, as she always did. Mordred was a liar. Mordred had manipulated her, had betrayed Arthur. Anything he told her—anything they had done—was a lie.

She found her fingers tracing her lips of their own accord and willfully put her hands down at her sides.

"What was probably nothing?" Brangien stopped, forcing Guinevere to face her.

"I . . . dreamed last night."

"But that should not be possible. Should it?" By giving Brangien the ability to connect her dreams to Isolde's, Guinevere had given up her own dreams. Every knot, every spell, every piece of magic had a cost. This was one of the few Guinevere had been more than happy to pay.

"No, it should not."

"Could it be the fairy queen?" Brangien whipped around, like the Dark Queen would rise behind them, a shadow blurring out the sun.

"It did not feel like her. But it did not feel like me, either. It felt like someone else's dream, tugging me along in its wake."

"We will break the knot." Brangien reached up to her hair, searching for Isolde's strands.

"No! Then you will not be able to see Isolde!"

"But what if this magic creates an opening? Room for the Dark Queen to slip in? We cannot risk it." Brangien let go of her hair and took Guinevere's hands in her own. As always, Brangien's touch was a cool reassurance, full of everything that made her who she was. But this time it was flooded with sadness. Brangien sighed and released Guinevere. "I will take one more night to tell Isolde, so she will not fear that something has happened. If that is all right."

"Of course." Guinevere leaned close. "You are my dearest friend. I want you to be happy, however you need to be. I will figure this out as quickly as possible."

Brangien nodded, but there was distance in her expression. Her smile appeared, the old one. The one Brangien wore when she did not want to be seen. "We will sort this all out. We will defeat our foes. And we will survive the coming terrors."

Guinevere was alarmed. She had not told Brangien the details of her dream. "Do you think it will be that bad?"

"Oh, I am not speaking of magical menaces. I am speaking of Dindrane's wedding."

Guinevere dissolved into relieved laughter, and Brangien feigned a stern voice. "I warned you from the beginning to avoid Dindrane. But you did not listen, and now look where we are. But back to the less immediate threat of the possible fairy attack of your mind. What should we do?"

Guinevere resumed walking. "If it does not happen again when I have my dreams back, we will know the knot was the opening and will have to figure out another way to connect you to Isolde. We will manage. We are the two cleverest women in Camelot, after all." Guinevere tried to sound more confident than she felt.

"My queen!" Lancelot joined them with the slight metallic jingle of chain mail. Her dark brows were furrowed in anger.

"Yes?"

"I left you with Sir Gawain. But then he came to the training arena alone."

"Yes, we finished our work."

Lancelot looked at her with an intensity that implied Guinevere was missing something important. "And now you are alone."

"No, Brangien and I are going to Dindrane's."

"And on the way there, who is protecting you?" Lancelot's hand was on the pommel of her sword. Even as she spoke, her eyes swept every street and window, searching for threats.

"I hardly think I'm in danger walking in Camelot."

"You were taken in Camelot."

Guinevere flinched at the memory. She still got headaches she suspected were from the blow that knocked her unconscious so Maleagant's man could abduct her. Her answer came out sullen. "On the field during the chaos of the tournament!"

"Because no one was paying attention. That will never happen again." Lancelot's fierce tone was informed by her own experiences rescuing Guinevere. Lancelot had been willing to sacrifice everything, even before she was a knight.

Guinevere softened and put her hand on Lancelot's arm. "I know."

"But I can only guard you as well as you allow me to, and if I do not have the correct information, I cannot do my job." Lancelot seemed angrier than the situation called for. Guinevere wondered if the fight they had been forced to leave to others was nagging at her valiant knight.

"You will regret finding us," Brangien said. "We are going to visit Dindrane and sit for hours as she examines cloth."

Lancelot did not so much as blanch, a credit to her noble devotion to duty over personal comfort.

Guinevere stopped on the walkway outside the steps to Dindrane's room. The young woman's voice already drifted toward them with a litany of demands. The room was too small for even one woman, much less five of them plus all the materials, and it was situated on the side of her brother's house that got the most direct afternoon sunlight. With autumn still warm, it would be sweltering. "Maybe Sir Lancelot could rescue us?" Guinevere asked.

Finally, Lancelot broke, a smile claiming her lips. "I am afraid even I cannot protect my queen from this."

Guinevere sighed. She imagined herself in a forest, fighting evil side by side with Arthur, wielding magic with all the confidence and earth-shaking power of Merlin. But she was not in a forest, wild with power. She was in Camelot; she was queen. She could not fight like Merlin, and she did not want to. Not really.

She took a deep breath and drew strength from her friends on either side. Brangien was right. They would face whatever was to come, whatever horrors awaited them. Starting with Dindrane's wedding plans.

CHAPTER FOUR

After being trapped in Dindrane's room until the impending curfew finally gave them an excuse to leave, Guinevere wanted to be anywhere but the castle. No, that was not true. She wanted to be only one other place. At Arthur's side, fighting the Dark Queen. She paced nervously along the outer walkways, but the forest was too distant to be seen. A few reports had been sent back—nothing that caused alarm. Still, she would not feel settled until Arthur returned. She should have insisted on staying. At least if she could not help, she could bear witness. Could be nearby should something terrible happen.

Cross and anxious as the sun set and night brought no answers, Guinevere tried to distract herself with her own small problems. She had dreams to attend to. Brangien was somber and distant as Guinevere helped her prepare for bed. She combed Brangien's straight, thick, nearly black hair, careful to avoid the section with Isolde's knotted auburn strands. They would remove them in the morning.

"How did you meet Isolde?" Guinevere asked, wanting something new to think about. Then she hurriedly added, "We do not have to speak about it if you do not wish to."

"No, it . . . it would be nice to speak openly about her. I held her as a secret for so long, it became instinctive." Brangien released a breath and some of the tension in her shoulders disappeared. Guinevere continued combing, the soft rhythm of it soothing them both. Normally Brangien was the one to prepare Guinevere for bed, but Guinevere wanted to offer this kindness and was grateful that Brangien accepted.

"I hated her when we first met. My father worked hard to get me placed in a good house as a lady's maid, but I had been spoiled by my mother and resented that I would now have to perform all these minor tasks for someone my own age. And Isolde—" Brangien laughed. "It is funny to think of it now. All the things about her I hated that eventually would become so dear. Isolde was dreamy. Forgetful. She would leave tasks half-finished. I was constantly picking up her sewing throughout the castle, left in the oddest places. I would find Isolde curled up in a window, asleep there like a cat in the sun. I thought she was the laziest girl I had ever met. What did she need to sleep so much for? After a month of finding her napping in odd places, as though she was hiding from me, I decided to stay up all night in secret and watch her. Perhaps she was not sleeping well. I had tricks for that, you know. And I had potions, as well. I do not do those here. They cannot be hidden like my sewing.

"That night I pretended to sleep on my cot in the corner as usual. After an hour, Isolde slipped out of the room. If she were going to visit someone—a guard, perhaps—and she fell pregnant, I would be blamed. I followed her. When she went to the kitchen, I assumed she was there to eat. I watched through a crack in the door as Isolde tiptoed around her ancient nurse. The woman had been moved to the kitchens when I came on as Isolde's maid, and she was fast asleep in the corner. Isolde made dough and set it to rising, tended the fires, then cleaned and scoured and prepared everything for the morning so that when her nurse awoke, all her duties would be done. It took Isolde nearly four hours to complete everything. When I could see that she was almost finished, I stole back to our room. Everything I thought I knew about her was wrong. She was not lazy or dreamy. She was constantly leaving her tasks undone because she saw that her nurse needed help, or that a page was lost, or that a maid was being berated for her work and needed help. Isolde was the kindest, most generous person I had ever seen.

"After that, I tried to emulate her. I found ways to make her life easier, the way she did for others. And she noticed, and did the same for me wherever she could. We would work together, and she sang or told me stories. We were no longer lady and maid. We were best friends. And then one day, laughing as we cleaned out the fireplace and sneezed on ashes . . . we were more. It was as natural as breathing." Brangien stopped, and Guinevere paused her combing. Doubtless Brangien was thinking of their parting. But Guinevere wanted Brangien to fall asleep with the memory of love, not loss, foremost in her mind.

"How, though? How did you know you were more than what you had been?"

"When I looked at her, everything felt right. And her hand in mine . . ." Brangien looked down at her hand, her fingers curling over something that was no longer there.

"It felt safe?"

Brangien laughed. "No. It felt anything but safe. It still felt right, though." Brangien turned and stole the comb, starting on Guinevere's hair.

Guinevere wanted to know more. Needed to know more. She

had crossed that line with Mordred, but he had never been bound by the same rules she was—or at least, that she was trying to be. He had always been there to disrupt and undermine Arthur. It hurt most of all, that maybe he had never seen her as anything but a means for attacking Arthur. She had felt things when they touched, and they had *felt* true. But even though he had begged her to come away with him, she could not trust that his motives were anything other than causing further pain to Arthur.

No more thoughts of Mordred. Only thoughts of Arthur. Arthur, her friend. Arthur, her husband in name only. Arthur, who was out fighting their battles alone because they could not fight them side by side. "How did you cross that divide between what you were and what you became? Were you scared?"

"Scared of discovery? No." Brangien scowled. "Love between women is seen as harmless. Encouraged sometimes, even, as a means for high-born girls to expel excess energy with no threats to lines of succession. As though what we had was a child's game instead of more real than any of their arranged unions."

Guinevere had not even thought about being afraid of discovery. That had not been what she meant at all. "Were you scared that once you made it clear you loved her, what you had before would be lost to you forever?"

Brangien's strokes were distracted. "All I knew was that I wanted Isolde—all of Isolde—in my life, beside me. There was no fear in that first kiss. Only hope. We were both surprised, I think, but there was no fear. Not then." Brangien stopped. "Have you— Guinevere, this morning when I asked about your night, you were upset. Have you and Arthur not been . . . together yet?"

Guinevere closed her eyes. If it was known that she and Arthur had only shared a bed as friends, their marriage would not be considered legal. Not to mention the need for heirs to solidify Arthur's reign and protect him from usurpers. But she trusted Brangien with her life, and with almost all her secrets. "I keep thinking—hoping—maybe one night he will be tired, or perhaps have had too much wine, and that will make it easier for him to kiss me and it will just happen and then we can move forward."

Brangien put down the comb. She took Guinevere's chin in her hand and lifted her face so they were looking at one another. In the low candlelight Guinevere could almost see herself reflected in Brangien's dark, pretty eyes.

"Would you really want a kiss that was not meant?" Brangien asked.

Guinevere felt the misery pooling in her stomach. "But we are already married."

"Give him time. He loves you."

"But not like you love Isolde."

"I should hope not." Brangien laughed. "I am selfish and vengeful and jealous. The king is . . . honest. I think he will never offer you anything that he cannot commit to fully. I do not wish to dismiss your worries, but I promise it is better than a husband who treats you as a possession." Brangien's face darkened once more.

"Maybe *I* should kiss *him*," Guinevere said.

Brangien smiled, twisting her lips into a teasing shape. "That is the best way, I think. Your first kiss is special. Why should you not be the one to choose when it happens?"

Guinevere cleared her throat and stood hastily. It would not be her first kiss. She had not chosen the first one, but she had not rejected it.

Brangien turned down Guinevere's bed and then tended to her own. "I will tell no one, of course. You and the king are young. You have time to find your way to each other as husband and wife."

Brangien lay down and Guinevere tucked the blankets around her. "So much time."

Brushing a kiss against Brangien's forehead, Guinevere draped a cloth with a sleeping knot across Brangien's chest, and her friend was gone to say goodbye to her true love.

Guinevere envied her—both the true love and the sleep. Guinevere would not risk another dream invasion, and so had resolved to stay awake. She could not sleep this night anyway, knowing Arthur was out there fighting their battle alone. After wrapping herself in a cloak, she slipped out of her rooms. There was an exterior door next to them. She unlocked it and walked out onto the stairs that encircled the castle, winding and soaring to the very top. Perhaps from the alcove near the top she would be able to see the distant line of fire. Regardless, she could work.

A figure peeled itself from the darkness and she screamed.

"My queen!" Lancelot held her hands up.

Guinevere covered her mouth, her heart racing. "Lancelot!" She leaned against the wall, trying to calm herself. "What are you doing?"

"King Arthur is not in the castle."

"That does not explain why you are lurking out here."

Guinevere could not see Lancelot's face in the night, just an impression of her. But Lancelot's voice was as clear and purposeful as her gaze would have been, had it been visible. "King Arthur is not in the castle, which means Excalibur is not in the castle. I always watch this door when the king is gone."

"But you must be exhausted. Do you do this every time? He is away so often."

"I am never exhausted. I am always ready."

Guinevere laughed. "Well, that makes one of us. I feel always exhausted and never ready. Come on, then. We are climbing." Lancelot

followed her as they carefully wound their way up the side of the castle to Mordred's favorite alcove. The night was cloudy and felt even
darker than usual. Guinevere was glad for the unexpected company.

Other than Arthur, Lancelot was the only person in Camelot who
knew the truth about Guinevere. She also knew the full extent of
Guinevere's magic, having seen her perform the worst of it in the
hollow of trees where she revived the Dark Queen. If the story were
known, Guinevere wondered, would she have an epic tale like Arthur and the Forest of Blood? Perhaps it would be called Guinevere
and the Dread Hollow. But she would not be the hero of that story.

Sighing, she settled into the alcove. Lancelot stood at attention
to the side. A thought struck Guinevere. "Did Arthur ask you to keep
watch while he was gone?"

"I am the queen's protector. He does not need to ask me to do
my duty."

Although she would have been delighted to know Arthur had assigned it—that he thought of her when he was not here—Guinevere
was happy that Lancelot had chosen this, rather than being commanded. It was no small task, either. Arthur was constantly riding
out, tending to borders. He always took knights, but never Lancelot.
Lancelot was *her* knight, specifically, but Guinevere wondered how
that made Lancelot feel. She had earned her place among Arthur's
knights, the same as any of them. Better, even. She had gotten further in her tournament than any other knight ever, fighting Arthur
himself to a draw. And yet she was always left behind. Just like
Guinevere.

They were here, alone in the dark, while the rest of the knights
fought actual darkness.

"You should get comfortable," Guinevere advised, focusing on the
task at hand. "This will take some time, and will look like nothing but
finger wiggling and intense staring to you."

"What are you doing?"

"Searching."

"For what?"

"I might not be able to be there, but I can get a sense for how the fight is going and make certain there are no other areas of the Dark Queen's magic we have not discovered." She yanked out two hairs and tied them around her fingers, similar to the knot for seeing. She had always been able to feel more than was readily apparent, and she used this knot to extend that ability—at painful cost.

Sensation left the rest of her body, and she leaned against the alcove's low stone wall for support. She felt light and disconnected. For a heady moment she wondered whether she had fallen into another dream and would rush along the streets or, worse, up the side of the castle to the hidden drop into the lake and the waiting Lady. Closing her eyes, Guinevere took a deep breath, trying to anchor herself.

When she was steady, her hand pushed outward. There were few sparks in Camelot. A warm glow from where Brangien slept. A few cold bites from where her iron knots protected the doors in and out of the castle. The warning that her seven anchored stones along the borders of the city would send should something come near. She shuddered as her hands passed over the void of the dead lake. It still bothered her that no magic existed there whatsoever, no hint of life or warmth. The fields had it, the smallest amount suffused throughout, though nothing that was not natural. To the south she felt the sparks of Rhoslyn's camp, filled with women banished from Camelot for practicing magic. It was almost like visiting a friend, and she was glad nothing had changed there. She had not seen Rhoslyn since the Dark Queen attacked Guinevere in the forest with a possessed boar and then a spider's infected poison. Lancelot saved her from the boar, and Rhoslyn saved her from the poison. And then Lancelot had taken Guinevere to Merlin and hidden with her as they watched the Lady of the Lake seal Merlin away. That had been the day that cemented Lancelot's and Guinevere's fates at each other's sides.

With a burst of affection for the knight still at her side, Guinevere pushed north and west, sweeping farther and farther out, but other than the tiny pinpricks of wildlife moving through the night, she felt nothing alarming. Nothing new. Nothing threatening.

Finally, reaching the edge of her endurance, Guinevere threw her sense of magic toward Arthur. There was the line of fire. It was not magic, not in the same way the knots were, but fire was its own sort of energy. Hungry and chaotic and quite close to what the Dark Queen was. Life that could turn to death with a shift of the wind. Unpredictable and brilliant and beautiful and terrible.

She could almost feel it singeing her hands, could feel the dying trees and vines, those lives snuffed out. A retreat of energy, almost like smoke being drawn back into lungs. This was a fight Arthur was winning. And Arthur was—

She had found Excalibur. *And Excalibur had found her.*

The hairs wrapping her fingers snapped and blood rushed back in spikes. She was staring up into Lancelot's face, held in Lancelot's arms.

"My queen? Guinevere!"

"I am—I am fine." Guinevere was not fine. This was even worse than when Arthur had unsheathed Excalibur beside her just last night. For one brief, horrifying moment, she had felt the cold, empty expanse of Excalibur. It was nothing like the fire or the Dark Queen. Those were hungry, active, bursting with life and destruction.

Excalibur was a void. It was not hungry, and therefore could never be filled.

And there had been a moment—a single heartbeat—when Guin-

evere had been certain she would be the one to snap out of exis-
tence, instead of just her magic. Her silly little knots.

Lancelot did not release her, and Guinevere did not ask to be released. She did not think she could stand on her own. Not yet. Lancelot's steady presence was the foundation she needed right now. The
rock seemed to sway beneath her as if she was on a wretched ferry.
She could not tell how tightly she clung to Lancelot's arm. There was
no sensation in her hands, and would not be for several days.

After a few minutes, Guinevere felt capable of sitting. She moved
gingerly, resting against the rock, shoulder to shoulder with Lancelot.
"They are winning the fight."

"That is good."

"But this cannot be it. The Dark Queen is still out there. I would
have sensed if she were in the trees. And Mordred, too." Guinevere was certain she would know him simply by feeling his presence.
"They are out there, and with this failure, doubtless they will hatch a
new plot, and I do not know how I can prevent it."

"Do you need to prevent it?"

"Of course!"

Lancelot was quiet for a moment. "Some things you cannot prevent. Not every foe can be predicted, not every move can be anticipated. You can only face them when they appear, as we did today.
Successfully. So we do everything we can to be ready. We watch, and
we wait."

"I *hate* waiting."

Lancelot laughed at Guinevere's petulant tone. "Do not imagine
us whiling away our days in foolishness. Imagine us as the adder,
curled and coiled in anticipation of the strike."

Guinevere laid her head on Lancelot's shoulder. "I cannot sleep
tonight." Her hands were somehow both numb and in agonizing

pain. It hardly seemed fair, but such was the cost of magic. She shuddered, unbearably cold as she remembered that brief brush against Excalibur.

"We will keep watch together, then."

"Next time Arthur is away, you can sleep in my sitting room. That way you will be close enough to hear if anything is wrong. And you will not be standing outside in the dark, alone."

Lancelot shifted so that Guinevere's head was at a more comfortable angle against her shoulder. Her low voice was softer than normal when she answered, "I am never in the dark when I am protecting you."

They passed the night secreted away in the alcove in companionable silence. For once, Guinevere did not fret over everything that was out of her control. Arthur had won this fight and Brangien would help her figure out what had taken over her dreams.

Lancelot was right. They would be ready for whatever came. Together.

CHAPTER FIVE

At dawn, Guinevere and Lancelot saw a ferry approaching and rushed down from the castle. They arrived at the dock just as it drew near. Guinevere's chest felt tight and painful—as though she had been breathing in smoke instead of waiting safely—as she searched the soot-stained faces. Then she found what she was looking for.

Arthur.

Guinevere closed her eyes, half tempted to pray as she had been taught in Arthur's church. But why should she send this gratitude elsewhere, to an invisible god? She liked it right where it was: in the center of her heart, warm and hopeful.

She opened her eyes and waved, but there was commotion in the middle of the knights. Arthur had begun stripping off his chain mail and leather, right down to his underclothes. He climbed onto the railing of the ferry, stood silhouetted against the brilliant morning sun just now defeating the horizon, and then did a flip into the water.

Guinevere shuddered, imagining how it would feel to submerge herself in that cold, dead thing. Like sinking into a grave. But Arthur emerged with a joyful whoop and lay back, floating, face turned up toward the sky.

With shouts and jostling, several of the younger knights did the same. Sir Bors, thick and dour, shook his head. Sir Tristan laughed, grabbing Sir Bors's good arm and pretending to tug him toward the edge. Sir Bors threw Sir Tristan over the side to uproarious laughter. Then, blowing out a sigh from beneath his ponderous mustache, Sir Bors peeled off his layers and joined them.

Soon all Arthur's knights were in the water, splashing each other and washing off the soot and smoke of their victory. Even young Sir Gawain, who had ridden to the fight after filling his duties yesterday evening, swam alongside them.

No. Not *all* Arthur's knights. Lancelot stood perfectly still beside Guinevere, at attention, hand on the pommel of her sword. Separate from both the fight and the celebration.

Guinevere did not know how long it would take the knights to finish bathing. She should get back to Brangien to comfort her and to discuss the dream and what they should do about it. And it could not be fun for Lancelot to stand here, observing. Apart.

"Come, we should—"

"Guinevere!" Arthur shouted, and Guinevere could hear the smile in his tone. She turned toward the lake. He was walking toward her, the water up to his waist.

"My king." The water clung to him as though it would claim him, drag him back under. It rolled off him like a lover's caress. She wondered briefly, sharply, what his relationship with the Lady of the Lake had been. He never spoke of her without tones of wonder, but he also rarely spoke about her. Because there was nothing to say, or because it was personal?

"Three cheers for my queen, who found the threat and warned us of it!" Arthur raised a fist in the air and led his men in a disorganized cheer. Guinevere shook her head demurely, smiling. But it was a performance. She did not feel this was her victory. Even if she had discovered the threat, she had done little to fight it except *leave*.

And the threat was her fault. Every incursion of the Dark Queen, every time they found and fought her—anyone who was hurt or lost in the battles—would be Guinevere's fault for trusting Mordred. For trying to fight as a witch, not as a queen.

Arthur splashed free from the lake. His underclothes clung in interesting ways that were they not surrounded by knights and ferry workers and the men who guarded the dock, might have required further observation. As it was, Guinevere felt her cheeks warming.

Arthur chose this moment to be observant. He took in Guinevere's blush and smiled with a playful, nearly wicked edge that took Guinevere's breath away. For the first time she saw the resemblance between Arthur and his nephew, Mordred.

Arthur held out his arms. He was dripping with lake water. "Can I get an embrace from my queen?"

Guinevere stepped back, raising her hands defensively. "Not covered in that water, you cannot."

"Just a quick hug!" Arthur lunged, and Guinevere shrieked, dodging him. She knew they were playacting—that he was as aware of their audience as she was—but her laughter and her horror were not feigned. She loved seeing Arthur like this: relaxed, happy, *young*. And she loved that he had figured out a way to involve her in this celebration even though she had not been able to fight. And she absolutely was not going to let him touch her while he was covered in that fetid, wretched, seeping water.

Guinevere ducked behind Lancelot, keeping her knight between them. "Save me, Sir Lancelot!" she said, laughing.

Lancelot stayed perfectly still. Guinevere had placed Lancelot between her king and her queen. It was an impossible situation.

But then Lancelot reached up and undid her cloak—blue, with a simple golden sun emblem in the center. She bowed and held it out to Arthur.

He wrapped it around himself. "Now?"

"Very well." Guinevere stepped from behind Lancelot and put her arms around Arthur's waist. He pressed a kiss to the top of her head.

"We won," he whispered.

"We did," Guinevere agreed.

"I did not find her there. Or him."

Guinevere did not need to ask whom he referred to. The Dark Queen and her grandson, Mordred. "We will find them."

"Sir Lancelot is rested," Sir Percival grumbled, climbing out of the lake. "She can take my place at the aspirant training today." He walked past Lancelot without a glance and without asking her if that was okay. Guinevere wanted to turn to her knight, to check on her, but Arthur took her hand. He might have squeezed. She wished she could use her touch sense to feel him, to draw some of his strength into herself. But her hands were ruined from last night's magic, and would be for days.

They walked toward the castle, Lancelot behind them.

The crowd cheered, startling Guinevere out of her doze. If she was this tired, she could only imagine how tired Lancelot must be.

Guinevere was sitting in the stands and the knights were on the arena floor, organizing the day's aspirant matches. The least Guinevere could do was stay alert. Arthur had filled her in on the details when they got back to the castle, but then he had been pulled away by the return of scouts he had sent north. Guinevere had wanted a distraction for poor Brangien. She had dismissed Guinevere's questions perfunctorily as she shook out clothes, insisting that everything was fine after her last dream with Isolde. But her eyes were red and swollen, and so Guinevere had suggested they attend the training. Really all she wanted was a nap, but even that was an uncomfortable prospect. Would the invasive dream still have access to her mind?

Guinevere blinked, focusing on the arena's dirt floor and the various players there. The cheer had not been for Lancelot, who did not have the admirers she had once enjoyed as the patchwork knight. Guinevere knew many in the city did not accept Lancelot and could not fathom why Arthur had agreed to knight a woman.

Guinevere wondered, sometimes, if Arthur *would* have knighted Lancelot had things gone differently. Lancelot had won her tournament without question, but during the celebrations afterward Guinevere had been kidnapped by Maleagant's man, and Lancelot had been revealed as a woman. If there had not been the complication of Guinevere's abduction, how would Arthur have addressed it all? As it was, in the confusion and scrambling to get information, Lancelot was simply forgotten. Which left her open to join with Brangien and Mordred in a rescue mission that Arthur could not pursue without risking war.

It had been Lancelot's bravery in rescuing Guinevere from the island where Maleagant was holding her and then Lancelot's help in fighting Mordred and the Dark Queen that had given Guinevere the opportunity to demand that Lancelot be her very own knight. Arthur could not put Camelot second to Guinevere, ever. Lancelot could put Guinevere first, always.

But without the leverage of Lancelot's real-life heroics, would she have been knighted? If Maleagant had not abducted Guinevere, would Mordred have found a different opening to trick Guinevere into helping him? Or would he still be here, perhaps sitting at Guinevere's side today, making her laugh?

It was useless, thinking about how things might have gone differently. Maleagant was dead. Mordred was a traitor. And Lancelot was a knight. *Her* knight. Guinevere sat, visible in red and blue, wearing a crown of braids and cheering for her so that everyone would see Lancelot was supported. It was her own sort of vigilant protection; the only type she could offer Lancelot. Lancelot was not usually in rotation for this task, so Guinevere was excited to watch.

Lancelot sparred with Sir Tristan and Sir Gawain as they waited for the aspirants to finish selecting their gear and begin trials. Guinevere waved a handkerchief, beaming, and then sat back into the shade with Brangien. The handkerchief fell to the wood floor beneath them. At least her fumbling fingers had held it while people were watching.

Brangien did not notice, either. She looked haunted. It hurt Guinevere to be unable to fix it yet. She would, as soon as she could.

After the aspirants were finished for the day, they were due back at the castle to finalize preparations for the travel to the estate of Dindrane's father. As tedious as it was planning caravans and supplies, Guinevere was looking forward to the wedding. The travel would bring them across land she had not yet visited. And it was a week—at least!—with Arthur at her side. Maybe, away from the stresses of Camelot and the duties that pulled him away, they would finally be able to . . . something. Guinevere could never quite finish the mental image of what she hoped would happen beyond a kiss.

Had the way Arthur smiled at her at the lakeshore made her think they were getting closer because it had been intimate, or because it had reminded her of Mordred?

Brangien offered her a strip of cloth to practice knots, but Guinevere shook her head. She could not feel her fingers other than pins and needles, which made her useless at actual needlework. But she would be recovered by the time they left. On the road, outside of Arthur's lands, they would be vulnerable. She would not be caught unaware or indisposed.

She remembered Lancelot's description of her as a waiting adder and smiled, picturing herself coiled up not with knots and tension, but with deadly power.

A rumble of noise in an unusual tone drew her attention to the ring. One of the aspirants was holding his sword, tip down, his back to the knight who was giving instructions. His back to *Lancelot*.

Lancelot did not talk about how the other knights treated her. When she was with Guinevere, she was always on guard, scanning for threats, doing her duty. Guinevere had no idea how things went for Lancelot elsewhere. But Lancelot had been excluded from a fight and a celebration, and then Sir Percival had dumped his own work on her without even asking. And now this insult! Guinevere stood, livid.

Brangien's hand on her arm stopped her from speaking. "Let her address it," she murmured. "A queen commanding them to show respect will only prove to them that Lancelot is not worthy of their respect on her own merits."

Lancelot said something and all the knights—and aspirants other than the one with his back turned—laughed. They moved into their various rings, no one else hesitating to follow Lancelot's instructions. The sulking aspirant was left alone. When he tried to move into a ring where Sir Tristan was instructing, Sir Tristan shifted so that his back was to him. Sir Gawain did the same thing. Guinevere held her breath when the man got to Sir Bors, one of the oldest and by far the surliest of the knights. But Sir Bors shifted and did the same.

Guinevere let out a breath of relief. "They know Lancelot's worth."

Brangien was more practical in her views. "They will protect their own. King Arthur made Lancelot a knight, and if they disrespected that, they would be disrespecting their king and themselves. Besides, you are the reason Sir Bors is about to enjoy matrimonial bliss. You are Dindrane's champion. He will not do anything to offend you."

Perhaps Brangien was right and it had less to do with the knights' feelings about Lancelot's worth and more to do with their pride about their own. But at least in public they were united. Guinevere settled in and watched Lancelot work. It was funny to think of how certain she had been that Lancelot was a threat back when Guinevere only knew her as the patchwork knight. What had seemed supernatural about Lancelot's talent then filled her with pride now. It was soothing to watch her own knight continually best the men around her, then patiently instruct them. She had seen only two people beat Lancelot. Arthur—who fought her to a draw—and Mordred.

Who won.

A shadow loomed at the entrance to their covered booth. Guinevere looked up, half expecting Mordred to be there with his wry smile and his knowing eyes, but it was only a servant page, offering them refreshments. The rest of the afternoon dragged. Guinevere was uncomfortable in the late-afternoon heat, exhausted, her hands painful. At last they finished and Guinevere and Brangien could leave. They walked slowly back up to the castle.

"Buckets," Guinevere muttered to herself.

Brangien laughed. "What woe are you comparing to the idea of having to haul buckets up this endless, cursed hill?"

Guinevere sighed, looking forward to undoing her tight braids, letting her hair down. "I am just tired."

"I will guard your sleep tonight."

Guinevere patted Brangien's hand distractedly. They were nearly to the castle gate. Guinevere debated entering through the gate and climbing the narrow, claustrophobic internal stairs, or cutting to the side and taking the exterior stairs that soared and swept along the outside of the castle. Too confining, or not confining enough always seemed to be her options these days.

"Guinevere!"

Guinevere turned. A girl was running toward them from the gate. She had long golden hair that streamed behind her with all the luster of a field ripe for harvest. Her wide-set eyes were almost the same honey color, and she had a smattering of freckles across her nose and cheeks. Her dress and cloak were lovely, all in pinks. Guinevere had never seen her before.

She looked at Brangien in confusion, but Brangien seemed equally puzzled.

The girl stopped before them. "Sister!"

"Sister?" Guinevere nearly laughed in confusion. She did not have a sister. And then her stomach dropped in horror. *She* did not have a sister. But Guinevere—the real Guinevere, dead Guinevere—did. Her name was Guinevach, if memory served. Was this . . . Guinevach? Here to visit a sister she no longer had?

Guinevere could barely think through her panic. This would be the end of everything. All they had fought for, all she had chosen, ruined because of a girl deciding to visit her sister. The deception had worked because no one in Camelot or the surrounding regions had ever met the southern princess Guinevere. No one had known what she looked like. But no amount of jewelry or fine cloaks would convince Guinevach she was seeing her own sister.

Guinevere braced herself. But it did not matter. Nothing could have prepared her for what Guinevach did next.

CHAPTER SIX

Guinevere stood perfectly still, arms pinned to her sides by Guine-vach's hug. "I am so happy to see you again!" Guinevach laughed, then drew back a few inches. "And look! We are the same height now. When you left I only came up to your freckled nose." She wrinkled her own freckled nose in delight. "Do you remember how our nurse would make us sit side by side in front of the fire as she brushed our hair and lectured us for letting the sun ruin our complexions?"

"I—" Guinevere did not remember. Of course she did not re-member. And she could not wrap her head around this development. Guinevach was fourteen, perhaps fifteen now, which meant she had been eleven when her sister—the real, dead Guinevere—had left for the convent. But surely even a child could tell the difference be-tween her own flesh and blood and an imposter. Though Guine-vach's embrace was loose, Guinevere could not breathe. She did not know what to say. What expression to put on her face. What to think of any of this. She stepped away. "I am so sorry, I am not well. Brangien?" Guinevere turned toward her maid.

Brangien, who knew nothing of Guinevere's false identity, swooped in to the rescue regardless. "The queen needs rest. We will schedule some time with you when she is well." Brangien stepped between Guinevach and Guinevere, took Guinevere's arm, and led her into the castle. Guinevere risked one glance over her shoulder. Two women were hurrying to catch up to Guinevach, whose face was carefully set in a neutral expression with only the slightest narrowing of her eyes.

"Get me Lancelot, or King Arthur. Both. Whoever you can find first." Guinevere paced the length of her room, hands over her stomach. She had not lied: indeed, she felt quite sick. Brangien did not ask for more details and hurried out of the room. Guinevere longed to tell Brangien the truth of her identity, but this was a secret too dangerous to inflict on anyone who did not already know.

Guinevere leaned out the door and called after Brangien. "And if you see my sister, do not speak to her. If she speaks to you, tell her I am ill!"

She felt like she was trampling through her own mind, trying to dig around for crucial details. What did she know of the real Guinevere's sister? She was two years younger. Her name was Guinevach. Their father, King Leodegrance, ruled over a small kingdom named Cameliard. And . . . that was all. The extent of her preparation on that front.

"Thank you, Merlin," she muttered through gritted teeth. Yet another way in which the wizard who saw all of time had failed spectacularly to prepare her for any of it. For many reasons, she hated him for allowing himself to be sealed in that cave by the Lady of the

Lake. Being unable to shout at him for this was added to the very long list.

It made her sad to think about Merlin, though, and everything he had not—and *had*—done. But she had other things to worry about now. She touched her nose, the freckles undetectable to her fingers. She had never let herself wonder what the real Guinevere had looked like. What she had been like. It was too sad, too uncomfortable.

The door burst open and Lancelot strode in. Her sword was already half-drawn, as though she expected a battle. "Brangien said you needed me." Though Lancelot no longer wore her familiar patchwork leather and metal armor, her hair remained wild, dark curls, worn plain without any of the braids or ornamentation that were the style for women.

Guinevere sat, then stood. The flock of birds always living in her chest these days had been startled. They flung themselves against the confines of her ribs, beating and flapping in a frenzy inside of her.

"What is the threat?" Lancelot stood in a fighter's stance, feet apart, perfectly balanced.

"Not one you can fight with a sword. Guinevere's sister is here."

Lancelot frowned and then looked appropriately alarmed. "Wait. Guinevere—the princess you are supposed to be—was a real person?" Lancelot had never asked for more details about where Guinevere had come from. She had guessed that Merlin was her father, but beyond that, had merely accepted Guinevere as Guinevere had accepted her.

Guinevere nodded and resumed pacing. Where was Arthur? "She died, and I took her place. She really was from Cameliard, and she had—*has*—a younger sister. Who is here now." It was hard, speaking and thinking about the real Guinevere, having gotten so used to being Guinevere herself. The confusion was more than verbal.

"That is . . . not good."

Guinevere answered with a high-pitched laugh. "No. It is not good. I just met her."

"Did she—"

They were interrupted by the door opening. Arthur strode in.

"Guinevere! What is wrong?" He took her by the shoulders, peering into her face as though looking for some hurt there.

"My *sister* is here."

Arthur's face wrinkled in confusion, then smoothed out with deliberate understanding. "Oh. Your sister. I was not aware she was coming for a visit."

"Neither was I."

"Lancelot, will you wait outside?"

"She knows everything," Guinevere said. Arthur did not revise his statement, though, so Lancelot bowed her head to her king, then closed the door behind her.

Guinevere started babbling. "She saw me. She saw me!"

"What did she do?"

"Embraced me."

"She—wait. She saw you as Guinevere?"

Guinevere sat on the edge of her bed, throwing her hands up. "Yes! No. I do not know. It would have been three years since she had seen her sister, and of course no one is aware that the real Guinevere is . . ."

She trailed off. She hated the cruelty of letting the family think their daughter and sister was alive and well when in reality the girl had died in the spring. It was demanding a price of people who never agreed to pay it, all to keep the false Guinevere safe and at Arthur's side.

But as she had learned, much of Merlin's magic had a breathtakingly cruel edge. So much smashed and broken and discarded on the way to an end only he could see. An end only he chose.

Arthur reached for her hands and she let him take them, wishing again she could feel what he felt. She would give anything to siphon some of his calm assurance into herself right now. "Did Merlin do something to change your appearance?" he asked. "To make you more like Guinevere?"

"Not that I remember, but you could fill a thimble with what I remember and still have room to spare. Curse that faithless wizard!"

Arthur flinched and let go of her hands. Whatever Guinevere's own complicated feelings toward Merlin, Arthur revered him as his oldest friend and protector. Guinevere rubbed her face, then stopped, her numb hands making everything feel off. Strange. *Was* it her face? What secrets did it hold?

She shook her head. "As far as I know, he only changed the memories of the nuns so they would think I was their own Guinevere." The information was just there, in her head, much the same as the knot magic and her few memories of growing up in the forest. There was no lead-up to it. No planning with Merlin, no discussions, no memory of it actually happening. "He could have done something to my appearance. I do not think he did, but he could have."

"So either Guinevach truly recognized you, or . . ."

Guinevere leaned back and stared at the ceiling. "There are two options. The first, that Guinevach is only pretending to recognize me. Either because she was young enough when the real Guinevere left—" Arthur flinched again. He did not like it when Guinevere referred to the other one as the real one. But was it not the truth? *She* was the imposter. "Because she was so young that there is enough room for Guinevach to convince herself she misremembers what her own sister had looked like."

"You said 'either.'"

Guinevere made a clumsy attempt to undo her tight plaits. The braids were tugging at her scalp, but her fingers struggled uselessly.

"Either that, or she is pretending to recognize me because she has some reason to pretend. We have had enemies in fine clothes in the castle before."

Arthur reached out, taking one of Guinevere's braids and slowly undoing it. "But how would she have known it was you arriving at the castle? You were not accompanied by heralds. And you were with Brangien. She did not assume Brangien was the queen."

"Brangien looks like no one else here." Her father had walked across the world to change his fortunes. Brangien's features favored him, with beautiful big eyes and a round face.

"True. But if she truly could not remember her own sister's appearance, she would have asked. Not flung herself at you."

"She did call out my name before I turned toward her. And I reacted. So maybe by the time she reached me, she convinced herself, or was too confused? But no. That is not right. She was comparing our heights to what they had been and talking about our freckles. She seemed confident."

Arthur paused. His fingers ran down the waves left behind in her hair. "Maybe *Guinevach* is not Guinevach. Magic can—magic can alter faces. Perhaps yours was not the one altered."

Guinevere knew exactly what event he was remembering. The betrayal of his mother. His father, Uther Pendragon, wearing the face of Lady Igraine's husband through magic. Merlin's magic.

"True. But if that were the case, my knots at every doorway would undo the spell. Mordred is aware of those knots, though. And if whoever sent her knows I am not the real Guinevere, they would not need to change her face. I cannot recognize a sister I have never met, either. It would be easy to send someone pretending to be her." Perhaps, after the fairy queen's failure with the forest, Guinevach was another method of attack. If she had been sent here for Guinevere, that would explain how she knew exactly who to look for. She would have been prepared. "The Dark Queen cannot enter Camelot, so she created someone who we would never turn away."

"It is a possibility. But you said two options. What is the other option?"

Guinevere tapped her chin, wondering. The second option made even less sense. "That Guinevach did in fact recognize me. There were only a few days between when I took the real Guinevere's place at the convent and when I left with your men. Merlin changed the nuns' memories. I cannot imagine him slowly walking south for a month just to change Guinevach's memory. But then again, Merlin saw all of time at once. So he would have known Guinevach would come to the castle."

Arthur sounded dubious. "If Merlin walked—and he always walked, I never knew him to use a horse—or even if he had ridden, would he have had time to get to Guinevach and then come back before you saw him be sealed into the cave by the Lady of the Lake?"

Guinevere did not think so. But she could not be sure. And even though she had memories of looking at her face—seeing it reflected back to her in water, trees overhead coloring both with greenish tinges, a black pool of . . . no, that one slipped from her and she let it—she knew better than to trust her own mind. "Merlin could have changed my face. It would be the simpler option for him."

"Would you know? Could you sense if he had?" Arthur put the backs of his fingers against her cheek, stroking softly down it. He looked sad, as though the idea that Guinevere's face was not real hurt him.

It hurt her, too. She could not claim her mind, or her memories, or now even her face.

"Maybe. I doubt my knots could undo his work. But I am afraid if I actively tugged too hard at anything Merlin did, it might unravel.

And then where would we be? Your wife would have a new face. That would be difficult to explain to the kingdom."

Arthur let out a dry laugh, joining her by lying back on the bed. "It would."

"So what do we do?"

"I will assign Sir Gawain to her and have him watch her closely."

"Brangien can spy, as well."

There was a light knock on the door. Arthur sat up. Guinevere followed his lead. "Come in," Arthur commanded, even though it was Guinevere's room.

Lancelot opened the door but did not enter. "Guinevach arrived in Camelot with three guards and two maids. One an older woman, one barely a woman at all. I have given her guards rooms on the far end of the castle and assigned guards to watch them. I put Guinevach on the sixth story and am locking the interior door. The exterior walkways will be guarded day and night, and her movements marked at all times."

Arthur nodded. "Very good. You may go." He turned back to Guinevere. "We leave for Sir Bors's wedding in three days. You can be ill and take to your bed until then."

"And I will do what I can to sense whether there is magic at play." Guinevere bitterly regretted rendering her hands worthless for the time being. She could not even grasp Guinevach's hands to feel whether there were any currents of threat or anger. "But if she is here to catch me, I will have to be careful. I cannot give her evidence that I use magic."

Arthur's shoulders were squared, his face determined but not worried. "Tonight I will visit the dining hall while she is there and unsheathe Excalibur. We can rule out whether she has fairy magic."

"Mordred could be around Excalibur, and his father was a fairy knight."

They both sat in silence for a moment. Mordred had explained to Guinevere how much pain he bore all the time living here. How patient and determined he must have been to endure it, to endure Excalibur. Guinevere saw the hurt on Arthur's face and regretted bringing Mordred up. "But that is a good idea. If she reacts to it, we will have an answer."

Arthur recovered, looking more confident. "Magic or not, we can handle this."

They could and they would handle it, together. If Guinevach was a threat, Guinevere pitied her. And if she really was just a girl trying to visit her sister, everything they were doing was cruel and Guinevere pitied her all the more.

But sending Guinevach away was no crueler than letting her know her sister was in a hole in the ground, her grave unmarked, her name stolen. Maybe even her face stolen.

Was nothing truly Guinevere's?

CHAPTER SEVEN

"Well?" Guinevere asked, looking up at the cliff face. They had come nearly to the top of the castle, carved from the mountain in levels. "Do you think you can climb it?"

Lancelot squinted in the darkening light, considering. Guinevere hated sitting in her room, stewing, waiting for more information about Guinevach—she wanted to *do* something. And she realized that in her search for magic, she had not looked east. The mountain behind them felt like safety. And it was—safety from men. No army could stage an attack from that direction. But a Dark Queen, fueled by magic? Guinevere could picture it, vines bursting overhead and spilling down the castle like the waterfalls on either side, creeping and choking.

She had used blood to knot magic onto a rock. It would link to her other sentinel rocks and tell her if any threat came from this direction. But she needed to get it up there.

"I think so." Lancelot held out her hand. Guinevere gave her the rock, and Lancelot tucked it into a pouch at her waist. She had stripped down to her tunic and breeches, removing even her boots. She wore a coiled length of rope across her body, from right shoulder to left hip.

"I saw you climb, once. Straight down to the lake, to get to your boat."

"My boat?" Lancelot stared upward and considered her path. "I have never had a boat."

This was surprising. "How did you get back and forth for the trials, then, without using the ferry?"

"There is a cave. I spent many years there as a child, when—" Lancelot stopped. Guinevere wished she would continue. She wanted to know more. How Lancelot had survived as an orphan. What it had been like. Guinevere was ravenous for details of other childhoods to tuck in around the blank spaces of her own.

Lancelot cleared her throat. "Well, and I can swim."

"Across the whole lake?" Guinevere asked, horrified.

Lancelot laughed. "It is not so far if you start on the cliff sides. Now, we are losing the light."

Before Guinevere could counsel caution, Lancelot had begun to climb. Her speed was breathtaking. While Guinevere did not particularly fear heights—preferring, apparently, to divert all her terror to water—her heart beat faster watching. There was one breathlessly infinite moment when Lancelot's fingers slipped and she dangled by one hand, but she quickly recovered and finished the ascent, disappearing over the top of the cliff face.

Then the rope cascaded down, reminding Guinevere of her imagined vines. But this rope brought no threats, only protectors.

"I placed the rock away from the edge, so it should warn you before anything reaches the cliff face," Lancelot called, dangling casually from the rope by one hand as she looked down over Camelot. She dropped neatly to the walkway, then gave the rope a sharp tug. It slithered free and fell to a pile at her feet. Lancelot gathered it back up. "I did not see anything amiss, and I could see for a fair distance."

"Good. Thank you. Tomorrow I would like to ride out and scout the eastern borders just to be certain."

"We can find an excuse for that. You look tired. Shall we return you to your rooms?"

Guinevere sighed, sitting and putting her back against the rock. She looked out over Camelot as candlelight began to flicker in windows and along the streets. From up here it was so simple, so tidy. She knew that running a city was anything but simple and tidy. Still, it was a pretty picture with the gray shops and homes, the slate and thatch roofs, the organic pathways of the streets running through everything like seams. If she closed her eyes, she could imagine pulling the whole city over herself like a blanket.

She turned to Lancelot, annoyed to see that Lancelot looked as Lancelot ever did: ready. "You *should* look tired, too. I need to sleep, but I am afraid of what I will dream."

"Tell me about the dream that frightened you."

Guinevere had told Brangien some of it, but she went into more detail now. "It felt like I was experiencing someone else's dream, or memory," she said, after explaining it. "It was foreign."

"But it does not sound like the Dark Queen."

"No, I agree. I have felt her magic, tasted her power. This was different."

"The Lady." Lancelot said it matter-of-factly. Hearing her state it like that made it feel more real. Guinevere doubted herself less. "Did the dream seem threatening?"

"Yes!" Guinevere stopped herself, putting one hand against the stone. She could feel nothing now, which was both a comfort and an annoyance. *Had* the dream been threatening? During it, she had not been frightened. Even the plunge into the abyss had seemed necessary and welcome. All her terror had been upon waking. "Maybe. I do not know. But why would she invade my dreams? Because Merlin hid me too well?"

"I wonder if . . ." Lancelot trailed off, hesitant.

"Go on."

"We heard her, when she trapped Merlin. She accused him of stealing something precious, and she wanted it back."

"Yes. The sword."

"That is what we assumed. But what if we were wrong?" Lancelot stared out at the twilight. The lake reflected the sky, luminous with the last, lingering moments of daylight. Guinevere could almost love the way it held on to the light. She wished the lake were the mirror it appeared to be, so she could look into it and discover her own face. Map it like she could map this city. Label and understand and claim it as her own.

"Why would we be wrong about that?" she asked. In the approaching night, her skin looked bled of color, the same shade as the lake. She stared at the lavender veins of her hands, so like the natural channels of a river, feeding the landscape of her body.

"Why would she attack Merlin over the sword, when Arthur is the one who has it? Why would Merlin be afraid she would come after *you* to get it back?" Lancelot said.

"Well, because . . . to punish Merlin. He let himself be sealed in the cave so she would not find me and come after me to hurt him."

"If an ancient power like the Lady of the Lake wanted Excalibur back, she would have it. She allied herself with Arthur. Took his side against the Dark Queen. It does not seem like her."

"What does she *seem* like?" Guinevere asked, genuinely puzzled. The light was quickly failing, and she could not see Lancelot's expression anymore, only an impression of her face, as though viewing her through thick, warped glass.

"I mean, she has no reputation for capriciousness or cruelty."

"Other than entombing Merlin alive," Guinevere added wryly.

"Well. Yes. She was devastated over what he stole. But she has never come after Arthur. And you have nothing to do with the sword. You cannot even be around it. Is there another reason Merlin would work so hard to keep you from the Lady?"

Merlin had begged Lancelot to hide Guinevere that day when the Lady attacked him. And he had sent Guinevere to Arthur for protection. Guinevere was also nearly certain that Merlin had put the debilitating fear of water into her so she would not go where the Lady could get to her.

The lake beneath them was dead, devoid of any magic or life. What if Merlin had done that? Had somehow made it inhospitable to the Lady of the Lake as further protection? Guinevere wondered if perhaps Arthur had helped, using Excalibur.

The stars began to pierce the fabric of the sky like tiny needle points. Guinevere did not remember the stars so much as she knew them down to her soul. She had stared up at them for so long they were written on her mind where no one—not even Merlin—could erase them. "What else could he have taken from her, though? And why does it involve me? I— Oh. Oh no."

Who took care of you when Merlin was with me all those years?

Merlin is not your father. You cannot even say it without stumbling on the words.

Magic runs through your veins.

You have stolen something precious from me.

She had so few memories. Everything else—her childhood, her life, her mother—had been wiped away like fog from a window. Someone had taken them from her so she would not know. So she would not ask.

Guinevere put her face in her hands, hiding from the stars and from the lake beneath them. "Lancelot. I think the Lady of the Lake is my mother."

"Say nothing to Arthur." Guinevere sat on the edge of her bed, taking deep breaths and imagining her face like her mind: easily wiped clean of everything inconvenient or painful or dangerous. "Until we know more, I do not want to trouble him with this."

"But if she is your mother—"

"All I know—*all I know* in the altered landscape of my mind, damn that wizard—is that I believe in Arthur. That I chose him. I have known it from the start." Not in the way she "knew" Merlin was her father—a fact that she knew but that never felt or settled right. Her belief in Arthur was part of her. Nothing could have placed it there, and nothing could take it away. "Right now, that is enough for me. There is the threat of the Dark Queen out there, and there is the threat of Guinevach right here. Those are the threats I am ready for. Those are the questions I can answer. And until we have answered them, I can let questions about myself lie." She looked up, desperate for reassurance.

Lancelot offered her none. Her knight's face was clouded with worry and something else. She seemed on the verge of speaking, but the door opened. Arthur entered, followed by Brangien. Lancelot gave a quick bow. "I will be outside if you need me."

Guinevere did not want her to leave, but she did not have a chance to call her back.

"No reaction to the sword." Arthur gestured to his belt out of habit, but he had thoughtfully left the sword somewhere else before coming to Guinevere's room.

It took several seconds for Guinevere to understand what he meant. Guinevach had not reacted badly to Excalibur. "How was she at dinner?"

Arthur seemed hesitant to answer. Guinevere waited for the bad news. If only Guinevach were a cursed forest. A possessed wolf. A magically venomous spider. All those Guinevere could fight.

"Charming," Brangien said, rummaging through the chests in the corner. She was already planning and packing for their trip to Dindrane's family estate.

"And by charming, you mean . . ."

Brangien frowned at a yellow tunic as though it had done something to personally offend her. "Excellent manners. Back as straight as a sapling, swaying gently toward whoever was speaking. Mouth like a rosebud and a laugh as pretty and sweet. Sir Gawain certainly seemed to agree. Even Sir Bors spoke with her." Sir Bors had never had a conversation with Guinevere. At least, not one that was more than absolutely required to give or receive necessary information. "*Why* are we spying on her?"

"It is . . . complicated."

"There is a chance she is in league with the Dark Queen," Arthur said. It was the truth, or at least a sliver of it.

Brangien directed her frown toward Guinevere, holding up the yellow tunic thoughtfully. "She hardly seems the type. She wears a lot of pink."

"Because she wears pink she cannot be in league with evil?"

"No, sorry. That was a separate thought. I like her in pink. It is flattering. But I do not think it would suit you."

Guinevere turned back to Arthur, giving up on Brangien's assessments. "And the sword did nothing? How did you unsheathe it? How close were you?"

Arthur watched Brangien's actions with a furrowed brow. "Guinevere would look very nice in pink."

"She does not have the coloring for it."

"What does that mean? Guinevere always looks pretty."

"Because she has a maid who is careful to dress her in colors that will flatter her complexion."

Guinevere snatched the yellow tunic from Brangien and tossed it onto the bed. "Can we focus on the threat?"

"Right. Yes." Giving one last frown to Brangien, Arthur turned his full attention to Guinevere. "I unsheathed the sword as I walked in. Held it at my side and passed directly behind her. She did not react. And she was using a specially prepared iron goblet."

Guinevere slumped, disappointed. "That was clever."

Arthur laughed. "Try not to sound too proud of my cleverness."

"I am proud of you! It just would have been so much simpler if she had, I do not know, dissolved into flowers or gone up in a puff of smoke." Guinevere gestured toward the ceiling where puff-of-smoke Guinevach would have gathered.

"You *want* her to be evil?" Arthur asked.

"What? No! No. Of course not. But I need answers. And she is a threat, evil or not. If she is sent by the Dark Queen, or if she can tell everyone that—" Guinevere cut herself off. Brangien did not know that Guinevach could reveal the truth of Guinevere's identity.

"She has two lady's maids," Brangien said, laying out jewelry and pretending like she was not curious about why Guinevere had stopped talking. "A young maid, barely old enough to have her monthly courses, if that. She seems quite dim. And an older maid, who appears to be doing the bulk of the work. She is always sewing." Brangien held up a hand. "I looked. It is actual sewing, no knot magic."

There was a knock at the door. Brangien crossed the room and opened it, then stepped into the hallway and closed the door behind her.

Arthur spoke quickly. "I had Sir Tristan interview her guards. She came with three. One was familiar with a cook in the kitchen, who confirmed that the man was from Cameliard. So that would seem to confirm that Guinevach is indeed from Cameliard, which means she is actually Guinevach."

"Guards can be bribed."

Arthur nodded, sitting next to Guinevere. "That is true."

Brangien came back in. "The older maid. Guinevach sends her regards and hopes you feel well enough to meet her tomorrow morning. Dindrane is furious, by the way." Brangien swept the jewelry that did not meet her approval back into a box. "She is taking it personally that you are 'sick' and unable to help her finalize her preparations for the wedding. We leave in three days."

Three more days of avoiding both Guinevach *and* Dindrane? Any potential magical threats paled in comparison to Dindrane's wrath. It would take an entire contingent of knights and guards to keep Guinevere safe from her demands.

Guinevere felt the stones of Camelot closing in around her. It was less like a refuge and more like a cage, now that Guinevach was here. "Lancelot and I will go scout the eastern borders tomorrow. The river—"

"Is impassable," Arthur said.

"For human armies. I would like to see that region for myself, just to be certain."

"I cannot come."

"I did not ask you to."

Arthur frowned. "What if there is a threat? It could be dangerous."

"*I* am dangerous." Guinevere raised an eyebrow, daring him to challenge her. This had been their agreement. She came back as queen, but also as the first line of defense against the Dark Queen. Arthur relented.

"Can we leave early?" he asked, watching Brangien sort through Guinevere's things. "For the wedding, I mean."

"Early?" Brangien's face became a mask of horror at the suggestion. "Impossible."

"You can follow after with the main train so you have time to finish preparing. I will leave tomorrow night with Guinevere and a few guards." Arthur sounded excited the more he spoke. "Go tell Sir Caradoc and the captain of the guard. And the kitchens. We will let the main party catch up with us in a day or two, so we do not need too many provisions."

Brangien looked like she would rather strangle her king than follow through on his plan. But when she turned to Guinevere, some of the aggravation had a hint of anguish. "But how will you *sleep* on the road?"

Guinevere's dreams. They needed to see whether, with her own dreams returned, the invasive dream of the city returned. And until Guinevere sorted it out, Brangien would not be reunited with Isolde in her own dreams.

Guinevere tried to smile reassuringly. "I will sleep as well as I can tonight."

"Once you leave, I will not be there to help."

Arthur waved away Brangien's concerns, not understanding how complicated they really were. "I will be with her. You have nothing to fear."

Guinevere stood and took Brangien's hands. "I will be fine, and as soon as we are reunited, I will catch you up on everything."

Brangien bit her lip and then hurried from the room to fulfill her king's orders.

Arthur was almost bouncing on the balls of his feet. "Problem solved. I will rescue you from Guinevach and whisk you away to a very dull wedding filled with strangers!"

Guinevere laughed. She wanted to be excited, too. She had been looking forward to this journey, and leaving early with so few people meant even more time with just Arthur. But she could not be selfish. Arthur was trying to protect her from the potential threat of Guinevach and all she could reveal. But who would protect Camelot?

"We cannot leave the kingdom unguarded." Guinevere gestured toward the space on Arthur's belt where Excalibur should have been.

"We were going to be away from Camelot regardless. Guinevach's presence does not change that I am not always in the city. Besides, if she is a threat to anyone, it is to you, specifically. So the best way for us to combat any potential danger is to remove you from the situation."

Guinevere considered it. If Guinevach was soaked in magic, their combined efforts to protect Camelot would have already harmed her. And if she was here to reveal the truth of Guinevere's identity, she had not done so yet. "We leave early, and we send Guinevach home," she said.

"Write her a letter that you have to attend this wedding and do not know how long we will be away, and that you will visit her in Cameliard next. I will inform Sir Gawain he is to escort her and her traveling party beyond the borders of Camelot as soon as we are away."

"It does not answer any of our questions, though." Why Guinevach had come. If she was truly Guinevach or an imposter, like Guinevere. And why she pretended to recognize Guinevere. Guinevere put a finger against the side of her nose, tracing the freckles she could not see. How could she have freckles if her mother was the Lady of the Lake? Had her father been human? Was Merlin her father been human? Was Merlin her father after all? There had been an entire history in the way he had addressed the Lady. *Nynaeve, my Lady, my love.*

"Do we need those questions answered? One way or another, Guinevach is a threat to you. If the threat is gone, the questions are, too." Arthur stood, striding to the door. "I will make preparations!"

Guinevere disagreed. Threats could be vanquished or disarmed, but questions lingered as long as wounds. And with no answers, she had no way to heal them.

CHAPTER EIGHT

If Guinevere dreamed, she did not remember it. Her suspicions about the Lady of the Lake plagued her as she rode slowly alongside Lancelot, swinging around the southern end of the mountain of Camelot. Ferrying across the lake that morning had filled her with the usual dread and terror, this time compounded by wondering what she was not remembering.

What was missing.

How could she be a person when so much of who she was . . . was *not*? Not spoken. Not remembered. Not true.

It would take half the day to get to the other side of the mountain and see terrain flat enough to allow passage. They would stop at the enormous bisected river that came down as waterfalls on either side of Camelot. Guinevere did not have it in her to cross a river, and did not feel it was necessary. The land in this direction had been tamed fields where possible, but it was rocky and barren closer to the mountain. They were alone. The sun beat down, the heat less intense than in summer but somehow more unbearable because of the promise of autumn's cooler embrace. A petulant last assault of discomfort with no breeze or shade to offer relief.

"My queen?" Lancelot prodded, steering her reliable blind steed closer to Guinevere's gray mare. "You seem distracted."

Guinevere laughed, releasing some of the tension inside her. She imagined it escaping like a burst of steam from a boiling pot. "I realized yesterday my mother might be the Lady of the Lake; I have an enemy in Camelot who threatens my place; we do not know when the Dark Queen will strike again; and my best friend is in mourning because she cannot use my magic to visit her true love every night."

"And you have to go to Dindrane's wedding."

"*And* I have to go to Dindrane's wedding. What should I expect?"

Lancelot glanced at her, trying not to smile. "I have never been to a noble wedding."

"Oh, I forget. You are so good at being a knight, it seems as though you have always been one." Guinevere shrugged off her cloak and set it across her lap. It was oppressively warm. She wished she could shrug off several more layers. "The only wedding I have ever been to is my own."

"I watched from across the lake. The lights were beautiful."

"That was my favorite part." The whole day had been overwhelming. Terrifying, even. Guinevere had been determined not to make a mistake. It felt like remembering a different person. That Guinevere had not yet been Guinevere. She still had her name. And she still thought she was coming to Camelot as Merlin's daughter to be the protector of Arthur.

Did everyone feel such sadness thinking back on who they had been? Lancelot certainly did not seem to want to dwell or speak of her life before now. Brangien, too, rarely spoke of her past. Guinevere knew she and Sir Tristan had been banished because of something to do with Isolde, but the details of it were never shared. She had felt the pain inside Brangien. The pain inside so many people, now that she thought about it.

Perhaps it was not such a bad thing to have so few memories.

Lancelot scanned the countryside. She was more at ease now, guiding her horse without conscious effort. Seeing her out here made Guinevere realize how tense Lancelot always was in Camelot.

"Do you miss being the patchwork knight?" Guinevere asked.

"Why would you ask that?"

"The freedom of it. Going where you wished. Doing what you wanted. Not accountable to anyone save yourself. It was a very different life from the one you have now."

She expected Lancelot to protest, but her knight looked thoughtful as she considered the question. Finally, she spoke. "There were some aspects of it that were better, yes. But everything I did was to become what I am now. Who I am now. I gladly accept any struggles or restraints, because it means I get to wear my king's colors and stand at my queen's side. This is exactly what I wanted."

"But is it what you expected?"

At this, Lancelot turned away. There was something evasive in the way she suddenly needed to resume scanning the horizon for threats. "Nothing is ever what we expect."

That, at least, Guinevere understood.

The river was wide, white and foaming as it rushed around jagged rocks and tiny islands that reminded Guinevere too much of where Maleagant had kept her prisoner. She could almost smell the damp space, hear the sneering replies of the guards. They were all dead now.

Guinevere looked away from the hungry river, focusing instead on the trees around it. It had been a steady uphill ride to get here, and they were letting the horses rest.

Choosing a shady spot beneath a soaring oak, Guinevere pricked one finger and carefully knotted her blood onto the stone, connecting them. If something passed this way that was a threat to her—and therefore Camelot—she would feel it. She set the stone beneath the tree, then closed her eyes, breathing in the scent of green things and ancient, patient life.

How unfortunate that nature was both the most peaceful and the most dangerous place possible. But that was its duality. It gave life and it took it, provided and withheld, offered beauty and danger in equal measure. Camelot was safe and ordered and structured, so many things put in place to separate people from nature. Roofs and walls. Pipes for water. Swords with men to wield them. The separation was a protection but also a loss.

Still. Better to protect what they had built, and now she would have a warning of impending danger.

Was it enough to know that a threat was coming, though? Guinevere remembered the feeling of the trees lashing her arms. Her blood dripping to give life. To feed. To create a new form for terror and death.

Her eyes closed as revulsion flooded her. Not at the memory of what had been done to her in that hollow, but at the idea for a knot creeping across her mind. She did not want to think it through, but she owed it to Arthur, to Camelot. Knight or not, she was still a soldier in the fight to protect this kingdom.

She considered the potential knot with as much detachment as she could manage. If she added hunger, if she added her own fear, if she twisted them all together in exactly the right way . . .

She could see it coming together, the twists and loops of the knot re-forming. It would work.

It was the worst kind of knot. She wanted to open her eyes, to look away, to imagine anything else. But how many decisions did Arthur make that he wished he could look away from? That he could avoid?

If she had a way to protect Camelot, she owed it to Camelot to do so. And what was more valuable than a warning of danger? Something to end the threat before it ever arrived.

She pulled several hairs from her head and reopened the cut on her hand. Coating the hairs in blood, she knotted and tied them around the sentry stone. Ugly, harsh knots and hungry magic. If anything passed this stone with the intent to harm her, the hunger would be unleashed and the land itself would draw blood until all was drained.

The worst part was that it took almost nothing from her. All spells, all knots, all magic had a price to pay. But this one demanded the price of whoever triggered it. Guinevere stared numbly at the weapon in her hand. That was the nature of weapons. The person who wielded them never paid the cost. Only the victims.

"I can swim it," Lancelot said, dropping out of a tree next to her.

Guinevere jumped, startled, and set the rock behind herself guiltily, as though Lancelot would be able to see what she had created. "Swim what? The river? No!"

"I will start upstream. The current will carry me down, but I can do it. And then I can place a rock on the other side, too. We can save ourselves the trip to secure the northern side of the river."

Guinevere hated this plan as much as she hated what she had just knotted into the stone. "I do not mind coming back."

Lancelot laughed. "You do not have to swim, or even watch. It will take me an hour at most. Besides, there is no real farmland to the northeast. An excuse for that trip will be harder to come by."

Guinevere sighed. Lancelot was right. It was the smarter choice to get it all done now, and then they could journey to Dindrane's family estate with more confidence. She would not leave Arthur's kingdom unguarded.

"Could you get to one of the islands?" Guinevere did not want to tie another of those terrible knots. Water was a powerful force of magic. That was why she never used it. But with water connected to the island and both shores, placing the knot in the middle would encompass the whole region.

It would set a trip line of death across the land. Guinevere twitched. She should destroy these knots, but they would only hurt those seeking to hurt her. Seeking to hurt Camelot, and Arthur. She shoved the rock into an oiled pouch and tied off the top. "Keep it dry, if you can."

Lancelot took the pouch, not knowing what she carried. If Guinevere told her, would her knight—her noble knight—still do what she was asked? "I have to go upstream a ways. Give me an hour. Stay right here."

Guinevere pulled her knees up and wrapped her arms around her legs. She watched Lancelot stride away with purpose. How did Arthur feel when he was about to go into battle? Dread? Guilt? Or determination?

She closed her eyes. The knot she had tied was branded on the darkness inside her eyelids, tying itself over and over. It was not the cost of the magic. It was the demand of her soul, forcing her to face what she had done, the choice she had made. She did not flinch. She watched and accepted. Minutes passed, and she could look at the knot without horror.

"For Camelot," she said, opening her eyes, her voice steadier than expected. If anyone came this way with the intent to harm, all she was doing was defending herself and her city and her king.

And then a thought struck her. The enemies before had been

faceless ideas. But there was one they knew. She imagined Mordred approaching from this direction, with his moss-green eyes, his clever lips, his promises and lies and spark and passion. Walking this way. Triggering the magic. Mordred cut down without a witness, without a mourner, without a chance to defend himself. Without Guinevere ever seeing him again, or even knowing that she had killed him.

She stood, sick. "Lancelot!" she shouted, rushing through the trees toward where Lancelot had disappeared. How long had it been? Would Lancelot already be in the water?

"Lancelot!" She pushed through the undergrowth, dodged around trees. She ran until she was out of breath. Lancelot could not have gone this far. Guinevere turned to double back. Maybe she could catch Lancelot swimming. A twig snapped behind her and she let out a cry of relief as she spun. It was not too late. It was—

A wolf, black and mangy, growled as its hackles raised, making it grow in size until it blocked out everything else. Its eyes glowed a familiar red, just like the possessed wolves she had encountered before. The growl doubled, then tripled, then became an entire chorus of death as six other wolves prowled in and out of the dappled shadows of the quiet trees above them.

This time she had no knights. No Excalibur.

Only herself.

The wolves' jaws parted, yellowed teeth revealed in twisted imitations of a smile.

CHAPTER NINE

The triumph of guessing right about the possibility of a fairy queen attack from over the mountain would hardly comfort Guinevere when she was dead, torn apart by a pack of wolves.

She could run. If she could get far enough fast enough, she might overtake Lancelot in the river, triggering the magic and killing the wolves. But she was wearing long skirts and delicate boots, and they were wolves. She did not like her odds.

"Go tell your queen she is not welcome here," Guinevere said, steeling her trembling voice. She had told Arthur she was dangerous. Now was her chance to prove it.

The wolves took a step toward her. Guinevere lit her hands on fire.

Fire magic did not come easily to her. It was a struggle to control the flames, to command them. She had the easiest time extinguishing them. Having hands that were still numb did not help the situation, but at least if she was burning herself, she would not feel it.

The wolves hesitated. Even in their magic-controlled state, they knew to fear fire and what it could do.

"Please." Guinevere locked eyes with the lead wolf. She bore wolves no ill will. They were beautiful creatures, predatory by nature but not out of viciousness. This radiating malice did not belong to them. "Do not make me hurt you."

The wolf snarled and leapt. Guinevere raised a hand, releasing the fire. It jumped from her to the wolf, hitting it midair. A natural fire would take time to catch. This was a magical fire, though. It consumed the wolf in a brilliant blaze of heat and fury. Guinevere cried out in dismay.

Even worse, the wolf had given the flames a taste and a target. Guinevere had guided the strike, but now released, the fire would follow its chosen path. A spark drifted in the air, then shot toward the nearest wolf. The creature went up in a blaze.

"Run!" Guinevere shouted, but the other wolves did not or could not understand.

A flare of pain alerted her to the fire spreading up her arms, burning her sleeves. She had taken her attention away from controlling it. She swatted at the flames before having the presence of mind to command them. Her power rushed forward, channeled in a wild and free way, the opposite of her binding knots and nothing like the struggle of controlling the fire. This was a deluge of cool, cleansing magic, running down her arms and extinguishing the fire, leaving behind only her unharmed skin and the charred remains of her sleeves.

When she looked up, seven piles of smoldering ashes greeted her, tiny fires spreading along the forest floor. The wolves were gone, the fight won.

Guinevere wept as she put out each lingering fire.

She mourned for the animals, and she simmered with hatred for her true enemy. If the Dark Queen had not stolen their will, these wolves would be alive. Free to roam the forests, hunting.

But there was so little forest left in this region. Perhaps the Dark

Queen had found all the wolves left, clumped and crowded and starving, driven from the fields that were slowly overtaking the land.

Guinevere wiped her eyes. She had been given no choice but to protect herself. Still, the smell of smoke and ash clung to her like guilt, permeating her to her core. Even if she had not burned the wolves, they would have died once they crossed the threshold of her protection knots. Was it worse to end lives that had already been stolen? Cruelty upon cruelty.

Guinevere trudged back toward where she would meet Lancelot. Halfway there, a sensation like walking through a spider's web blanketed her and then was gone. She knew her own touch. The killing magic was in place.

"Guinevere?"

She whipped around, fists raised.

Mordred was bisected by darkness, half in the shadow of a tree, half revealed by the early-afternoon sun. "What happened?" He pointed at her ruined sleeves and soot-stained dress, worry in his voice.

"The wolves are dead." Her voice was cold, raw from crying.

"All of them?" Mordred's face fell, and he lowered his hand. He held a clay pitcher. His clothes were not the brilliant-colored fine fabrics he had worn in Camelot, but simple browns and greens. Somehow he looked equally regal. His hair curled against his shoulders, darker than the shadows. She knew how soft it was. And she hated him for the knowledge.

"Your plan will not work."

"No, not if they are dead." He stared down at the pitcher. There were bruised hollows beneath his eyes as though he had not slept, but it could have been the shade playing tricks. "I thought I could get here in time. They did not deserve this."

"And Camelot did? We deserve to have cursed wolves descend on us? How could you?"

Mordred shook his head. "I am here to—"

"Do not lie to me." The pain in his face gave her vicious pleasure. She wanted to hurt him.

"I was trying to save them. The wolves." Mordred tipped the pitcher. The liquid that streamed from it was milky and strangely luminous. It pooled on the forest floor and quickly disappeared. "I am sorry you got there first. Sorry for both the wolves and for you."

"Save your apologies. You should run. I have men coming." She had only Lancelot, and Lancelot could not best Mordred in a sword fight. They had already learned this.

"You are hurt." Mordred took a step forward and Guinevere let out a sharp cry.

"Stop! You will die." Guinevere drew a line through the air with one hand. "If you come closer—if any of you come closer, if she comes closer, if any of her tortured familiars come closer and try to attack Camelot from above, you will die. Anyone who crosses this line with intent to harm me will be ended."

Mordred had stopped, frozen in movement as though he would take another step at any moment. "Then why warn me?" His voice was soft, the familiar playful tones completely gone, replaced with an earnestness that was far worse. "You left me in the forest. You made your choice. I betrayed your beloved king. And—and I hurt you."

"You did." Guinevere put her hands over either wrist, covering the dozens of thin white scars that marked where the trees had drawn her blood to renew the Dark Queen. Mordred's grandmother. Mordred's plan.

"So bid me cross the threshold."

"I do not want to watch you die!" Guinevere turned her back on him, away from the intensity in his eyes, the clear focus there. Mordred had always seen her in a way she longed to be seen. She had trusted him, and he had betrayed her. But he had also stopped short of killing Lancelot, even dragging her unconscious body into the trees so she would be safe from the newly rising Dark Queen. And though Mordred had ample opportunity, he never tried to kill Arthur.

She did not understand him, and she wanted to, and she hated that she wanted to. "Go," she commanded.

"Guinevere." A hand rested on her shoulder and she spun, heart racing, hand over her mouth. She was about to watch Mordred die. Mordred stood close to her, over the border of the magic. There was no pain in his expression. Only anguish.

"I do not wish to harm *you*. I am so sorry for the hurt I have caused. You have my vow I will never do it again."

Guinevere stumbled backward, away from him. Relief that she was not about to watch him die warred with panic. Either her magic did not work or Mordred genuinely wished her no harm. She did not know which was worse. "Get away from me," she choked out.

There was nothing of the eel in his expression, nothing secretive or slippery. Only sad resignation as he bowed his head, turned, and walked back the way he had come.

Lancelot rejoined her, nearly dry. "I know you hate water, so I stayed in the sun to— Guinevere, what *happened*?"

Guinevere shrugged, picking at the burned sleeves that barely covered her shoulders. She was sitting on the forest floor, utterly spent. "There were wolves. There are not wolves anymore." She should mention Mordred, but she could not bring herself to do it.

He had crossed the threshold. He could lie to her, but he could not lie to the magic. He meant her no harm. What did it mean?

Nothing. It meant nothing. He had used her. He had betrayed them all. Whether or not he believed he meant her harm, everything he was threatened them all.

"I should never have left you." Lancelot fell to her knees, her head bowed.

"You were doing your part. I did mine." Guinevere stood and held out her hand to Lancelot. "We have a long ride back to Camelot, and then we leave for Dindrane's estate tonight."

"Tonight?" Lancelot frowned in confusion, accepting Guinevere's hand and standing.

"Yes, Arthur and I are leaving early. He did not tell you?"

"No."

"It must have slipped his mind. Can you be ready in time?"

"I always have a bag ready." Lancelot walked at Guinevere's side, sword drawn, protective glare in place as her eyes swept the trees. Guinevere suspected she half hoped more wolves would come so she could protect Guinevere this time, but there would be no more threats. Not from this direction.

Guinevere herself half hoped Mordred would appear and challenge her knight. A simple, clean fight. No questions of loyalty, no magical tests. Sword against sword. Perhaps that was how Arthur did what he did. There was no wrong or right in a sword battle. Only victor and loser.

But she already knew Mordred would win that, too.

To Guinevere's surprise, they had been riding for only an hour or two when a man on horseback appeared on the trail, riding to meet them. Her heart knew his shape before her eyes could make out the details. Arthur.

She spurred her horse forward to him. "What is it?"

"I wanted to see how things were here, and— Guinevere, what happened to your sleeves?" He reached out and took the burned and ragged ends between his fingers.

"There were wolves." Guinevere gave a condensed version of what had happened. And just as with Lancelot, she left out Mordred entirely.

She could imagine exactly what would happen. Arthur would feel compelled to ride after Mordred. To confront him. And one of them would get hurt, or worse, killed. The brutal simplicity of swords as a solution. Mordred was not a threat right now, at least not to Guinevere. He was probably still a threat to Arthur, but their eastern border was secure, the wolves were dead, and whatever—whoever—that attack had been, it was thwarted.

Arthur tapped his fingers against the hilt of his sword, staring back at where Guinevere and Lancelot had come from, unaware of the missing parts of the story. "So no one can come over the mountain."

"Not if they mean harm. To me, specifically, but anyone seeking to attack Camelot would, by extension, be trying to harm me. I think it is broad enough." She hoped it was. It had not kept Mordred out.

"You are a wonder." Arthur considered her with wide eyes. Normally Guinevere would love to feel so seen by him, but right now, covered in the ashes of stolen life, leaving behind a death trap, she wanted to be invisible. To disappear. "And next time we will send you with more men. You should never have been alone."

Lancelot was riding behind them. Guinevere was certain she overheard Arthur equating Guinevere with only Lancelot to Guinevere being alone. "No, that would have been worse. I could not have fought the wolves with witnesses. Lancelot and I managed everything. We are a perfect team."

Arthur frowned, but said nothing. They rode back toward

Camelot. By the time they reached the far edge of the lake, it was nearing dusk. Guinevere nudged her horse to go faster, but Arthur clicked his tongue, slowing it again.

"We will miss curfew!" Guinevere reminded him. No one was allowed in the streets after full dark. It was the best way to keep down crime and mischief.

Arthur laughed. "We are the king and queen."

Guinevere raised an eyebrow. "So we are above the law?"

At this, Arthur looked sheepish. "Well, no. But it does make enforcing the law against ourselves a little more flexible. Who is going to put us in a holding chamber for being in the streets too late?"

She could not imagine any person in Camelot demanding the king spend the night in a cell for being out past curfew. When they reached the ferry, she was tempted to stay and let Arthur bring her things for their trip rather than add yet another lake crossing to an already overwhelming day. But she needed to change her dress and her boots, and wipe away the soot and ash. She wished she could wipe them from her memory, as well.

No. Never that. She would not wish away any of her memories. Not after having so many taken.

She wrapped herself in her cloak to hide her missing sleeves and let Arthur wrap his arms around her to hide her from the lake as they crossed. On the other side, Arthur stopped to instruct the ferryman to wait at the dock so he could transport their traveling group back across the lake. Guinevere had no desire to stay on the boat for the conversation. She had only just stepped free of the dock when a vision in pink rushed toward her.

"There you are!" Guinevach stood before her, smiling, her braided golden hair wound around her head like a crown, the way Guinevere so often wore hers. "Your maid—she is very rude—told me you were sick. But Anna, my lady's maid, saw you leave the castle this morning. I have been waiting all day! You must— Guinevere, what happened to your dress?"

Guinevere had tensed against attack as soon as she saw Guinevach, but this day alone she had created a magical barrier against their enemies, destroyed seven creatures that would have killed her, and faced the man who had broken her heart. What was Guinevach to any of that? Threat or not, changeling or real, Guinevach was a girl. Guinevere was a queen.

Arthur was right. They were not above the law; they *were* the law. Even if Guinevach stood on the dock and screamed that Guinevere was not really Guinevere, who would believe her? Who would challenge their beloved king when he took Guinevere's side?

If Guinevach was here as a plot against Guinevere, it was a weak plot indeed. And if her only threat was showing up where she was not wanted and where she might ruin things inadvertently, best for them all that she return to where she belonged.

Getting rid of Guinevach was the least cruel option. The longer she stayed, the worse it would be for everyone. Guinevere was not her sister and never would be. There was no place in Camelot for Guinevach, no matter who she really was.

Guinevere squared her shoulders. "I do not have the luxury of time right now. Tomorrow you will return to Cameliard and I will visit you when I can." A perfect solution. Guinevach sent home where she would be safe if she really was Guinevach, and where she could not go if she was not.

"Who *are* you?" Guinevach hissed.

Guinevere startled at this admission. Guinevach did not truly know her! But before she could say anything, the other girl's eyes filled with tears and she fled up the hill to the castle.

For a day filled with victories, Guinevere felt anything but victorious.

CHAPTER TEN

Arthur sent instructions to Sir Gawain. He would oversee Guine-vach's packing and escort her and her party to the borders of the kingdom in the morning. Guinevere would never have to worry about her again. Although Guinevere suspected that would not stop her from wondering about who Guinevach really was and what she had hoped to accomplish.

When they arrived back at the stables, ready to begin their journey in spite of the late hour, Arthur stopped short, surprised. "Lancelot," he said.

Lancelot did not hear him; she was directing the guards on which horses to pack. She shook her head. "A cart will be too cumbersome and draw attention. Until the rest of the group joins us, we should be able to move quickly if needed. Two extra horses for rations and bags. We can hunt along the way."

Arthur cleared his throat. Lancelot and the four guards turned and bowed. Sir Tristan appeared from the depths of the stables, arms full of gear that he awkwardly bowed around. Guinevere had never been to the stables this late; it was already evening, and almost all the stalls were full. The scent of hay itched her nose, but the gentle sounds of horses settling in for the night, stamping their hooves and letting out tired huffs of air, were soothing. She found her favorite gray mare was already being prepared for her. Of course Lancelot had chosen that one.

The four guards were vaguely familiar to Guinevere. They were older than Arthur—older than Lancelot or Sir Tristan, too—and Guinevere wondered if it ever rankled them to serve under knights and a king several years their juniors. If so, they did not show it. All four men were bustling about to appear as busy as possible, their faces so serious that Guinevere could see their excitement through the sheer effort it took *not* to show it. Being a guard was a coveted job in Camelot. It guaranteed housing within the city—within the castle, if the man had no family—and paid well. Being chosen to accompany the king and queen was a tremendous honor.

Guinevere actually wished it was less of an honor. The guards would be so *formal* about everything. And that would mean Lancelot and Sir Tristan would feel they, too, had to be formal.

"Where is Sir Caradoc?" Arthur asked.

Lancelot took some of the gear from Sir Tristan. "His hip has been paining him. We thought it best I take his place, as the queen's protector. The captain of the guard will remain in Camelot to oversee things in your absence, so Sir Tristan will manage the guards. That way I can focus on the queen's safety." Lancelot said it lightly, but there was something almost accusatory in her stance, her shoulders straight but angled away from Arthur. Arthur had not told Lancelot about this trip. Had he not intended for her to come? But of course he would have wanted that. Lancelot was Guinevere's knight.

Arthur nodded, any surprise pushed to the side. "Very well. We will be on our own two days at most until the rest of the attending knights and the traveling party catch up to us." Arthur reached up and removed his crown. "I think it best to look anonymous until we have our full force." He was wearing a plain green tunic. Guinevere had changed into a blue dress, unadorned, and a green cloak. For a moment one of her most well-worn imaginings—what it would be like if she were just a girl and Arthur just a boy, together in the countryside—surged to the front of her mind. But if that were the case, they would not need to disguise themselves, or ride with a guard. This was not the same thing.

But it was close.

She vowed to leave behind her fears and worries and questions. If Arthur could be satisfied with ending a threat and not worrying about what it all meant, she would be, too. Camelot would be safe in their absence. Guinevach had been met and dismissed with no harm to the kingdom. And whether Guinevere was the Lady of the Lake's daughter or whether Mordred was still out there somewhere, some-how intending her no harm whatsoever, well, none of that mattered. She was where she was supposed to be. Who she had chosen to be, and whom she had chosen to be with.

Lancelot pulled her old armor from a bag. "Very wise. Everyone, remove the king's colors."

All the men wore Arthur's colors on tunics over their chain mail. A golden sun in the middle of deep-blue fabric. Guinevere loved the simplicity of it, the hope. Arthur had always felt like the sun to her. The tunics were removed, and within a few minutes they were on the road, mounted, the extra horses trailing them.

Beneath the sturdy fabric of her plain cloak, with her horse gently plodding and the tree line growing ever closer, Guinevere felt sur-prisingly free. She found herself glad for this reprieve from being stuck in Camelot. It was easier not to dwell on things when there was so much to look at and experience out here.

Though it was night, they kept riding. Guinevere could always feel Camelot and the mountain it occupied, even when they were too far away to see it. It was a constant presence, almost a tug on her. She wondered if that was because she had left behind so many knots tying herself to it, or if Camelot was simply that powerful for all who lived there.

Guinevere pulled a bunch of leaves off a low-hanging branch. Pressing them to her face, she breathed in the scent of life, already altered by the dry approach of winter. There was no bite in these leaves. There was hardly any sense of them at all.

But perhaps that was the lingering numbness in her hands. They had dealt the Dark Queen two blows in a short time. She was trying the same old things, but Arthur and Guinevere were not the same old defenses. They were strong and determined and *together*. Guinevere tried to let go of the shame of what she had done to the wolves and replace it with pride in her king, and in herself. And she tried not to think about Mordred.

She was glad to be riding without the sullenly aggressive presence of the afternoon sun. She even enjoyed the bite in the air. The roads were well maintained, cleared and not muddy this time of year. The men rode watchfully but did not seem particularly concerned. Travel was safer within Arthur's kingdom than anywhere else. They kept traveling into the night, finally stopping when they were well into the trees just beyond the borders of Camelot's lands.

Guinevere tried to help as they set up camp. "Let me," Arthur said, taking the flint from her. She had no desire to use fire magic unless she had to, and apparently she was terrible at lighting fires without it. "Go sit. It is late."

Guinevere wanted to feel useful, but the men were so busy she did not know where to start. The day had been long—physically and emotionally—and she was sore from all the riding. She found herself missing Brangien, her feminine ally who would have sat with her and chatted as she undid Guinevere's braids and brushed her hair. Even though Lancelot was also a woman, she had a place here among the men that Guinevere did not and never would.

Also, sitting on a felled log after a full day riding really, *really* hurt. How did the men stand it?

Guinevere reached into her pouch. Brangien would bring most of her jewelry with the next group, but Guinevere had a few small stones that could hold magic, the worn dragon's tooth she liked to hold in her palm when she was worried, and her sewing supplies. She dug through them, marveling at how Brangien was always so organized, before finally finding her brush.

As she tried to undo her braids and brush her hair out with hands that now felt like they were being stabbed by needles, Guinevere missed Brangien even more. The bite in the air had moved from invigorating to stinging. And, worst of all, she had no one to complain to. She did not want to appear weak or cross in front of the guards, and she always wanted Arthur to be impressed with her. She shifted as surreptitiously as possible, searching for relief for her bruised bottom.

After coaxing the fire to life, Arthur sat beside her and soon she forgot her weariness. The guards had not served with Arthur before he became king. He talked differently to them than he did to her, and she liked seeing him like this. Arthur the king, approachable and funny and warm but always in command, even if it was only over conversation around a fire.

Arthur was midstory, and the guards—and Sir Tristan and Lancelot, though Lancelot hid it best—were listening raptly. "We rode into the woods, weary from the day's battle. I wanted nothing more than to rest before we had to face King Lot again. Sir Lucan—"

"Sir Lucan?" Guinevere asked, puzzled.

"He is on a quest," Arthur said with a tone of wistful longing that suggested he envied the quest that had taken Sir Lucan from Camelot for at least as long as Guinevere had been there. Sir Tristan cleared his throat, an uncomfortable expression on his face, and turned to watch the perimeter of the camp.

"As I was saying, Sir Lucan, having come into possession of a magic spear, found he could not stop walking. He did not know that the spear would never rest, demanding fight after fight until the wielder had conquered all or been killed. I was setting up camp before I noticed Sir Lucan was gone. I heard his cries for help and rushed into the trees to find him. After some time, I tracked him to a clearing. He had managed to drop the spear, but was facing one of King Lot's allies. King Caradoc's arm was lifted to deliver a fatal blow, when—"

"King Caradoc? Like your knight? Is Caradoc a common name?"

Arthur gave Guinevere an exasperated smile. "You will find out."

"Yes! Sorry. Continue."

"King Caradoc's arm was lifted to deliver a fatal blow, so I picked up a rock and threw it. It bounced off his forehead, stunning him and giving Sir Lucan enough time to get out of the way. I rushed King Caradoc and we fought a mighty battle. Our blades sparked and sang in the night. I had been fighting all day, but King Caradoc was fresh, and it was an even match. Finally, after an hour, his hands rose in surrender. He sat on the ground, winded, and looked at me in astonishment. 'Never have I had such a fight. Tell me, what is your name? For your honor in allowing me to surrender, I swear I will serve you for the rest of my days.' I bowed, accepting his offered sword, and told him that I was Arthur Pendragon. His astonishment was extreme. He had been in the woods hunting to kill me on behalf of King Lot. But now he had sworn allegiance to me! I understood his plight. To fill one holy vow, he would have to betray another. I bowed and offered to let him return to King Lot. We would part as friends but meet again as enemies on the battlefield. King Caradoc was again astonished. King Lot was a hard and vicious ruler, demanding fealty even from other kings. That very moment, King Caradoc removed his crown and became Sir Caradoc, leaving behind his birthright to embrace a higher calling of justice and truth. The next day, side by side, we defeated King Lot, bringing us one step closer to overthrowing Uther Pendragon and winning Camelot."

"Is Sir Lucan the brother of Sir Bedivere?" asked one of the guards, a blocky man with an incongruously delicate nose in the center of a face like a boulder.

"No, that is Sir Yvain," another guard answered.

"Yvain the bastard?" the blocky guard asked.

"No, Yvain the . . . not-bastard."

"The one Sir Gawain injured?"

"Which one?"

"Yvain the not-bastard."

"Is he not Morgan le Fay's son?"

"No," a third guard interjected. "She is a sorceress and can only give birth to demons."

"She is Mordred's mother," Guinevere said, frowning.

"Exactly," Lancelot muttered.

Guinevere noticed Arthur's easy smile had become a stiff mask. He did not like this topic. Morgan le Fay was Arthur's half sister. She had tried to kill him when he was a baby, as revenge for the rape of her mother, Igraine. The rape committed by Arthur's father, Uther Pendragon, and magically orchestrated by Merlin. Arthur and Guinevere had never spoken of Morgan le Fay.

"Yvain and Yvain the bastard have different mothers," Arthur said, obviously wishing to steer the subject from murderous half-sister sorceresses and other traitorous relatives. "Thus *the bastard*. Though he quite dislikes being called that, so if you meet him in person, I would recommend addressing him as simply Yvain, or Yvain the younger. Unless you wish to find out how much a bastard he is with the blade. And Sir Bedivere is the brother of Sir Lucan, not Sir Yvain."

The blocky guard scratched his head. "I am still confused about who is the brother of who and who is the son of who."

Arthur clapped him on the shoulder. "We would need a diagram to work it all out. Tell me, have you heard the story of the Black Knight?"

Guinevere leaned back and half listened to the new tale. She would rather hear about Morgan le Fay and Arthur's feelings about her, but he seemed determined to change that topic. It was astonishing how much life Arthur had lived before she ever met him. She often felt that her own life began the day they met. And while it was true she had few memories before that, it was also because there was something about Arthur that made him instantly the center of any life. Sir Caradoc had given up a crown after one meeting. Lancelot had trained her whole life to serve at his side. And Guinevere had chosen Camelot over all else to help him.

She stood, needing to stretch, and found Sir Tristan at the edge of the camp, standing guard. "Are you well?" she asked, puzzled by his tense silence.

"Sir Lucan," he said, his voice soft.

"What about him?"

"He is not on a quest. During my tournament, I faced him. He was hurt so badly he retired to an abbey to heal. We have not heard from him since. He must have lied to the king to save face. But I am the reason he is not here."

Guinevere put a hand on Sir Tristan's arm. "You all know the risks."

"We do. But it is easier to risk yourself in pursuit of glory than to accept that you have hurt someone else beyond repair. And not even an enemy. A friend. Sir Bedivere has not forgiven me, and I think he never will."

"I thought all the knights got along?"

"All the knights love our king, and that unites us. But it is a complex hierarchy with much history, a lot of it soaked in blood." Sir Tristan sighed. "Sometimes I envy Sir Lancelot."

"What do you mean?"

"Well, she is not—" He gestured vaguely. "She is removed from the politics and the drama. You know."

Guinevere did. She had seen as much at the dockside celebration. She looked back at her knight, standing just out of reach of the firelight, watching and listening as Arthur told his stories. When she rejoined the fireside, Guinevere sat nearer to her knight than to her king.

As the fire died down, bedrolls were unfurled. Lancelot, who had volunteered for the first watch, frowned. "We should have brought you a tent."

Guinevere gestured up at the stars. "I like this much better." In the absence of a moon, the constellations were so thick and bright that they almost felt like a ceiling; a brilliant, glittering dome holding them all safely in the dark.

Arthur unrolled his bed next to hers and was asleep almost as soon as he was horizontal. From the soft snores, nearly all the men were. Guinevere supposed it was a necessity. If they could not sleep in unusual circumstances, they would never be fit for their tasks on the road.

She tried not to fret about what they had left behind. Arthur clearly was not worried. Camelot was protected. Guinevach would be escorted out in the morning, averting whatever intentional or accidental damage she might have done. Mordred was out there, somewhere, but the Dark Queen was more than matched by Guinevere and Arthur, and Mordred had to know it now. Had he been there leading the wolves in attack, or had he really been trying to release them from their magical bonds, as he claimed?

And how did he genuinely mean her no harm, after all the pain he had caused her?

No. She did not want to think about him anymore. She was ready for this infinite day to be over.

Guinevere turned on her side to face Arthur, who was barely visible even this close. He always felt so far away when he was asleep. She rolled onto her other side. Lancelot moved like a shadow in the darkness, pacing the perimeter of the camp.

Guinevere watched her knight pacing as she kept watch, and forgot to worry about nightmares.

He is just ahead of her on the pathway. She can hear him laughing, low teasing notes in contrast to the brilliant summer sun winking through the foliage. She runs to close the distance, but when she breaks into the clearing, it is empty.

An arm circles her waist from behind, lifting her into the air and spinning her. She screams, but it quickly turns to laughter as the meadow whirls around them. They fall into a heap, face to face, his moss-green eyes fixed on hers with an intensity she can never ignore.

There is something she should be doing. Someone she should be with. But it is summer and the clover beneath them is soft and his hair is softer and his lips are softest of all.

"You made the wrong choice," he murmurs, his lips against her neck, and she cannot remember the choice or why she made it. She can only

feel this fire, this giddy, dangerous release of wanting and being wanted, and she does not care about anything else.

Guinevere awoke with a gasp. "Mordred," she whispered, blinking against the expected sunlight and finding only the cold blanket of an autumn night. The fire had burned low, and next to her Arthur slept, oblivious. The dream had not been like the dream of Camelot, where it had belonged to someone else. This was her own dream. Which worried her even more.

Guinevere stood, wrapping her blanket around her shoulders like a cloak. It was not simply the feeling of Mordred's lips and hands she needed to clear from her mind. The sunlight, the meadow, the freedom. It was all a lie. And she hated her sleeping brain for telling it to her.

A dark figure paused nearby.

"My queen?" Lancelot whispered.

Guinevere stepped to her knight. "Is it still your watch?" So much more of the night stretched in front of her. Guinevere eyed her bed-roll with trepidation. She did not want to wander in any more dreams tonight. Somehow the dream of Mordred upset her even more than the dream of the Lady of the Lake. Perhaps because she had memories of Mordred, and none of her mother. Or perhaps because the plunge into darkness held no allure in her real life, but the touch of Mordred . . .

"Third watch," Lancelot answered. "It will be dawn soon."

"But you had first watch!" That hardly seemed fair.

"I slept some."

Guinevere did not think the number of men present required

Lancelot to take two watches. Sir Tristan had not. He was sleeping nearby. Guinevere tightened the blanket around her shoulders. "Can I keep watch with you? I do not want to sleep again."

Lancelot did not ask why. She nodded, turning outward toward the forest and sweeping her eyes back and forth. "My queen, there is something I need to talk to you about." Lancelot sounded hesitant, almost worried. "It has to do with our conversation about the Lady of the Lake."

"I have been thinking about it, as well." Guinevere braced herself. Lancelot was going to suggest she tell Arthur. And she would. Eventually. But she was not ready to discuss it, to share the information and therefore make it feel even more real than it already did.

"I—" Lancelot froze.

"I heard it, too," Guinevere whispered.

There was someone—or something—in the trees.

CHAPTER ELEVEN

"Go to Arthur as though you are going back to sleep," Lancelot whispered. "Get some rest," she added in a louder voice, pitching it lower than normal so her naturally husky voice sounded like a young man's. "It will be morning soon."

Guinevere returned to her bedroll, certain that her stiff, nervous walk would give the charade away. She knelt, loath to lie down. That felt too vulnerable. What could she do to help? Fire magic? But fire was hard to control, and she worried about hurting the guards. The memory of those smoldering remains of what had once been wolves made her sick. And she had to keep her magic a secret. If it were revealed, getting rid of Guinevach would have been for nothing. Guinevere herself would be kicked out of Camelot.

Guinevere lay down and sidled up to Arthur. She put a hand on his shoulder and nuzzled his cheek. "Arthur, wake up," she said softly. "Do not react, but there is someone in the woods and we may be under attack soon."

The way every muscle Guinevere was pressed against became

taut and ready was the only indication Guinevere had that Arthur was no longer asleep.

Lancelot began whistling. It sounded distracted, like she was whistling without realizing it. From her limited vantage point, Guinevere noticed several hands stealing from bedrolls to grip the weapons that were never more than an arm's length away.

"Now!" Lancelot shouted. Sir Tristan leapt to his feet, bow in hand, arrow nocked. More than half the guards did the same. The rest, not fully awake yet, scrambled to catch up. Arthur stood. Excalibur was still sheathed on the ground.

"Sword!" Arthur shouted, holding out a hand. A guard tossed his own through the air and Arthur caught it neatly by the pommel, twirling it once to test the weight and balance.

"We know you are there." Lancelot's voice was clear and strong. Guinevere recognized it as the voice she had used as the patchwork knight. Lancelot had let her voice relax and go higher since then, so it was a surprise to hear her old one. Perhaps she had settled back into it because she once again wore her old armor. Or perhaps it was safer out here to use that voice rather than one that was obviously a woman's. "However many you are, this is not a fight you want."

"You sure about that?" a man sneered through the darkness. "Because— Oh."

The voice cut itself off. All the guards were ready, and faced the trees in a circle. Guinevere's heart was racing. She should be able to help, but she felt powerless. It reminded her of being in that terrible shack in the middle of the river, held there by Maleagant, unable to do anything as he used her as a pawn against Arthur. She could still feel the sting of his hand against her cheek. The terror at being held above the river, only his grip between her and the water.

"You—you are the patchwork knight." The man said it as a statement, not a question. Guinevere could not see him, but he sounded close.

"I am," Lancelot answered.

"We thought you were dead. No one has seen you. Not in months."

"I assure you I am quite alive."

"We did not realize this was your camp. We, uh, were just inspecting. Seeing who was nearby. Leaving now, no harm done. You have a nice morning."

Lancelot did not shift from her ready stance. After what could have been minutes or hours, fear distorting the passage of time, Lancelot finally turned toward the camp.

"They are gone."

The guards let out a collective sigh of relief. Sir Tristan laughed. "They had no idea the king is here. Your reputation precedes us."

The blocky guard's face was alight with awe. "Sir Lancelot's reputation *saved* us."

"I used to patrol this territory. It was good practice." Lancelot crouched to stoke the fire, effectively cutting off any further discussion about how her prowess alone was enough to frighten off would-be thieves and murderers.

Arthur took a step toward the trees. "We would have won the fight. We should go after them."

"If the queen were not here, I would agree," Lancelot answered. "I do not like those men going free to prey on others. But we cannot split our force, and I will not leave her without a full guard."

"Of course. Yes. Neither would I." Arthur returned the borrowed sword, then lay back down with his arms behind his head, his relaxed appearance belied by the slight frown pulling at his eyebrows.

Guinevere could see how it nagged at him to let those men go free. And she wondered, too, if his pride was a bit stung. It was Lancelot's name and reputation that had scared them away. Or at least who Lancelot had been before she became a knight.

"I do not like it, either," Guinevere said, sitting beside him. "I wish I could chase them down and . . ." Hurt them? Kill them? She had killed men before, drunk on magic and power. She did not like the way it had felt—because it had not felt like anything, which was terrifying. The men had not mattered at all. She had been channeling the Dark Queen's power then, which meant she understood some of how the Dark Queen viewed humanity.

Like ants. Ignored until they became pests, and then eliminated without a thought. It was how the fairy queen viewed all life, if the wolves were any indication. She stole their free will and sent them to their deaths.

Guinevere sighed and lay back, shoulder to shoulder with Arthur. "I almost wish it had been the Dark Queen," she whispered. "Or a magical attack. Dangerous, greedy men are so much more complicated."

Arthur actually laughed, turning to look at her, his pretense of going back to sleep gone. "And fighting the fairy queen would be simple?"

"We know she has to be eliminated."

Arthur looked less certain. "I keep imagining facing her again. But every time I picture it, Mordred comes between us. And I do not know what I would do then. If I would kill him. If I could. I know he betrayed us, but . . . he is family. And I still love him."

Something in Guinevere loosened. Not a magical knot tying her to one of her spells, but an emotional one of fear and anxiety. She was right not to have tried to kill Mordred. And perhaps she was even right to have hidden his presence from Arthur and Lancelot. If they had known he was nearby, they would have felt duty bound to go after him. She did not want to put Arthur in that position. It had been hard enough for her to kill the wolves. How much harder for Arthur to decide whether or not to kill his own nephew?

Mordred was a traitor. He was made at least in part from fairy magic and had brought the Dark Queen back to physical form. He was also Arthur's nephew, had fought side by side with him, had laughed and made Guinevere feel welcome, had comforted her when she was injured, had kissed her, had hurt her, had proved he did not want to harm her again. How could one person be so many things? And how could they ever make a decision about him that would take all those things into account?

"If you and I leave right now we can still catch those men," Guinevere said.

Arthur raised an eyebrow. "You want to hunt them down and kill them?"

Guinevere shrugged. "I could figure out a knot that would addle their brains so badly they would not remember which end of a sword to pick up. Though I would be *very* silly and confused for a few days as a result."

"As fun as that sounds, Sir Lancelot is right. We have no reason to risk it." But Arthur sounded more cheerful. Just the idea that they could go after the men if they wanted to seemed to make him feel better about letting the men escape. If Guinevere felt occasionally trapped by Camelot and its stone and its rules, perhaps Arthur did, too. His stories from last night had been all adventures and travel, making friends and defeating enemies.

Maybe that was why he spent so much time patrolling his own lands, doing things that most kings would assign to their knights or soldiers. He had after all grown up a parentless servant and page, not a prince. Being king was not a natural role for him.

It was another thing that bonded them. She had not grown up a princess, and still felt more at home out here than she did in Camelot.

Guinevere was hit with a sudden longing for what her treacherous dream had presented: a moment in a meadow in the sunshine. She wanted a blissfully free, giddy escape with someone. But she was determined that it should be Arthur.

CHAPTER TWELVE

They started traveling late that morning. Guinevere half suspected Arthur had delayed in hopes the thieves would come back and he would get his fight, but the brigands wisely stayed away.

"Tell me about your sister," Guinevere said as they waited for the men to finish packing camp. She kept thinking about his stories from the night before, how simple they were. How straightforward. Surely there had been more to Sir Caradoc's willingness to give up his crown. And she knew there was more to Mordred and Morgan le Fay than any of the stories told.

"My sister?"

"Morgan le Fay."

"My half sister," Arthur corrected her. "There is nothing to tell. She hates me. She has wanted me dead since I was born, and she tried to kill me several times when I was a child."

"How?" Guinevere had never heard about that. She had heard only bits and pieces of Arthur's childhood, most from Sir Ector and Sir Kay, his foster family. His *terrible* foster family.

Arthur shrugged. "I do not know the details. Merlin told me about it when I was older."

"But you let Mordred fight at your side, knowing he was her son?"

Arthur rubbed his face. He stared toward the trees as though looking for a threat, or for an escape. "We are not our parents. I wanted him to be more than what he came from. He disappointed me."

Arthur had always fought against what his tyrant father stood for. Of course he would have generously extended that same opportunity to Mordred and hoped for the best. "You never met Morgan le Fay, though? Even now, when surely she could not hurt you?" Guinevere was curious what a sorceress was like. She had known a wizard, and she had known witches, but a sorceress seemed special.

"Merlin told me I should never let her speak to me. I should put a sword in her heart before listening to a word from her mouth."

Guinevere was mildly horrified. It seemed extreme. She knew Arthur had to kill enemies, but to strike without question or hesitation the moment he saw someone? "Does she have some sort of power? Could she enchant you just by speaking?"

Arthur shrugged. "I do not know."

"But why else would Merlin tell you to kill her rather than letting her speak?"

Arthur shrugged. "If Merlin tells me something, I do it. He has only ever protected me."

Guinevere had no response to that. She did not agree with his trust in Merlin, but she did not want to quarrel or to keep digging at painful parts of Arthur's family tree. She let the conversation drop as they began to ride.

After only an hour on the road, though, they were interrupted by the sound of pounding hooves. The company stopped, swords drawn to greet whoever was coming, but the rider was revealed to be none other than Brangien. She rode white-faced and clinging to the reins. None of the swords were put away, all the men staring down the road beyond Brangien to see who was chasing her.

"My queen," she gasped, stopping her horse.

"What happened? Is it Guinevach?" They never should have left! If anything had happened in the city in their absence, it was Guinevere's fault. She had shown too much compassion. To Guinevach. To Mordred. If her compassion cost a single life, she would never forgive herself. Those lives would be on her head.

"No, it is—I am—I did not want you to be alone." She glanced at the guards around them. Guinevere intuited her meaning and dismounted, helping Brangien down and drawing her far enough away that they could not be overheard.

"What is it?"

Brangien's voice came out a whisper. "News arrived for Dindrane. King Mark will not be attending her wedding because there is to be a trial for his wife."

Guinevere frowned. Why this necessitated Brangien flinging herself through the countryside in a panic, she could not understand. Until she did. King Mark was the king Brangien and Sir Tristan had fled from. The king who had married Brangien's beloved Isolde.

Guinevere took Brangien's hands, feeling them tremble in her own. "A trial for what?"

"Witchcraft. I think—I think she was trying to find a way to connect to me without your help. Guinevere, he will kill her." She collapsed into tears and Guinevere drew her close.

Arthur, Sir Tristan, and Lancelot joined them. "What happened?" Arthur asked, alarmed.

"King Mark. He is going to try his wife for witchcraft."

Sir Tristan's kind brown eyes widened with horror. "Isolde," he whispered.

"Isolde? Your Isolde?" Arthur asked.

Guinevere shook her head. "Brangien's Isolde."

Arthur frowned, puzzled. "I do not understand."

"We have never told the truth," Brangien said, pulling back from Guinevere. "But it is time to. I will tell you the real story of Tristan and Isolde."

"And Brangien," Sir Tristan added, his voice soft with sadness.

Tristan and Isolde and Brangien

The tale was not as polished as that of Arthur and the Forest of Blood, or as funny as Sir Mordred and the Green Knight. It was not a tale that had been traded between bards, or even shared beyond Brangien and Sir Tristan, now clasping hands, united in the telling. It was a secret tale of love, betrayal, and failure.

King Mark desired a bride. He had been through three others, all disappointments. He charged his nephew, Sir Tristan, with riding the land and finding the fairest maiden for him.

Sir Tristan took his calling with all the earnest devotion a young knight could. He knew his uncle to be a jealous man, quick to rage, feared in his household and kingdom. And so when Sir Tristan heard of a woman noted not only for her beauty but also her kindness, he sought her out. Isolde was exactly what his king needed. Sir Tristan saw her and hoped that she would temper King Mark and bring much needed light and compassion to the kingdom.

Isolde's father saw King Mark's offered price and knew his daughter would bring much needed gold to his own household.

The deal was done before Isolde and Brangien knew about it. The entire household went into mourning when they discovered they were losing their Isolde. Sir Tristan saw how they loved her and had even more hope that he had made the right choice. He loved his uncle's people, if not his uncle, and he wanted to do right by them.

His uncle had requested only youth and beauty, and Isolde was youthful enough. She was beautiful, too, according to everyone, which mattered nothing to Tristan. But she was kind. Even though she was sad about leaving her home, Isolde had only gentle words for him. Her maid, less so.

Brangien had known this day would come. But somehow she thought it would be later. So much later that she did not have to think about it. Then this stupid, lovely boy showed up with his king's gold and Isolde—her Isolde—was sold like a breeding mare. Brangien became a creature of wrath and spite. She considered poisoning Isolde's father, but the deal had already been made and Isolde had a brother who would honor it, so that would solve nothing. She considered poisoning him anyway, but knew it would hurt Isolde.

So she packed her true love's belongings, and in her rage almost did not notice Isolde crying herself to sleep.

If Brangien was hurting, how much more must tender Isolde be hurting? Brangien would have to be at Isolde's side and watch as she married another, but Isolde would have to do the marrying. For once in her life, Brangien realized she could not bear to see someone else suffer. She would do whatever it took to make certain Isolde was happy. Even if it meant losing her.

Brangien packed, and Brangien prepared. Her mother had taught her many things. She was a practical witch who had a solution to any problem, including love. Brangien slipped the

*love potion—a magic that would make Isolde, her Isolde, be
happy with another—into her pouch and set out on the journey
to the end of her own happiness forever.*

*But as they crossed land, forded rivers, and camped day in
and day out, Brangien saw that the young knight at their side
matched Isolde for kindness. He was gentle and respectful and
good. And she did not doubt he was skilled as a fighter, having
been entrusted with such a task.*

*Isolde asked about King Mark, and Sir Tristan answered as
diplomatically as he could. But Brangien could feel the shape
of the man in the things that were left out, and she began to
fear. Even if she could make Isolde and King Mark love each
other, she could not change a cruel man into a good one. There
was no potion capable of that.*

An idea occurred to Brangien.

A terrible idea.

*If this valiant knight fell in love with her precious Isolde,
would he not do whatever it took to protect her? To keep her?*

*They boarded a ship that would take them along the coast
and deliver them to the king. Brangien had two potions. One
to make two people fall in love, and one to make a person
appear dead.*

*Her plan was simple: Give Sir Tristan and Isolde each
other. And then remove herself from Isolde's life to make
certain Isolde could be happy. As long as Brangien knew Isolde
was out there somewhere, she could never truly love another.
Potion or no, she suspected Isolde would feel the same way.
But Isolde had only ever seen minor potions; she had no idea
the power Brangien could brew and would never suspect such
a devastating act was deliberate. Isolde would have love, and
Brangien would be "dead."*

It was not fair to any of them. But Isolde always took care of those around her, and this was the only way Brangien could see to take care of her.

It would have worked. But as Brangien poured the cups of wine and readied the love potion, she wept for all she was losing. And Sir Tristan, hearing the weeping, came into the cabin too soon. She was caught. She expected violence, rage, or cold judgment.

What she got was worse. Sir Tristan listened with compassion and understanding, but forced Brangien to face the violence of her intentions. Isolde had already had her choices stripped away, and Brangien had decided to take away even her ability to love who she chose.

Brangien was ready to throw herself overboard, but Sir Tristan held her. He swore he would do whatever it took to protect Isolde, and Brangien, as well. He would help them find a way to be happy. And, in an act of supreme generosity, he promised not to tell Isolde what Brangien had intended to do.

They were bonded by secrecy and united in determination to protect Isolde. They stayed up late into the night, making plans to sneak Isolde to freedom as soon as they landed.

Unbeknownst to them, someone else stayed up late into the night, listening. When they landed, King Mark was there with a contingent of men. He condemned Brangien and Sir Tristan to death for conspiring against him. Isolde threw herself at his feet, weeping, begging for their lives as her wedding gift. King Mark granted it, banishing Sir Tristan and Brangien.

Brangien's plotting and magic, Sir Tristan's bravery, both amounted to nothing. In the end, Isolde had saved them and condemned herself with her kindness.

CHAPTER THIRTEEN

Brangien wiped her eyes. "After that, we ran. Tristan knew King Mark's forgiveness was only for show and that he would send men to kill us. Sir Tristan did not have to help me any more than he already had. I destroyed his life. But he stayed with me and we ended up in Camelot."

Sir Tristan put an arm around Brangien. "You did not destroy my life. I was knight to a king I could neither respect nor trust. And now I am knight to the greatest king in Christendom. If anything, you saved me. I am only sorry we could not save Isolde."

Guinevere understood why Brangien was ashamed to tell the story. It reminded her of Merlin. Taking another's free will was an act of tremendous violence. Brangien had been motivated by love, but she was no better than the wizard had been, even if *he* had been motivated by the good of mankind.

But people are more than their worst impulses. And Guinevere herself was not innocent. She had manipulated Sir Bors's memories to protect a dragon. She had killed the possessed wolves to save

herself. And she had released herself to magic and killed Sir Maleagant and his men.

The memory of their bones snapping as the trees devoured them
haunted her. She felt repulsion and horror now, but the worst part
was at the time she had felt *nothing*. She would never again view
human life as a means to an end, or as a price worth paying. That
was what Merlin had done with Igraine, Arthur's mother. There was
always another way. There had to be. Even if they had ultimately
failed, at least Brangien and Sir Tristan had tried to find that better
way to protect Isolde.

Arthur's brow was furrowed in a deep frown. "Brangien and Isolde
love each other . . . as a man and a woman love each other?"

"Yes," Brangien said. She held herself as an aspirant in the arena,
braced for a blow.

It did not come. Arthur still looked vaguely confused, but there
was no judgment in his expression. "I am sorry you lost her. And I am
even sorrier for this news."

No. Guinevere refused to allow this to happen. Isolde had done
nothing wrong. She had lost everything to protect Brangien and Sir
Tristan. She deserved to be protected in turn. And Guinevere would
not see Brangien's already broken heart irreparably damaged.

There was so much suffering in the world. So much that Guinevere had been involved in, directly or by association. Merlin's deeds
hung on her like chains. Daughter or not, she was linked to him, and
therefore linked to the terrible things he had done. She could not go
back in time and save Igraine, or protect anyone else he had hurt,
or even prevent him from doing whatever he had to her mind that
ripped away her past, her mother, her self. All Guinevere could do
was move forward and do as much good in this world as she could
manage.

"Did you ever get to go on a quest, Sir Tristan?" Guinevere asked. Brangien looked confused by the change in subject. Sir Tristan shook his head. Guinevere continued. "I know you have not, Lancelot."

Lancelot turned sharply toward her, eyes narrowed. "Rescuing my queen from Sir Maleagant was not a quest worthy of note?"

Guinevere cringed. "I meant as an official knight." She had not meant that. Quests were the things of stories. Fights against magic, against fairy knights, against wicked kings, dreamy and romantic and exciting. Her own rescue had been terrifying and terrible. "What if we rescue Isolde?"

Arthur sighed. "No."

"What do you mean, no?"

"I mean that I cannot do this. Much as I want to—and I *do* want to. But King Mark is a powerful man. If I were to lead men into his country and steal his wife, Camelot would pay the price. He has allies among all the southern lords and kings. I would be creating a war."

"You cannot fight a war over one woman," Brangien whispered as silent tears streamed down her cheeks.

"You misunderstand," Guinevere said. "I am not inviting you. This is not a quest for a king. It is a quest for two knights and two witches."

Arthur's expression was as swift and sharp as his sword. "No."

"King Mark will never trace it back to Camelot. We will go in disguise." Guinevere bit her lip, puzzling out the details. "We will need to get Isolde out without anyone knowing. And in a way that will prevent pursuit." She laughed, clapping her hands. "Brangien already had the perfect idea! We will kill Isolde!"

"Is that—is that not what we are trying to prevent?" Sir Tristan looked at Guinevere as though she had lost her senses.

"We will not really kill her. We will use Brangien's potion to make it appear as though she is dead. And then we will steal her before she wakes up and anyone is the wiser."

Sir Tristan's frown shifted into something more thoughtful. Something more hopeful. "King Mark inters his wives' bodies in seaside cliffs. It would be simple to retrieve her once they placed her there."

"You do not have enough time." Arthur did not sound triumphant. If anything, he sounded regretful. "If King Mark has sent word that he will not be at the wedding, that means the trial is imminent. His kingdom is on the southern tip of the island. It is at least a week's ride there. And if you were missing from Dindrane's wedding, there would be talk. It is not unreasonable that he could connect you to Brangien and Sir Tristan and realize what had happened, leading him back to Camelot."

Guinevere wanted to pull out her hair in frustration. There had to be a way. They could not let Isolde die.

"A ship," Brangien said quietly. She looked at the ground instead of Guinevere. "If we struck east right now we could be at the coast this afternoon. A ship could get us to the southern tip within two days, and then back up the coast with enough time to make it to the wedding."

"A ship," Guinevere repeated, her voice hollow.

"Guinevere." Arthur put a hand on her arm. "Imagine the lake, expanded until it swallows the horizon. Waves taller than you constantly crashing. Unknown fathoms beneath you. More water than you can comprehend. Water *everywhere*."

"I can do it." She met his eyes, forcing her voice to be steady. "We can do it."

"But—"

"If you were not king, if this had happened three years ago, would you have hesitated to rescue an innocent woman in peril at the hands of an evil king?"

Arthur's jaw twitched, then his shoulders dropped and he shook his head. "I would have gone in a heartbeat. I still would, if there were any way I could without hurting my people."

"We have a way. Let us do this." Guinevere did not want to ask permission. She did not need to. But she wanted to do this with Arthur's blessing. If not for herself, then for Lancelot and Sir Tristan. Tension made their expressions wooden and their posture equally stiff. Because if their king said no, they could not do it. Not without breaking the sacred vows they had taken to obey him. Not without giving up the knighthoods they had both worked so hard for.

Arthur turned to the knights. "If anything happens to her . . ."

Lancelot bowed her head. "I will let no harm come to her."

"You have our word." Sir Tristan took a knee. "I swear it. If it gets too dangerous, we will get the queen out. She is our first priority."

Resignation settled reluctantly over Arthur. "Very well, then. Your quest has my blessing."

Brangien let out a sobbing gasp and dropped to her knees. "Thank you, thank you, thank you, my king."

"I will cover for your absence," Arthur said. "I will tell the guards I want to range wider and explore more of the land, so you four are going to wait for the bigger party. Then we can tell a story about how you missed the bigger party and so continued on your own. But you *must* be to Dindrane's family estate on time."

Lancelot and Sir Tristan hurried back to the group to retrieve their horses and some supplies. If this was going to work, they could lose no time.

"We will be there." Guinevere threw her arms around Arthur's neck, pulling him close. His cheek was warm against hers, only a hint of roughness where he had not shaved that morning. "Thank you."

He put his hands on the small of her back, pressing her against him. "Be careful."

She pressed a kiss to his cheek and then let him help her onto her horse. As they rode away, she looked over her shoulder. She only felt a little guilt over her thrill of pleasure at being the one leaving instead of the one left behind.

CHAPTER FOURTEEN

The roads east were in poor condition. Sir Tristan and Lancelot both rode warily through the scraggly farmlands and slumping villages, ever-braced for attack. They had ridden hard but not so fast it would put the horses at risk; they would be at the coast soon.

Though it was quite obvious they were not within Arthur's borders anymore, Guinevere sensed no threat from the land itself. There was no indication of the Dark Queen or her magic. Just the threat of men, frightened and vicious with desperation, but she trusted in Sir Tristan and Lancelot.

She understood her companions' tension, but she was almost elated. Arthur was always ranging out to save people, to rescue towns, to protect the innocent. Guinevere was not made to sit in a castle, to ride to and from celebrations in comfort, to be protected. Perhaps this was a bad idea, but it *felt* right, like reclaiming missing parts of herself. If she could not remember more than a glimpse of her past, she could fill in her present with whoever, whatever she chose to be.

Lancelot had her eyes on the horizon. "There are many Saxon settlements along the eastern coast. They are a fishing people, so we should be able to find a ship without too much trouble. If it takes us more than a day to secure passage, though, we will have to turn around."

"We will find a ship." Guinevere sounded confident. This was their quest. They would not fail. She would use her magic for good. To help people she loved, people who deserved her help. She would be better than Merlin in every way.

"And if we do not?" Brangien asked. She looked more troubled than hopeful. "I should go alone. This is too much to ask of you."

"You did not ask. We chose this. Because we can. We have the freedom to decide what we want to do with our lives and our skills. Igraine had that taken from her."

"Isolde," Brangien interjected softly.

"Yes, that's what I said."

"You said Igraine."

Guinevere froze. Her tongue had betrayed her. This was about more than Isolde, even if she did not want to face it. But did it make her quest less noble, if part of it was motivated by anger at Merlin? He had taken and taken and taken. Lives and innocence and memories. She would not take. She would give.

Sir Tristan straightened in his saddle. "Do you smell that?"

Guinevere breathed in deeply. He was right. Something had changed, but she could not say what. Dust and heat and drying green were now overlaid by something else. It smelled like . . . life. Sharp and bright and cold, with a hint of decay.

"The sea." Brangien hurried her horse forward. It was another league before they saw it. At last they came over a rise and the horizon disappeared.

"Oh." Guinevere could think of nothing else to say. The blue stretched as far as she could see, to the end of the world. There was land, and then there was water. And nothing else.

A hand at the small of her back made her realize she had been lost, frozen, staring at the water. Lancelot had dismounted and was right next to her. She half expected to see judgment in her face.

Instead, she found sympathy and support. "Are you well, my queen?" Lancelot asked.

Guinevere nodded, still dazed but at least able to focus. She kept her eyes on Lancelot to avoid looking at the sea again.

"Ships," Brangien said, breathless.

If Guinevere was going to do this, she would have to face it. She turned toward the water and took it in, bracing herself. While she still felt overwhelmed, it edged toward awe. Maybe the Lady held no sway over the sea. Even if she did, how could she find Guinevere on something so infinite? Guinevere laughed, closer to hysteria than delight, but at least she could move. Whether the sea really was not the same as the rivers and lakes or whether her body simply did not have enough space to contain that much fear, Guinevere steeled herself. Along the shoreline was a series of wooden buildings, and bobbing in the water like a sad copse of lost trees was a series of masts attached to boats.

"Ships indeed. Shall we go find one?" Guinevere grasped her reins.

Brangien burst into tears. Lancelot looked at Guinevere, alarmed. Guinevere nudged her horse next to Brangien's and reached out to take her friend's hand.

"Thank you," Brangien said.

"We will save her."

Brangien nodded, taking her hand back and wiping under her eyes. To give her time to compose herself, Guinevere turned toward Lancelot, who was remounting her horse. Sir Tristan rode ahead to scout the road.

"Are you at least a little excited for a quest, Lancelot?"

Lancelot did not smile. "I am not here to rescue Isolde. I am here to protect you. I will do whatever that requires, even if you do not like it. Even if it means this *quest* fails."

"Come on!" Sir Tristan called, guiding their pack horse. "We can hire a ship and be on our way before nightfall."

Lancelot clicked her tongue and her horse followed the command. Guinevere watched Lancelot's back as she rode, worry tight in her chest. Nothing was allowed to go wrong. Lancelot would not have to make the choice to save Guinevere over anyone and anything else.

If the smell of the sea from far away was invigorating, this close it was invasive. Guinevere raised a sleeve to her nose to filter out the riot of rotting fish, wet wood, and refuse assaulting her.

"That one." Sir Tristan pointed. The ship he had picked was not the largest, but it looked big enough to transport the horses. The horses could not be left behind. Besides being more valuable than anything else they carried, Lancelot's horse was her most important possession. Guinevere knew there was no way they would continue without it. She did worry about the faithful blind steed and how it would handle something as unfamiliar as a sea voyage, though.

They had decided Sir Tristan should do the bargaining. He was the least remarkable of their company. Lancelot *could* be mistaken for a man in her clothing and with her short, unadorned hair, but when she spoke at length it made the mistake less likely. Guinevere and Brangien unfortunately looked nothing like each other or either of their companions—Sir Tristan was the darkest complected, his family having been brought here by the Romans and then settling, and Brangien's features favored those of her father, who had walked across the world from the farthest east of it to make his fortune. Guinevere was paler than Lancelot, and none of their faces spoke to relations. There was no pretending that any of them were siblings.

Guinevere hoped that there would be no questions when payment was offered, but if there were, Sir Tristan was a traveling knight, Guinevere his wife, Brangien her maid, and Lancelot Sir Tristan's . . . well, they had not figured that part out yet. Squire? Fellow knight? Very distant cousin?

Sir Tristan flagged down a young man hauling a tangle of nets out of the bottom of a small boat. "Who does that ship belong to?" He pointed to the one they wanted. It seemed absurd to Guinevere to trust a few planks nailed together against the might of this endless expanse of water. She had to turn her back on it before she began thinking about it too much. She could still hear it, though. Waiting. Waves lapping against the shore, stretching out toward her.

"Wilfred." The young man wiped his nose along the sleeve of his much-patched tunic.

"Where can I find him?"

The fisherman shook his head, then pointed toward a shack clinging precariously to the rocks on the shore.

The group exchanged confused glances. Shaking his head and then pointing seemed contradictory, but there was a language barrier. Sir Tristan shrugged, then picked his way across the rocks to the indicated shack while the rest waited with the horses.

"I will try not to speak," Lancelot said. "It is best if they assume I am a man." Lancelot's voice was low, but not as low as a man her height should have. "Once we are on the ship, we are at their mercy to a certain extent. We will hope this Wilfred is honorable, but if he proves otherwise . . ." Lancelot's hand tightened on her sword pommel. "I will allow no harm to come to either of you."

"We are not without defenses, too." Brangien had pulled out a strip of cloth and was industriously sewing. Guinevere could not see the knots, but she doubted the piece was decorative.

"I would not wish to cross any of us." Guinevere said it with joking enthusiasm, but she felt formidable.

Sir Tristan emerged from the shack and hurried toward them. The rocks along the shore were gray, nearly black with the clinging moisture and littered with items deposited by the incessant waves. Guinevere tried not to imagine that the saltwater-soaked hunks of wood were from other ships.

Sir Tristan had an odd expression when he reached them. "Wilfred is not home. But his sister, Hild, will take us. She can transport the horses, as well. I have retained her services for the next seven days."

"How much will it cost us?" Lancelot asked. They had a handful of Guinevere's jewels to bargain with, safe in her bag alongside her brush and her dragon's tooth.

Sir Tristan looked flushed. He scratched the side of his neck in a nervous gesture, staring back at the shack. "Less than it should, I think? She was excited by the prospect."

"Intending to kill us and take the horses?" The matter-of-fact way Lancelot stated it made Guinevere stare in shock, but Sir Tristan took it as understood and shook his head. Did they really have to anticipate this level of violence whenever they left Camelot? How were men any worse than the Dark Queen? Her violence was random, at least. In a way, that felt kinder than men preying on each other for profit.

"Hild does not seem the type, and we are both larger than she is. I told her we would pay half now and half upon landing, delivered to our companions who would be waiting for us. It seemed the wisest lie. She said two days to sail to the southernmost point, and then another day and a half to sail to where we will disembark. She did not ask questions about why we chose our route."

"That is probably for the best," Guinevere said. A thrill of excitement spread up her spine. Everything had been theoretical, but now it was real. They were going to do it.

They were going to get on a boat. For two days.

She felt less excited and more ill.

Hild was younger than Guinevere had expected. She could not have been more than eighteen. They had not seen her until after she had rowed out to her boat and then maneuvered it as close to the shore as she could. A long gangplank was dragged out and placed in the water. The horses would have to wade to it. Lancelot went first, to stay aboard with the horses in case Hild planned to load the horses and then leave.

"Welcome, welcome!" She spoke their language, but with a heavy accent. Her hair was almost yellow, her cheeks ruddy, her bright-blue eyes already hinting at how they would line from years of squinting in the sun. There was something inherently cheerful about her, and if appearances were anything to go by, she was absolutely thrilled to meet them.

She chattered happily as Lancelot guided her horse up the ramp and then returned for the others. "The horse cannot see? That is good! Very good!" She laughed. "Beautiful horses. I hate horses. Too-big teeth." She gestured at her own teeth and then bit down in an exaggerated manner. "Never trust a beast that can fit your—" She gestured to her shoulder, looking at Sir Tristan.

"Shoulder."

"Yes! Shoulder. Never trust a beast that can fit your shoulder in its mouth." She snapped her teeth again for emphasis and then laughed and leaned a little closer to Sir Tristan. "I never bite."

Sir Tristan's eyes widened with alarm. Guinevere did not much know what to make of the comment, either. Perhaps it was an issue of language. Or perhaps . . .

Well, Sir Tristan *was* very handsome.

Sir Tristan cleared his throat. "That is all the horses. Should we board? Where is your crew?"

Hild gestured at the four of them, then at Lancelot. "Crew! My brothers all hired out for harvest. Last sail of the year. Good time."

That would explain her eagerness and her willingness to go along with their requests. It gave her a chance to earn money that she was not expecting to have again until the spring.

"How do we get to the ship?" Guinevere asked.

Hild squinted at her. "I do not understand."

"How do *we* get to the ship?" Guinevere gestured to herself, Sir Tristan, and Brangien, and then pointed at the boat.

Hild turned to Sir Tristan. "Is she . . ." She pointed to her forehead and then made her eyes go wide and unfocused while tilting her head vacantly to the side.

Guinevere folded her arms. "No, she is not!"

"We walk to the ship? Like the horses?" Hild laughed. "Boots will dry. Everything dries. Everything gets wet. It is the sea." She stretched out her arms and spun once, then sloshed toward the ship.

Brangien looked at Guinevere with alarm. There was a loud splashing as Lancelot hurried from the ship toward them. Without a word, she scooped Guinevere up and carried her through the water toward the ship.

"Have to beat Hild back, in case she decides to sail away with our horses," Lancelot said.

Guinevere put as much weight into her arms around Lancelot's shoulders as she could to relieve some of the strain on Lancelot's arms. "Thank you," she whispered. The gangplank creaked alarmingly when Lancelot set her down, and she rushed up onto the deck.

The movement did not stop there, though. The whole boat
bobbed and dipped with the waves. Guinevere had hoped that since
it was bigger than the ferries it might be steadier, but her hopes
were dashed. The center of the ship was covered with a grate and
the horses were whinnying in alarm beneath her. There was a small
cabin on one end, a mast in the middle, and entirely too little wood
separating her from the sea. She did not know whether it was the
wood groaning or herself.

"Bucket," Hild said, pointing to a battered bucket shoved in a
corner between the side of the boat and the cabin.

"What?" Guinevere's head was swimming, and the thought of
anything swimming made her feel even sicker.

Hild pantomimed vomiting violently, then pointed again. "Bucket.
Then dump." She took the imaginary bucket she was holding and
pretended to toss the contents overboard. She then began barking
out commands, but Guinevere knew she could be of no use.

She fell more than sat, arms around her legs, head resting on her
knees. Her breath was too fast, too sharp; her heart pounded. She
could hear the water everywhere. Smell it. Feel the damp of it. It was
too much. She could not do it. She had told Arthur she could, and
she had been wrong, and the whole quest would fail because Merlin
had made her afraid of water.

"Guinevere?" Brangien put a light hand on Guinevere's shoulder.

"Put me to sleep," Guinevere said through gritted teeth. "Put me
to sleep. I cannot do this. Please. Put me to sleep."

"But—"

"Brangien!" Guinevere's whole body shook. She could not stand
this, could not handle the fear, felt herself falling into a dark hole.
Not the one in Camelot from her dream, but another deeper, darker
hole, one she walked into of her own free will, only to—

CHAPTER FIFTEEN

"Drink this. Come on, you have to drink."

Something pressed to Guinevere's lips and she did her best to swallow. Half of it dribbled down her front. It was dark. Guinevere did not know where she was. A door opened and shut. The room was moving. Why was it moving?

"Keep drinking. Did you need something?" Brangien was talking.

Sir Tristan answered. Why was he in her room? And why was her room moving? "Hild is very . . . friendly."

"Are you interested in that type of friendship?"

"All I want to do is serve King Arthur. Go on quests. Fight for goodness and take care of my friends."

"I will do a better job of intercepting Hild," Brangien said. "I am sorry. I should have helped more. Just tell her you are faithful to your unconscious wife." Sir Tristan was not married. When did he get a wife? Why was she unconscious? *Why was the room moving?*

"I did not want to embarrass her and risk her stranding us. But she seems good-natured."

A boat. They were on a boat. She was in the middle of the sea.

There was water around her, beneath her, everywhere. Guinevere's heart picked up. She could not breathe, could not—

"Finish drinking this if you want to go back to sleep." Brangien's tone was firm. Guinevere drank as quickly as she could.

The door opened again, bringing with it the scent of the ocean. Guinevere wanted to die. But not here. Not where the water would claim her body.

Lancelot spoke. "Hild said we will weigh anchor in a few hours. She will bring us ashore an hour's walk from King Mark's castle. How is she?"

"Her heart is racing so fast she may as well be a rabbit. *Finish*, Guinevere."

Guinevere choked down the rest of the drink and felt the strip of cloth settle back into place, her relief outweighing her shame over being so useless.

"Come on. I need you awake." Brangien's tone was brusque. Guinevere reached up to pull the blanket over her head and block out the light, but there was no blanket. She sat up, startled to find herself on dry ground. She had been set on a patch of earth covered with pine needles. The light was weak, dappled and broken up by the branches overhead, but it still dazzled her to the point of tears. She could hear the ocean but she was on land.

"And you will stay here." Lancelot sounded firm. Guinevere could not make her eyes focus enough to see individuals. She felt shaky and wrung out, like a tree whose leaves were about to fall, trembling with the smallest of breezes.

"I will!" It took Guinevere several seconds to place Hild's voice.

"She is alive! That is good. I thought maybe she died, and then I would get no money."

Someone held a canteen to her lips and Guinevere drained the whole thing. She tried to orient herself. She was on land. They were on their way to rescue Isolde. She had been asleep for two days.

"Thank you, Hild," Lancelot said. "We will be back by nightfall."

"I will wait until tomorrow."

Guinevere accepted the bread put in her hand and ate it ravenously. Her stomach was uncertain, but now that she had her wits about her, she refused to take longer than needed to recover. Even though she was on dry land, the dregs of panic were still draining from her. She could swear the solid earth beneath her had the slightest pitch and roll. Reaching into her pouch, she clutched the dragon's tooth, rubbing her thumb along it. It grew warm to the touch.

A sense of an intelligence somewhere nearby tickled the edge of her consciousness. Was it her touch magic, or something from the dragon? She dropped the tooth and it disappeared. Then she picked it up again and the sense returned. The dragon was nearby. It must have ventured south, following the sun before winter fell.

It did not matter. She needed to focus.

Sir Tristan crouched nearby while Lancelot got the horses ready. He spoke quickly, filling her in on the plans she had missed. "King Mark is not a sentimental man. When his previous three wives died, they were entombed within hours. No ceremony. Brangien will sneak into the castle and deliver the potion, and then we will wait near the cliff tombs for Isolde to be placed there."

"Is the potion ready?" Lancelot asked.

Brangien crumpled something to dust between her fingers and sprinkled it into a leather canteen. "It will be by the time we get there."

"No." Guinevere shook her aching head. "Brangien might be recognized. King Mark has seen her, and many of his men have, as well."

"I could—" Lancelot's voice was strained. She cleared her throat and continued more purposefully. "I could dress as a woman." They had spoken of it before. Lancelot was herself in armor; wearing women's clothing felt like lying.

"You stand out." Guinevere gestured. "You are tall and strong and you do not carry yourself like a servant. I do not know if you could convince anyone. I will do it."

"No," all three said at once, but Guinevere stood. It took everything in her not to sway or tremble, but she managed.

"I am best suited to the task, and you all know it. I can imitate a maid and draw no attention, and even if I do, I have plenty of tricks that will give me enough time to escape. But those will not be necessary because I will do such a good job of walking with exasperated purpose through the castle that no one will dare stop me. And when I find Isolde and explain who I am—"

Brangien interrupted. "She will know who you are. We have spoken of you."

Guinevere was touched that Brangien took her into the dreamspace and shared that part of her life with Isolde. "Good. Then she will know she can trust me when I give her poison and tell her to drink it and die."

"But what if she is in a cell?" Lancelot asked. "What if you cannot find her?"

"Then I will improvise. I am good at it." Guinevere gave Lancelot a meaningful look. She had been improvising since the day Arthur's men retrieved her from the convent. She mounted her horse, accepting Lancelot's help as though it were appreciated but not necessary, though she doubted she could have gotten up on her own. Hopefully she would be fully recovered by the time they arrived at the city.

Brangien finished her potion as they rode, then passed the leather canteen to Guinevere. Lancelot eyed the exchange warily. Guinevere was careful not to make eye contact or look anything other than ready and confident. She was certain Lancelot would change her mind about this plan at the slightest indication of danger or hesitation, and Guinevere would not let that happen.

"Right, left, through the hallway, up the back stairs, second door, right, last door." Guinevere repeated the instructions to herself. Sir Tristan had explained the castle's layout to her and given her directions to the royal chambers. And Lancelot had made her swear that if Isolde was not there, she would come right back out.

Sir Tristan led them along the shoreline, avoiding the city. But even from this distance Guinevere could smell it. Woodsmoke, animals, a tannery. It was wretched. So bad that Guinevere would have preferred even the smell of the sea over it. She was awash with gratitude to Arthur for having so much foresight in how he took care of Camelot. It was not enough to have a city that functioned. Arthur made certain his city was *pleasant* for everyone who lived there.

This castle, too, was less than impressive. Guinevere could not see details from this far, but it was a squat, inelegant building with only two stories. The foundation was stone, but the rest was wood and vulnerable to fire. It was built along a cliff overlooking the water, so at least it had a natural defense on one side.

Sir Tristan led them to a rocky outcropping. They dismounted, tied up the horses, and climbed until they reached a good vantage point. Sir Tristan pointed to a cove where there was a cave halfway up the cliff. "Those are the tombs. When you have done your part, meet us here."

Brangien tucked a small purple thistle behind Guinevere's ear.

"I have told Isolde about you in our dreams, of course, but this will prove who you are and that you come on my behalf."

"Guinevere," Lancelot said, her voice low but commanding.

"I will come back at the slightest hint of danger," Guinevere said, quickly clambering down the rocks before Lancelot could say anything else.

Squaring her shoulders and lowering her cloak's hood—no one working inside a castle would wear a hood—Guinevere walked with purpose, keeping well away from the edge of the cliff, her eyes on the ground. She entered the castle through a side door and then followed Sir Tristan's directions like she knew exactly where she was going.

And she did. She was going to rescue a damsel in distress. Arthur was not the only hero in Camelot.

CHAPTER SIXTEEN

Guinevere had not accounted for the fact that she was really only used to one castle, and was rarely alone in it. The castle at Camelot was shallow but with many stories, so no single one was that complex. Some had only a handful of rooms, and she did not even know what many of the areas held because she never had reason to visit them.

Not ten minutes inside King Mark's castle and she was lost. It was a squat labyrinth, a lifeless, breathless forest. And it all felt so fragile. So temporary. Half the floors she walked across were rushes, crunching beneath her feet. A few sparks and the entire castle—and with it, King Mark's authority—would be gone.

No wonder Arthur was succeeding. Camelot itself lent him credit and status. The permanence, the order, the beauty. Arthur was young, yes, but how could anyone not be inspired by his city? Of course everyone who came to him wanted to be part of it. Between that and the sword that had waited for him in the heart of Camelot, it was as though someone had lovingly prepared it all for him.

The sword *had* been prepared for him, but no one knew where

the city came from. It had always been there. The Romans had used
it, as had Uther Pendragon. Guinevere wondered whether Merlin
knew who first built it, but Camelot was far more ancient than
he was.

She suppressed a shudder, remembering her dream about the city
when it was new, which triggered thoughts of the Lady of the Lake.
She did not have time to dwell on those questions. Arthur would not
fail his quest because he was thinking about impermanent castles
and ancient cities. She tried remembering Sir Tristan's instructions,
but without being able to retrace her steps to her starting point, they
were worthless. She had no idea where she was or how to get to
where she was supposed to go. No wonder Arthur always opted for
the straightforward method of battles and sword fights.

"Excuse me?" A young man in King Mark's livery—black, with
what was either a red spear or an odd tree in the center—put out
an arm to stop her. She was in a long, dim hall. There were no windows to help orient herself. Her eyes watered from the smoke of
something cooking nearby, the smell hanging heavy all around them.
"What are you doing here?"

Guinevere had sworn to Lancelot that no one would notice her or
question what she was doing. Panic served no purpose, so she set it
aside. She could not control having been seen, but she could control
how she was seen. If she could convince an entire city that she was
a queen, she could certainly convince one round-faced young man
she was a lady's maid.

She immediately burst into tears.

The young man's eyes widened in alarm. They were muddy brown
with thick eyelashes. His teeth were crooked where he bit his lip before speaking. "What—what is wrong?"

"I only arrived last night, and my father had to trade ever so many
favors to get me a spot in the castle, and he was so proud and he told

everyone, including my aunt, and she *hates* me, she is always telling me I am a useless, stupid thing, and how my father would have been better off having no children at all than only having a daughter like me, and she is right because I was supposed to fetch some wine from the kitchen but I got lost on the way and my father will be so disappointed in me when I am sent home." She stopped, sniffling, letting her lower lip tremble. "Do you think they will even send me home, or will they lock me up for failing?"

The young man's face turned red as he tried to hold back laughter. "Well, it is your lucky day. I know where the kitchen is. And you can dry your tears. No one will notice you this evening. They are going to burn the queen." He offered his elbow and she took it, grateful the movement covered her shocked horror. *Tonight!* Isolde was to be executed that very evening. She had not a moment to lose.

"Thank you! My aunt told me I would find no kindness in the castle, not one drop, but she was wrong. What time is the—what time is the—the bonfire?" Guinevere stumbled over the atrocity of saying *bonfire* in relation to Isolde, but she did not know what else to call it.

He turned them toward the kitchen. "At sunset. Did you miss the whole trial? It was very sad. The queen wept and the king raged. So, nothing unusual there." He laughed good-naturedly. "But it is too bad she is a witch. She was always nice to us. My sister thinks it has more to do with King Mark wanting an heir than any witchcraft, but I think she must have been up to something, always locked in her rooms, sleeping all hours."

"Is she in a cell? I hate to think I am in the same castle as a witch." Guinevere shuddered. It was not hard to fake. She already felt sick with dread at how little time she had and how complicated her task had become. She had promised Lancelot she would come back.

She was going to break that promise.

"At sunset, you will never have to worry about her again." He made a whooshing noise and waved his fingers through the air in a gruesomely cheerful imitation of fire. "Kitchen is there." He pointed to a door. Guinevere could have followed the smell of smoke and burning grease quite easily on her own. "I have to go now. It is my shift to be outside the king's door." His chest puffed with pride.

"Thank you. My hero." She smiled as he turned away, then her smile fell away like a curtain being drawn. If she could not find Isolde, she could find the man who knew where she was. She followed the young man and tore several threads free from her tunic as she walked, knotting them viciously into confusion. It made her vision swim and her steps unsteady, but it also made anyone who might stop her or ask questions simply slide right past without noticing her.

After a narrow flight of stairs and in another dim hallway he paused to spit at a door before continuing on.

It was a gamble. Follow him to the king, or examine the door that triggered his derision? Guinevere paused. The door was bolted from the outside. She could find the king after, if she needed to. She slid the bolt free, then considered the lock. Inside her pouch she carefully moved aside the potion and examined her options. She had thread. Bits of cloth. The tooth from the battered dragon, which certainly would not help. She had none of her iron thread, which was unfortunate. That would have done the trick quite nicely.

With a sigh, she reached into her boot and withdrew the iron dagger Arthur had gifted her. She did not like this magic, either its tolls or the way it felt. She cut the tip of one finger and pressed it against the lock, tracing a simple knot for age. Then she let her blood drip into the keyhole. There was nothing dramatic or showy. After a few seconds, the lock simply fell open, a fine dusting of rust sprinkling

out of it. If anyone looked closely, they would think the lock had succumbed to age and the ocean-damp air.

Guinevere leaned against the door, resting her head there. Blood
magic asked more than any other type did. She did not know the
exact cost of this one. She suspected she had just given up several
days of her own life to concentrate the passage of time on this one
tiny object. Magic always had a price, paid now or paid later.

She opened the door. The room was dim, its single window shuttered. A cot was in one corner with neatly folded blankets. There
were no paintings, no carpets. Sitting on a plain wooden chair near
the wall was a woman.

"Who are you?" a voice as soft as a spring bloom asked. Guinevere
stepped inside. The woman's hair was long and full. Her eyes were
wide set over a small nose and lips like a budding rose, her cheeks
full, her hands dimpled, her generous curves swathed in green cloth.
It was impossible not to be a little breathless when faced with such
beauty.

"Who are you?" Isolde repeated. "What is happening?" She stood,
alarm on her face as she tried to focus on Guinevere but could not
manage it because of the confusion knot. "Who are you?" Her voice
was rising. She would get them discovered. Guinevere pulled her
tunic to her mouth and bit off the threads of the knot, releasing
the magic. Her head cleared, like the pressure before a sneeze is
released. Isolde took a step back, blinking rapidly as her eyes finally
settled on Guinevere.

Guinevere pulled out the purple thistle. "I am here on Brangien's
behalf."

Isolde's face drained of blood as she reached out a trembling
hand. "Brangien's flower. Beautiful not in spite of its spiky nature but
because of it." She held the thistle against her chest. "Who are you?"

"Guinevere."

"The queen?" Isolde's expressive eyebrows raised nearly as high as her hairline. "Brangien sent King Arthur's *queen* to me?"

"Well, it is a group effort. I am here to set you free."

"And Brangien?" Isolde's voice shook.

"Brangien is waiting to help. There will be a place for you at Camelot if you want."

"I could not." Isolde put her hands over her heart, shaking her head. "It would put everyone there at risk. Brangien and I will have to run. We will have to run forever."

"We had a plan. It was a good plan. But the timetable is more complicated now that you are due to be burned at sunset." Guinevere tugged on the window shutters. They were nailed shut. The room was on the second story, and they could probably manage to climb down. But could they do so without being seen? Guinevere was afraid if she used the false-death potion on Isolde now that she had been found guilty of witchcraft, they would simply burn her body instead of interring it in the cave tombs.

Guinevere reopened her finger wound and used up precious time on several of the nails until she managed to pry the shutters open. It was nearly twilight. The execution loomed. She thought she could smell woodsmoke; it was probably a constant scent, but it hung like a promise of death. Luck was finally on their side, though. A tree was near enough to the window that they could reach it and climb down. It would also shield their descent from being observed.

"Come on. We will run, and then we will figure it out." It was not the right plan, but it was better than being burned at a stake. Guinevere held out her hand and Isolde took it.

In the time she had spent asleep, Guinevere's sense of touch had restored itself. She was privy to the year of torment and terror this gentle woman had experienced at the hands of her husband.

Isolde carried the pain just beneath the surface, so much that it took Guinevere's breath away. And somehow under the pain and around it was hope and goodness and light. All the little ways Isolde had found to give kindness in a life that denied it to her. And the bright burning core of love that Guinevere knew was for Brangien. Doubtless, that core had sustained Isolde.

"Maybe when we get down we could burn this castle to the ground," Guinevere said, gritting her teeth against the pain still washing over her. She helped Isolde onto the windowsill.

The door burst open, revealing a man in a crown.

CHAPTER SEVENTEEN

Guinevere was face to face with King Mark, the man they had created this entire plan to avoid. Everything was ruined. Guinevere was surprised at how calm she was. Everything that could go wrong had gone wrong; all she could do now was respond to whatever he did. She shifted so she was between Isolde and the king.

King Mark surprised her, though. He closed the door behind him, sealing them off from the rest of the castle. "Who sent you?" he asked. She had imagined him looking like Maleagant, a hard man with a hard face. Instead, King Mark's face was puffy, bloated. Veins webbed out from his nose, and there was something deeply unpleasant about his wet and swollen lips.

Guinevere was well aware of what this man was capable of. She had only brushed Isolde's skin, but what that woman had endured . . . King Mark was a monster. But Guinevere had meant it when she said that she and Brangien were formidable. In place of fear was *fury*.

Guinevere allowed a half smile that did not touch her eyes. "You know who sent me."

"If my brother thinks he can win the throne by taking what is mine, he is sorely mistaken. I will burn him to the ground," King Mark growled. "But first, I will burn two witches tonight." He grabbed Guinevere's wrist. Thankfully the cloth there blocked his skin, as she had no desire to feel what this man was like. She did not need to.

Isolde stayed perfectly still on the windowsill, like a deer frozen in terror.

There were options. King Mark had not called the guards because he did not think Guinevere was enough of a threat that he could not deal with her himself. If she could somehow force him to drink Brangien's potion, his "death" would cause enough upheaval to cover their escape. And she relished the idea of him waking up in a tomb. But how to do it?

"He should not have sent a woman," King Mark said, eyeing her. "Not even big enough to keep around for fun. Tell me, Wife, did you really think you could get away?"

Isolde let out a small whimper.

"Get down, now, or I will hurt her and make you watch."

"Climb out," Guinevere said. "He cannot hurt me. Go. She is waiting." Guinevere turned, forcing Isolde to look at her instead of at King Mark. "Trust me."

Isolde hesitated only a moment, then leapt for the tree.

"Insolent witch!"

Guinevere was ready to make her move as soon as King Mark ran for the window or the door. She could tie a sleeping knot and then—

She gasped, caught off guard as King Mark put his hands around her throat and squeezed. She had no weapons, no tools, no way to make him swallow the potion. He was hurting her—

Spots danced—

He was going to kill her—

No air, there was no air, everything was dark and all that was left of her were the bubbles fleeing upward toward the blackness above, the water waiting to rush in and—

Not again.

She touched her fingers to his forehead, gathered her power in a desperate rush, and *pushed.* It was an act of panic, animal in its intensity. She had lost sense of who she was, where she was. All she knew was that this thing, this creature in front of her, was hurting her. Killing her. And she would not let it happen.

Guinevere flooded through King Mark's mind like a river overflowing its banks, destroying indiscriminately. Her vision blurred with his hands still around her neck, and her will surged even stronger.

Only when King Mark fell did she come back to herself. Out of breath, with agonizing pain in her throat, she stood over him, tensed for another attack. He stared at the ceiling, glassy and unfocused, breathing in shallow, automatic gasps.

"Oh, no," she whispered. She had lashed out with magic. Not the careful, contained knot magic, but a wild and ferocious power she did not understand. Only once before had she used her touch magic on a mind, forcing Sir Bors to think he had killed the dragon so the dragon could go free. But she had been careful then. Cautious and precise. Even that had felt like too much, like an act of violence.

This time she had destroyed an entire mind.

She staggered and leaned against a wall, looking down at this man. This monster, yes, but still a man. Had she not hated him for using his power to hurt others? And had she not just used her own power to hurt him? She wanted to be better than Merlin, to do better than he did, and yet once again she found herself using magic for her own needs and leaving destruction in her wake.

Maybe it was not so bad. Maybe he was just sleeping. He was

breathing, after all. Guinevere crouched and brushed her fingers across his forehead, then recoiled as though burned.

There was *nothing* there.

Whoever—whatever—he had been, she had erased it. Washed it all away.

She stood, shaking out her hands, wishing she could remove them, separate them from herself. They felt so much, and they did so much, and she had not controlled them. She had been mindless with terror, whatever had roared to the surface at his attack now receding beyond her efforts to examine it. In truth, she did not want to. She wanted to forget this. All of it. What she had done but also what she had felt from this vicious, vile man when he had touched her. What she had felt from Isolde.

Isolde. Guinevere did not have time to dwell on her own horror. She leaned out the window. Isolde had navigated the branches to the center of the tree, and her face was pressed against its trunk.

"Stay there," Guinevere whispered.

Isolde looked up in shock. She had not believed Guinevere would win, not really. But at least she had hoped enough to get out of the room. "Guinevere!"

"Give me a few minutes. Do not move."

Guinevere ducked back inside. She had to do something. Anything. She had to fix this.

She could not fix this.

All their careful planning. All her insistence that she could do it without endangering Camelot. It had all been undone because she could not control herself. One sleeping knot and she could have drugged King Mark. He would have awoken thinking his brother had kidnapped his wife.

But no. She never would have had time to tie the knot. He was never going to let her leave the room alive. She should have walked away as soon as she realized the original plan would not work. It was what she had promised both Lancelot and Arthur she would do. She had betrayed them both.

She closed her eyes, trying to calm her breathing. Isolde deserved to be free. Guinevere could not have chosen to walk away, no matter what she promised.

Guinevere lifted her chin and opened her eyes. It was time to improvise. What was a little more chaos compared with what she had already done? She placed her palms against the far wall. The rough wood was old. Dry. Ready and waiting for Guinevere to destroy it.

She coaxed sparks out, not minding when they bit her hands. The pain kept her focused, reminded her of the costs of these choices. When the wood caught and began to burn, Guinevere threw open the door. She grabbed King Mark under his arms and dragged him into the hallway. His head bumped roughly along the floorboards. At least it was already empty.

"Help!" Her voice was raw and tortured from the damage to her throat, but with smoke already billowing out of the room, she had an excuse for sounding that way. "Help me!"

Three men came running down the hallway. They stopped short at the sight of the king on the ground, Guinevere still trying to drag him farther from the burning room.

"She burned herself alive!" Guinevere wailed. "The queen! She lit herself on fire! The king fainted. She would have killed them both!"

The guards stepped toward the door, but a rush of burning air and smoke greeted them and they shielded their eyes from the heat. Guinevere fought a surge of annoyance that their priority was to make certain the queen was actually dead rather than to help save more lives. "Where are the rest of the men?" she asked. "Where is everyone?"

"Already outside for the burning!" one of the men answered, staring wide-eyed at the flames devouring the room.

Guinevere still had some luck on her side, then. The castle was empty. "Hurry, we must get the king out. Sound the alarm before the whole castle burns!"

This spurred them into action. Two of them picked up the king, carrying him awkwardly down the hallway while the third sprinted ahead, shouting, "Fire!"

Guinevere followed, covering her face with her sleeve and coughing. It was only partly an act to keep anyone from looking closely at her and being able to identify her later. Mostly, it filtered her breathing. With this much smoke already, she doubted the castle could be saved.

"Fire!" she screamed. "Fire!" The stairway was emptying as people flattened themselves against the walls to let the unconscious king pass, then filled in behind them. "The queen is dead!" she shouted for good measure, to help that part of the story settle into place. "Fire! Fire! The queen is dead!" Others took up the call.

Guinevere twisted her hope like a knot, wishing she could encircle the whole castle.

Let everyone get out.

Let everyone get out.

Let everyone get out.

Panicked screams accompanied their passage. Several took up the call that the queen was dead. She also heard some exclamations about witchcraft and, inexplicably, several about a dragon. What if they thought the dragon had done this? It would be in line with all the other damage she had done if this led to a dragon hunt and put her friend at risk.

But she could not very well interrupt those cries with "Only witchcraft, no dragons at all!" She could not draw any more attention. She cut away from the guards carrying the king, breaking off to a side hall where several servants were fleeing. Guinevere used the chaos to tumble out a door with a couple of maids and then sneak to her right, following the side of the castle around to the back.

It was not difficult to find the tree she had left Isolde in. It was framed by brilliant orange as that whole wing of the building was consumed by flames. "Isolde!" Guinevere shouted. Isolde was still clinging to the tree, keeping the trunk between herself and the intense heat. The dry leaves were curling, some beginning to smoke. "Come on!"

Isolde clambered awkwardly to the ground, dropping the last few feet and landing in a tangle of skirts.

Guinevere helped her up. "Are you hurt?"

Isolde shook her head, eyes wide. "What happened in there?"

"We have to go. Now. They think you are dead." Guinevere took her hand and they ran. They did need to run, but she also did not want to tell Isolde what had happened. She did not want to tell anyone. She never wanted to think about it again.

The evening was blessedly dim and cool once they escaped the reach of the flames, but it was difficult to navigate the rocky cliffside terrain in the growing dark. Guinevere had a moment of terror that she would not be able to find the meeting place. That she would be stuck here forever, her guilt a beacon as smoke billowed into the sky. But after a few strained minutes, she recognized the particular jutting rocks.

"It is us!" she tried to call, but her throat was too damaged from King Mark's violence, the shouting, and the smoke. It came out a tortured croak.

A figure emerged from behind the rocks. Isolde let out a cry like a wounded animal, racing past Guinevere and throwing herself into

Brangien's arms. They collapsed onto the ground, cocooned in quiet cries and murmured words that belonged only to the two of them.

Lancelot and Sir Tristan stepped out, as well. Guinevere was grateful it was dark, that they could not see her expression. She felt removed from herself, as though the whole nightmare was something she had heard about instead of seen and done. A story told by someone else. Guinevere and the Wicked King.

She did not like the story.

"What happened?" Lancelot demanded, staring at Isolde, who should have been sleeping as though dead at this point in their plan.

Guinevere was freezing. She shivered, trying to keep her teeth from chattering. "Complications."

"Why are you talking like that?" Lancelot leaned close.

The night was a shield, protecting Guinevere from revealing the truth. "Smoke. Had to set the castle on fire."

"You had to *set the castle on fire*?"

"They think she is dead. We are finished here." Guinevere brushed past Lancelot and began walking toward where they had hidden the horses. She forced herself not to look back. Part of her wanted to return to the castle, to make sure everyone got out alive. She honestly could not decide which would haunt her more: knowing people had died because of her, or spending the rest of her days afraid they had.

She suspected she deserved to be haunted.

CHAPTER EIGHTEEN

As they rode away from the fire, Guinevere tore out several strands of hair and knotted them around the dragon's tooth in a spell for connection. She could not go back to make certain no other people were hurt, but she could at least protect this one creature. As soon as the magic was in place, a sense of awareness of another mind settled around her. For once the cost of the magic was a comfort. She was not alone.

If all went according to plan—which was not a given, especially not this night—the dragon would feel the pull of her knot and trail their ship up the coast. She would undo the knot when they were in an uninhabited place. Though those were harder and harder to come by.

It made her think again of the wolves she had faced behind Camelot. The dragon had felt the call of the Dark Queen and had resisted. Would the wolves have rejected her if they had the safety of a dark wooded retreat with free range to pursue their natural prey? With no refuge, was it any wonder they had succumbed to her magic?

Guinevere rubbed her eyes. They were red and raw from the

smoke; closing them offered little relief. There were too many other images she did not wish to see, clamoring for her mind when it was unfocused. So she would focus. Once they were back at the ship, she could sleep. Oblivion had never been so tantalizing.

Though they had brought an extra horse for Isolde, she and Brangien rode together, Brangien in front and Isolde's arms around her waist, head resting against her back. If they spoke, Guinevere could not hear it, and she was glad. This reunion belonged to them. Lancelot rode close to Guinevere and several times looked as though she would ask for more details, so several times Guinevere hurried her horse forward to leave Lancelot behind.

Finally, as they were drawing near to the ship—a merry campfire burning in the darkness like a beacon from Hild—Lancelot maneuvered in front of Guinevere, forcing her to stop.

"Before we get back to Hild, we need to decide how we will explain Isolde. Both to Hild and to Camelot. And you need to tell us what happened."

"She will be my cousin," Brangien said. "A new maid, brought on through my recommendation." Isolde peered at their party over Brangien's shoulder. Sir Tristan had ridden near them, close enough for companionship but far enough to give them privacy. Guinevere could see his smile in the darkness, could *feel* the happiness radiating off him. He had completed a quest. He had saved the woman he could not before and reunited his best friends. His joy seemed the simplest. Brangien's and Isolde's would doubtless be tempered by the pain Isolde had endured to get to this point. And Guinevere could feel no joy at all, happy as she was for her friend.

"Is that what you want, Isolde?" Guinevere had gone from a forest witch to a queen. She had enough struggles with that. She did not assume going from a queen to a lady's maid would be any easier. The first night of this trip without Brangien had taught her how easy it was to become accustomed to having others help her with the most basic things.

"It is more than all right. It is so generous." Isolde sounded sincere. And Brangien's stories had made it clear Isolde was not opposed to work. She had often done it to ease the loads of those in her own home. At least in this new home, she would have something she had never had before: true freedom.

Sir Tristan was as cheery as the night was dark. "We can say Brangien wrote ahead and Isolde met us on the road. It is normal for a queen to have more than one lady's maid. No one will question it."

"Isolde is a common name where I am from," Isolde offered. "Though we can change it, if you think that will be safer."

Sir Tristan answered. "Some people know your name, but they think you were, uh, my lover." He cleared his throat, uncomfortable. "I could not wrestle the story from them. But you will obviously not be with me. I do not think anyone will assume you are the same Isolde."

"I am certain the story of her death will spread quickly," Guinevere said. It hurt to speak.

"And what *is* that story?" Lancelot nudged her horse even closer.

"They were going to burn her alive. It was too late to carry out our plan. So I improvised."

"I am not sorry to see that castle burn," Isolde said. Brangien shifted, reaching a hand back to rest against Isolde's cheek. "Though I hope no one got hurt. Guinevere was so brave!"

Lancelot did not comment on that. Doubtless she would have preferred more caution and less bravery. "And their king? He will be convinced?"

"King Mark will not be a problem. I am tired. Let me pass." Guinevere clicked her tongue and used her horse to force Lancelot aside.

She arrived at the camp first. Hild was sitting near the fire.

She looked up, surprised. "You are early. We cannot set sail until morning."

"We are happy to camp here for the night." Guinevere dismounted and let Sir Tristan take her horse along with the others to be fed and watered.

Lancelot orbited her, close enough to hear everything she said, but with an extra, deliberate distance. Guinevere had hurt her. But Guinevere could not imagine how much worse it would be if Lancelot knew the truth of what she had done.

She sat near Hild. The ocean raked its fingers along the coast, trying to drag the land into its depths. A cloak was draped over her shoulders, and Isolde patted her once, softly, before sitting across the fire from them.

"New one." Hild gestured at Isolde.

"My cousin," Brangien said.

Hild frowned dubiously. In the firelight Isolde's hair was revealed to be a burnished copper red. Her skin was fair, and her curving shape nothing like Brangien's angular one. A rose to a thistle.

"On her mother's side," Isolde offered, as though that cleared everything up.

Hild grunted, uninterested now. "In the morning, we sail. I know a river. I can get you closer. No extra money. But"—she looked at Lancelot, a shrewd expression on her sunburned face—"my brothers are there. They need work. They all do. Good men. Strong. They can do farming. Fishing. War. Good men for your King Arthur."

Lancelot's eyes widened. She coughed to cover her surprise.

Sir Tristan took a few seconds too long to respond. "I am afraid we cannot help there. We do not know King Arthur."

Hild shook her head, impatient with the deception. "Lady knight." She jabbed her finger toward Lancelot. "We hear things. A lady knight is a good story. No one else has one."

Lancelot did not move or react, frozen. Guinevere knew how mortified Lancelot would be that she was the reason their disguises had failed. But then Hild turned to Guinevere.

"And you are queen."

"What?" Guinevere sputtered.

Hild nodded, confident. "You sleep. For days! Everyone else works. Only a queen could do that."

It was Guinevere's turn to be embarrassed. She wanted to defend herself and explain, but being too terrified to function was hardly a better excuse than being a lazy queen.

"We can help King Arthur. Transport things. Transport men." Hild pointed at Sir Tristan. "Like this one! I want more like him. But who want—" She paused, frowning thoughtfully, then made several gestures Guinevere did not quite understand and definitely did not want to think about long enough to understand. And now Sir Tristan was as embarrassed as Guinevere and Lancelot.

There was no point in denying who they were. Better to have Hild on their side than angry that they still insisted on lying to her. Guinevere sat up straight, lifting her chin, adopting the posture she used during dinners with the knights and their wives. "You can tell no one where we have been. It is extremely important."

Hild nodded eagerly. "I keep secrets, you help my brothers."

"Having men who know the coast and how to sail it would not be a bad thing," Lancelot said, her tone grudging.

"How do we explain our arrival at their village?" Sir Tristan asked.

Guinevere would resume her role as queen earlier than expected. It was disappointing to lose the freedom of being someone else, but at least it gave her something to train her mind on. An excuse to look forward instead of back. "We do exactly what Hild wants. We say we were nearby, met Hild, and are visiting to extend an invitation from King Arthur. Your people can meet with him and discuss ways to work together in the future. We can even take one of your brothers with us. We are going to a wedding."

Hild nodded eagerly, then squinched up her face in thought. "Maybe we get close to the village and then walk. I am not supposed to take the ship."

Guinevere laughed. "But you are so good at it!"

Hild frowned. "How do you know? You sleep the whole time." Hild set down her cloak, lay on top of it, and closed her eyes. "We leave at dawn."

Brangien and Isolde had their arms around each other. Brangien's head was on Isolde's shoulder, and Isolde rested her cheek against the top of Brangien's head. Their lips were moving, but they spoke so softly that Guinevere could not hear. Sir Tristan faced out toward the night, taking first watch.

Lancelot sat down next to Guinevere. "You have bruises on your neck."

Guinevere traced her neck with her fingers. Hopefully Brangien had something they could use to cover the evidence of King Mark's violence for the wedding. And for the meeting with Hild's brothers. She did not want any rumors starting.

Her fingers stayed on her throat. She wondered if she could get her hands around a neck tightly enough to do what King Mark had done. His hands were so much bigger than hers. He was so much stronger. Just like Maleagant had been. If Guinevere had not been able to draw on something wild and violent, if it had been only her, just a girl, how could she have fought either of them?

But if she were just a normal girl, Maleagant would never have known she existed. She would never have gone to King Mark's to rescue Isolde. He would never have attacked her. And he would still be a person, instead of an empty shell.

Maleagant would still be alive to destabilize Arthur's kingdom, and King Mark would still have Isolde. Guinevere watched through the sparks and flames as Brangien said something and Isolde let out a single short laugh. It was a small moment, but knowing what Guinevere did about the pain Isolde had been through, it was *everything*.

"I am fine," Guinevere said to Lancelot. She stood and strode a few steps into the trees. The wind had shifted, blowing the smoke toward her face, and it made her want to cry.

Lancelot followed. Her face was like a book that had been shut, revealing nothing.

"Are you angry with me?" Guinevere asked.

"I am angry with myself. And with that man."

"But it worked. We won."

"We did not win. You *survived*. That is not the same thing. How will I explain this to King Arthur? How can he allow me to continue as your knight when he sees this? My failure is written across your neck."

"This was my choice. All of it."

"It should *never* have been you who went. I was a fool to agree."

"Why should anyone else have gone?"

"Because you are the queen!"

"You know perfectly well that title is a lie. It means *nothing*." Guinevere was startled by her vehemence. But it was true. Not only because Guinevere was not really Guinevere, but because she was only one person regardless. Why should she matter more than anyone else? Why should someone like King Mark be in charge of an entire city? Because of who he was born to? Because of gold, or a sword, or—

Guinevere stopped her thoughts. *Arthur* was king because of a sword. And because of who he was born to. But he was so much better than that vile man.

Lancelot shook her head. "You may not have been born to be

queen, but that does not change the fact that you *are* the queen. It means something to me. And it means something to King Arthur. I was wrong to agree. He will take away my knighthood."

"Nonsense. You did what I asked of you. If King Arthur wants to be cross, he can be cross with me."

"I am the one who will answer for this! Did you never think of that?" Lancelot's expression was stricken. "He will make me leave, and I have to—I *need* to protect you. From the moment we met in the forest, I have known it was my life's duty to defend you."

Guinevere could not take this guilt on top of the rest. Lancelot needed to realize that Guinevere was not really the queen, and never would be. "But before that was it not your life's duty to kill Uther Pendragon? And then was it not your life's duty to become a knight to serve Arthur?" Guinevere did not want to be cruel, but she was so tired and everything hurt and she did not deserve to be protected. "You would do better to return to your previous sworn duty. Arthur is more deserving than I."

Lancelot looked as though Guinevere had delivered a physical blow. She stalked back to camp, leaving Guinevere alone in the dark.

CHAPTER NINETEEN

Mordred laces his fingers through hers, lying next to her. Flowers bloom around them as they stare up, the clouds writing unintelligible stories across the sky.

"Did I do the wrong thing?" Guinevere does not quite know why she asked. There is something hazy lingering on the borders of the meadow, a sense of unease. It smells like smoke. But when she looks to see it, there is nothing there.

"Define wrong." Mordred turns on his side to stare at her, tracing a finger down her profile, lingering on her lips. "Better yet, tell me who gets to define wrong, and why."

She turns to face him. "Arthur."

Mordred laughs. "But why?"

"Because I chose him."

"But why?"

Guinevere wants to argue the point, but she does not remember what the point was, or why they were arguing it. And Mordred's lips are so very close to her own.

Guinevere peeled her eyes open. There was no ship's deck beneath her, only solid, safe ground. Though being awake meant having to feel things again. Guinevere resolved not to. She sat up, accepting the canteen Isolde handed her. Isolde rubbed small circles on Guinevere's lower back, a simple, comforting touch that was both unexpected and devastatingly tender.

"Your knots are wonderful," Brangien said, examining the rope Hild was tying to secure the ship. They were not beside the ocean anymore but on a riverbank. It did not make Guinevere feel any better. "Did your brothers teach you?"

Hild laughed. "No. They want me to—" She gestured at her belly, then moved both hands outward like it was expanding. "But there are only men who smell bad and are bad." She looked regretfully at Sir Tristan, who was preparing the horses. "No good men. But a good ship. A very good ship."

"Come on." Brangien held out a hand to help Guinevere stand. "Time to make you look like a queen."

Guinevere accepted the help. She was shaky and needed to eat, but she had not been asleep as long this time. She reached into her pouch to get her brush. Her fingers bumped against the dragon's tooth.

"Oh! Is this area very populated?" Guinevere turned to Hild, worried. She had been asleep, so she had not been watching for a good area to sever the connection to the dragon. Now that she was awake she could sense her old friend. Not specifically how near it was, but that it was aware of her and their connection. And she could feel an extra warmth diffusing downward from the crown of her head where she had taken the hairs for the knot.

Hild gestured at the trees around them. "No farmland. Too rocky. My brothers stay in a village there"—she pointed vaguely upriver— "but only a few men."

Guinevere pulled out the tooth and bit the knot free. She let out a small, sad exhalation as the connection to the dragon disappeared. It was suddenly much colder. She felt alone in a sharp, painful way.

"Dindrane's family estate is half a day's ride to the west." Lancelot had already mounted. She did not look at Guinevere. "We should speak with Hild's brothers so we can be on our way and meet up with the king before he arrives."

Guinevere removed her plain outer tunic. Brangien handed her a pretty blue one, long enough that it would drape nearly to the ground. "I need a collar," Guinevere said as she fastened a belt made of linked metal squares around her waist. Brangien's eyes traced the bruises, but she said nothing. She was unusually gentle putting a cloak with a stiff embroidered collar around Guinevere's shoulders, pinning a jeweled broach in place so the collar would stay shut and hide the marks.

Though they had brought nothing for Isolde, she was wearing something befitting a lady's maid. Brangien must have spent the ship journey altering her own clothes to fit Isolde.

Sir Tristan helped Guinevere mount her horse. He always treated her formally, but now that she was dressed up, there was an extra distance. She wondered if he noticed. Becoming queen again was almost as isolating as breaking the connection to the dragon.

Hild led them along the riverbank. The trail darted in and out of the trees, rocky and indistinct. Hild rode the extra horse, and Isolde and Brangien once again shared.

"Not far now," Hild said. Campfire smoke drifted through the air. Someone shouted and Hild answered, a long string of words in a language Guinevere did not know.

A man appeared on the trail in front of them, loping toward them with long strides. "My brother Wilfred." Hild did not sound excited about the reunion, which surprised Guinevere since Hild was bringing good news. Wilfred looked a lot like Hild, if she were ten years older and twenty years meaner. Sun-bleached hair retreated from his red forehead, and his eyes were almost invisible beneath bushy eyebrows drawn permanently low. A thick beard obscured the lower half of his face. He said something to Hild. Hild answered, and they continued back and forth, unintelligible, with Wilfred increasingly angry and Hild sullen. It was a far cry from her cheerful demeanor before. Finally, Wilfred grunted and gestured for them to follow.

Hild dismounted and led her horse, so they did the same. The village more resembled a camp. The buildings were ramshackle, no order or sense to their placement. Several had already collapsed and been left to rot. If it was a harsh winter, Guinevere did not envy anyone living here. Maybe this encampment was temporary and the villagers went somewhere else for winter. But it made no sense to stay here during harvest; there was no farmland nearby.

Twenty or thirty men lounging around a firepit greeted them with eyes hooded in suspicion. They all had a similar look to Hild and Wilfred. Guinevere had heard of Saxons moving in and taking land, but these men did not strike her as the type motivated to conquer or marry into landownership. No one stood. Another heavily bearded man continued picking at the dead skin between his toes with a dirty knife. If they wanted to be soldiers for Arthur, they were in for a very rude awakening. He would not tolerate this slovenly behavior.

Hild started speaking, but Wilfred interrupted her. He gestured to their group, offering a few curt sentences. One word made all the men look at Guinevere and laugh. It was not a laugh like Hild's, one that invited merriment even if they could not understand her. It was a dirty cudgel of a laugh, and Guinevere wanted to be invisible.

Lancelot stepped forward, hand on her sword. "We are here on behalf of King Arthur of Camelot. If any of you wish to join his service, you can become soldiers and work for the chance to be a knight. It is not an easy path, but it is—"

The barefoot man belched loudly, scratching his stomach with the tip of his knife. "Sit." He gestured to logs placed around the firepit. "We eat. Then we talk."

The scent of whatever was cooking in the large iron pot was as appealing as slop for the market pigs. Guinevere did not want anything that came out of it. She sat on a log, with Brangien and Isolde taking up positions on either side of her. Lancelot remained standing, as did Sir Tristan.

"Ramm," Hild said, keeping her eyes on the ground. "He leads the camp."

Guinevere had often been around large groups of soldiers and knights. She had traveled with Arthur and his men on several occasions. But even though none of the men here had moved or even paid them much attention, she felt vulnerable in a way she did not like. The hairs rose on the back of her neck. She was afraid of these men. And she was also afraid of what she would be willing to do to protect herself.

She could no longer pretend that what she had done to Maleagant's men had been entirely due to the magic of the Dark Queen infecting her. There had been no Dark Queen in that room with King Mark. That had been Guinevere, and Guinevere alone.

Guinevere adopted her favorite queen posture. It was a way of reminding herself to be what people expected. To control what they saw and how they reacted. She sat straight, lifted her chin so even though she was shorter than the men, she gave the impression of looking down at them. Not in a disrespectful way but in a way that communicated she was not meek. Not afraid.

The posture gave her strength. Queen Guinevere would not wait on someone else's whim. She stood. "We are extending an offer for work in the fields or with King Arthur's soldiers. He is also interested in your reputation as excellent sailors. You have much to offer Camelot, and Camelot has much to offer you. You can accept this offer or not. If you accept, you may choose a man to accompany us and meet with the king to discuss terms."

Ramm's eyes narrowed thoughtfully. Then he grunted and stood. He walked to Guinevere and held out one enormous, dirty hand.

"Good," he said, his hand still extended. Guinevere realized she was meant to clasp it. She put her own palm against his. He smiled. And then he yanked her hand, spinning her so her back was against his chest, his knife held to her throat.

Lancelot's sword was already drawn, as was Sir Tristan's. Isolde screamed. Brangien stood in front of her, a dagger drawn from her skirts. The men around them were like cats, one second lounging and the next swollen in size and menace, brandishing weapons and ready for a fight. No one moved to attack, but everyone was ready to. They were a single breath from an eruption of violence.

Hild shouted in their language, gesturing frantically. Her brother tried to shush her, but she shoved him and ran toward Guinevere. A man punched her in the jaw. She sat roughly on the ground, dazed.

"Release the queen," Lancelot demanded.

Ramm laughed. His breath was rank and foul against Guinevere's face. He said something and Hild translated, her voice hollow. "Scraps for work, or gold for a queen. Ransom is easier."

"And making an enemy of a king?" Sir Tristan trembled with rage. "That is not so easy."

Ramm shrugged, the knifepoint scratching the skin beneath Guinevere's chin. He spoke.

"Nothing to lose," Hild translated as she gestured weakly at the camp. Then she spoke for herself. "I am sorry. I did not know. I did not know."

Lancelot raised her sword, flicking her eyes over the camp. They were outnumbered at least ten to one. She pointed her sword at Ramm. "I will fight you for her."

Ramm laughed again. Guinevere wanted to flinch from his beard, wiry and terrible, scratching the back of her neck, tangling in her hair. It was almost worse than the knife. "No."

"Are you afraid to fight a woman?" Lancelot delivered the words like a slap to the face.

Hild translated his answer. She was still sitting on the ground, legs splayed, back curved. "He says they are twenty-five, you are two. He is not stupid. Why fight one-to-one?"

"For honor."

Hild did not bother passing along Lancelot's words. She shook her head, expression sorrowful. "What honor?"

"Very well. I will kill you all, then." Lancelot smiled. Her calm demeanor was more frightening than any posturing or vicious snarling.

"I kill her first." Ramm jabbed the knife for emphasis.

Guinevere rose onto the tips of her toes, trying to get her throat as far from the blade as possible. "Take Brangien and Isolde." She kept her voice clear and steady, hoping she could make everyone else feel the same way by sheer force of will. "All of you go. Get the ransom."

"No." Lancelot spoke as sharply as the edge of her sword. "I will not leave you."

Guinevere wanted to strangle Lancelot and her bravery. She looked at Brangien instead. "Get the gold from King Arthur. It will be just like the time we helped Sir Bors free the dragon."

Brangien frowned, dagger still clutched in defense of Isolde. "What?"

Sir Tristan shook his head. "Sir Bors killed—"

"Remember?" Guinevere interrupted. Her throat felt dry, but she did not want to swallow, not with that horrible blade so close. "When Sir Bors freed the dragon, it felt loyalty to him, and then we all met two leagues to the west and celebrated. I am letting you all go free because I know you are loyal. Like dragons."

Brangien nodded, her expression still dubious but her eyes understanding. She knew what Guinevere was capable of. Some of it, at least. She might not understand the details, but she got Guinevere's meaning. *Leave. Wait two leagues west.* Guinevere should have told them she saved the dragon. But they had to trust that Guinevere could handle this and keep them safe.

Brangien turned to Lancelot. "We should go. The sooner we get the gold, the sooner we can finish this."

"No." Lancelot shifted into a fighting stance.

Brangien leaned close to Lancelot, whispering. Lancelot's eyes roved the camp, doing mental calculations of how many men she would have to kill before getting to Guinevere.

Guinevere wished Lancelot would look at her. She needed Lancelot to understand. "*Please.* As your queen, I am commanding you. As your friend, I am begging you. Take Brangien and Isolde. Get the ransom. Go now."

Lancelot finally met Guinevere's gaze. Guinevere was shocked to see tears in her knight's eyes. Lancelot did not sheathe her sword, but she backed up, gesturing for Brangien and Isolde to go to the horses. Sir Tristan moved so he was beside Lancelot, a united front, swords still raised.

"I will kill you," Lancelot said, pointing her blade at Ramm.

"If he harms her?" Hild offered.

"No. I will kill him no matter what. I will kill you *all* if anyone harms her." Lancelot clicked her tongue and her horse approached. She mounted, never sheathing her sword as she waited for Brangien and Isolde to get on their horses, Isolde taking Guinevere's gray mare. Sir Tristan mounted last, grasping the reins of the extra horse.

Guinevere offered a smile as tight as her chest. "I will see you soon."

Fury and devastation warred for prominence on Lancelot's face, but she tapped her heels and her horse broke into a gallop. Guinevere watched as her protector and her friends rode away, hoping that they understood her meaning.

And that she would be capable of saving herself.

CHAPTER TWENTY

The door closed behind Guinevere, and she was alone. They had taken her to what could only be called a shack under the most generous of imaginative leaps. The single room was dark and smelled of mildew and wood rot, and the only furnishing was a pile of what might have been clothes, blankets, or even a ship's sails in one corner. "Well then." Guinevere sat on the packed-dirt floor. They had not bothered taking away her bag or searching it. After all, she was only a girl, even if she was a queen.

Guinevere pressed one eye to a gap in the wood slats of the shack. Men were trickling into the camp. Some were greeted warmly, others with cautious distance. Word was spreading fast about Ramm's prize, and these men were taking no chances. They were forming an army. As near as Guinevere could guess, there were close to three dozen, with no telling if that was the lot of them or if more would come. She had to act before they did. Or worse, before Lancelot returned and risked her own life.

Guinevere emptied her bag onto the dirt and considered her options, dragon's tooth in hand. Sleep knots would have worked if there had been only a handful of people, but she could not manage dozens. Knotting confusion into her own cloak would not let her walk past so many people intent on keeping her. It only worked if someone was not certain what—or whom—they were looking for.

All her knot magic was not enough. It was, by its very nature, limited. Contained. But she would not use her own touch magic as wildly as she had with King Mark. A part of her never wanted to use it again. It was like the rest of her mind: so much unknown that she could not say what would happen.

Besides which, she could not ask three dozen men to line up and wait their turn for her to disable them.

She had lit a fire at the castle to create a distraction. The buildings here were made of wood, too. Could she run fast enough to get free? Once in the woods she could leave confusion knots scattered to disrupt her trail.

She would only have one chance. She could not waste it. And she could not do it alone. The dragon's tooth was smooth and warm in her hand. Maybe the dragon had always meant for her to use it if she needed it. And she had drawn the dragon all the way here already. Fate had set up this convergence. She pulled out a few hairs, then redid the same knot she had used before. She felt the connection immediately, even stronger than before. The dragon was nearby. She tugged the knot tighter, increasing the pull.

For a few minutes nothing happened. Guinevere strategized what she could do on her own, trying not to give in to despair. Perhaps her magic had not worked, or the dragon simply did not understand.

But then she *felt* the dragon. It shifted and stirred in the morning sun. This was its last autumn, and it had been luxuriating before winter came. After winter, Guinevere knew it would burrow deep into the earth and never come back out. She had made the deal with the dragon when she saved it from Sir Bors, granting it one last visit of the seasons.

She gripped the tooth. It warmed and so did she, with something like a fire kindling in her chest and getting hotter.

The door opened and Guinevere dropped the tooth into her bag.

Hild's eyes were focused on the ground. "Too many men." She gestured behind herself, her hand limp. "Too many ideas. Money! Fights! Make your king hire us! Kill your king and take Camelot!" She saw Guinevere's alarm and held up her hands. "Stupid. No ports there. Bad fighters without ships. Ramm wants money." Hild sagged against the doorframe, which made the whole shack lean slightly, as well.

"Do they really think King Arthur will simply hand over gold and leave them be?" Guinevere felt the tooth against her side, warm through the bag.

Hild shrugged. "Good ships. Good sailors. They can get away. King Arthur might still want them, too." She gestured vaguely around herself to communicate expansion. "Faster moving, more wars won, more land."

"But we could never trust you."

Hild slid along the wall to the floor. Guinevere was still worried about how to get away, and more than a little scared of Ramm, but Hild seemed so *sad* about everything. Guinevere wanted to comfort her. Hild shook her head. "You can never trust anyone. Only trust yourself."

"I trust a lot of people."

"Yes. And you are here. Trust is bad."

"You did not violate our trust. This is not your fault."

"I knew Ramm is bad. I thought he was gone. Wilfred would listen alone. Maybe. But not with Ramm here."

Guinevere saw the opening. "Then go speak with Wilfred. Convince him to help us get out. I will take you both to Camelot with me. You can have your own ship."

"No." Hild looked over her shoulder with a wistful expression. "It is all broken now."

Guinevere slipped her hand into her bag. The tooth was growing steadily warmer. Guinevere was half-afraid it would singe a hole through her pouch. She had used a similar knot to what Rhoslyn, the woman banished from Camelot, had performed on her stones so women could locate each other in secret. The closer the dragon got, the hotter the tooth would become.

"Can we go outside, at least?" Guinevere asked. "I am hungry."

Hild shrugged, then stepped aside so Guinevere could leave the shack. The men were gathered around the fire, talking and laughing and arguing in that same rough language that Guinevere did not understand. Ramm passed around a jug of something and they took turns drinking from it. They barely glanced at her, which was a relief. No one seemed worried that she would run, or that they would be unable to catch her if she tried.

Hild led her to a table and handed Guinevere a hunk of rough, hard bread. Trees pushed in all around. The river curved away from them, winking in the sunlight. On the other side of it, portions of the forest had been felled. Eventually it might be good farmland, but it would take time. Much easier to ransom a queen than to invest in the future through backbreaking labor. Arthur's way was better. He always put in the time to create a future worth striving toward.

Guinevere turned to Hild. "Run away with me. Please."

Hild shook her head. "This is my family."

"They are a bad family. Choose a new one. I did." That was a lie. Guinevere had not chosen to forget the Lady of the Lake. Merlin had chosen it for her. But she *had* chosen Arthur. Brangien. Lancelot. Sir Tristan. Dindrane. Camelot.

Hild stared at Wilfred, who was taking the jug from Ramm, drinking so much that it ran down his throat and soaked into his shirt.

Guinevere slipped her hand into her bag. The tooth was scalding; she could only brush her fingers against it. She heard a rustle somewhere in the woods behind them.

"Ramm!" Guinevere shouted. "Let me go now or you will regret it."

Ramm wiped his mouth and pulled out his knife. His smile was obscured by his beard, but the hair hid none of his malice. He said something and pointed to Hild to translate.

Hild shook her head desperately. "No."

Ramm strode forward, knife raised.

That was when the first bright burst of flame roared from the trees.

CHAPTER TWENTY-ONE

"Drachen!" the men screamed, running. Another stream of fire engulfed the buildings. Ramm was half on fire, flailing as his clothes burned and his beard began to smoke. There was no pleasure in watching this, no victory. Only horror. Guinevere needed to flee and to take the dragon with her so it would not cause any more damage.

Guinevere grabbed Hild's arm. "Come with me!"

Hild took a step with Guinevere, but then looked over her shoulder. "My brother!" She ran back into the camp.

Guinevere could not drag Hild or force her to come. She had to go. Now. Guinevere ran into the woods, dodging around a burning tree.

"Stop!" Hild shouted, but her shout turned into a scream.

Guinevere turned to see what had happened, but a leathery wing whooshed through the air, cutting off her pathway. The wing shoved her against the dragon's body and she scrambled onto its back to avoid being crushed. It ran, lumbering and crashing through the trees. It had one damaged leg—she remembered that from their last meeting—but its gait seemed more chaotic than the old wound would account for. Screams from the camp were quickly muffled by the forest.

Guinevere clung to the dragon, wrapping her arms as well as she could around its thick neck. It was far larger than a horse and there was nowhere for her to get a good grip with either her arms or her legs. She slid back, terrified she would fall, and managed to grasp it at the wing joints. Hoping she was not hurting the dragon, she held on with everything she had.

After a few minutes' mad dash through the trees, the dragon slowed, stumbling. Then it tripped and crashed to the ground. Guinevere rolled free, one arm caught beneath her. She heard a loud pop and her shoulder lit up with pain. She gasped, on her back, staring up at the sky through the autumn flames of the leaves. There was a rasping noise she could not place.

She used her good arm to push herself onto her knees, whimpering as she tried not to move her injured shoulder. And then whimpering again at what she saw.

The dragon was on its side, the terrible rasp issuing from it. Its poor body, already battered and scarred from so many years fighting to survive, twitched. A spear was lodged behind its front leg. Blood, thick and black, dripped from the wound.

"No," Guinevere whispered, her hands hovering above the dragon's chest. "No, no, no." She looked at the dragon's face. One golden eye beneath a drooping eyelid fixed on her. She did not want to touch the dragon, did not want to feel what it was feeling, but she owed it to the creature. She put her hand on its forehead beneath one of its great curling horns.

The leaves. The season of peaceful fire, the whole world burning brilliant and bright. Guinevere calling. Guinevere coming with the dragon so it would not sleep alone. The dragon answering the call. And then—

Men.

The men Guinevere had saved it from so it could have one last winter.

Sleep, it implored her, sending her images of darkness and rest. It wanted her to come with it, still.

"We have to split up," Guinevere said. "I am sorry. Please, go. *Hide.*"

The dragon answered her call because it thought she had changed her mind and wanted to burrow deep into the earth and sleep, letting the changing world go on without them. She had promised it peace, and instead she had tricked it into another fight.

She stepped back, her face wet with hot tears. She held out the tooth with her good hand. "Go. I am sorry." The dragon rolled out a long purple tongue, taking the tooth from her. It limped away into the trees, alone and injured, body and soul.

Fight like a queen, Merlin had said. Merlin, the liar. Merlin, the monster. Merlin, whose advice she should not want or heed. But she kept fighting like a forest witch, like herself, like *him,* and everyone and everything around her paid the price.

It was for the best. The dragon would be safe from her reach. She leaned against a tree, looking back at where they had come from. The dragon's trail was impossible to miss, a patch of lumbering destruction. She imagined Ramm, his beard smoldering, his dirty knife ready, stalking toward them.

Cursing herself, she tore out hairs and tied knots of confusion, throwing them over the dragon's trail. It cost far more than she could afford to cover it up, but she would not let the dragon be found.

Clutching her injured arm to her chest, she began to move in the opposite direction. The dragon had gone east toward the coast, but Guinevere was going west. She tied more knots, dropping them behind her as she went. The world spun in a dizzy blur. It was too much. Her own sense of direction, even her sense of balance, were thrown off by the confusion she had created. She stumbled as far as she could. Minutes or hours passed. She was too disoriented and in too much pain to know. Finally, when she could no longer smell smoke or even see it, she collapsed next to a tree and closed her eyes to rest for a minute. Just a minute.

"Guinevere? Guinevere! What are you doing here?"

She peeled her eyes open. Everything was fuzzy, as though viewed through a veil. She lifted her good hand to her face to pull away the veil but there was nothing there. Mordred leaned closer and she patted his cheek. "What are *you* doing here?" she asked.

"I was looking for something. I saw smoke so I came to investigate, and then I found a very confusing trail that demanded I not notice or follow it, so naturally I followed it. What happened?"

"I do not want to say. Not right now." She tried to stand, then gasped in pain and sat back down.

"Your arm." Mordred sounded upset. She did not like it. He was supposed to be smiling, trying to kiss her. "Try to relax." He took her wrist in one hand and her elbow in the other. "I did this for Arthur, once. And he did it for me. Twice. So now we will be even, I suppose."

"Did what?" Guinevere asked.

Mordred pulled and twisted.

She gasped in shock as the pain flared incandescent and then lessened to almost nothing. Whatever had been wrong with her shoulder was fixed. "That hurt." She slapped Mordred's side while he wrapped a strip of cloth around her shoulder and bound her arm to her waist. "I like it better when we kiss."

"What?" Mordred paused, his fingers light against the skin of her wrist.

"This is a bad dream. I do not want this one." The edges of her vision were still hazy. When she tried to speak, it took several seconds for her tongue to catch up to her words. She wanted to wake up.

"You prefer the ones where we kiss." The laughter in his tone made her smile. She had missed the way he could say things without saying them, could laugh without laughing, could confuse her in the most aggravatingly delicious ways.

"Yes. This is— Mordred, I hurt the dragon. It is sad now, and it is my fault. And I hurt someone, he was bad but what I did might have been worse, and the dragon burned another bad man, and—" She could not see anymore, but this time because of tears. She hated this dream. Hated that her feelings had invaded this space, too. She wanted an escape, a sleep without guilt. But her guilt was too strong and it followed her here. "I am as bad as Merlin."

"Far prettier, though."

Guinevere glared, or tried to, but then the world was spinning again, blue and brown and orange, and she could not focus. She anchored herself to the green of Mordred's eyes. "I am being serious."

"As am I. You are not as bad as Merlin." Mordred shifted closer and she lost his gaze, but it was nice being next to him. She felt less like she was about to tip off the edge of the world and tumble into the sky.

She rested her head on his shoulder. "You asked me who gets to define wrong and why."

"I did? And what did you tell me?"

"I did not have an answer. I still do not. But I can feel it. Right and wrong. Only after, though. Why can I not feel what will be wrong before I do it?"

"Because then you really would be Merlin, and you would do

it anyway." Mordred shifted as though he would stand. "Are your friends looking for you, or only enemies?"

Guinevere reached for him, wrapping her arm around his neck and pulling him close. "Lancelot and Sir Tristan and Brangien and Isolde are waiting for me when I wake up. I think. I hope. But stay. Can we just stay here for a little while? I do not want to go back. It is hard and confusing." Camelot was dreams of the Lady of the Lake, questions about her mother, politics and stress even when she was not faced with dangers like Guinevach. And when she saw Arthur—oh, she would have to tell him, she would have to say all the terrible things she had done.

The trees were not safe, but at least they were simple.

"Are you certain?" Mordred's voice betrayed nothing, but his forehead rested against hers.

"I am not certain about anything. Why are you asking me so many questions? Can you just kiss me?"

Mordred let out a long, slow breath. "No. Not yet. But I will the next time you ask me." He gently removed her arm from around his neck, tucking something into her hand where it was wrapped against her torso.

She leaned back against the tree and closed her eyes. A scent of smoke found her and she wept again, thinking about how she had used the dragon. How sad it had felt, trying to convince her to go with it. "I keep trying to be clever, and it works, but it causes so much damage."

"Ah. Yes, that is the price of being clever. We win, and we hurt other people, and we always, always hurt ourselves. Better to be dull and good, barreling through the world like Arthur. It makes things simpler."

"You told me I made the wrong choice."

"That sounds like me." He did not rejoin her and she was cold and her shoulder ached and she wanted him back at her side. Branches snapped and broke, and then there was the scent of smoke again. Always smoke. Reminding her of what she had done. Who she had hurt.

"I wish you would stay with me," she whispered.

"And now you know how I feel." A soft brush of his fingers ignited sparks along her cheek that did not fade as she drifted away on delirium.

"My queen? My queen!" The voice got softer, more worried. "Guinevere?"

Guinevere peeled her eyes open. "Lancelot."

Lancelot pulled her into a fierce hug. It hurt. Guinevere's face was smashed against the leather armor of Lancelot's shoulder, a comforting scent. When Lancelot released her, the vulnerability that had been communicated by the rib-crushing intensity of the hug was replaced by determination. Lancelot stomped out the remains of a small fire that was smoking heavily from too much green wood. "That was smart," she said. "But we do not want anyone else finding you. Are they pursuing you?"

Guinevere used the tree to leverage herself up. One of her arms was bound against her, keeping it from moving. Her shoulder hurt, but not as much as it should. She did not remember binding it, or starting this signal fire.

"You are hurt." Lancelot was careful this time not to make it sound like an accusation as she examined Guinevere's arm. "You did a good job with this dressing."

Guinevere looked at the ground where she had been propped against the tree. There, among the fallen leaves, was a single delicate purple-and-yellow blossom, just like the one Mordred had given her after soothing her burned hand beneath a tree a lifetime ago.

"Not a dream." She picked up the flower and stared at it with both wonder and horror. Mordred had been here. He had fixed her shoulder, set up a signal so she could be found by her knights, and then . . . left. Again.

Maybe she was still delirious. Maybe the confusion knots she had tied had been far more powerful than she meant them to be. She held up the flower. It was an impossible bloom, far too late in the season for something like it. "Do you see this?" she demanded.

Lancelot looked alarmed. "Yes?"

Guinevere tucked the flower into her bodice, pressing it against her heart. It felt like it would disappear if she did not keep track of it, melting in the light of reality like her dreams always did.

"What happened?" Lancelot asked.

A spike of guilt pierced Guinevere, as though Lancelot would know she had once again been with Mordred and had not fought him. She could not explain their encounters. First, he proved he wished her no harm. And now he helped her and then walked away.

Why had Mordred said he had been there? She could not remember. If he was following her or stalking them, why help and then leave? The whole encounter had the quality of a dream, nebulous and impossible to remember details.

It did not matter. She could not let Lancelot be distracted by chasing Mordred. They had to get to Arthur. And once again, Mordred had done no harm. The opposite, even.

"I . . . I got away. There was a fire." She could not bring herself to tell this truth, either. That she had used the poor dragon and then sent it away. Lancelot would not understand. Hild's scream echoed through her memory, and she shuddered. She hoped Hild was not hurt. "I used magic to confuse them so they could not track me." The memory of Ramm rolling on the ground to put out flames that could not be extinguished made her shudder so hard it hurt her shoulder. "I should have waited for the ransom," Guinevere whispered.

Lancelot lifted her onto her horse, then climbed on behind her. "After you are safe with Sir Tristan, I will go back and deliver a message." Lancelot's voice was cold.

"No!" Guinevere half turned, nearly falling off the horse. Lancelot grabbed her and readjusted her seat. She did not want Lancelot to see what had happened. The cost of her ransoming herself. "Ramm has paid. They all have." Everyone paid the price of her magic.

Guinevere let her head hang heavy, her mind a jumbled mess of Hild's scream, the dragon's sorrow and confusion, and Mordred's inexplicable kindness.

"Your safety is all that matters," Lancelot said firmly, brooking no argument. "If we hurry, we can meet Arthur and his party on the road before they reach the estate."

Guinevere's stomach dropped. With all the terrible truths she needed to tell—and the ones she already knew she would not—for the first time, she wanted to see anyone but Arthur.

CHAPTER TWENTY-TWO

Guinevere and Lancelot rode for an hour before joining a relieved Sir Tristan and a frantic Brangien and Isolde. Guinevere slid to the ground too quickly, nearly falling.

"You said two leagues to the west!" Brangien's face was red with anger. "We were supposed to wait two leagues to the west. That is what you meant, is it not?"

"It is. You did exactly what I asked you to." Guinevere was exhausted in body and spirit. The price she had paid for the confusion knots had mostly worn off, but it did not change the pain in her shoulder, the lingering unease over Mordred's actions, and her sadness at leaving Hild behind with men who would never listen to her.

"Why did you talk about the dragon, though?"

Guinevere closed her eyes and rubbed her forehead. The dragon was better off without her. Surely it knew that now. "In case they could understand some of my words. They would focus more on the dragon than on the detail of waiting two leagues to the west."

"How did you get away?" Isolde asked. There was something

gentle but knowing in the way she watched Guinevere. Isolde saw all the pain Guinevere was not discussing. Guinevere did not like being so seen, so understood. Not right now. It reminded her of Mordred, which was the last thing she wanted.

"I started a fire. It is turning into my signature. Come, we should be on the move." Guinevere mounted her own horse and urged it forward without waiting.

They rode quickly, only stopping near evening to change Guinevere's smoke-scented clothing and fix her hair. There was nothing to be done about her arm, but Brangien used nicer cloth that matched Guinevere's dress to redo the wrapping.

When they hit a road, Sir Tristan ranged out to get their bearings. He surprised them by returning with more men. Guinevere's heart sank when she recognized Arthur riding alongside him. She was not ready. Arthur's broad smile froze as he looked closer at her. Her neck was covered, but she could not hide her arm or the strain of what she had been through.

"Guinevere." He dismounted and held his arms up to help her. She did not want to get off her horse and lose that barrier preventing them from speaking too closely. But she slid down and let him half catch her and set her on her feet. He embraced her, careful of her arm, and whispered in her ear, "What happened?"

"Too much." Guinevere pulled back, smiling. She raised her voice so everyone around them could overhear. "We had good fortune. We were going to wait for Dindrane's party, but Brangien's cousin, Isolde, was traveling to Camelot. We crossed paths. She will join my service as a lady's maid. We decided not to look for the other travelers. I missed you."

"What happened to your arm, my queen?" asked the earnest young guard who had been so confused about Yvain and Yvain the Bastard's knightly lineage.

"I fell from my horse. It is harder to ride in skirts than you would think."

He frowned thoughtfully. "I think it would be very hard."

Guinevere laughed. "Then it is exactly as hard to ride in skirts as you think."

Arthur took her good arm, angling them toward the trees and privacy. "We can make camp here. No reason to push on today."

The earnest guard spoke. "But Aron scouted and said we are only an hour away and the wedding party is already there. They must have left early, too." Realizing he had just contradicted the king, he bowed his head. "Whatever my king thinks is best, though."

"We should push on," Guinevere said. "I would like to sleep in a bed tonight." She wanted more time to collect herself. To decide what to tell, and how to tell it.

Arthur glanced toward the solitude of the trees, clearly torn and wanting answers now instead of waiting. But he was too kind to deny Guinevere's request. Besides, it would draw attention and perhaps more scrutiny to her story if Arthur seemed worried. "Very well," he said, lifting Guinevere to his own horse and then climbing on behind her, putting one arm around her waist to steady her. He was so solid, so real behind her. She let her head lean back and rest on him, surprised by how much it relieved the tension in her back and neck.

"I missed you, too," he said, his breath soft on her neck.

She should tell him the truth. All of it.

As soon as Guinevere dismounted inside the heavy wooden gates of Dindrane's family estate, before she could even get a proper look around, Dindrane was at her side.

Dindrane's anger was delivered with a smile, her hand possessively gripping Guinevere's good arm. "I *wish* you had *told* me you were going to *leave early,*" Dindrane said, each emphasis accompanied by an almost painful squeeze. Guinevere was certain Dindrane did not realize she was doing it, but she also could not hold it against her friend. Without Guinevere there, Dindrane had been forced to ride for days with her vicious sister-in-law, Blanchefleur. That was not a happy start to a celebration.

"I am sorry. Truly. To make it up to you, I want you to wear my jewels." Guinevere embraced Dindrane and kissed her cheek. It was a shockingly intimate display of affection by a queen, and Guinevere knew everyone there would remark on it. She lowered her voice to a whisper. "And if anyone here is cruel to you, find me immediately and I will sing your praises until the roof falls down on all their heads."

"Thank you," Dindrane whispered back, then straightened, nothing on her face revealing the vulnerability Guinevere had heard in those two words. "Oh, Father, hello." Dindrane waved to a baffled-looking older man. Even though he had known they were coming, he seemed unable to reconcile his daughter standing arm in arm with a queen.

Guinevere was hyperaware of Arthur's presence, knowing what awaited her as soon as they were alone. So much to tell. She let the introductions wash over her, smiling and nodding when appropriate. Sir Bors was almost adorably awkward, bowing so low to his future father-in-law that he nearly fell over. Guinevere had never seen him so eager to please, which provided some balm to her wounded soul. He truly did love her friend, and that, combined with the public respect he gave Lancelot, helped her like the gruff knight.

One man glared at them all, his bushy white eyebrows wild with stray hairs. He looked as though he would rather stab Sir Bors than bow to him.

"My father's cousin," Dindrane whispered, her voice tight. "Sir Bors has cheated him out of his bride."

"His—what?" Guinevere looked at the old man in horror, then back at Dindrane.

"There is a reason I went to Camelot without any prospects. Anything was better than what had been assigned me here." Dindrane nodded with a haughty expression on her face at an aunt who greeted them.

Dindrane was one of several children, three of whom were also female. It seemed cruel to Guinevere that she should have been betrothed to that old man. It explained, though, why she was willing to endure Sir Percival and his wife. At least in Camelot, she had been free to make some of her own choices. Sir Percival had gone there for the same reason. As the second son, he stood to inherit nothing, and chose to make his fortune as a knight.

It was hard for Guinevere to gauge whether or not Dindrane's family estate was impressive. Her first introduction to cities and castles had been Camelot, and compared with that remarkable place, everywhere seemed lesser. There was certainly a lot of mud. Ladies' maids here must spend hours of every day cleaning it from hems. Guinevere tried to negotiate her way through the mud as carefully as possible, mindful of not taking more of Brangien's time than necessary. But the house itself looked solid, with small windows and a red-tiled roof that contrasted nicely with the surrounding rolling golden fields.

"Who is that?" Dindrane asked, glancing back at Isolde. "She is very pretty." It did not sound like a compliment, but rather a judgment.

"Brangien's cousin, Isolde. Brangien sent word ahead and she met us on the road. She is to assist Brangien as my maid."

"I am so relieved!" Dindrane's exuberance for the topic surprised

Guinevere, until she continued. "It is absurd for a queen to have only one lady's maid. And it sets a bad example for the rest of us. Sir Bors kept saying if the queen had but one, surely I only needed to hire a woman for a few days a week. This is much better. Now he cannot tell me I should not have one in the house with us. Isolde should have brought sisters. Though I would never allow a maid that beautiful into my home. Ladies' maids should be respectfully plain." They walked from the sunny outdoors into the dim and breathless interior of the manor. The walls were whitewashed and covered with tapestries. The floors were stone, rough and uneven but clean.

"Pardon me, Dindrane," Arthur said, putting a hand on the small of Guinevere's back. "I am certain my queen is tired after so long on the road. She had a fall and will need to rest until tomorrow. Show us to our rooms."

"Of course! I will make your excuses at supper." Dindrane appeared surprised as she noticed Guinevere's wrapped arm for the first time. But Guinevere's cloak was heavy and covered most of her. Dindrane snapped her fingers at the nearest person who looked like a servant. "You. Take my special guests, King Arthur and Queen Guinevere of Camelot, to their rooms." She whispered conspiratorially to Guinevere, "You have my father's own rooms. No others in the manor were good enough to host a king." She looked downright gleeful at this displacement of her father.

Brangien and Isolde made to follow Guinevere, but Dindrane waylaid them. "Brangien! We have to finish my dress. Can your cousin sew? She does not look like she can sew. Isolde, is it?"

"Yes, my lady," Isolde said, curtsying prettily.

"Well, you have a lot to live up to. Your cousin is the finest lady's maid in the entire kingdom. We have had ever so many . . ." Dindrane continued as she led Brangien and Isolde away.

Brangien shot a look sharper than an arrow over her shoulder at

Guinevere. Guinevere would have loved to rescue her, because then she would not be alone with Arthur. She was not ready for this conversation. She did not know if she ever would be.

Lancelot and Sir Tristan accompanied Arthur and Guinevere. Arthur held up a hand when they got to their door and the servant left. "Doubtless you are tired, but I do not know this man or his household. I do not want the queen unguarded at any time."

"We are not tired, my lord," Lancelot said, bowing her head. "We will not leave this post." She did not make eye contact with Guinevere. Guinevere wanted to reassure her knight that, however Arthur reacted to Guinevere's revelations, she would make sure Lancelot was not punished. But then they were in the room and the door was closed and it was just the two of them. The two of them, and the truth.

CHAPTER TWENTY-THREE

The room was dim, the windows shuttered against the late-afternoon sun. A large bed took up most of the space, with a fireplace and two chairs in one corner. Guinevere would have preferred a smaller room that did not belong to Dindrane's father. She removed her cloak, moved to one of the chairs, and sat on it, curling her legs beneath her.

Arthur let out a small cry of dismay. Then, to Guinevere's surprise, a wave of anger crashed over his face. She had never seen him look this formidable, not even when he had been confronting Mordred and the Dark Queen. She found herself shrinking, but it was not her he was angry at.

"Who did that?" He pointed at her neck.

Guinevere had forgotten about those wretched bruises. There were so many other wounds she carried, inside and out. "King Mark." She intoned the name like she was speaking of the dead. She might as well have been.

"He hurt your arm, too?" Arthur's hands were clenched into fists.

"My shoulder. And no. That was—you should sit down. There is

no one you can fight. No vengeance to be had. I have seen to that."
Her voice was dark, her memories darker.

Arthur did not follow her advice, choosing to pace instead. "You
were never supposed to see King Mark. How did you convince him
to let Isolde go?"

The beginnings of a tremble plagued her bottom lip. She remembered the pain of his fingers around her throat to steel herself against
it. "I did not convince him. I—he was choking me, and I felt what he
did to Isolde, what he made her go through, and he was—" Guinevere stopped, took a deep breath. "I used magic. I was not careful.
Whoever he was, whatever he has done, it does not matter now."

Arthur was aghast. "Did you *kill* him? How could Lancelot and
Tristan let you go alone?"

"It was my plan. They are in no way accountable."

"They most certainly—"

"You taught me that the king is always accountable. Does that not
apply to the queen, as well?"

Arthur finally sat. He closed his eyes and repeated himself. "Did
you kill him?"

"No. But I might as well have. He is gone regardless. Whatever
Merlin did to me—to my mind—I did far worse. Arthur, I—I erased
him."

Arthur was still for a long time; then he nodded. "Did anyone see
you? Will they be coming for Isolde?"

"No. They think her dead in the fire."

"The fire?"

"I also burned down the castle."

"*Guinevere.*"

"I know. It was—nothing went how I had planned. It was a good
plan. A safe plan. But he was going to burn her at the stake. There
was no time."

"You should have left."

"I could not. Would you have?"

"That is beside the point."

"It is exactly the point! Why should I have valued my life over hers?"

"Because you are the queen!"

"Actually, I am *not!*"

Arthur looked as though she had struck him. But she was too upset to comfort him or to take her words back. She was not the queen. Both because she was not actually Guinevere, and because their marriage was not legal. Arthur seemed determined to pretend that they had a normal marriage, but she could not and would not allow it any longer.

She clasped her hands tightly so she would not reach out to him. Even this angry, her impulse was to comfort him. To support him. "She could not save herself. I could."

Guinevere wished she sounded triumphant as she said it, wished it sounded like the tales of Arthur's quests, but she just sounded tired. Remembering everything did not feel like a victory. It felt like a tragedy, even though she had won.

"What did they think happened to the king?"

"They already condemned Isolde as a witch. They believed she did it."

"You made them think a woman destroyed their king?"

"He hurt women. They are better off without—"

"No, Guinevere, *this* will hurt women. If any men are inexplicably sick, or die unexpectedly, they will blame the wives for being in league with the witch who broke the king. We banished magic to weed out the chaos of the Dark Queen, but we also did it so people will *forget*. So they will stop using it as an excuse to accuse women of wrongdoing, to blame them for the unknown and unexplained. You used fear as a tool, but fear and terror only lead to violence."

"With a king like that, they were already living in violence!" Guinevere stood, panicked and angry. Arthur was wrong about this. He had to be. She could not have made things worse than they already were.

"I know. But violence can never beat down violence. Only justice can replace it."

"No one was coming to bring them justice! No one was saving Isolde! No one was fighting King Mark! I am sorry if they did not have their own King Arthur to bring peace and goodness. All they had was me, and I used what I had to and I hurt who I had to in order to—"

A flicker of memory. Had she discussed this with Mordred? What had they said?

Mordred had told her she was not like Merlin. But the truth hit her so hard she could scarcely breathe. She was *just* like Merlin. She wanted to do something, and she did it using magic. Violent magic. She changed things to be the way she thought they should be, and she hurt someone permanently. But unlike Merlin, she could not see the end result of her actions. Maybe she helped things. Maybe the next king would be a better ruler. But maybe she made the entire kingdom worse. Maybe women—innocent women—would die because of what she had said and done. And she had no way of knowing.

Just like she did not know how much devastation she left behind when she escaped with the dragon. She knew what it had cost her, what it had cost the dragon. But what of Hild? What of those men, greedy and lazy as they were? Would they freeze in the coming winter? Would they starve? Would their injuries fester and kill them?

She burned with shame. "I wanted to be different from Merlin. But I am not even the same. At least he knew what he was doing. When he hurt people, it was planned. I do it without any thought whatsoever."

"What happened to your arm?" Arthur asked, his voice softer. He guided her to his own chair, pulling her onto his lap.

"Hild—the ship captain's brothers tried to hold me for ransom. I made our friends leave me and called the dragon."

"The dragon? Sir Bors's dragon?"

Guinevere nodded, pressing her face against his shoulder, wishing she could slip into the darkness behind her eyes. "It burned the village and I escaped, but it—they injured it and I made it limp away into the woods alone and hurt. I could have left the dragon unbothered. I could have waited. You would have ransomed me. I was so determined to save myself, and it got hurt and I got hurt and I *used* the dragon. I never even considered how the dragon might feel. It was cruel of me, Arthur."

"But it is a dragon." He sounded confused about how she could have hurt a dragon emotionally.

Guinevere shook her head, trying to figure out how to explain it. And to tell Arthur the next part, the part about Mordred. But there was a knock on the door. Arthur slipped free, moving her gingerly, aware of her shoulder. Guinevere turned her back so no one would see her crying when he opened the door.

"Yes, of course. I can speak with him now. The queen is resting." Arthur closed the door softly behind him, and Guinevere was left alone. If Arthur could not understand about the dragon, how could he ever understand how complicated her feelings about Mordred were?

The room purpled with twilight. Guinevere did not wait for Brangien to come help her but fumbled and tore at her ties until she finally managed to get out of her dress. Her shoulder was stiff and sore, but she could move it. She curled into a miserable ball and tried to sleep.

Sometime after dark, Arthur climbed into bed. She had half expected him to be gone all night and was surprised. She was even more surprised when he pressed his body against her back. "You did what you had to," he whispered, cradling her. "Once we return to Camelot, it will be easier. Guinevach is gone. We know we can match the Dark Queen in whatever she attempts. You hurt people, yes, but you hurt *bad* people. Men who hurt you and others. Let these things you had to do go. Do not think on them anymore. As your king, I command it."

She let out a small laugh, closer to a sniffle. "Oh, you command me now?"

"I do. At least in this matter." His tone grew serious. "This is the pain of being king. Of being queen. Making choices that will hurt some but save others. And often not knowing until it is too late who will be hurt and who will be saved. I am sorry you have to share it, but I am glad to have the company."

"Me too," she whispered. It was unfair of her to think Arthur would not understand her pain. He might not understand everything, but he understood this. He did not see all of her, but he saw enough. And they were bad men, King Mark and Ramm both. Like Uther Pendragon had been. Like Maleagant had been. If Guinevere could not accept that she would have to hurt wicked men to protect others—and herself—she would not be a very good queen *or* witch.

The choices would always be hard, and she would have to live with the consequences. She could live with knowing King Mark and Ramm had suffered because they had stepped into her path and tried to stop her.

But Arthur did not know the whole story. The specter of Mordred rose behind her closed eyes. She had tucked the flower into her pouch and even though it was not magic, she could feel it pulsing nearby, declaring her duplicity.

She would throw it out in the morning. Mordred—dream Mordred, real Mordred, both—was wrong. She had made the right choice. And she was making the right choice now by not telling Arthur his traitorous nephew was more complicated than good or bad. If Arthur had to face Mordred someday, he needed to be able to do so with a clear head. Guinevere would feel conflicted enough for both of them.

CHAPTER TWENTY-FOUR

Guinevere stared out the thick glass of the sitting room window. She had awoken this morning with Arthur still beside her for once. It filled her with strength and determination to shrug off the haunting guilt. This was Dindrane's wedding, and she was here to support her friend. But supporting Dindrane through a wedding was almost as challenging as giving herself permission to accept what she had done to King Mark and Ramm.

The world was warped and distorted through the window, a vision of blue and gold she longed to be out in, instead of sewing in this stuffy room with a dozen women. The walls were stone, whiter than the gray of Camelot, but that made them look dingier with their years of stains from smoke from the fireplace. The rooms were all small and tightly crammed with furniture. This particular room was tightly crammed with women, as well. Guinevere wondered what it would be like to grow up in a building of labyrinthine hallways and tiny rooms, all access to the outdoors shut away by windows and bars and fenced courtyards. Was Dindrane ever allowed to run free? To explore?

She still longed to know what childhood looked like, what it felt like, all the different ways it was experienced. She knew the general shape of Arthur's—spent serving Sir Ector and Sir Kay and learning from Merlin—but Brangien had not spoken much of hers. She seemed to feel warmly toward her parents, at least. Guinevere knew so little of Lancelot's past. Or Mordred's. Was he raised by Morgan le Fay, his mother and Arthur's half sister, the sorceress who had wanted to kill Arthur when he was an infant? How well had he known his own father, the Green Knight, one of the Dark Queen's offspring and fairy protectors? Had he spent much time with his grandmother?

It seemed like vital information. She wanted to take their pasts and absorb them, make them part of herself, learn all the pieces that went into making the people she knew now. Maybe then she could understand them. Maybe she could even come closer to understanding herself. Fill all her gaps with other people. Push out Merlin and the holes where the Lady of the Lake had been removed.

"And then the queen asked me to be her personal guide to the complexities of Camelot. She found it quite overwhelming."

Guinevere looked up, lost to the flow of conversation, nodding only half a second too late to Dindrane's story. Because Dindrane had not been living here, she had not had time to gather the necessary things for a bride to take to her new home. And it was important that she have her own things. That, along with the money being exchanged between Sir Bors and Dindrane's father that evening, would ensure that even if something happened to Sir Bors, Dindrane and any potential children would not be left destitute.

Guinevere liked this practice in theory. She liked the part where she had to sit, sewing, far less. Still, she tried to smile and act pleased to be there to combat the air of resentment from Blanchefleur and other relatives. Brangien and Isolde had joined them, though they kept to the edges of the room and spoke with no one.

"I wonder what the men are doing," Guinevere said, trying to keep the longing to be anywhere else out of her voice.

"The men?" Dindrane did not pause from stitching a serviceable tunic. "Oh, I imagine they are drinking or bragging or fighting."

An ancient aunt looked up with a milky-eyed glare. "Sometimes they have tournaments, but I doubt the boys could really enjoy it with a *king* present. Everyone would have to be careful not to hurt him."

Guinevere felt a spike of defensiveness. "King Arthur is more than capable."

"Of course, Your Grace. Of course." The woman nodded, her neck skin folding like the cloth in her bony hands. "All men are serviceable with a sword or spear when they want to be."

"And when you would prefer they not be," one of Dindrane's sisters-in-law said, snickering. Her face was pinched around a prominent, bony nose. It gave her a hawkish profile, which was not helped by the way she watched them all with careful, predatory eyes.

"Always wanting to spar in the middle of the night," the other one agreed.

"Or first thing in the morning. Sheathe your sword, fool. No one wants to be greeted with that upon waking."

"Sword is generous. I was thinking knife. Or perhaps needle." The two women cackled. Dindrane blushed furiously red. Guinevere had some idea what they were talking about, but imagined it was much worse for Dindrane to hear, given it was her own brothers they were speaking of.

"Of course," Blanchefleur said, stabbing her needle into a piece of cloth and smiling with just as much sharp intent, "Sir Bors is so old, it will probably not be an issue for our Dindrane."

"He is only five years older than Percival," Dindrane snapped.

"Too bad you could not snag his son instead."

"His son is fourteen!"

"Still, you are fortunate to have found anyone willing to take you into their house at your age. Though we all know why he is doing it." Blanchefleur flicked her eyes over Guinevere.

Blanchefleur's meaning was clear: Dindrane was only valuable because of her connection to the king and queen. The women sparred, too, apparently. But not with weapons. Guinevere knew whose side she was on, and her mouth responded before she had time to think her words through. "Did you know Sir Mordred, the nephew of the king, also sought Dindrane's hand?"

Everything after this would be a lie, but it was a safe lie. No one in Camelot knew why Mordred had disappeared. Arthur had kept it a secret, only saying that Mordred had left and would not be returning. Why not give them a better story? The truth hurt too much. Better to replace it.

"What?" Blanchefleur frowned.

"Oh, yes. It was terrible."

"What was terrible?"

"Why, the fight." Guinevere set down her sewing, putting on her best confused expression. "You did not hear?"

Blanchefleur shook her head. The other women in the room leaned closer, except Brangien, who knew Guinevere was lying. Her knowledge was betrayed only by a slight narrowing of the eyes.

Guinevere looked at Dindrane, smiling affectionately. "You have always been too modest, my dear friend. Can I tell them? Please?"

Dindrane gave an uninterested lift of her shoulders. "If you wish." Then she turned her face so only Guinevere could see it, and formed the word *What?* silently with her mouth.

"Oh, it was thrilling!" Guinevere put one hand over her heart, where Mordred's flower had pressed before she moved it. "It was the night of the tournament in which Sir Lancelot proved herself. On the field that day, Sir Bors walked out wearing our Dindrane's handkerchief as his colors. We were not shocked—he had clearly been in love with her for years but was too reserved to say anything. Tournaments make all men braver. But they also make them more reckless. When Sir Mordred—King Arthur's nephew, and closest heir"—that was hardly true, but they need not know; it made everything sound more romantic—"well, when he saw it, jealousy flared. He, too, had long nurtured a secret affection for lovely Dindrane. That evening, as the wine flowed, so, too, did their passion and anger. Sir Mordred confronted Sir Bors, demanding he be allowed to court Dindrane, being of higher rank within Camelot. A lesser man—one more concerned with his position among King Arthur's knights—certainly would have ceded pursuit of Dindrane to Sir Mordred. But Sir Bors's love for her defied the bounds of rational thought. He immediately challenged Sir Mordred to a fight. The winner would be allowed to court Dindrane, and the loser would have to leave Camelot. Forever."

"What?" Blanchefleur looked aghast. "Percival has told me nothing of this."

"He did not know. You will recall that immediately after these events I was abducted and everything became very busy and confusing." Guinevere waved her hand as though those events were far less important than the fictional ones she was spinning. "Sir Bors and Sir Mordred faced off with nothing but their fists and their determination to be the one to win Dindrane's heart and hand. I was there, as was my maid, Brangien."

"Mmm, it was very exciting," Brangien murmured from the corner, not looking up from her sewing.

"Though Sir Bors's experience on the battlefield is unsurpassed,

Sir Mordred had never been defeated in single combat. He was considered the most deadly of all Arthur's knights."

"They hated him," Blanchefleur said, wrinkling her nose.

"With good reason," Guinevere said, not allowing the other woman to wrest the reins of the story. "Sir Mordred was arrogant and cold, and I was terrified he would win." Mordred appeared arrogant and cold, but really he was reserved and watchful, constantly in pain from being around iron because of his fairy heritage through his father. But when one got close to him, he was insightful and funny and heartbreakingly duplicitous.

She should never have gotten close to him. She could not let it happen again.

Back to the story. Stories were so much tidier. So much easier. "Sir Mordred loved Dindrane, but I knew he would not be half the husband to her Sir Bors would. We all watched as they battled. And though Sir Mordred was the younger and faster, Sir Bors's heart was pure, his every strike made true and powerful by his love for Dindrane. In the end, he stood alone on that dark field, battered but triumphant. He had defeated Sir Mordred and won the fairest maiden." Guinevere beamed at Dindrane, who had her lips pursed in what looked like modesty but was probably an effort to hold back laughter.

"What happened to Sir Mordred?" one of the aunts asked.

"Oh, he was banished. He had honored the terms of their agreement. And, I think, he could not bear to stay in Camelot and watch Dindrane wed another." Guinevere bit her lips, pretending to be worried. "I should not have shared this story. Sir Bors will not speak of it. He loves his king and would never exult in a victory that sent the king's nephew away. Please do not bring it up in front of him."

"But surely King Arthur was angry?" one of the sisters-in-law asked.

"He values Sir Bors too much to let this come between them. Sir Mordred made his choices." Guinevere smiled dismissively, but saying that cost more than she had anticipated. Mordred had made his choices, and he had made them for love of his family. It felt oddly like a betrayal to spin this story using him, knowing what she did of how fiercely he had also loved her. Had he, though? Twice now he had seemed to prove no ill intent. But she knew the Dark Queen was still trying to overthrow Arthur. Mordred had chosen her side. They were enemies, regardless of feelings.

Guinevere cleared her throat, trying to dislodge some of the pain stuck there. It was not just residual pain from King Mark's fingers. "And all ended up as it should so that we could be here to celebrate the beautiful Dindrane's wedding to valiant Sir Bors, the dragonslayer."

The dragonslayer story, too, was a lie. Were *all* the stories lies?

"Two suitors," Blanchefleur said to herself, staring in blank anger at the floor.

Dindrane set down her sewing. She beamed at Guinevere, then put on a prim expression. "Well, I certainly would not have told that story today. Bringing a tale of another man to my wedding celebration hardly seems proper. But I cannot command my queen not to speak when she wishes to. Now. We have another activity to get to before the men."

Relieved, Guinevere put her work away. At last this punishment would end.

Dindrane stood, straightening her skirts. "We are going to the bathhouse! They have none in Camelot, and I have missed it so!"

Guinevere repented of her haste to be finished with sewing. "A bathhouse. What does . . . what does that entail?"

"There are four rooms. Each gets hotter, with stoves and heated rocks the servants pour water on to make steam. And in the final

room they scrape you clean, then we all sit in the water and soak."
Dindrane clapped her hands. "Come now, we cannot let the men
have a turn before us. I will not sit in the same water they soaked in
after all their riding and wrestling."

The women bustled about the room to put away their projects.
Guinevere looked with horror toward Brangien.

Brangien stood and took Guinevere's elbow. "I am afraid the
queen cannot accompany you."

"What? Why?" Dindrane deflated.

"She is not allowed to be undressed in front of anyone but her
husband." Brangien delivered the same lie Guinevere had given the
first time Brangien had attempted to help her into a bath. As though
Guinevere could not hear or speak for herself, Brangien lowered her
voice conspiratorially to the rest of the women. "The rules are very
different for kings and queens in Camelot."

The women nodded as though that made any sense at all. Guinevere was escorted from the room. "Thank you," she whispered.

Brangien's smile was satisfied. "You do not always need a knight
to protect you. I can do it just as well."

"Could we go see what the men are doing?" Guinevere wanted to
spend time with Arthur. To take more of his strength and confidence
into herself however she could. They had been separated too early
that morning.

"They are probably haggling. We would not be welcome, and I am
glad. I do not want to hear what Dindrane is worth in terms of gold."

Isolde spoke, her voice soft. "That was an amazing story you told."

"An amazing lie." Brangien snorted a laugh. "It never happened."

Isolde looked alarmed and taken aback. "But why would you
say it?"

"Dindrane is my friend. It was the only way I could think to protect her from those horrible women."

Isolde slowly nodded. "They did seem . . . unkind."

"We all protect each other, in whatever ways we can." Guinevere squeezed Brangien's hand, and Isolde stepped closer to both of them.

"I am glad for it," Isolde whispered. Her lovely face had a haunted quality. Brangien noticed, too. She linked her arm with Isolde's.

That was the other lie of stories. Even when the stories told were true, they never talked about what happened after the quest. About all the wounds—visible and otherwise—that lingered long after the neat close of the tale. They had rescued the damsel. The end. But there was still so much pain there, and perhaps there always would be. Guinevere knew Brangien was unparalleled at taking care of others. She said she had learned it from Isolde; it seemed a gift of grace that Brangien now got to use it to comfort Isolde. Hopefully, with enough time and love and freedom, Isolde would be able to feel safe again. But Brangien needed space to care for her love.

"Do you two mind if I rest alone?" Guinevere put one hand on her door. "I did not sleep well last night. I would appreciate the solitude."

Brangien nodded, grateful, and guided Isolde toward the small chamber they had been given. At the other end of the hall, Sir Tristan and Lancelot stood guard. Guinevere longed to go speak with them, to spend the hours in friendly companionship. But they had a job to do, too.

Guinevere entered her room. Arthur had commanded her not to dwell on things. He was right. She would not wallow in guilt over the king she had destroyed, or the dragon she had betrayed, or the man she could not afford to think about or trust ever again.

She took Mordred's flower out of her pouch and crushed it in her palm until the delicate petals were nothing but smears of color on her skin. And then she sat, alone with only her thoughts and regrets, which felt like the greatest punishment of all.

CHAPTER TWENTY-FIVE

Guinevere sits at the table, a pleasantly blank look on her face as her mind wanders far from what is being discussed among Arthur and the other men. It does not really involve her and never will, but she is here because she is supposed to be. The walls of the room feel too close, the table too big, herself too small.

A laugh that does not belong in this space tugs her attention; she is caught on it like a fishing line. Mordred leans against the doorframe. His smile is an invitation and a promise.

Alarmed, Guinevere turns toward Arthur. He glances at his nephew, then at Guinevere. "Oh, go on. I can do this without you." He smiles, then turns back to the business of being king.

Giddy with nerves and excitement, half-certain what she is doing is wrong—but with Arthur's permission—she stands and takes Mordred's extended hand. Together they walk out the door into the pouring rain of a forest. Laughing and shrieking in surprise, Guinevere lets Mordred tug her to the shelter of an ancient, gnarled tree. They press against the bark, water streaming down their faces and mixing as their lips find each other's.

The bed shifted and Guinevere sat up with a start, her heart racing, the taste of rain and other lips still on her own.

"Sorry," Arthur said, lying next to her. "I did not mean to wake you." The room was dark, the air charged, whether in reality or because of the remnants of her dream clinging to her.

Without thinking about it, without giving herself a chance to stop, Guinevere put her hand out, found Arthur's chest, and lowered her lips to his. She felt him go rigid with surprise, eagerly anticipating feeling his heart begin to race beneath her hand.

But it did not.

And his lips did not move against hers.

He lay there, still and unmoving. Mortified, Guinevere withdrew, scooting away on the bed and pulling her knees up to her chest. Her shoulder ached and she felt like crying. She did not know whether or not to apologize. She did not want to.

"Guinevere," Arthur said, but it was not with longing or regret. It was with sadness.

"Why not?" It was the question she kept coming back to. Why not? They were married. She loved him, had loved him since the moment they met. Why could they not also love each other this way? She *wanted* to. It would make everything easier. And beyond that, it would make everything better. She wanted Arthur to look at her the way Mordred had.

No! Not that way. She wanted Arthur to look at her the way Brangien looked at Isolde, like there was no one else in the world. She would even take the way Sir Bors looked at Dindrane, always slightly confused but happy.

Arthur sat up, leaning against the wall behind the bed. "There is . . . there is no rush."

"What do you mean by that?"

Arthur sighed. He held out his arms.

Her eyes had adjusted enough so that she could make out his shape in the dark. She did not want to move to him, to be held like a friend or a sister. And she knew he was not inviting her back to try again. She stayed where she was. "What do you mean by that?" she repeated.

"It is—" He stopped, going quiet.

She wished it were not so dark. She longed to see his expression. But she could do better than that. She reached for his hand and took his fingers between her own. Her hands had finally returned to normal. Arthur was as he always felt—steady, warm, strong—but he also felt sad. And . . . scared. Had she ever felt him scared before? "Please tell me. It cannot be worse than what I imagine. That you regret marrying me, that you do not like me, that you wish—"

"No." He squeezed her fingers. "No, it is the opposite. You are my best friend, the only person I feel at home with." He tugged her fingers, pulling her close so she nestled against his side. She put a tentative hand on his chest and there, finally, was the skip and speed of a pulse that indicated he was not as steady as he sounded. "It is not that I do not want you like— Well, I worry. My mother, you know. And Elaine. Every important woman in my life has died in childbirth. And I cannot—I will not—risk you like that."

"But—"

"Not *never*. We have all the time in the world between us." He put his fingers beneath her chin, lifting her head and tilting her face up. This time when he pressed his lips to hers, there was a kiss there. It was gentle. Patient. She could feel the sparks of desire, but they were nothing compared with his determination to do the right thing. To protect her.

The kiss ended as it had begun: Thoughtfully. Softly. Carefully.

She squeezed her eyes shut against the tears that burned there and would betray her. She loved Arthur and treasured what they had and had no desire to lose it, but she also wanted to be *in* love. Wildly. Deliriously. Recklessly. Love *should* feel urgent. A rush of emotion, an inescapable need. A spark and passion that consumed everything, that burned away caution and fear and left only desire.

But Arthur had been hurt in ways she had not. And he did want her. She would try to be patient, for his sake. And for hers.

The next day during wedding festivities, Arthur seemed more aware of her than usual, taking extra time to speak with her or even stand near her in a deliberate way. It somehow made everything hurt worse.

Dindrane was lovely. She had insisted on Guinevere matching her so that everyone would see them as the same. They were dressed in belted white tunics with blue-and-red cloaks. Guinevere had loaned her best jewelry to Dindrane, though, wanting to be certain Dindrane shone in every way possible on her wedding day. And Brangien had quickly sewed a delicate collar to add to Guinevere's dress and cover the slowly fading bruises.

In spite of her awful family, in spite of everything she had been through to get to this point, Dindrane was luminously happy when she and Sir Bors exchanged rings. Sir Bors was flushed red and beaming, and Guinevere could swear there were tears in his eyes as he kissed Dindrane. Guinevere was satisfied. Dindrane was married to a man who would certainly work hard to make her life a happy one. And Guinevere did not question that it would in fact be a tremendous amount of work.

But after the wedding there was the feasting, and the drinking, and the dancing, all in a crowded, airless hall. The scent of too many bodies and too much wine set Guinevere's head aching. She found herself looking longingly at the door, as though Mordred really would show up to rescue her.

It was the worst kind of dream, because every part of it was destructive. The Mordred of her dreams was not the real Mordred, and she did not need rescuing. Not from this.

Arthur lingered close to her at the table where she sat watching the dancers. But she sensed his tension as he glanced toward a gathering of lords and kings from the region. Allies and information just a few steps away.

She elbowed him gently in the side. He wore relatively simple clothes. A vest of deep blue over a clean white tunic. The silver crown on his shorn head was his only adornment. He turned toward her with a questioning smile and she felt the familiar pulse of affection. Her handsome, *good* king. She would work on patience.

"Go on, talk politics."

He grimaced guiltily. "I do not want to leave you alone."

"How can I be alone?" Guinevere gestured to the packed room. It was like a battlefield, with combat fought in dance and gossip and drinking contests. She was not skilled in any of it. "Alone would be gloriously preferable at this point."

"Can we dance later?"

"I do not know any of these dances. Merlin never saw fit to push that information into my head." She flashed a quick smile at Arthur as he left. What would she have lost of her past if Merlin had taught her to dance? Did it even matter? At this point she had so little left of who she had been, it was like she had not even existed before becoming Guinevere.

She should pretend that was the truth. Forget the fear of what she did not know about herself, her mother, her past. Go back to Camelot with a clean slate. Free from both her own past and the real Guinevere's. No more Guinevach, no more Lady of the Lake, no more Merlin. Only Guinevere and the family she had chosen.

Brangien and Dindrane stood before her, each taking one of her hands and pulling her up.

"Where are we going?" Guinevere asked.

"To dance!" Dindrane laughed. "It is my wedding, you cannot tell me no."

"*You* are dancing?" Guinevere turned to Brangien, shocked. Isolde was sitting on a stool near the door, beaming as she watched Brangien.

Brangien lifted Guinevere's good hand in the air, then somehow shifted it to force Guinevere to spin in a circle. "I love dancing."

"You do not!"

"I do!" Brangien slipped into the circle of dancing members of the wedding party and mimicked their moves expertly. None of the other maids were dancing yet, but Brangien enjoyed special status as lady's maid to the queen. She was assured and graceful and *happy*. Guinevere wondered in that moment if she had ever seen Brangien truly happy before now, dancing in a room where her love was free to watch. Knowing at the end of the night, they could be together. At the end of every night from now on, they could be together.

Guinevere laughed, Brangien's happiness infectious.

"Come on." Dindrane eased Guinevere into the circle, constantly correcting her movements. But it was not done meanly. It was done as fun between friends. Sir Bors, who was not dancing, watched with the same lovestruck awe that Isolde did. Guinevere could not help but check if she was being watched with love, as well.

She wished she had not. Arthur was deep in conversation with a circle of men, not watching her dance. But in a way that made it easier. No one cared what she was doing. Guinevere relaxed and let Dindrane instruct and guide and correct her, and before long she was spinning with all the other dancers as musicians filled the room with as much noise as there was drink and talk. Her shoulder was sore, but that did not lessen her enjoyment.

Laughing and clasping hands with Dindrane and Brangien soothed some of her fears. They had their own loves now, but they were still her friends. She had gained a new friend in Isolde and, if not a friend in Sir Bors, someone she respected. And her role in creating this match assuaged some of the guilt she felt around Sir Bors for what she had done to his mind to protect the dragon. At least one of them had come out on the other side better off.

As Brangien twirled her out of the group and then back in, Guinevere discovered that someone *was* watching her. Lancelot never took her eyes off them. Guinevere, giddy with movement, stuck out her tongue and crossed her eyes. Lancelot's watchful gaze cracked and she smiled, shaking her head.

Guinevere wished she could pull Lancelot into the dance. But she was the queen and Lancelot was her knight, and she had to respect that. The smile shared between them finished sealing away the pain of the past few days.

She chose this life, and she loved it and was loved in turn by so many people in it.

Guinevere danced until her feet ached as much as her sides did from laughing. She retired to the table with Brangien and Dindrane, joined by Isolde. They formed an island of sisterhood, sealed away from everyone else as they ate and drank and giggled. There were jellied fruits and nuts in crystalized honey. Even the gossip was sweet, Brangien and Dindrane filling Isolde in on all the wonders that awaited her in Camelot. Guinevere forgot that they were there for a wedding until the men started banging raucously on the tables.

"To the bed!" they chanted, over and over. Sir Bors looked at the men with such aggressive displeasure the chanting faltered.

He walked to Dindrane, then bowed and held out his hand. "If you are ready to retire?"

Dindrane, who did not seem nervous so much as excited, stood and took his hand. "I am."

A few brave souls shouted encouragement and whistled as they left, but Sir Bors's glower had managed to defeat any of the more crass sentiments and certainly cut short any ideas about following the couple.

Guinevere remembered her own wedding, how odd and new everything had felt. How determined she had been. Scared, but certain of who she was and what she was doing there. It made her feel sad, thinking about that girl. That was the night she had given her real name away to a flame, snuffing it out forever to avoid the temptation of revealing it. If she knew then what she knew now—the layers of Merlin's manipulations, the false premise of her entire role in Camelot, the damage already done to her mind—would she have made the same choice to willingly sacrifice what little she had of herself?

"Come on, to bed," Brangien said, sensing the shift in mood. Sir Tristan was staying at Arthur's side, and would until he retired. Brangien and Isolde accompanied Guinevere back to her room, Lancelot padding silently behind them. The knight checked the room to make certain it was empty, then stepped back out as Brangien and Isolde helped Guinevere undress, unlacing and untying her from the layers. Brangien brushed Guinevere's hair while Isolde carefully repacked the clothing into a trunk.

From the hallway, a conversation filtered to them with a male voice getting louder. There was a smacking noise, and then the wall shuddered as something slammed into it. Guinevere and Brangien rushed to open the door. Lancelot was standing guard, hands clasped in front of her. An unconscious man was sprawled on the floor next to her.

Lancelot shrugged. "He had too much to drink. Perhaps it is best if Brangien and Isolde stay in your room tonight. There will be many drunk men."

"Thank you." Guinevere agreed with Lancelot's assessment. If Arthur was bothered to find his bed filled by two others when he returned sometime in the middle of the night, he did not express it. Guinevere awoke to find him on the cold floor, using one arm for a pillow. She was flushed with affection as she stared down at him. She could not imagine another king who would sleep on the floor while two maids took his place in the bed.

Brangien and Isolde tiptoed around the still-sleeping Arthur to prepare themselves for the day. When breakfast was delivered by a servant, Guinevere peered into the hall. The unconscious man was gone, but Lancelot still stood in the same position. Sir Tristan was farther down the hall.

"Did you stand there all night?" Guinevere asked.

"Yes, my queen."

"Come in and have breakfast, then."

Lancelot frowned. "Should I?"

"You should." Guinevere did not wait for Lancelot to follow. She pulled another cushion to the low table where their breakfast was waiting. Arthur had awoken and was stretching.

"How was your night?" Guinevere asked, breaking pieces off the large, rough loaf of bread.

"Interesting." Arthur joined them. If he thought it odd that Lancelot was there, he did not say. "There was much discussion of the Saxon settlers. They are pushing in everywhere. Where they cannot outright take over, they marry into the families and take over that way. Actually, Dindrane's father seemed relieved that she was married now, so he could refuse them. I had thought the Picts were our biggest problem, but there has been no movement or conflict from them in weeks. That border seems firm without Maleagant around to stir up trouble."

There was a heavy silence as the three of them—the only ones in Camelot who knew the truth of Maleagant's demise at Guinevere's hands—remembered what had happened.

Arthur pushed on as though to prevent them from thinking on it. "The men here warned me to watch out for the Saxons, which we have already learned thanks to your would-be ransomers. These people already crossed the water to get here. Crossing a king is no great challenge after that. Should I range out to get more information, or do I wait for them to come to me?"

Lancelot sat straighter. "When we sailed along the coast, I took note of every settlement. I will give you locations and numbers. Though we did not go north, it should give us some idea of what the landscape looks like now."

Arthur nodded, his strong features thoughtful. He rubbed his jawline where there was a hint of stubble. He did not grow much facial hair, but he kept it shaved clean. "Thank you. That was good thinking."

A smile as quick and brilliant as a flash of lightning struck Lancelot's face and was immediately replaced with her best stoic-knight expression. Guinevere felt a similar surge of pride. Lancelot was clever and smart, and she was glad that Arthur recognized it. Hopefully this fixed some of the damage her quest to rescue Isolde had done. Though Guinevere had claimed all responsibility, she knew Lancelot felt guilt over her injuries, and she wondered if it had strained things between Arthur and her knight.

Arthur took a bite of an apple. "I would say we should hire the ship again, but I think that is out of the question."

"I *did* burn down their village." Guinevere tried to say it lightly, tried to make a funny anecdote out of one of her most painful

memories. It almost worked. Maybe that was why they told the stories the way they did. Tell them often enough, and they could become the truth.

"Horses it is, then. We will leave tomorrow for home."

Guinevere was surprised at the sudden, sharp longing she felt at
the word. This trip had been exhausting mentally and emotionally.
As eager as she had been to leave Camelot, she now found herself
equally anxious to return to where things were, if not ideal, at least
easier. To embrace and explore who she was as Guinevere the Queen.

CHAPTER TWENTY-SIX

Guinevere had taken breakfast in her own room, but on the last morning there, she went to the great hall for one final sociable appearance. Arthur had left before sunrise to speak with local rulers. Brangien and Isolde were busy packing and preparing everything for travel. Lancelot stood guard by the door. Guinevere wished she could have Lancelot dine with her, but she had resolved herself to being beset by Dindrane's awful relations.

Dindrane saved her before any others arrived. "Come on, we can eat breakfast in the gardens. Much nicer than here." Dindrane glanced dismissively at the smoke-stained hall. She gestured for the servant to attend them and led Guinevere outside. Lancelot followed, then took up a post near the door where she had a full view of the gardens. The sparse green space clung to the back of the estate, more an afterthought than something lovingly tended. But there was a nice view of the rolling fields spreading out in front of them like a blanket of gold and green. Guinevere and Dindrane sat on a stone bench and waited as the servant set out the dishes.

Breakfast was a simple affair of bread and cured meats, a chore more than a celebration. Guinevere picked over the food, wishing for more of the honey-crystalized nuts. "How are you?" she asked Dindrane. They had not seen each other the day before. It had been the most muted day of the trip, with most of the wedding party suffering from too much drink.

"Wonderful. I am— Oh, I am so happy." Dindrane laughed brighter than any of the surrounding blossoms. "I am finally free."

Guinevere could not quite understand the sentiment. After all, Dindrane was married now. Legally tied to Sir Bors forever. And husbands had far more rights than wives did.

Dindrane ticked the facts off on her fingers, one by one. "I have a husband, so no one can look down on me. I never have to endure Blanchefleur again, or live in her home. My father was not generous, but between what he was forced to contribute and what Sir Bors gave, I have a chest big enough that I will never have to wed again should something happen to Sir Bors. Which I hope it never does! He was—he is— Guinevere, he . . . appreciates me." A blush crept across her cheeks. She looked bashful, an expression Guinevere had never before seen on her face. "I know I can be off-putting. I have been told as much my whole life. But Sir Bors likes me. I make him laugh. And not because he is mocking me, but because he is—"

"Delighted by you?"

"Yes! That is it exactly."

Guinevere plucked a scarlet blossom and tucked it into Dindrane's chestnut hair. "I am glad you found someone who knows he is lucky to have you at his side. And I am glad I was able to be here to celebrate it with you."

"Thank you. I could not have faced this alone." Dindrane's shoulders tightened; she did not look back at the house, but she did not have to. Guinevere could tell she felt attacked by it, even outside.

"I am sorry to say we are leaving this afternoon. Camelot needs us. I know the celebrations will continue for—"

"I will come!" Dindrane stood immediately.

"But you—"

"I came here to force my father to pay, and to show them that I do not need them and never will again. I cannot wait to leave. I will go tell Sir—my husband. I will go tell my *husband*." She laughed, spinning in a happy circle, then pulled Guinevere up and made her twirl, as well.

"Time to go home," Guinevere said, laughing with her friend.

"Home!" Dindrane shouted. She kicked the foundation of her old home for good measure as they walked back inside.

Feeling no duty toward these people to offer them gratitude or whatever she should as queen, Guinevere hurried back to her rooms. "Do you need to pack?" she asked Lancelot as she resumed her post outside the door.

"No, my queen. I am ready."

"Of course you are." Guinevere felt a surge of affection. Lancelot had made this whole trip possible. She had sacrificed and risked and protected. Guinevere could not imagine life without her. How had it been only a few months since Guinevere suspected Lancelot was a fairy threat?

She entered to find the room efficiently stripped of any evidence of their stay. Brangien and Isolde had worked quickly. Guinevere turned to visit them and see if they needed any help, when the door opened and Arthur walked in. One glance at his face and Guinevere's happy mood was punctured.

"What?" she asked.

He did not bother trying to smile. He waved toward the hallway and Sir Tristan and Sir Bors entered. "You, too, Sir Lancelot," he said.

Guinevere moved to the side as the three knights entered and stood awkwardly. There were not enough chairs for everyone, and barely enough space for so many broad shoulders. "What is it?" Guinevere repeated.

"Sir Percival informed me that other lords of the region have heard I am here and want to speak with me about treaties. There is the issue of King Mark's successor"—he had the grace not to look at Guinevere as he said it—"and everyone is on edge about the Saxons. I cannot pass up this opportunity to speak with them and leave with our southern neighbors firmly on our side. I have had to focus on the Picts to the north for so long, I have neglected this region. This is my chance to fix that."

Guinevere sat down, politeness abandoning her along with her hopes. "Oh. How long will we stay?" She hated Dindrane's family, hated having to be a foreign queen in an unfamiliar place. At least in Camelot she knew how to play her part, and there was a reason for it. Pretending for these people was a waste of her time. She resented all of it. She should be back in Camelot, protecting her own people. Who knew what the Dark Queen might get up to in their absence?

"I do not want you to stay."

Guinevere looked up sharply; there was an almost physical sting to Arthur's words. Was he still angry about what she had done to rescue Isolde?

Arthur paced, hands clasped behind his back. "Sir Bors, I want your counsel. You and Sir Percival have ties to this area, and it will lend Camelot credibility when they see we are connected to these southern families at the highest levels."

Sir Bors nodded, bowing. "I will go inform my wife. She will . . ." He had a moment of fear cross his face.

"She can return with us," Guinevere offered, trying not to sound as hurt as she felt. "It will give her time to prepare your home to her liking without interference."

Sir Bors smiled, a combination of alarm and affection. "That is a good idea. Thank you, my queen." He bowed again and left the room.

Arthur continued to pace. "I do not know how long this will take. I do not like being away during the harvest. When you get back to Camelot, I want you to rule in my absence."

"What?" Guinevere stood, surprised. He was not sending her away because she had failed. He was sending her away because she was *capable*? "But you left Sir Gawain and Sir Caradoc in charge."

Arthur took her hands in his. "I want it to be you from now on. When I am gone, Camelot still has a ruler in its queen. You know the city now. You know how it works, what it needs. And it needs you."

Guinevere's emotions churned. Disappointment over Arthur staying, pride and elation over Arthur's vote of confidence. But also worry. Because if she was left in charge of Camelot, that meant she was *left* in Camelot, whenever Arthur was away.

But that was a conversation for another day. Already Arthur and Sir Tristan and Lancelot had moved on to discussing travel logistics. Arthur wanted to know all the details—perhaps partly to make certain Guinevere did not improvise again. Brangien and Isolde appeared and retrieved the trunks waiting by the door. With everything settled here, the timeline for leaving had been moved up.

Guinevere wanted a few minutes to speak privately with Arthur, but in the bustle of activity there was not a chance for it.

It was only as she was leaving that he caught up to her and drew her aside. "Be careful," he said. "No quests this time, please. If there is a new threat from the Dark Queen, wait for me if you can. And if you cannot—"

She smiled as playfully as she could manage. "I will try not to have too much fun defeating her without you."

Arthur laughed. "Leave some heroics for the rest of us." He drew her close in an embrace. "*Please* be careful this time."

"We know we can handle the Dark Queen," Guinevere said, placing a hand on the back of Arthur's neck. "There are no threats in Camelot that we have not thwarted. The biggest risk is that I will be bored waiting for you."

"Here is a wish for boredom, then." Arthur drew back and, with a surge of impulse Guinevere felt like a flush from his skin, kissed her. It was like a patch of sun on a cold day, warm and bright and welcome.

The memory of his lips lingered on hers as she rode toward home, where she would rule as queen.

CHAPTER TWENTY-SEVEN

By the time they arrived at the pier at the bottom of Camelot, Guinevere's head ached and her still-healing shoulder was stiff. They had pushed to make good time back, having no reason to delay. The trip across the lake felt exceptionally cruel after so much travel. She did not even have Arthur to cling to and draw strength from. Lancelot, Brangien, Isolde, and Dindrane formed a barrier around her, blocking both the lake from her view and Guinevere from the view of anyone who might criticize how badly the queen handled water.

When she stepped off the ferry, Guinevere put her queen face firmly in place. Regal. Responsible. Not a girl who was terrified of water, nor one who did not know her own history, nor one who had left a path of damage and destruction and death in her wake from a simple trip to a wedding.

Arthur had commanded her to leave it in the past, and she would do her best.

No one had expected them back this soon, but the citizens who noticed them waved and bowed. Guinevere smiled graciously in acknowledgment. Tonight she could rest, but tomorrow she would have to speak with Sir Caradoc and Sir Gawain about what had been done for the harvest in her absence and what still needed to be accomplished. And she would inquire how Guinevach had acted when Sir Gawain escorted her out of the kingdom. Though that threat was averted, now that Guinevere was back home, she was curious to know what the threat had *been*. Innocent, or deliberate? Guinevach's attitude about being kicked out might offer some clues.

When they reached the castle gate, Guinevere lowered her hood. Isolde craned her neck to stare up at the castle carved straight from the mountain. Guinevere remembered her awe seeing it the first time, too. "Home," she said, squeezing Isolde's arm companionably. "Welcome to it."

"As soon as you are rested, you must all come visit me," Dindrane said, pointing to Sir Bors's house, which was prestigiously located very near the castle. She smiled in satisfaction. "I can host you whenever we wish, in my own rooms. *All* the rooms are my own."

Lancelot was speaking with the guards, giving instructions. The castle's grand main entrance, a large wooden door reinforced with scrolling swirls of metal—and with a hidden iron knot that undid any magic crossing the threshold—opened. Guinevere blinked in confusion as her tired brain processed what she was seeing. Sir Gawain, as pleasant as ever with a smile on his round, ruddy face as he gazed, besotted, at his companion.

Guinevach.

"Oh, Guinevere!" Guinevach smiled blandly, dipping into a curtsy. "How wonderful that you are back."

Dindrane, unaware of the tension, embraced the girl. "Guinevach! You stayed. I wish you had been able to come to my wedding. It was wonderful. You must visit me, too, of course."

Guinevach returned the hug, staring at Guinevere over Dindrane's shoulder. "I could not go home, not without spending some time with my beloved sister." Her hair shone with the last rays of the sun, but her gaze was as cool as the coming evening.

They had underestimated her.

"Call on me tomorrow morning, Dindrane," Guinevere said, then swept inside the castle past Guinevach and Sir Gawain. "Sir Lancelot, please follow."

Brangien and Isolde flanked her, and Lancelot covered their retreat.

"She was supposed to be gone. Arthur arranged it," Guinevere hissed as she hurried up far too many stairs to their level of the castle.

Brangien huffed, pushing open a heavy door on the second floor and glaring at a guard posted there. "You might want to go ahead of us and open all the doors instead of simply standing there like decoration!" The guard looked terrified as he scurried in front of them. They usually took the exterior staircase, avoiding the narrow interior flights and the unwieldly doors. "Yes, well," Brangien answered, now speaking to Guinevere, "King Arthur is a king and a man and when he tells people to do things, he assumes they will be done." The guard was lingering next to Guinevere's door when they got to the fifth floor. "Yes, *thank you,* now go fetch food and drinks for us."

"But I am not a—"

"You are not willing to do whatever your queen asks of you?" Brangien's tone was the verbal equivalent of a swat on a naughty child's bottom. The guard practically ran. "Honestly," she said, undoing her cloak and throwing it onto the dresser, then unfastening Guinevere's cloak and collar and carefully putting them in their place.

Isolde stood in the center of the room, looking around. She had no idea who Guinevach was, or why it was troubling that she was still there. "It is remarkable," Isolde breathed, eyes wide. She danced to the window and pressed her face against it. "So high!"

"Brangien can take you to explore." Guinevere had anticipated a little bit of pampering—she had gotten spoiled—but now she wanted to be alone so she could quiet her mind, currently buzzing like a disturbed hive of bees. And she needed to speak with Lancelot, who was waiting in the doorway. "Come in," she said, gesturing.

Lancelot strode into the room, taking up a position in the center of it.

"We will not leave until you are settled." Isolde's hands fluttered as she glanced around the room, trying to figure out what to do with herself to be useful.

"Please!" Guinevere paused. She tried to soften the edge her desperation had given the word. "Please. When I first came to Camelot I could not believe it, either. My shoulder is bothering me. All I want to do is rest. Go see your new home."

Brangien seemed suspicious as she undid some of the laces of Guinevere's outer dresses so that Guinevere would be able to undo the rest on her own when she chose to. "I will pick up some things that may help with the stiffness. No magic!" she said, predicting Guinevere's worry. "Nothing that a good lady's maid would not know about."

Guinevere turned to Isolde. "There is no magic allowed in Camelot."

Isolde nodded. "Brangien told me as much. I never had any talent for it anyway, in spite of what they said at my—" She stopped, her expression far away and vacant, doubtless remembering her trial. Her condemnation. Her husband. She blinked rapidly, forcing a smile. "It was always Brangien who was good with those things. She is the special one."

"There are many ways to be special." Brangien squeezed Isolde's hand as she passed her. The way they moved, always reacting to the other, was almost like a dance. Brangien opened the door at the first knock and took the tray from the guard, then shut the door without thanking him. She placed the food—some fruit and meat—along with a pitcher of watered wine on the table, then steered Guinevere into a chair.

"Rest. There are no problems that will not keep until tomorrow." She narrowed her eyes, doubtless wanting to demand Guinevere tell her what the real problem was with Guinevach. But Guinevere could not. Would not.

Guinevere nodded, smiling. "Show off our city. Impress her."

As soon as the door was closed, Guinevere addressed Lancelot. "Find out what happened. Sir Gawain was supposed to make certain Guinevach left. Did she bewitch him? Bribe him?"

"Smile and bat her eyelashes at him?" Lancelot shrugged at Guinevere's frown. "He is very young. She is very young. I cannot imagine he took much convincing to disobey his king's orders. But I will find out the exact course of events."

Guinevere nodded. Tomorrow, she would hold a council of war. Perhaps, having failed on two fronts already, the Dark Queen was well into her third. Guinevach had drawn first blood by staying. She would not win.

Guinevere had assembled her fiercest allies: Lancelot, the best knight in Camelot; Brangien, a formidable witch and endlessly clever maid; and Dindrane, the most accomplished gossip Guinevere had ever known.

"You want us to *what*?" Dindrane asked, leaning forward intently. They were in Guinevere's sitting room, which was being converted to a bedroom for Isolde and Brangien so they could have some privacy. Guinevere had promised it to Lancelot, but that was before they had an addition to their ranks. Lancelot could have a cot in her own bedchamber when Arthur was away. That way she could get some rest while protecting Guinevere.

For now, though, it was still a sitting room. Guinevere sat on a cushion, leaning back against the wall. Dindrane had taken a chair, while Brangien sat on a stool and Lancelot stood near the door.

"I want you to spy on Guinevach. Gather any information you can about her. Why she is here. Who she is talking to. What she is doing." Guinevere expected demands for details or a refusal to help without explanation. She braced herself.

"That is easy," Dindrane said, her tone pleasant. "I can have her over for a meal this evening. Do you want to be there, too, or would you like me to work on her alone?"

Guinevere almost questioned why Dindrane was not questioning her request, and then she remembered what it had been like at Dindrane's wedding. Dindrane knew being related did not necessarily make people *family*. "Alone. She might open up without me there in ways she would not if I were present. And thank you," she said.

"You are very welcome." Dindrane smiled, then leaned across the space to Brangien, brushing her fingers along Brangien's pale-blue sleeve. "Do you think this color would look good in my sitting room? How could we incorporate it?"

Brangien tugged her sleeve from Dindrane's touch. "A cushion or two will bring in enough of the color without being too expensive. I brought this with me, but a woman on Shi—Market Street"—Brangien corrected herself from using the old name—"sells something in a similar hue."

Dindrane stood, excited, and excused herself. "I will let you know how the visit goes!" she called as she left the room.

"My queen," Brangien said, settling onto the more comfortable chair Dindrane had vacated, "it would help if I knew why we need to watch Guinevach so carefully. How can I find something if I do not know what I am looking for?" Brangien demanded the information Dindrane did not care about.

Guinevere toyed with a heavy silver ring on her finger. She was still not used to wearing things like it, though Brangien was more insistent lately that Guinevere wear her jewels and finery. It felt distracting. "I am afraid this has something to do with the Dark Queen."

Brangien's face shifted, horrified. "Your *sister?*"

Guinevere could not admit to Brangien that she had no idea whether Guinevach was in fact Guinevach. "Arthur's own nephew was in league with her. And we do not know the scope of her power and influence. Guinevach could be under her sway without knowing it. Or she could be entirely innocent. I do not know. But the timing of her arrival and her insistence on staying are both suspect. We trusted Mordred. We will not make the same mistake with Guinevach."

"There is still something you are not telling me." Brangien's gaze was cool.

Guinevere sighed. "Yes. There are several things I am not telling you. And, just as before, I need you to trust that I would tell you if I could, but what I am not telling you does not put you in any danger."

"But does it put *you* in danger?"

"Not immediately. You will be the first to know if that changes. For now, we all watch Guinevach and gather whatever information we can. Look for any attempt to undermine me or the king. Any whispers or rumors that start, whether they can be traced to her or not. And let me know at the slightest hint of magic."

"Very well." Brangien looked determined, if not happy. "Leave Isolde out of it. She is a terrible liar."

"That is not a bad quality," Lancelot said.

"It is a very good quality," Guinevere agreed, an ache in her chest making her wish she had the same problem, or that she could even afford to. Her whole life was a lie. She had to be the best at it.

CHAPTER TWENTY-EIGHT

Even with the Guinevach complication, Guinevere had not forgotten that Arthur put her in charge of Camelot. She would not shirk the tasks that had piled up in Arthur's absence.

Guinevere set herself up in the dining hall. It was the best space for meeting with large groups, and there were many people to meet with. Arthur tried to engage his subjects on the same level they existed, and she would do the same. No thrones or daises.

It was hard to focus as several merchants argued that their stalls in the preharvest market should get better placement. She promised them better spots in the much larger harvest festival, provided they lend their horses and wagons to the harvest effort for reduced cost.

After that, it was a city engineer with an issue with one of the aqueducts. Guinevere did not understand what he was saying, but she knew that Arthur would only trust the city's water supply to an expert, so she approved all his requests for funds and man power. If the aqueducts failed it would not be disastrous—they still had the lake—but it would definitely make life harder for the servants. She remembered that long-ago tour of the city at Brangien's side, and her comment about Camelot's favorite saying when things went wrong: Could be buckets.

She kept repeating it to herself as issue after issue was listened to and dealt with as close to what she could imagine Arthur doing. *Could be buckets.* She could be Ramm's prisoner, waiting to be ransomed. *Could be buckets.* She could be married to a monster like King Mark, unable to protect herself or anyone else. *Could be buckets.* She could be sitting in her room waiting for Arthur to return, nothing to occupy her time or mind except worrying.

Sir Gawain sat to one side, taking careful notes about the line of curfew breakers currently giving excuses and seeking pardons. Lancelot had confirmed her own suspicions: the young knight was deliriously in love with Guinevach and had made no secret of it. When Guinevach told him that she would rather stay and wait for her sister to return, he had hastily agreed. Her guards had left, stranding her with her two maids. She could not be sent home unaccompanied. It was a clever move.

Lancelot stood near the door, watching everything. There were a few officials, as well, there to consult should Guinevere need them. As much as Guinevere accomplished, though, the work never ended. As soon as the curfew breakers were pardoned or punished, there was a land contract to be discussed between two farmers. After that, the captain of the guard needed her to approve the rotation of men to protect the roads for the preharvest market, and then she had to look at and agree to funds for the extra forces for the harvest. There would be more goods and money in Camelot then than at any other time, meaning they had to be extra wary.

After the details were hammered out—fortunately, Arthur had had most of the plan in place already—it was down to the harvest festival. "Would you prefer to discuss it tomorrow?" asked one of the officials, a slight man with wispy hair and skin so pale it was nearly blue.

Guinevere wanted nothing more than to be done for the day. But Arthur trusted her. She needed to convince these men that his confidence was not misplaced. And to do that, she could give them no excuse to take over, no reason to think her weak. Even if they meant to spare her out of kindness, it was not what Arthur would ask of or accept from them.

"No, thank you. We are all here. We should use our time well." She would ask Arthur for a crown similar to his own. Her jeweled circlet was too ornate, decorative. She did not want to project beauty and wealth. She wanted to project confidence, assurance, dependability. Like her king. How often had she tried to absorb those same feelings from his touch?

Guinevere looked down at the notes for the festival. "What will we do if we have latecomers who want to sell goods at the festival?"

"We cannot give them the best spots!" One of the merchants from earlier was still lingering at the back of the room. His face was red with resentment at the idea.

"Of course not." Guinevere lifted a hand to reassure him. "I thought we could reserve a section on the lakeside of the grounds. It is not the best land—too muddy—but we are not using it for anything else. That way we can accommodate them without inconveniencing any of our own trusted merchants who have applied for their spots and aided the city in invaluable ways." Guinevere offered the merchant a smile and he accepted it with a relieved sigh and a nod.

The door opened and Lancelot stood to block it, but a golden flash of hair announced Guinevach's arrival. "Oh, hello!" She dipped a pretty curtsy, a smile as bright as her hair beaming across the room. Guinevere noticed several men sit straighter in response. Sir Gawain practically fell out of his seat with the physical force of his response.

"I am sorry, I had hoped to visit my sister, the queen." Guinevere wondered if perhaps Guinevach had emphasized the words *my sister* too much, or if it was all in her head.

Sir Gawain stood in a flurry of paper. He grimaced in horror as all his work fluttered to the floor, but then bowed stiffly. And then just as stiffly tried to bend over while his spine remained perfectly straight as he gathered the notes he had most likely ruined.

Several of the officials looked at Guinevere expectantly. Guine-vach had forced her hand. Guinevere *had* to introduce her. And by introducing her, claim her and give her power. "This is my sister, Guinevach of Cameliard."

Guinevach's smile became even prettier. It was as though her cheeks could pinken on demand. "At home, they call me the Lily of Cameliard. You may all call me Princess Lily, if you wish."

"Princess Lily," Sir Gawain whispered to himself. His face had gone a shade of red like it had been left too long in the dye vat. He fixed his papers and kept his eyes on them.

Guinevere refused to call Guinevach *Princess Lily.* It sounded absurd. And why was she claiming a new name? Guinevere remem-bered how tempted she had been to tell Arthur her real name. It had been part of why she had given it to the flame and snuffed it out. If she did not know it, she could never reveal it. Was Guinevach not really the other woman's name, and she wanted to go by her true one? And why was she insisting on that title? Was Guinevach in fact a princess? Guinevere had been. The *real* Guinevere had been. Guinevere shook her head, trying to keep track of the lies. Trying to remind herself that she was not in fact the real Guinevere. Some-times even she forgot. She would ask Dindrane whether Guinevach was a princess now that Guinevere was married, or if Guinevach had always been a princess. Guinevere had no idea how it worked in Cameliard, which was a problem, since she was supposed to have grown up there.

"I am not available right now, Guinevach." Guinevere saw Guinevach's eyes tighten with a flicker of displeasure at the use of her name. "We are discussing the upcoming harvest festival."

Whatever anger had been on Guinevach's face was replaced by wide eyes and clasped hands. "Oh, wonderful! Will there be a tournament?"

"We have not—"

"Even in Cameliard we have heard of Camelot's tournaments! I have always wanted to see one! King Arthur's knights are the best in the whole world." Guinevach beamed at each of the knights in the room, lingering a few extra seconds on Sir Gawain, whose face had not recovered from the deep-red hue any merchant would pay to capture for their cloth.

"The festival is not about our knights. It is about our people. It is to celebrate the harvest," Guinevere said.

"But what is the harm in a tournament?" Guinevach took an empty space on a bench next to an official, who eagerly shifted to give her room. "The knights are the pride of Camelot, and the people are from Camelot, so celebrating the knights is a way of celebrating the people and their harvest."

"Tournaments do lead to higher attendance, which means we sell more," the eager merchant in the back said.

Guinevere forced a smile, keeping her voice even. "Yes. But this is the *harvest* festival. There will be food and drink, minstrels, dancing, and—"

"Oh, will you have animals?" Guinevach broke in. "Once a man with a bear came to Cameliard. He had raised the bear from when it was a cub. The bear could dance, and balance a plate on its nose! Oh, such a dear, wondrous thing."

Guinevere found the entire concept horrifying. But several men were looking at Guinevach raptly, and the wispy-haired man was nodding eagerly as he spoke. "My sister wrote me about a trained bear once! Perhaps she knows where we can find the man, and we could—"

"Yes, thank you," Guinevere said firmly. "We will discuss entertainment at more length tomorrow. Right now we are discussing the particular details of how to organize the festival."

"But there must be a tournament. Even a small one." Guinevach locked eyes with Guinevere, her golden ones flashing with intensity and what Guinevere suspected was aggression in spite of her plum-sweet tone. "You cannot very well have a tournament of farmers competing to see who can plow the straightest line or thresh the fastest."

"Actually," Guinevere said, "that is a wonderful idea." She turned to the official in charge of the festival planning, a calm, meticulous man in his late twenties with tightly curled hair and a brown complexion similar to Sir Tristan's. "Could we create a tournament field with tasks similar to the tournaments, but to celebrate our farmers and field workers? A competition of strength, seeing who can lift the heaviest bales of hay and carry them across the field. A tree-felling contest—we will have to bring in the trees, of course. Oh, and we can have a show of livestock! And a milking race."

The men in the room laughed imagining it, but they were also nodding. It was a good idea. Guinevere knew it was. The people would love it, and would love the chance to be in the spotlight in front of their king. The fact that it went against what Guinevach had barged in and demanded was only a small part of Guinevere's satisfaction.

"Excellent. See to it. Now, back to the planning. How far in advance should we send the guards out, and how many miles of road should we cover?" Guinevere did not look at Guinevach again, expecting her to slink out of the room. But Guinevach stayed seated until the end of the meeting, a full two hours longer, every minute of which Guinevere could feel two angry golden eyes on her.

Finally, it was time for evening meals. Guinevere was pleased. She had accomplished as much as any king. Probably more than Arthur, if she was being honest. He had a shorter attention span than she did. "Thank you, good sirs. Until tomorrow."

They all bowed and filed out. Guinevach stood, too. Guinevere turned toward Sir Gawain to ask about some detail from earlier in the meeting. She knew Guinevach had plans to dine with Dindrane that evening and would not want to be late. Guinevach hovered for a few moments before turning and swishing out of the room.

"Will you be eating in here?" Lancelot asked. Already servants were shifting the benches and moving tables back into place. Several of the knights ate every meal here. Guinevere occasionally joined them, but after that many hours sitting as queen, she had no desire for more time spent in the company of expectations.

"In my rooms." Guinevere stood, her injured shoulder creaking in protest at movement after so long being still. Lancelot offered her arm and Guinevere accepted it. Once they were alone in the hall, Guinevere steered them in the opposite direction from her chambers.

"Where are we going?" Lancelot asked.

"Guinevach is not here, and knowing Dindrane, she will not be released until it is almost curfew. We are going to search her room."

CHAPTER TWENTY-NINE

The castle was carved out of the mountain, so it was shallow and soaring, many stories tall. Guinevere's rooms next to Arthur's were on the fifth story. The first floor was an entrance hall and several small rooms held by the knights without families. The second was the great hall—also used as the dining hall—and the kitchens. The third and fourth were servant quarters and storage rooms. The fifth was the royal bedrooms, along with more storerooms and small chambers used by the pages. The sixth was where Uther Pendragon, Arthur's father and the previous king until Arthur defeated him, had kept his favorite companions. Guinevere had never had much reason to come to the sixth floor. Most of the stairs from one floor to the next were outside the castle, narrow stone flights that crisscrossed its exterior, winding around it, sometimes leading nowhere, sometimes leading to things like Mordred's favorite alcove and nothing else. Fortunately, the sixth floor could also be accessed by an interior passageway, which meant Guinevere and Lancelot could go from the fifth floor to the sixth floor, where Guinevach's room was, without being observed from outside the castle.

Without any windows, the passageway was pitch-dark. As they reached the top, Guinevere felt a swell of pity for the women Uther had favored. Lancelot had to use all her significant strength to push the heavy door open. Arthur had mentioned that the exterior door and stairway had been blocked. The only way in and out when Uther was king was through this black tunnel. The women had been prisoners.

Arthur had, of course, unsealed the exterior door. Guinevach and anyone who visited and stayed here could come and go as they pleased. But the door remained an uncomfortable reminder of who had been here before Arthur. Of what this castle—wondrous and strong—could be in the wrong hands. Protection turned to prison.

Guinevere followed Lancelot up the last few steps to the hallway. It had been a prison, but a beautiful one. The windows had colored pieces of glass, and nicer rugs than Arthur had in his own room lined the stone floor to make it softer, warmer, and less echoey.

"I do not know which room she is in," Guinevere said. There were three doors, one on either end and one in front of them. That room would have no exterior windows; Guinevere could not imagine anyone putting Guinevach in it. The windowless rooms were used for storage or as servants' quarters.

"On the right." Lancelot pointed.

Guinevere looked at her, surprised. "Did you already find out?"

"I assigned her room strategically." Lancelot looked almost offended. "She has no guards anymore. Only her two maids are left. One is a girl of twelve, the other an older woman. I do not know if you—if Guinevere—would have known either of them in Cameliard. The page I spoke to was unsure how long they had been in Guinevach's service."

Guinevere nodded. It was important information. The servant

girl, being only twelve, would doubtless question her own memory before she would question Guinevere's identity, assuming she had ever met the real Guinevere. It was unlikely she had been working in the castle at Cameliard before the real Guinevere left for the convent. The older woman was far more likely to be an issue. Guinevere would have Brangien interview her first to ascertain how well she had known the real Guinevere.

"Can we not just banish her?" Guinevere stared at the door uneasily.

"Not without answering questions about why. Especially now that she has established herself here and forced you to introduce her as your sister." That detail had not escaped Lancelot, either. "Did she seem threatening today at the meeting?"

"No. Just . . . annoying. She undermined me and tried to take control of the discussion."

"You were right to decide on something other than a tournament. The harvest festival is not about knights or soldiers. It is about what we all do, together. But she seemed less confrontational to me and more . . ." Lancelot paused so long that Guinevere prodded her.

"More what?"

Lancelot shrugged. "Young. Very young."

Young or not, Guinevach was still the biggest potential threat to Guinevere's safety. Guinevere strode forward and opened the door to Guinevach's rooms. They were set up much like her own. The main bedroom had a bed, several chests, and two chairs. Everything was in shades of blue, elegant and feminine. The bed was neatly made, nothing out of place.

"We know any magic would be undone coming in, but she could do magic once she was inside," Guinevere said, "provided she did not cross the thresholds of the doors again." It was a flaw in her protection system. She had only anticipated magical threats coming from the outside in. It had been a failure of imagination on her part that allowed Mordred to fool them all.

Her hand drifted toward her heart, where she had pressed his flower. The flower was gone now. Trusting Mordred had been a mistake she would not make again. Guinevere certainly would not trust this girl, whoever she was. She stepped toward the trunks to look for evidence of magic or evil intent, when the door to the dressing room opened.

The woman was middle-aged, her dark curls kissed with silver framing a square jawline. Her eyes were rich brown, accented by high arched eyebrows and lines from both worry and laughter. She was beautiful in the way a stately evergreen is: efficient and strong and towering. Her dress and cloak were gray, simple and serviceable but with excellent stitching and a few graceful details.

"Oh, hello, I—" She paused, taking in the sight of Guinevere and Lancelot. Guinevere silently cursed herself. She had assumed that Guinevach would take both her lady's maids to the meal with Dindrane. But Guinevere probably depended on Brangien more than most ladies depended on their maids, because most ladies were actually ladies and therefore understood what was expected of them in various social situations.

The woman frowned. "Please forgive me, but . . . are you the queen?"

Guinevere nodded, unsure what to say. This did not look like a woman who would question her own memory. If she had met the real Guinevere, they were in trouble. Guinevere's fingers twitched. She could fix it, if she had to. But she did not want to.

Fortunately, the woman bowed. "Queen Guinevere. My name is Anna. I am delighted to make your acquaintance. I have heard your praises sung since I joined your father's household."

"And when was that?" Guinevere tried to keep her tone pleasant and light, as though she were making conversation and not interrogating the woman. Anna not knowing her was a benefit, certainly, but it was also suspicious. Guinevere could leave for another kingdom today with Brangien and Isolde and introduce herself as anyone she wished, with two lady's maids to support her claims.

"Three months past. Before that, I served in Lady Darii's house. You may know her? Her family ruled a day south of Cameliard, near the black beaches of the western shore."

"I am familiar with the name," Guinevere lied. "What brought you to Cameliard?"

"With your marriage, Princess Guinevach was ready to prepare for marriage, as well. Your father wanted a maid with more experience than any in his household."

"Did he not wish to send her to the convent to be prepared, as I was?"

At this, Anna's mouth twisted. It was subtle, but Guinevere wondered what Anna was holding back with the expression. "She is older than you were. And with you married, she is eligible to be wed now."

Guinevere wanted to ask about Guinevach's father, King Leodegrance, but not knowing him herself—and with no one in the castle familiar with the man—she had no way to check whether Anna's information was correct. "And how was your journey from Cameliard?"

"Long." Anna smiled. "You will forgive your sister for wishing to stay. She was so disappointed when you left; she could not bear to have come all this way and not be reunited."

Guinevere offered a tight smile in response. "Yes, I am glad my father was able to spare her for a bit longer."

A shadow crossed Anna's face. Her smile tightened like Guinevere's. "As you doubtless remember, it is no great sacrifice for him."

She was angry about something, but the way she said it was intimate, as though her anger should be shared by Guinevere.

Guinevere chose not to respond. "I can see that my sister is not here. I will call on her later. Perhaps tomorrow or the next day. Please keep her out of the great hall when I am holding counsel, though. I have the duties of the king while he is away, and cannot take time for social calls."

"Yes, my queen. I will make an effort to redirect her attentions. Though you know Guinevach." She said it fondly. Again, Guinevere was expected to be in on some shared information between the two of them.

"After all these years, I am afraid I do not. Good evening, Anna." Guinevere held out her hand. It was the best way to get a sense of someone. She would do it to Guinevach as soon as the opportunity presented itself. She should have done it at the gate, but she had been so flustered she had not even thought of it.

Anna took the extended hand. The older woman felt much the same as she looked: stately, calm, intelligent. But there was a strong undercurrent of intense curiosity. No threat or violence or darkness that Guinevere could sense. Alongside the curiosity was sadness, but Guinevere found most women carried far more of that than they ever showed.

Guinevere released her hand. Anna bowed and Guinevere left, followed by Lancelot. "Bar the stairway door," Guinevere said, once they were safely back on the fifth floor. "I do not want her to be able to come down to our rooms unless she goes outside where she can be observed and where she has to cross the magic thresholds." There was always a guard at the entrances to these rooms when Arthur was home, and Lancelot was here whether Arthur was home or not.

Isolde was in Guinevere's rooms, sewing. She smiled but said nothing as Guinevere lowered herself into one of the chairs, exhausted.

"Shall I direct that your food be brought here?" Lancelot asked.

Isolde stood, a determined look on her lovely face. "I will do it! That is a job for me. Please remind me if I am forgetting something a lady's maid would do. I thought I understood the job, but there is so much to learn. It is very exciting." She seemed genuinely delighted by it. "Sir Lancelot, I will bring food for you, too!" She hurried from the room. Brangien was out, apparently. Guinevere did not know what she was doing but did not doubt it was something that needed to be done.

Brangien beat Isolde back, though. She rushed in carrying the scent of the evening on her cloak. Her cheeks were flushed and her eyes bright. "News! Several pieces." She nodded in greeting to Lancelot. "The first: King Arthur will be back in three days."

That was good. Though Guinevere did not trust him to deal with Guinevach, she wanted him back in the city so they were fully armed against all threats.

"The second: your sister's young maid is worthless. I have never met such an empty-headed young thing. She claims she has known Guinevach for three years now, but she could be lying. I am afraid I do not know enough about Cameliard or your family to verify anything she said. She does not seem bright enough to be a good liar, so either she is not one, or she is the best I have ever encountered."

Guinevere nodded. She did not know enough about Cameliard to test the girl, either, but Brangien did not know that. "If she is lying, she will have been coached, so we cannot rule anything out."

"I thought as much. Dindrane will come by in the morning to tell us about her meal with Guinevach. And speaking of Princess Lily"— Brangien said it with exaggerated disdain, which made Guinevere snort with laughter—"it appears she was quite busy while we were gone. Rumor in the castle is that no fewer than three knights are considering courting her."

"What?" Guinevere frowned. "She is only here for a visit. And she is a child."

"She is nearly fifteen. Old enough for a betrothal, certainly. Regardless, she visited every lady still here and flirted with every knight under the age of twenty-five. Already she is the talk of Camelot."

"In a good way, or in a bad way?"

"Who can say? But everyone loves gossip, which means they love Guinevach. She has meal invitations for every night this week, and the next, as well."

"Interesting. Thank you, Brangien." Whatever Guinevach was here to do, she was playing a more complicated game than Guinevere had anticipated.

It takes so long to create the city. Everything is shaped just so. Everything is ready. Waiting.

The darkness takes form at the bottom of the city. She looks around, and then she laughs.

Why?

Because they are coming.

Why do you care?

The question makes no sense. It is not a matter of caring. It is a matter of fact. They are coming, and they will need this city, and it will be ready for them. For him. There will be a wizard, and he will help with the sword. And then—

Well. When the infinite now *became the future and then, the Lady would choose.*

I am bored, *the darkness says, buzzing and humming and thrumming.* Come and dance with me. *She is movement and chaos, brightest life and sharpest death. There is no patience in her, no sense of the power of performing the same action over and over and over until eventually a different result is achieved.*

Still, the Lady loves her, because the darkness is life, and the Lady loves life above all. She nourishes it and makes it possible. It is painfully dear to her, even if she is always separate from it. The Lady flows down her silent and waiting streets and greets the darkness at the end in a joyful embrace. And for that moment, the Lady feels alive.

CHAPTER THIRTY

Guinevere awoke and sat up with a gasp, looking down at her hands. They were hands. She was real. She blinked until her eyes settled on her own room, her own bed.

She lay back down, trying to calm her racing mind. Another dream that belonged to someone else. The Lady of the Lake. If the dream was to be believed, Guinevere officially knew where Camelot—the mysterious city on the hill, the wondrous waiting miracle—came from. The Lady of the Lake carved it herself. When Guinevere had mused that it seemed like Camelot was designed to give Arthur status and power, she had not realized how close she was to the truth.

The joy the Lady had felt at embracing the Dark Queen shocked her, though. And it made her deeply, uncomfortably sad. Because she knew how that story ended. On the shore of the lake, with the Dark Queen calling for her ally and receiving no answer.

Apparently they had been more than allies. They had been so unalike, and yet capable of understanding each other in a way no living creature could. And the Lady had turned her back on that in favor of Arthur and Merlin. What had the wizard done that undid centuries

of the Lady's careful anticipation and work? She had betrayed the
Dark Queen for Merlin and Arthur, and then she had betrayed Merlin, as well. Was it really all because of Guinevere? If Merlin had
gone to such lengths to erase the Lady from Guinevere's memories,
there *had* to be a more sinister reason. Something more complicated.

But what was more complicated than families?

Doubtless done with sleeping for the night, Guinevere sat and
lit a candle at her bedside. Normally she did not mind the dark, but
with the embrace of the Dark Queen lingering in her mind, not as
something terrible but as something joyful, she wanted the distraction of fire.

"My queen? What is it?"

Guinevere startled. She had forgotten that Lancelot would be
sleeping there until Arthur returned with Excalibur. "Another dream."
Guinevere stared at the tiny flame a few seconds longer, wishing
with desperate, painful longing that she could get it to whisper her
real name to her. One thing—just one—that truly belonged to her.

But she had given it up when she came here, and that was that.
She blew out the candle.

"Of the Lady?" Lancelot asked.

"Yes."

"Was there anyone else in it?"

"The Dark Queen." It made Guinevere sad, remembering.

"No one else?"

"It was a long time ago. When Camelot was new."

"Oh, when she made it."

Guinevere almost answered yes, but she froze. She was glad
she had already extinguished the candle so Lancelot could not see
the horror on her face. How did Lancelot know that the Lady of the
Lake had made Camelot? No one here knew where it had come
from. But Guinevere's silence gave her away. She heard Lancelot

cross the room. In the darkness she could see only the silhouette of her knight, standing next to her bed.

"There is something I should tell you. Something I should have told you a long time ago." Lancelot sat on the side of the bed. "I know the Lady of the Lake. Or at least, I knew her."

"How?" Guinevere whispered.

Lancelot and the Lady

*Excalibur was returned to the Lady of the Lake without
ceremony, thrown over the side of a boat as its occupants fled
the king who would kill young Arthur before he could fight
back. It was not his time yet. She would wait, as she had
waited.*

*But he was not the only child she had chosen, or the only
one she cared for.*

*Lancelot stood on the shores of the lake, threadbare tunic
not covering knobby elbows. Knees scraped beneath too-thin
leggings. Boots stuffed with grass so she could fill her father's
steps. She was tall for her age, underfed but with a frame that
could be strong, given time and food and training that she
would never have.*

She was alone, and she was about to die.

*Behind her she could hear the band of men, soldiers
under Uther Pendragon's banner but criminals and rapists
with or without those colors. They had chased her here, her
knife sticky with the blood of the man she had stuck it into*

*while her mother's body was still warm in the shack they had
shared.*

*She knew she needed to care for her weapon. To keep
it clean. Her father had taught her that, at least. She bent
down and carefully washed the blade in the lake as the men
approached. Maybe she could get one more of them. It was all
she had left. She wished Uther Pendragon were there, that he
were the one who would feel the knife as it cut away his life.
But she never got anything she wished for.*

*Her hands under the water looked distorted. Smaller than
they were. Delicate, like her mother's. A shout from behind
her was more animal than man, a sound of rage and violence
and hatred of their own weakness, turned to hatred of anything
weaker than them. Lancelot closed her eyes and gripped the
knife. And then two hands, translucent, circled her wrists and
pulled her under.*

*When she awoke, she was in a cave. There was a shining
expanse of lake between her and the shore, and her attackers
were nowhere to be seen. Water dripped along the back of the
cave, sounding like laughter as it fell.*

*A wave rolled her knife onto the floor of the cave, along
with three bruised apples and one flopping, gasping fish.*

*The Lady of the Lake had saved Lancelot. Over the next
few years, Lancelot retreated to the cave whenever she needed a
safe space. She grew strong, fed and protected by the Lady. She
trained and worked with single-minded purpose. The Lady had
saved her and Lancelot knew what it meant: She was chosen.
Chosen to kill the king. To get her vengeance.*

*Lancelot got her first sword, old and rusted as though it had
been dredged from the very bottom of the lake. No Excalibur
for her, shining and perfect, but a flawed, heavy sword that*

*would force her to compensate. To get stronger. Piece by piece,
armor was delivered to her from the water, plucked from
bloated and rotting bodies left behind in attacks or retreats.
And always she had the gentle lullaby of waves lapping the
edge of the cave, the extra push of the water as she swam,
buoying her and speeding her to and from her excursions into
the mad violence of the world beyond the lake.*

*When Lancelot was not out training or working, she
returned to the cave. But it tormented her, knowing who lived
above. When she was sixteen, she tried to climb the cliff to
Camelot for the first time.*

She fell a third of the way to the top.

*The water rushed up to meet her, breaking her fall and
depositing her with a thump back in the cave. She tried again,
and again, and again, until she no longer needed to be caught.
She could climb that cliff in her sleep. The cliff to Camelot.
The cliff to Uther Pendragon.*

*She was ready. She had a better sword now, hard-won in a
fight. It seemed most days like everything about her, from her
muscles to her voice to her soul, had been hard-won in fights.
Strapping on the armor cobbled together from less fortunate
fighters, Lancelot tipped her head to the lake and whispered
her gratitude. The Lady had given her everything she needed.
She was ready.*

*It was midnight with no moon, but Lancelot had climbed
the cliff so often she did not need to see. She pulled herself
over the top and prowled through the alleys, toward the castle.
Toward the king she would kill. She turned onto the main
street and was surprised to hear a splash. She looked down. The
street was flooded.*

Not flooded. Flooding. And the water was rising. Lancelot

ran to get ahead of it, but it followed her, swelling into a river and sweeping her off her feet. It carried her from the castle, down a street, twisting and turning until she slammed against a rock. Her breath was knocked from her and she feared she would drown, but the river stopped as suddenly as it had started. Lancelot stood, in pain and furious, using the rock as support.

She felt the words beneath her fingers. This was no simple rock. It was the stone that had held Excalibur until someone had claimed it. A boy. A stupid child, gone now.

Lancelot pushed her hair from her eyes, which were blurry with tears of pain and rage. She turned back toward the castle, but her way was blocked by the river, now in the form of a woman rippling in front of her.

Lancelot, *the Lady said.*

Lancelot stumbled backward against the stone in shock. She had been alone for so long. Sometimes she wondered if she was mad, if she was imagining the Lady so she would not have to be lonely. So she could pretend someone out there cared whether she lived or died. Whether she killed Uther Pendragon.

It is not you, *the Lady said, her voice so familiar. Cold and clear and sad and joyful all at once.* It is not you, *she repeated, and Lancelot hung her head in shame and despair. All her work, all her training, had been for this. But the Lady had chosen someone else.*

I will leave soon, *the Lady said, unaware or uncaring that Lancelot's entire life had led her to this point and was now over. Worthless. Why had the Lady saved her, if Lancelot was not chosen for this?*

You will return my kindness. *It was not a question. It was a command.* You will know when. *The water surged forward,* warm and overwhelming, surrounding Lancelot before splashing to the ground and running downhill, no longer the Lady, eager to become the lake once more.

That night, as Lancelot carefully climbed back down to her cave, she knew with a certainty that nothing would catch her if she fell. She was alone, again. And she would be alone until she found her calling, her quest from the Lady of the Lake. Because she had not been chosen to defeat this evil, but surely, surely out there was some other reason she had been saved.

CHAPTER THIRTY-ONE

"When Arthur defeated Uther Pendragon and I found out the Lady of the Lake had given Excalibur to him, I decided he must be what she had been talking about. So I set out to become a knight. And then I met you, and . . . and she was right. I *knew*."

Guinevere sat with the story wrapped around her. "Why did you never tell me?" It hurt that Lancelot had kept this from her. As though Guinevere would judge a past tainted by a creature of magic.

"Because you were so scared of her. Her actions at Merlin's cave scared me, too. I had never seen that anger, that rage. It did not even seem like her. And I worried that if King Arthur knew about my connection to her, he would not let me serve as your knight." Lancelot was quiet for a long time. When she spoke again, her voice was tentative. Searching. "May I still be your knight?"

Guinevere reached through the darkness for Lancelot's hand and squeezed. "The first time we clasped hands, it felt right. Like we were meant to be in each other's lives. Almost like we always had been. You will *always* be my knight."

The Lady of the Lake and Merlin. Both of them had put Arthur and Guinevere and Lancelot on these paths. This collision course. But what did it mean that the Lady and Merlin—who had in one way or another created all three of them—were now enemies?

The next morning, Guinevere brought up the dream to Brangien.

Brangien combed and plaited Guinevere's long black hair. "Your mind was not empty this time. You have your own dreams back."

"Yes," Guinevere said, toying with a selection of rings. She had three, all the real Guinevere's. Normally she did not think twice about them, but she wondered if Guinevach recognized any of them. If any of them meant something to her, and therefore had meant something to the real Guinevere. "So our theory that something was pushing the dreams in since mine were empty is wrong. But now that we have Isolde, I suppose it does not matter."

"Hmm." Brangien frowned thoughtfully. "Do you think it is because you have been in the castle for so long? If what you saw is true, then the Lady of the Lake spent a lot of time with these stones. And your touch thing"—Brangien gestured vaguely toward Guinevere's hands—"could be building up memories of her as you live and touch things here."

That had not occurred to Guinevere. It was true that a few times as she touched the stones of the castle she had almost felt something. Perhaps when she was asleep, she was relaxed enough that the full memory of the stone could come through.

"That may very well be it." That, and her connection to the Lady. It was Guinevere's own magic, manifesting in an unexpected way. It was both comforting and worrisome. Her memories were a void. Could it be that it was not her dreams that were being filled, but her own mind? Was she absorbing a little of everyone and everything around her and using it unconsciously to rebuild what had been so damaged by Merlin?

It was yet another unknown, and there was no one she could ask about it. Certainly not the cruel and culpable wizard sealed away by the very Lady she had dreamed of, or the Lady herself. Guinevere would sooner have no answers at all than any delivered by water.

There was a knock. Lancelot had gone to bathe and change, promising to be back before Guinevere had to go anywhere. Brangien opened the door, angling herself in such a way that she blocked the view of the room. Isolde peeked in from the sitting room to see who it was.

"Yes?" Brangien said.

"I wondered if my sister wanted to go on a walk with me this morning before her meeting." Guinevach sounded as hopeful and bright as a morning after rain.

Brangien did not glance back to check. She did not have to. "The queen is feeling indisposed this morning. She has to stay in and rest until her duties claim her."

"Oh. Yes, of course. What time will she be attending the meeting? Perhaps I could assist her."

"Do not trouble yourself. She would rather you go out and enjoy the city. The bakers on Piss—on Castle Street are quite good. I recommend honeyed buns if you can find any." Brangien closed the door. They waited in silence for a few moments to give Guinevach time to wander away, then Brangien sat next to Guinevere.

Isolde had joined them and was sorting through Guinevere's dress options for the day. "Guinevach is very earnest and sweet. She must be so excited to be here."

"Yes, I am sure she is." Brangien gave Guinevere a narrowed-eye look that made it quite obvious she was sure of no such thing.

"Oh, this is lovely!" Isolde held up one of Guinevere's prettiest dresses, a flowing gown of pale green that Brangien usually paired with a blue cloak.

"It is. But I need something that conveys authority." Guinevere was working on behalf of Arthur and needed to project the same assured strength. She could not carry a sword, which seemed to be the biggest indicator of power.

"Right. Yes. Of course." Isolde went back to sorting. She held up a gray tunic dress whose bodice was embellished with red and blue threads that looked almost like chain mail in their pattern.

"That is perfect."

Isolde beamed at the praise, then chose a sleeveless robe of deep blue.

"The matching gray hood," Brangien said. "We can attach it. It looks like silver, and we will arrange it so it frames her face like a crown or a halo."

"But she is not going outside today." Isolde held up the hood. It was not connected to a cloak, but would lace on at Guinevere's shoulders, holding it in place.

"We are not being practical. We are being purposeful. Guinevere cannot look like the king, but we can make certain no one forgets she is the queen." Brangien put the hood in place, fussing with it and adjusting it until she was satisfied with how the stiff fabric surrounded Guinevere's face without shadowing it. Then she took the two blue strips of the robe front and, instead of draping them straight down, crisscrossed them and pinned them in place on Guinevere's shoulders so the swath of blue elegantly pooled above her chest and then fell behind her arms like a cloak or a cape.

"She looks like Camelot!" Isolde gasped. "The gray of the city, the blue of the lake, the twin waterfalls."

Guinevere did not particularly like imitating the water she hated so, but she could not deny Brangien's cleverness with the visual. "You are a genius."

Brangien made a few more pins and tucks. "I know," she said, stepping back to consider her work before nodding. "Now, whatever you do, do not push the hood back or pull it forward. It is a halo, not a cave."

Caves were almost as bad as water. Guinevere stood straight, afraid to move. "I will do your work the honor it deserves, even if my back never recovers."

"Good."

There was another knock on the door, but before Brangien could reach it, it opened to reveal Dindrane. "Good morning, I—oh, my queen!" Dindrane paused, her mouth open as she took in the sight. "Brangien, are you certain I cannot lure you from the queen's service?"

Brangien did not even acknowledge the remark. She set about cleaning up with Isolde as Dindrane sat on a bench near where Guinevere stood.

"Sit," Brangien commanded Guinevere. "You will have to figure out how to sit at the meeting, so you may as well practice here."

Guinevere stepped lightly and gathered her skirts, lowering herself with a straight spine into her seat. Everything stayed where it was supposed to, and she breathed a sigh of relief. "How are you?" she asked Dindrane.

Dindrane waved the question away. "Your sister is charming and elegant and sweet and graceful. She brought me this belt she sewed herself. I have never seen such tight stitching."

Brangien's voice was sharp. "Can I see it?"

Dindrane frowned, but undid the cloth belt from her waist and passed it to Brangien. Guinevere knew what Brangien was looking for: knots of magic, evidence that Guinevach was using sewing the same way Brangien did, to anchor spells and to do so under the noses of everyone around her. After a few seconds of examining the belt front and back, Brangien shook her head and returned it to Dindrane. "Beautiful," she said.

"Are you jealous?" Dindrane laughed. "The girl can sew better than you."

"I am not jealous." Brangien lifted her eyes to the ceiling in exasperation, then resumed her work alongside Isolde. "Isolde, will you fetch some food for our guest?"

Isolde nodded, smiling warmly at Dindrane before leaving.

Brangien sat down, joining them. "How was she really?"

"Exactly as I said." Dindrane smoothed the belt back into place. "Honestly, I have never met such a lovely young woman. Were I not happily married and satisfied with my life, I might have hated her for her youth and beauty. As it is, I only found it mildly annoying. But even I caved by the end of the meal. She is endearing. I spoke to a few of the other wives and they have all received similar gifts and visits from her. She knows how to carry a conversation and when to listen. She has clearly been educated in all the ways a princess should be." Dindrane paused as though she had said something wrong. Guinevere did not realize what it was until Dindrane's failure to look at her felt deliberate. Dindrane had been comparing Guinevach with Guinevere, and it was obvious which of the two fell short of what a princess should be.

"We had different tutors." Guinevere wanted to shift in her seat but was afraid of disturbing her hood. "And I spent years in the convent before coming here. Tell me, what did you speak about?"

"She wanted to know all about my house, my wedding, Sir Bors, my clothes, the decorations I chose. Her praise was as artful as her stitchwork. And she steered the conversation back to you many times. How long had we known each other, how did we become friends, what were you like when you were not being the queen."

"Hmm." Guinevere frowned.

"I would not have noticed it if you had not asked me to spy on her. She is subtle. But it was clear the entire visit was aimed at getting as much information about you as she could. I told her nothing useful, of course. Only that you were my dearest friend and everyone remarked on what good friends we were and how wise you were to choose me as your friend." Dindrane tossed her hair over her shoulders, her smile wicked. "I am afraid I was not helpful. But she never acted frustrated or chagrined. She just pivoted and tried a different path of conversation to find a way to her goal. Very clever. I like her immensely. I hope she is not here to destroy you and steal your husband, but if she is, you should be flattered at such a skilled foe."

Guinevere could not help but laugh. Everything was confusing and dire, but Dindrane managed to make it sound more like a game than anything. Dindrane stayed for another hour, gossiping and telling stories as they ate the food Isolde brought. It was exactly what Guinevere needed after a restless, disturbing night. It made her feel normal, made her feel like she really was who she was pretending to be.

"We should go," Brangien said, looking at the sun's location in the sky. "They will be waiting for you."

Guinevere sighed. Back to the business of being the queen. She bade Dindrane a fond farewell. Lancelot entered the room as Dindrane left, then escorted them down to the hall. There was a hum of conversation coming from behind the closed door. Guinevere thought nothing of it until it was punctured by a sparkling stream of laughter.

Guinevach. Guinevere pushed open the door to find the girl sitting in the queen's seat, midsentence, as the entire room of men leaned forward intently, hanging on every word.

"Oh, hello!" Guinevach waved. "Your maid said you were indisposed, so Sir Gawain helped me call the meeting early. We have just finished! Everything is settled." She smiled, a row of pearly teeth daring Guinevere to demand her seat back.

"How wonderful." Guinevere stood there in her carefully strategic outfit, as Guinevach, her golden hair braided like a crown around her head, dismissed the men, and ended the meeting.

CHAPTER THIRTY-TWO

Guinevere had been waiting for three hours, sitting on the ground plucking plants and stripping them to pieces. Lancelot had finally given up standing and was sitting beside her. They were waiting for Arthur outside the city, across the lake. He was due back today, though they had no idea what time.

Guinevere could not stand to stay in the city, or the castle. She felt hunted. The past two days everywhere she had gone Guinevach was either there or had already been, her presence lingering like the embroidered lilies she left in her wake. On pillows. On sashes. On belts. Wherever Guinevere went, the ladies wore evidence of Guinevach's popularity. The knights were no better. Sir Gawain wore a kerchief embroidered with one of Guinevach's lilies, either unaware or uncaring that several of the other knights hated him for it. They had all received them, but only he acted like it was a badge of honor to be displayed.

Guinevach had taken over plans for the harvest festival. Guinevere did not even know how it had happened. Somehow between one day and the next, the festival became Guinevach's. She took

Guinevere's idea and made it bigger, better. Now they would have milking contests for the maids, a display of sewing where women could show off their skills, a pig-wrestling contest. Even the knights were in on it. They were no longer competing as knights, but competing alongside the farmers. They knew the farmers would win most of the contests, but that was part of the celebration. A chance for the regular men to best Arthur's knights in fun and jest.

"Chicken-catching contest. I could have thought of that." Guinevere tore another blade of grass from root to tip.

"My queen?" Lancelot leaned her head toward Guinevere.

"There he is!" Guinevere stood. Arthur and his men were visible in the distance, a cloud of dust in their wake. She was sure he would be exhausted and ready to go back to the castle, but she needed to speak here where they were not observed. Where they would not be haunted by the specter of Guinevach hovering somewhere nearby, smiling and pink and lovely.

It felt like it took forever for Arthur to reach them. When he did, he smiled wearily, dismounting and pulling Guinevere in for a hug. "I did not expect you to meet us."

"I wanted to speak with you. In private."

Arthur waved his men on. "Go ahead without me. My queen and I will take the long way home." The knights all went ahead, toward the city, save Lancelot. She gave Arthur and Guinevere a respectful distance, moving out of earshot. Arthur sat on Guinevere's blanket.

Guinevere sat, too. "How did it go?"

"As well as can be expected. It was useful information, and I am glad to have more connections in that region. You were right that the Pict peace gives us an opportunity to focus elsewhere. How have things been here? Have you accomplished all my duties so I am not required for anything at all?" Arthur smiled, then lay back, his arms behind his head. He was dusty and road-worn but did not seem eager to return to the city. Guinevere lay next to him, closing her eyes against the glare of the sun.

"I have not accomplished them. Someone else has. Guinevach is still here."

"No!" Arthur shifted to his side, propping himself up on an elbow. He blocked the sun so Guinevere could see again. "What happened?"

"She sent her guards home without her. And now the whole city adores her. Which makes her much more difficult to shuffle out quietly. I have found no evidence of magic, but I was not able to search her rooms very well. Her lady's maid has only been with her a few months. Allegedly. They could all be lying." Guinevere shook her head. "I do not know. I cannot know. And that is what is so terrible. I have no idea what Guinevach is up to because I do not know her, but I cannot admit I do not know her!"

"What has she done? She did not reveal your identity, did she?"

"No. But she is everywhere. Talking to everyone. Taking over the harvest planning. Making friends, flirting with knights, giving presents."

"Is that . . . bad?"

"Yes! She is very good at all of it!" Guinevere sat up, unable to contain her frustration. "I have had to keep my distance from everyone as I learned what my role was, how to behave, how to do the things that a princess would know. And she already knows it all. She is better than I am at everything, and everyone loves her, and if she is plotting against me, I cannot see how, which means I cannot fight her!"

Arthur took Guinevere's hand and tugged her back down. She acquiesced with a huff of breath. "I am here now," Arthur said, keeping her twitching hand in his warm, comforting one. "We will see if there is a threat. But the biggest threat—that she would reveal the truth of your deception—did not happen. And that is a relief," he said, as if the matter was concluded. "Tell me, how did you like ruling Camelot in my absence?"

Guinevere was not as reassured as Arthur. He had been wrong about how easily Guinevach could be dealt with. In Guinevere's mind, this meant something more sinister and complex was at work. But Arthur was back, and they would face it all together.

But to his question. How *did* she like ruling Camelot? "It is a lot of details. Land and crops and storage and market stall space. Who knew what an outrage a single shift in market stalls could ignite?"

Arthur laughed. Guinevere could not help but laugh, too, happy to have this shared moment.

"I will admit," he said, "it was perhaps not a kindness giving you my tasks. I did not miss those meetings."

"Let me tell you my ideas for the harvest festival, though!" Guinevere rushed to fill him in before he returned to the castle and Guinevach took credit for everything. Dindrane's joke about Guinevach stealing her husband had made more of a mark than Guinevere expected. But Guinevach could not lure Arthur to her side. He was Guinevere's. Arthur listened, commenting and praising, and for that bright hour they were king and queen *and* Arthur and Guinevere, and everything was going to work out.

CHAPTER THIRTY-THREE

It was a relief, having Arthur back. Guinevere had relished the idea of authority, but the reality of it was more of a grinding monotony. Though she vowed to make an effort to be more involved in the actual ruling of Camelot, she was not sorry to pass back the bulk of duties to Arthur.

The next day she made her slow way to the combat arena with Brangien. Isolde did not like crowds and had volunteered to stay behind and see to the day's work.

"How is Isolde adjusting?" Guinevere asked, leaning on Brangien's arm. A guard, a cheerful fellow named George whom Guinevere was fond of, walked at a respectful distance, Lancelot having gone early to the arena. Because it was harvest season, there were likely to be few aspirants; it was more of a training day for younger boys who hoped to become soldiers and whose families were merchants, allowing them the freedom to train instead of work fields.

"It is good to be back together. But she has a lot of healing to do. Some things I think will be different forever. King Mark was— Well. I am not sorry about what you did to him."

"I am," Guinevere whispered. "It was wrong."

"He would have done worse to you. But if it takes the rest of our lives for Isolde to feel safe, then I am committed to that task. She will *never* be threatened again."

"Does she like Camelot? Or do you think she would do better somewhere secluded?"

Brangien shook her head, which was a relief. Guinevere wanted what was best for Isolde and hoped to support Brangien in whatever the two women needed, but she did not want to lose her friend. "No, part of what was so horrible for her was that he kept her isolated, allowed her no friends, nothing to do. She was not what he wanted, so he refused to let her be anything at all. Helping others is part of her. This castle, bustling but open, makes her feel safe. And she loves Sir Tristan and Lancelot and you, and is finding a good rhythm with her new work. I think the routine, the busy tasks, they are all helpful. She is sleeping better."

"I am glad. Let me know anything I can do to help, or to make her life easier."

Brangien squeezed Guinevere's hand where it rested on her arm. "I will. Thank you. And how are you? Any more dreams?"

"Nothing to report." Guinevere and Arthur had returned to the city together, then stayed up late into the night discussing in detail what Arthur had learned and what it all meant for Camelot now and in the future. If Guinevere had dreamed after falling asleep in Arthur's bed while he wrote letters, she remembered nothing, which suited her fine.

Guinevere and Brangien walked into the arena, climbing the wooden benches until they reached the covered section reserved for royalty. It was built out so it overlooked the arena floor, giving them the best and most comfortable view possible. Today, however, there were additions. Anna was sitting in the back, mending stockings.

And Guinevach was sitting in Brangien's seat, leaning forward and waving a kerchief.

Brangien froze. Normally she sat next to Guinevere, but with another lady here, it was not her place anymore. Guinevere could feel the tension in Brangien as Brangien led her to the seats at the front and then walked back and sat stiffly next to Anna.

"Oh, hello!" Guinevach beamed at Guinevere. "I heard you never miss watching your knight in the arena. You have been very hard to spend time with!" Guinevach said it lightly, patting the chair next to her.

Guinevere sat. "I told you I did not have time for you. I told you to go home. You did not listen. I owe you nothing."

Guinevach did not so much as flinch. "I am glad your husband is back. That must make you happy. Is he away often?"

Was she fishing for information? She had to know Arthur often left the city. "The city is always protected."

"All those knights! I like them very much. But none is as good as King Arthur. He is so handsome." Guinevach's expression went soft and dreamy. "Imagine being betrothed to a stranger and riding to discover *him* waiting for you at the end! You are the *luckiest*." The way she emphasized *luckiest* made it sound less romantic and more like a criticism. "Do you remember what Father always used to say to us?" She fixed her golden eyes on Guinevere, waiting.

It was a trap. Guinevere was sure of it. "I am afraid you will have to be more specific. He said many things."

Guinevach raised one delicately expressive eyebrow. "Not to *us*." She paused, but when Guinevere did not respond, she pitched her voice low and raised her chin, glaring down at Guinevere as though she were a mess to be cleaned up. "Pray you are beautiful and fertile; the world has no other use for a girl."

Guinevere must not have hidden her shock well enough.

Guinevach's brow furrowed. "You really do not remember? He would say that, and then *you* would cry."

"It has been a long time since I thought of Father." Guinevere looked out at the arena, trying to end the conversation. She could not trade memories she did not have. And this one felt particularly cruel. Whether it was made up or not, Guinevach was obviously trying to communicate something. Maybe commenting on the fact that Guinevere was not pregnant yet? Until she provided Arthur an heir, she was not a good queen. She knew it. The kingdom knew it. Only Arthur did not care.

"How fortunate for you." Guinevach's voice was as cold as a winter midnight, but she followed Guinevere's lead and focused on the arena.

Soon she was again cheering, waving her embroidered kerchief whenever one of the knights did something particularly good, or even when they did not. Lancelot led a group of boys through a drill to make certain they all knew how to wield a sword. If they did not have basic proficiency, even the blunted training swords could pose a threat to someone who had no idea how to block a blow.

"Sir Lancelot," Guinevach said. "That is funny."

"What is funny?"

"That she is called sir."

"That is what knights are called, and she is a knight."

"Yes, of course." Guinevach rested her pretty pointed chin on one fist. "But it is odd. It is also odd how close you two are. You spend so much time together. She even sleeps in your bedchambers sometimes, does she not? Does that bother the king?"

"Why should it bother him?"

Guinevach shrugged. "I do not know. That is why I asked whether it does. But she is a knight, and he certainly would not let any of the other knights sleep in your chambers. Why should the standard be any different for Sir Lancelot?"

"She is a woman."

"But she is a *knight*. People are talking."

"Who is talking?"

Guinevach brushed a hand dismissively through the air. "I cannot remember. It has been remarked upon to me is all. People find it odd that the queen spends less time in the company of other ladies than she does with her knight and her maidservant."

Is that what the little vermin was doing? Stalking through Guinevere's city, gossiping about her? Gossiping about Lancelot and Brangien? As though she had any right! As though any of them had any right. Guinevere would never choose to spend time with horrid Blanchefleur, or Sir Caradoc's insufferably snobbish wife. Besides which, everyone knew Dindrane was one of Guinevere's closest friends. But somehow that seemed not to count. Or at least, Guinevach was pretending it did not.

"*People* find it odd, or the ladies find it odd? Have you spoken to anyone in this entire kingdom who does not hold a rank or title?" Arthur treated all his people equally, and Guinevere had always endeavored to do the same. It helped, of course, that she felt more at home with waifish chicken maids and blacksmiths and knights who raised themselves in the wilds than she did with most of the ladies.

Guinevach actually laughed. "I am the Lily of Cameliard. I am a princess. Unlike your maid back there, *I* know my place."

"Well, *Lily,* I am the queen of Camelot, and I choose my own company."

"Yes. I have noticed." Guinevach glowered. Then that rosebud smile bloomed firmly back into place. She turned to the arena. Sir

Gawain waved at them and Guinevach stood, waving back. "Oh, good, it is time!"

"Time for what?"

"Our turn!" Guinevach took Guinevere's arm and forced her to stand, half dragging her from the booth and down the steps to the arena floor. The boys had finished training and were putting gear away and shuffling out, rubbing bruises and flushed with exertion and, in most cases, happiness. "Sir Gawain!" Guinevach released Guinevere and hurried toward him.

Guinevere walked a few steps behind her, unsure how to get out of the situation, or what the situation even was. She had never been on the arena floor before. It smelled like packed dirt and sweat, and there was a hint of iron, as well, whether from the weapons or the not insignificant amounts of blood that had baptized this space over the years she was not sure. It had not always been used for training bouts. Before Arthur, its purposes were far more violent entertainments.

"Princess Lily." The young knight bowed. As an afterthought, he quickly added, "Queen Guinevere." His bow was much less deep. Lancelot looked over at them from where she spoke with Sir Caradoc and Sir Percival, but it did not look like a conversation she could easily escape from.

"Did you bring them?" Guinevach asked.

"Yes, of course!" Sir Gawain rushed to the other side of the arena and dragged two bales of hay into place. Then he used a couple of daggers to pin up cloths painted with targets. Sir Gawain loped past them and returned with two small bows and two quivers of arrows, which he presented with a flourish. "As requested!"

Guinevach took a bow and a quiver, then looked at Guinevere. "Well?"

"Well, what?"

Guinevach laughed. "I could not believe it when Sir Gawain told me they had never seen you shoot! My sister, who could best all the men by the time she was twelve! Come, I have waited years for you to teach me."

Guinevere looked at the offered bow and arrows with horror. She had never touched one in her life. This was a test, and she would fail it beyond question.

Guinevere had wanted to be a viper lying in wait for enemies, but Guinevach had her beat. Guinevach knew she could not declare Guinevere a fraud, not with King Arthur supporting his queen. But she could slowly and surely poison everyone against Guinevere, undermine her place here, point out her deficiencies until no one could deny that their queen was an imposter.

It was genius. And short of accusing Guinevach of witchcraft and having her driven out of Camelot, there was no way Guinevere could combat it. She had already publicly declared Guinevach her sister. Everyone adored her. Guinevere was trapped.

She had faced an evil king, rescued herself from kidnappers, stopped the Dark Queen's forest attack and her wolves, and yet this girl was outmaneuvering her.

"There you are!" Arthur's voice flooded Guinevere with relief. She watched as he strode across the arena floor to them. He looked puzzled at the scene. "What is this?"

"King Arthur!" Guinevach curtsied prettily. She really *could* blush on command. "I wanted my sister to teach me how to shoot. No one is better with a bow than Guinevere."

Arthur took in Guinevere's panicked expression. She could see the wheels turning as he tried to think of a way to get her out of the situation.

"I have not practiced since leaving for the convent," Guinevere said. "It was not allowed."

"Oh, come now. Some things you do not forget." Guinevach's smile faded as Guinevere did not move to take the bow. Her voice dropped, the sweetness turning sharp. "Why will you not do this?"

Arthur stepped forward and took the bow and arrows from Sir Gawain. "Not today, Guinevere. I do not want you to risk increasing the injury to your shoulder. Being so out of practice, you could be hurt even worse. I will teach Guinevach."

"That is very kind of you." Guinevere retreated to where Brangien and Anna had come down from the booth and were sitting nearby.

"Forgive her," Anna said, not looking up from the stockings she was darning. "She likes an audience."

"Yes, I had noticed." Guinevere watched as the knights gathered, smiling and laughing jovially as they offered pointers. Guinevach was terrible. But there was something artful to her absolute lack of skill. The worse Guinevach shot, the more she pouted, and the more the men consoled her and offered tips and praise for the slightest improvements. Even Arthur was drawn in, laughing at an arrow that failed to go more than two feet. He placed his hands on Guinevach's arms, standing close behind her as he corrected her posture and guided her position. That arrow flew absolutely true, hitting the center of one of the targets. The men cheered, and Guinevach's smile as she glanced at Guinevere hit its intended target as well, striking deep.

It had all been an act, and every single man, including Arthur, was falling for it.

CHAPTER THIRTY-FOUR

"That was wonderful!" Guinevach lowered her bow and beamed at Arthur. "Soon I will be as good as you, Guinevere!"

Guinevere was ready to leave. She had been ready to leave for some time. "I am certain you will surpass me. King Arthur, shall we—"

"There is a play this evening!" Guinevach interrupted. "It should be starting soon. My maid told me about it."

Guinevere shot a glare at Anna, who shook her head and mouthed, *The other maid.*

"Please, can we go? I have not been to a play in ages. Father did not approve of them." Guinevach turned to Arthur, eyes wide and shining with hope. She was not asking Guinevere. She was appealing directly to Arthur.

"It has been a while since I saw a play. I could use an evening of laughter sitting next to my beautiful queen." Arthur smiled warmly at Guinevere, who was forced to smile back. How could she say no now? Maybe this was part of Arthur's trying to make more of an effort with her. And if she refused to go, Arthur might still go. With Guinevach.

"Oh, hooray! I am so happy! Guinevere, I know your shoulder is hurt, so the king and I will go ahead and get our seats. That way you can walk as slowly as you need to." She put one hand on Arthur's elbow and expertly spun him, already walking toward the exit. Arthur glanced back at Guinevere, helpless amusement on his face as he let himself be led away.

Her shoulder required she go slowly? Guinevach *was* a witch. But she was a witch of words and emotions.

"Can we go, too?" Sir Gawain blurted, staring after Guinevach.

"The more the merrier," Guinevere said through gritted teeth. Sir Gawain and a few other knights hurried after the king and his captor, Sir Gawain stripping off his armor and tossing it at a poor squire as he jogged to catch up to Guinevach. She noticed they did not even ask Lancelot if she was going. That, combined with Guinevach's words, seized hold of Guinevere's mind.

Brangien stood, glowering. "Now we have to go to a play? I have a lot of work to do. It is unfair to leave it all to Isolde." And, doubtless, she did not wish to be apart from Isolde more than she needed to.

"I can attend the queen." Anna tucked the stockings into a pouch at her hip. "Guinevach will be fine without my attention."

"Yes, she has plenty of other people to give her attention." Guinevere hated the petulant tone in her voice, but Anna laughed good-naturedly. Guinevere waved to Brangien. "You go back to the castle. I will manage with Anna and Sir Lancelot."

"I would have dressed you differently for a play." Brangien frowned thoughtfully. She pushed Guinevere's hood back, letting it drape down her back. Then she undid two of Guinevere's braids so her wavy hair framed her face. Finally, she pinched Guinevere's cheeks.

"Ouch!" Guinevere swatted Brangien's hands away.

"What? You need a pretty blush." Satisfied, Brangien left.

Lancelot stepped toward them, but Guinevere took Anna's arm

instead. She would not walk arm in arm with any *other* knight. It was something to think about, much as she hated to admit it. And there was more than that to think about. Her special treatment of Lancelot separated Lancelot from the other knights even more than her gender did. And Guinevere had created additional problems for Lancelot by using their closeness to convince Lancelot to do things and take risks no other knight would.

She was being selfish. Being a knight was Lancelot's dream, and Guinevere had been unknowingly sabotaging her the entire time. It was a devastating realization. Whatever they felt for each other, whatever closeness they had, it was getting in the way of Lancelot's knighthood. Among King Arthur's knights, Lancelot did not deserve to be on the sidelines.

Lancelot said nothing, but walked a few paces apart from them to the theater. It was at the lowest part of the city. It was cheap entertainment, in many senses of the word, attended and enjoyed by anyone who could manage a coin to get in.

"Have you been to a play before?" Anna asked as they joined the main street and followed it down toward the lake. The water shone distractingly, and Guinevere remembered rushing down this same street to embrace the Dark Queen.

The *Lady* rushing down this street to embrace the Dark Queen. It was not Guinevere's memory. She tried to shake off the sensation of remembering something that had not happened to her. Had the Lady of the Lake been as invasive as Merlin? Flooding her mind with memories that were not her own, while Merlin took away memories that were? "Yes, I went to one with Mord—I went to one, once."

If Anna noticed her slip, she did not remark on it. She would not know who Mordred was anyway. "Did you like it?"

Guinevere sighed. "Yes. It was one of the happiest nights I have ever had."

"Then why do you sound sad, remembering it?" Anna paused. "Pardon me, my queen. I overstep."

"No, it is all right. It does make me sad, remembering. So much has changed since then." Everything had felt so hopeful and full of promise that night, as she laughed beside Mordred and Brangien. An image of Mordred walking backward in front of them, eyes twinkling with mischief as he almost suggested something that could not be taken back. He had been good at that, at implying more than he said and watching for her reaction.

And she had always reacted, had she not?

Mordred could have handled Guinevach, Guinevere had no doubt of that. He would see right through her. They would have laughed together about Guinevach's lack of subtlety. Guinevere wanted that right now more than anything.

It was the cruelest thing Mordred had done yet, making her miss him instead of hate him.

"Can you believe her?" Guinevere demanded. They were in Arthur's room, sitting across from each other. "Pretending she could not shoot to force you to fuss over her. And then making us all go to a play."

"Guinevere." Arthur's voice was soft, his eyes tired. "I think she just wanted to go to the play. She seemed to enjoy it. Have you considered that she is exactly who she says she is, and is here to visit her sister?"

That was the brilliance of this attack. No one else could see it. Arthur had no idea of the little battles women waged every day—to be seen by men and respected, and also to navigate all the other women fighting for a place in this world. And Guinevere was not good at it. She thought she was improving, but Guinevach was proof she was not good enough. This was the most ingenious attack possible, because only Guinevere saw it.

She paced. She needed Arthur to understand. "No. No! She is— she is more than that. I cannot say if there is magic at work, but how can you explain her pretending to recognize me?"

"We have theories. We talked about them."

Guinevere waved that away. "And all her little tests. Earlier today she was quizzing me on things *our* father said to us. Then she tricked me into that absurd bow and arrow competition. If I had shot, it would have proved I was not the real Guinevere. She knew she could not expose me outright. I confronted her and told her to leave, so she changed tactics. Now she is proving to everyone that she is better than I am at everything. Being friends with the important ladies. Taking over the harvest festival. Making all the knights love her. Flirting with you."

"She was not—"

"She *was.*" It had taken Guinevere months of *marriage* to get Arthur to even kiss her. Guinevach doubtless could have done it much faster. Perhaps she still would. "It is all deliberate. After she has shown everyone what an amazing princess she is, she will reveal that I am not Guinevere. She is trying to replace me!"

Arthur leaned back in his chair and rubbed his face wearily. "Even if that is her goal, it would never happen."

"Why not? If she revealed that I am not who I say I am, why would they not want a real princess of Cameliard instead?" Guinevere laughed bitterly. "She would probably make a better queen than I do anyway. She has all the education and training and manners for it."

Arthur's answering frown was immediate and worried. "I do not care about that."

"You do not care about much of anything as far as your queen is concerned!" Guinevere held up her hand to cut off his protest. "I did not mean to snap. But it is true. I do not know how to be a queen. All this is pretend. *I* am pretend. And the one thing a queen should do—that everyone in the kingdom is waiting for, whether you notice it or not—is something you do not want."

Arthur's quick, guilty glance toward her midsection—a glance she received from everyone she passed whenever she was out among the people—indicated he knew exactly what she was talking about. But he did not live with the glances and the whispers. She did.

"Do you really want a baby?" he asked, not meeting her eyes.

Guinevere sat across from him and slouched. "No, not yet." Maybe not ever. She had not really considered it. And she had to admit Arthur was right. She was only seventeen. Or was she sixteen? She did not know, not really. Regardless, there was time. And she was *not* ready. "I am tired, and I need you to understand this is every bit as real a threat as possessed wolves or vengeful forests or even armed, expanding Saxons."

"You really feel threatened by her?"

"Guinevach is so good at all of this. And I am pretending every moment of every day." Even with those closest to her. Even with herself.

Arthur took her hands in his and locked eyes with her. "Guinevere. I think you are looking for a threat where there is none because you are afraid. Not of magic or the Dark Queen, but of your place here. There does not have to be danger for you to matter. No one can replace you, because you are who I want at my side. For both the dangerous moments and the dull days."

Tears burned behind Guinevere's eyes and she did not know whether she was angry or hurt or happy, or an impossible mess of all three. Then, to her surprise, Arthur closed the distance between them and pressed his lips to hers. It was a kiss like a fire on a cold afternoon. Warm and soft. Familiar, even. Longer than their last one. It was both comfort and exploration. When he finally pulled away, they were both smiling.

There was a knock on the door. Arthur stood and opened it to find a guard with several letters. Arthur had work to do this night, and so did she. Buoyed by the kiss, carrying the feel of his confidence and assurance with her, she used the guard's distraction with listening to Arthur and slipped out the hall door to the exterior walkway. She wound up and around the outside of the castle, stone on one side and a plunge into darkness on the other.

Whether or not the Lady of the Lake was malicious, she certainly had little regard for safety when she made Camelot.

Guinevere did not realize she was heading to the alcove until she was almost there. It was time to check for magic again. It had been too long. Maybe Guinevach would be burning like a torch and Guinevere would have an excuse to banish her. Or maybe the Dark Queen would be tumbling toward them like an avalanche that only Guinevere could protect Camelot from.

It might not have mattered to Arthur whether Guinevere had something to fight, but it mattered to Guinevere. She needed something to push against, otherwise she was worried she would be . . . nothing at all.

She needed work. Something to occupy herself. Maybe this was why Arthur kept himself so busy, why he was always out riding to check on things or to see to a threat. If he was always *doing,* he did not have to be *thinking.* Thinking about ladies and queens, or, worse, about Ramm and King Mark.

As she neared the alcove, Guinevere's breath caught. There was a flicker of candlelight. Someone was already there. The only person she had ever seen there was Mordred. He had already appeared to her twice. Was it such a stretch to imagine he could find a way into the city?

And what would she do if it was him?

The last few steps felt like an eternity. "Hello?" she called, her voice soft and tentative.

"Oh! My queen." Anna, Guinevach's maid, answered. She turned, a hand pressed in surprise against her heart. "I am so sorry. I did not know anyone came here. I will go."

Guinevere was disappointed. *No.* She refused to be disappointed. She was relieved. Of course Mordred could not get into the city. Not without her knowing. "There is no need to go. What brings you here in the dark?"

Anna shifted to let Guinevere in. The candle illuminated the small space, which now included a cushion and a bag of supplies. "I love the princess, and her young maid is very . . . earnest. But they are both energetic in ways I occasionally need some space from. If I have to hear one more ranking of the knights in order of handsomeness and wealth, I will stick my needles through my ears."

Guinevere snorted an inelegant laugh. "I can imagine it would be a trial to be paired with two such young women."

"You are not so old yourself, my queen. But you seem much . . ."

"Wiser?" Guinevere suggested, hopeful.

"More burdened." Anna smiled to soften the word. "I get the sense you see much more of the world and its complexities than young Guinevach does."

Guinevere sat, refusing the offered cushion. Anna joined her and pulled out a strip of cloth the color of which Guinevere could not make out in the dim light. The older woman sighed as she began embroidering. "I see lilies in my sleep. I wish she had chosen something simpler. Or that she gave out fewer favors."

Guinevere barely contained her triumph. Guinevach was not even embroidering the favors herself! She would be certain to tell Brangien and Dindrane. She liked Anna very much, and not just for this information. There was something about Anna that Guinevere trusted. A quiet, experienced intelligence. "You are right about my burdens," Guinevere said. "I have a lot of problems I cannot find solutions to right now. Or even determine if they are actually problems, or if I am making them into problems to give myself something to do."

Anna did not pause her sewing. "Who do you go to for advice?"

Arthur, but he disagreed with her. Brangien, but she was busy with Isolde and had no more insight into this than Guinevere did. Dindrane, but only when Guinevere needed help navigating the world of ladies and their infinite rules for engagement. Lancelot, but she could offer no solutions, only support, and Guinevere was depending far too much on that—to Lancelot's detriment. The only person who would know more than she did was someone she would never trust again, and could not speak to even if she wanted to. He was sealed in a cave. Guinevere shrugged, miserable.

Anna nodded sympathetically. "Camelot is such a *young* kingdom. There is much value in years well used, just as there is much value in the passion and energy of youth. Do you know anyone who might have advice or have gone through something similar? Someone with experience?"

The sentiment echoed how Guinevere had felt about Anna just moments before. But she could not ask Anna about the Dark Queen, or what Guinevach was up to. In spite of her inherent trust of Anna, she was still Guinevach's maid, and therefore suspect. Guinevere did not dare use her own magic on Guinevach after what had happened with King Mark, but she did not agree with Arthur. Something was going on there, and she had to find out what. She needed Merlin, curse him.

"A woman," Anna added. "Men are problems unto themselves and rarely solutions."

Guinevere laughed, and then she realized exactly whom she could speak with. She had once suspected Rhoslyn of conspiring against Arthur, as she had suspected Lancelot was a fairy back when she only knew her as the patchwork knight. But just as Lancelot had been revealed to be much more, so had Rhoslyn been revealed to be a woman who loved her chosen family and did what she had to in order to create a safe home for them. One where they could continue to practice the magic Camelot denied them.

Rhoslyn had saved her once, from the poison of the Dark Queen. She knew what the touch of chaotic magic looked like, how it worked. If the Dark Queen was moving in a new way against Arthur, Rhoslyn might have information. And Rhoslyn's magic was smaller, subtler, which meant she also might have safe ideas for how to deal with Guinevach.

"Thank you." Guinevere stood. "This was helpful. I will leave you to your solitude."

Anna smiled and bid her good-night. With Arthur's kiss on her lips and a plan, Guinevere felt better. Tomorrow, she would go to the woods and visit a witch, and it would be the beginning of the end for whatever Guinevach was plotting.

CHAPTER THIRTY-FIVE

Guinevere desperately missed the secret passage. It had been her decision to stop using the tunnel that led from the shore behind one of the waterfalls directly to the castle—Maleagant, that evil man, had figured out she had another way in and out of the city. If he noticed, others would, as well. She would not put Arthur or Camelot at risk that way. Besides which, Mordred knew about the passage, so Arthur had blocked the door and she had placed magical wards that would warn her if anyone was in the passage.

It had all been necessary. A responsible decision. But oh, she hated this wretched ferry.

Lancelot gave her a few moments to collect herself after the interminable ride. It was always easier with Arthur. She could cling to him and try to absorb some of his confidence and strength. And in the past she had done something similar with Lancelot. But awful Guinevach's words had needled their way under Guinevere's skin. No matter their past, no matter what brought them together, Lancelot was a knight. Guinevere would protect that. She had to treat Lancelot the same way she treated the other knights, because otherwise she was signaling to everyone that Lancelot was different. And she could not let them think Lancelot was anything other than a full knight of King Arthur.

Even this trip, though, was evidence that Lancelot had different rules from the other knights. Guinevere could not imagine going into the forest with just Sir Tristan, or Sir Gawain, or Sir Bors. There would be gossip. Scandal, even. It was both convenient and unfair that the same rules did not apply to Lancelot simply because she was a woman.

Their story today was that they were checking on the harvest. And Guinevere's story for Arthur was that she was making certain there were no tendrils of the Dark Queen's magic growing closer. Which she would do. But she did not think he would approve of her visit to Rhoslyn, so she had left that out.

Lancelot retrieved their horses from the stables on the grassy shore of the lake. She rode her own trusted blind mare, and Guinevere rode the gray mare she favored whenever she could. The horse was calm and soothing, and Guinevere rode with one hand placed on its neck, enjoying the sense of an animal that could exist in this moment of movement without desiring anything else.

It would take a few hours to reach the border of Camelot's lands and the deep woods where Rhoslyn lived. Fortunately, with Arthur back, no one would miss Guinevere. If Guinevach had her way, no one would *ever* miss her.

They rode in silence for the first hour before Lancelot spoke. "Have I done something wrong, my queen?"

"What?" Guinevere removed her hand from the horse's neck, breaking the calming reverie she had let wash over her. They were still in farmland, the gold dotted with brown as men and women moved among the stalks, harvesting. The day was pleasant, but there was an increasing hint of bite to the air, a cool note on the wind promising the winter to come.

"Last night you seemed distant. And on the ferry you stood apart, too. Is it because of what I told you? Because you have to know— you must know—my loyalty is to you. My time with the Lady of the Lake is history."

"I trust you." Guinevere stared at the horizon, where a dark smudge indicated the start of the forest on this border. "It is not you who have done something wrong. It is me. I demand that the other knights treat you as an equal, and that the people see you as no different from any of King Arthur's other knights. But *I* treat you differently. And people notice, and they talk. I will not allow anyone to question your place, or your honor, or your right to wear King Arthur's colors."

"Who has been talking?" Lancelot sounded ready for a fight, and it made Guinevere smile.

"I do not know, and it does not matter. You protect me. If this is how I can protect you in return, then I will be more careful."

"Is King Arthur unhappy with me?" Lancelot frowned, her dark curls falling over her face. "I have failed you. You were hurt under my watch."

"No! No. Arthur knows you do more than any knight could be asked to, and that my . . . adventures were either my own fault or out of our control."

Guinevere thought the conversation was over, but after a few minutes Lancelot spoke again. "But you still trust me. Even knowing my past."

"At least we know your past. That is more than I have. And I come from as much magic as you, if not more. You are my friend, Lancelot, one of the only people in the whole world I trust completely. In private, we will continue as we always have. But we will be more careful with appearances."

Lancelot nodded, tightening her grasp on the reins and urging her mare to go a bit faster so that Guinevere could no longer see her face.

An arrow whistled past Guinevere and lodged in a tree behind her.

"Down!" Lancelot shouted, drawing her sword and maneuvering her horse between Guinevere and where the arrow had come from.

"The patchwork knight?" a woman shouted. "Is that you?"

"Yes!"

"Sorry! Sorry! No more arrows."

Lancelot rode forward warily, sword raised, keeping Guinevere behind her. A girl materialized from behind a tree. Guinevere recognized her from her last trip to the village. She was the one who had helped draw the Dark Queen's poison from Guinevere's veins. Guinevere did not remember her name.

"What was that about?" Lancelot demanded, scowling.

"I missed! On purpose," the girl added, slinging her bow over her shoulder. "I could have hit either of you."

"Ailith could only hit a target if she was trying not to," a young woman said, stepping out from behind a gnarled oak. "Come on, both of you. Your timing is terrible." She stalked through the trees and Guinevere and Lancelot followed, exchanging a worried glance.

The tiny village, once neat and orderly and clean, was in chaos. Women were shouting as they tossed things to one another, packing a cart. The fires had burned down to ashes. No one was cooking or talking or even sitting. Rhoslyn, her dark hair streaked with gray, seemed to have aged several years since she and Guinevere had last seen each other, during the summer. She ripped down a woven mat from where it served as a door to a hut and rolled it up.

"Rhoslyn?" Guinevere called, dismounting.

Rhoslyn frowned as she tried to place Guinevere's face. "The spider-bite girl?" she asked. "And our patchwork knight. Not *our* knight any longer." She nodded toward King Arthur's crest on Lancelot's tunic. "What are you doing here?"

"I need your advice," Guinevere said.

"I am afraid this is a bad time. Gunild, pack it tighter or it will bounce loose!" Rhoslyn gestured to a bundle in the back of the cart.

"Are you leaving?" Guinevere asked, following Rhoslyn's gaze. The young woman who had escorted them, her sturdy build contradicted by gentle eyes, did as Rhoslyn instructed, pushing a bundle down and wrapping a rope around it.

"We are."

"Not because of the king!" Guinevere could not imagine Arthur had told them to leave. He banished them out of necessity, but wanted no harm to come to them. Surely he would have told her if he had decided to push them out even farther.

"No, he does not care about us. But there are men in the forest who do. We made the mistake of refusing their offer to let us buy our place here with our bodies." The fire in Rhoslyn's eyes burned bright with hatred and anger.

"But they do not own this land! You are doing nothing wrong."

"We are existing independent of them, and that is enough reason for some men to hate us." Rhoslyn's narrow shoulders fell slightly, but she recovered. "So we will exist somewhere else."

Lancelot scanned the trees. "Are they coming soon?"

"They said they would be back tonight. We are not going to wait and see if they keep their promise."

"Come to Camelot," Guinevere said. "I can speak to the king."

"Why would he listen to you?"

Guinevere grimaced. "Because I am the queen."

Rhoslyn stared at her, openmouthed with shock, before recovering. "Well. That *is* interesting. And I appreciate your generosity, but I have been driven from Camelot once and managed to do so with my life only because of Mordred's kindness and your knight's intervention. I do not want to see what Camelot would do if I returned."

"This is my fault," Guinevere said. "If I had not taken Lancelot from you, then—"

"Then Lancelot would not be a knight, and that would be unfortunate." Rhoslyn smiled fondly at Lancelot, who had taken up a position at the edge of the huts where she could see into the trees better. "In the end, if we cannot keep ourselves safe, we will not be safe. And we cannot keep ourselves safe here any longer, so we will leave." She glanced up at the position of the sun. "Where *is* he?"

Ailith shouted a question and Rhoslyn turned away to answer her. Then she turned back to Guinevere. "You must have come here for a reason. What is it?"

"I—" It all felt so much less urgent in the face of what Rhoslyn and her people were going through. It was embarrassing to ask for help with a girl, so Guinevere chose the more obvious danger. "I wanted to ask if you have felt dark magic. The Dark Queen has physical form again."

Rhoslyn brushed her hair back from her face before she grabbed another mat and rolled it. Guinevere did the same, trying to be useful. "We leave well enough alone when it comes to her. We ask nothing and offer nothing and hope her chaos looks the other way. And it has, so far."

"But . . ." Guinevere gestured to the camp.

"This is not the chaos of nature's violence. This is the chaos of man's. They are very different things."

Guinevere nodded. "So, you have not noticed anything?"

"Not here. But if she were to show up right now, I would welcome her. I think she would take our side." Rhoslyn reached up to undo a hanging ornament made of glass shards tied to a string. It caught the light as it spun, creating flashes of beauty. A single tear traced down Rhoslyn's face, and she wiped it away determinedly. "We made a home here. We will make another."

"In the trees!" Lancelot shouted. "Movement!"

"Positions!" Rhoslyn commanded. The women dropped everything they were holding. One took the few children in the camp and ran into the nearest hut with them. The rest spread out along the borders, armed with bows and arrows.

Guinevere stood in the center, helpless and terrified. If she were Merlin, she could wield fire as a weapon, but she did not trust herself to be able to control it. Using it took tremendous focus and these were not ideal circumstances. She was as likely to set herself on fire as she was to set the whole forest ablaze, and neither would help these women. Maybe that was why Merlin had counseled her to fight as a queen, not as a witch. He had seen all this. He had seen what she did to King Mark. He knew she would lose control.

But he was not here.

She yanked several threads from her cloak and tied them into knots of confusion. Her head swam, but she had not done enough to incapacitate herself. She attached the knots to the hut where the children were hiding. If men did make it into the camp, they would bypass this hut, their eyes sliding right past it and finding nothing worth looking at.

"Stay in there," she whispered to the woman inside. "No matter what happens. You will be safe inside."

"Thank you," the woman answered. There was a child-sized sniffle, but otherwise only silence in the dim interior.

Guinevere wished she had a weapon, but it would be useless. She had no skill with any of them. She wished she were the real Guinevere, if Guinevach's claims about her sister's bow skills were true. She hurried to where Rhoslyn crouched next to a hut, scanning the trees.

"When you run out of arrows, go to the hut with the children," Guinevere told her. "It will be hard to find, so you will have to focus, but you will be safe there."

Rhoslyn looked at her with a question in her eyes, but there was no time. Guinevere ran along the perimeter, passing the message to each woman. There were only a dozen of them. They could fit. Then she placed herself outside the hut to help them find it should the time come.

"Little birdies," a man called from the trees in a mocking singsong, "we are here for you."

There was the twang of a bowstring, the pounding of hooves, and a woman's scream as all hell broke loose. Once the men drew closer, fighting with bows and arrows would not be enough. And if Ailith was any indication, these women were not trained for battle.

Guinevere clenched her fists, ready to call fire if she needed to. If she burned down the forest, or herself, at least she would take some of the men with her.

Gunild staggered past Guinevere, bleeding from one leg. She looked around, confused, unable to see where she was supposed to go. Guinevere shoved her into the hidden hut and then twirled, trying to keep track of where everyone was and what was happening. Lancelot charged into the trees, roaring, trying to draw the attackers to herself and away from the women.

"The hut!" Guinevere shouted. "Get to the hut!"

Eight, then nine women rushed toward her. Guinevere pushed

them into the dark space. Her magic was holding. Even knowing where it was, the women could not focus on it.

Rhoslyn staggered into the center of the camp, wielding a knife and an ax.

"Get in," Guinevere said, reaching for her.

"No. I will stand and defend them until my last breath."

Guinevere could not argue with that. She picked up a heavy stick and coaxed sparks to the end of it. The torch would burn brighter and hotter than a normal fire, lighting anything it touched. "I will stand with you."

Lancelot rode back toward them, breathing hard. Her sword was red and glistening. "I do not know how many there are," she said, eyes searching even as she spoke. "I am afraid—"

Another horse pounded into the village, stopping just short of them. Guinevere stared up at the rider, shocked.

"You!" Lancelot shouted, lifting her sword toward Mordred.

Mordred raised a spear and threw it with all his might.

CHAPTER THIRTY-SIX

Mordred's spear flew past Lancelot, burying itself in the chest of a fur-clad man running toward them with a raised mace.

"Four more!" Mordred shouted, drawing his sword. He rode to Lancelot's side. Guinevere knew it was more than the cost of the confusion magic making this scene hard to process. Lancelot, too, seemed shaken, but she did not have time to question it. She dismounted and stood shoulder to shoulder with Mordred, their swords up as the attackers shot free of the trees and ran at them.

Lancelot fought with the ferocity of someone who had battled her entire life to get where she was. Every movement was precise and brutal, every blow met and returned with twice the force. Mordred fought like a dancer, a reed bending in the wind, dodging and twisting until his foes showed a weakness and his sword found a home.

A twig cracked behind Guinevere. She whirled, swinging her stick like a club. It connected with the stomach of a man. He looked down in shock as the fire jumped from the stick to his body, licking up him with ravenous speed. He screamed, running and flailing, before falling to the ground and rolling in an ineffectual attempt to smother the flames. Guinevere knew how it would end and looked away. The hut was still safe. This price was worth it.

Mordred stood, a hand on one hip, his sword at his side. He surveyed the village, then turned back to the trees. "How many did you get?"

Lancelot glared. "It is hardly a competition."

Mordred gave her a witheringly dismissive look. "I am trying to account for all the enemies. There were three I killed before that one"—he pointed to the man with the spear planted in his chest, the shaft listing to one side like a tree whose roots were not deep enough— "then these four."

Lancelot's answer was gruff. "Four more in the trees."

"And one for Guinevere." Mordred flicked his eyes toward her, but she could not tell whether he was pleased or not.

"Were you following us?" Lancelot demanded.

Mordred ignored her. "Thirteen. Does that sound right, Rhoslyn?"

Guinevere turned to Rhoslyn, surprised that Mordred was on friendly terms with her. After all, he had overseen the courts and had been the one to banish her.

"We got two more with arrows. I think that is the lot of them. You are *late*, Mordred," Rhoslyn said, dropping the ax.

"All apologies. Sincerely." Mordred strode over to them. Lancelot hurried after, putting herself between Guinevere and Mordred, but Mordred paid her no mind. "In my defense, they were also early. Is everyone ready? Where are they?" Mordred looked around the camp, his eyes widening with panic. "The children and the rest of the women. *Where are they?*"

"Here." Gunild slipped out of the hut, followed by a line of women and children.

Mordred squinted, trying to see better. "Nice work," he said, glancing at Guinevere. "Very clever." What he had said before when tending her shoulder about being clever sparked in her mind. And then the things she had said, thinking he was a dream, also came back and she fought a humiliated blush.

"What are you doing here?" Guinevere demanded.

"I could ask you the same thing."

Guinevere folded her arms. "You expect me to believe it is a coincidence that you ended up here on the same day we did?"

"*You* expect *me* to believe it is a coincidence you ended up here at the very hour I was scheduled to arrive?" Mordred raised an eyebrow in an expression that Guinevere realized, with a sinking stomach, she missed. Terribly. "You did not bring enough help, though."

"Enough help for what?" Lancelot growled, still holding her sword.

"To bring me to justice. I do not mean to offend, Lancelot, but we have faced each other in combat before, and you were not the one to walk away."

Lancelot took a step forward, but Guinevere put a hand on her shoulder. "Stop." Mordred had spared Lancelot's life that terrible night in the meadow. He had even dragged Lancelot out of harm's way, making sure the Dark Queen would not kill Lancelot out of spite when she rose. "We did not come here for you," Guinevere continued. "I came to speak with Rhoslyn."

"Oh." For a moment, Mordred's face fell. Then his eyelids half closed, framing his moss-green eyes with night-dark lashes, as his mouth twisted into a lazy smile. "Well then, thank you for the help, and give my regards to my uncle."

He took his horse's reins and led it to the cart. Gunild and Ailith began hooking it up.

"Where are we going?" Rhoslyn asked, counting children.

"South and east. My mother has seen an island. Surrounded

by rivers of mud, but ancient and beautiful. You will be safe there. There is something special about it."

Ailith threw her arms around Mordred's neck. "Thank you."

He smiled and patted her shoulder. "No need to thank me." Every woman here looked at Mordred with shining gratitude. It was clear they all knew him, trusted him, and even loved him. He had been the one to banish women, but he had done that instead of having them killed. Maybe he had also helped them form and protect this little village. But why?

"Mordred, can we speak?" Guinevere gestured toward the trees. Lancelot's brow descended, her eyes flashing like the moment before a storm. "We will stay in sight," Guinevere told her.

Mordred followed her the few steps to the trees. "How is your shoulder?"

"Nearly healed. Thank you for that. I do not understand it. And I do not understand this." She gestured toward the camp.

"That is how I noticed your fire before. I was making certain my mother's vision of the island was true. Her visions are not always accurate. Though I suspect *you* are following me now. This is three times. Having regrets?"

Guinevere gave him a flat look, and he continued. "These women have always been kind to me. I help out where I can. I am glad you were here today. Lancelot especially, though please do not tell her." Mordred waggled his fingers mockingly toward where Lancelot stood watching them, her legs braced and her sword half-raised, ready to charge at the slightest provocation.

"But what are you *doing* out here? You were with the wolves, but not on their side. And then you helped me and just . . . left. And now you are, what, escorting these women to a new home?"

"I am doing exactly what I told you I would be doing." Mordred reached up and plucked a golden leaf free from where it dangled above their heads. He twisted it by the stem, watching it flutter and dance in his hand. He sounded less defiant than he did sad. "I am living. I am free. I am doing what I choose, when I choose, how I choose."

"But your grandmother. I thought—well, I thought you would be plotting with her."

Mordred shook his head. "Not being on Arthur's side is not the same as being evil. I wanted my grandmother to be whole. To reclaim some of the magic that was taken from the world. When she was unmade, she went mad. Her spirit and her power were uncontained, uncontainable. I hoped that, by restoring her body, she could be whole again. I could not do it for my father, but I could do it for her." He paused, a shadow flitting across his face. "She has not forgiven Arthur. I cannot blame her for that. But I do not serve her, or anyone. I am genuinely sorry for using you. For not being honest. I think if I had told you the truth—if I had been open—I think you would have chosen to help me."

"I would *never* have."

Mordred smiled, holding out the leaf. Guinevere did not take it. He let it drop to the ground. "We cannot know now, can we. But using you the way I did is the only thing I regret."

Mordred had betrayed Arthur. His own blood. His own king. He had helped build Camelot, and then he had defied them all and walked away. "The only thing? Really?"

"Well." Mordred shifted, leaning closer. "That, and that you did not come with me. I regret that every single moment of every single day. But that was not my choice to make." His eyes were the greenest thing in the forest, like the shade beneath an ancient tree, cool and secret and inviting. She did not have to wonder if his lips were as soft as they looked. She knew.

"Tell me," he said, "how did Arthur react when you told him I proved I mean you no harm, and when he found out I helped you in the forest?"

Guinevere flinched and Mordred's eyes widened, then narrowed slyly. "Ah. Tell me why you did not tell him."

She turned her back on him.

"If you will not tell me that, then tell me: What were you talking about when I found you before? Something about your dreams?"

Grateful she had already turned so he could not see her furious blush, Guinevere stomped back to the cart and the women. Lancelot was immediately at her side, eyes only on Mordred.

Ailith moved toward Guinevere. "Can you—can you really get me back into Camelot, like you told Rhoslyn? I want—there is a—"

Gunild joined Ailith, pulling her in for a fierce hug. "There is a stupid brother of mine that needs a woman foolish enough to love him. Are you sure?" They had all left lives behind in Camelot. And apparently some of them felt the loss more keenly than others.

Ailith nodded, the tears spilling down her face. "I was a child when I was banished. It was because of my mother, not because of me. I do not think anyone would recognize me or have reason to suspect me."

"Are you certain?" Rhoslyn said. "You know what you are giving up."

"I know." Ailith undid a necklace of smooth rocks knotted lovingly together. She passed it to Rhoslyn, pressing it into the older woman's hand. "Thank you. For everything."

Rhoslyn kissed Ailith's forehead. "Take care of yourself."

Gunild sniffled. "And take care of my stupid brother, and have lots of fat babies and name one after me. Name them all after me."

"Time to go," Mordred said. The camp had a few other horses, and they loaded the children into the cart and onto the horses where they could.

"Good luck," Guinevere said to Rhoslyn. She had not said goodbye to Mordred. She would not.

Rhoslyn smiled, the lines around her eyes both weary and kind.
"And to you, too." She turned and walked into the trees. Mordred
was the last to go. He shared one last, long look with Guinevere.
Almost as though he was waiting for something.

And part of her was tempted to run after him.

That was more terrifying than the attack had been. "Come on,"
she said, turning abruptly. "We have to go home."

Guinevere and Lancelot dropped Ailith off at the dock. The girl hurried into the city to find Gunild's brother, with a promise to check in
and let Guinevere know when she was settled and safe. Guinevere
could find her work in the castle kitchens.

"Perhaps we should leave Mordred out of our accounting of today's activities," Guinevere said.

Lancelot slowed, her emotional hesitation mirrored physically. "It
seems like something the king should know."

"That Mordred helped you? Protected a bunch of women who
are not citizens of Camelot, outside the boundaries of Camelot? Is
leaving to some island far away? We do not even know if he plans on
returning." Guinevere's heart sank as she said it. She had not considered it before. Had that been goodbye forever? She did not want it to
be. She hated that she did not want it to be, but she could not deny
it. "And we do not know where the island is, so if Arthur wanted to
hunt him down, he would have no more idea of Mordred's location
than he does right now."

"Are you protecting him?" Lancelot sounded hurt.

"He protected us!"

"*I* protected us!"

Guinevere stopped. They were near the castle gates. "Mordred is—complicated. It is all complicated. And if we tell Arthur, it will be even more complicated. There is no threat there. Mordred is gone. I do not think Arthur needs to know."

"How is it complicated?" Lancelot took one of Guinevere's hands and turned it palm up, then tugged Guinevere's sleeve, revealing the delicate white tracings of scars the trees had left. "He hurt you."

Guinevere yanked her hand back and pulled her sleeve down. "He did. And I have not forgotten, and will not forget. But there is more to it than that."

"There really is not, my queen." Lancelot motioned for the castle gate to be opened, then bowed stiffly. "Please alert me if you decide to leave the castle again today." Then she turned away and walked inside.

Frustrated and guilty for upsetting Lancelot, Guinevere slowly made her way up too many flights of stairs to her rooms. She could not stop thinking about what Mordred had told her. He *had* betrayed them, and hurt her. That much could never be taken back. But he also seemed convinced that if he had been honest with her, she would have chosen to help him.

She did not think so. But she did think she could have understood him. Maybe she could even have convinced him not to pursue that course. It made her sad, thinking that there was a sequence of events, of choices, that would have meant Mordred had stayed here. With her.

But with the memory of his kiss tingling on her lips whenever she thought of their few moments alone, she wondered if maybe that would have been the most disastrous path of all.

Rhoslyn had given her no answers to her Guinevach problem, but in a way, Mordred had.

Guinevere stopped only to speak with a page. She explained her plan to Brangien, who finagled a reason to make Isolde leave for the next two hours, then hid in the sitting room, ready. At last Guinevere had a plan. A knock on the door signaled the beginning of it.

"Come in," Guinevere said.

Guinevach stepped inside. She looked nervous. "You sent for me?"

"I did. Please, sit." Guinevere gestured to the chair across from her own. Guinevach settled into it, her pale-pink skirts draping around her like her beloved lilies. Guinevere pulled out the iron dagger that King Arthur had given her. She hated it, the way it seemed to trigger a ringing just outside her hearing. Guinevach's eyes widened and she stared in horror at the blade.

Guinevere held it tight. If Mordred had been honest, everything would have been different. Guinevere would be honest, and would drag honesty from Guinevach, too. She held out her free hand. "Give me your hand." Guinevach complied. "Now. It is time for only truth between us. Tell me: Why did you really come here, and why are you pretending to know me?"

CHAPTER THIRTY-SEVEN

Guinevach slumped in the chair, her perfect posture wilting like a lily in the summer heat. "Why am I *pretending* to know you? Because I do not know you."

Guinevere gripped the knife, triumphant, until Guinevach continued. "Not anymore. You are like a stranger to me now, and it breaks my heart." Guinevach dropped her head. Her voice trembled like her shoulders. Guinevere felt it all, the emotions that could not be lied, could not be faked. And she regretted *everything*.

"It is like—it is like our childhood never happened. I ran away to find you. I bribed the guards who brought me here with every last piece of my jewelry." She gestured to her crown of braids, her dress unadorned except for the elaborate lilies she had put there herself. "And when I got here, you left. Again. Just like before, when you got to leave and I had to stay in that castle, with him." Her voice turned to a snarl and when she looked up, her teary eyes were filled with rage. "You were always sad. You would cry and cry, and sometimes it was like you disappeared inside yourself. I felt so alone when that happened, but it was better than when you left. I begged father to send me to the convent after you, but he refused. I was his *spare*. I was the one he could keep around for decoration, because you were too precious. Too fragile. Too valuable. One daughter is a commodity. Two are just wasteful excess."

Guinevach leaned toward Guinevere, ignoring the knife, her jaw jutting out angrily as she chewed each word. "I hate you. You got away, and you did not take me with you, and you never came back for me. And when I got here, you told me to go home. Back to that place, back to our father. You swore—you *swore* you would come for me. Why did you break your promise?"

Guinevere let go of the knife and of Guinevach's hand. She had not been prepared for this. Not for any of this. There were no lies in this girl. Only incredible pain and hurt and desperate determination. "I—I could not."

"You *could not*? You married a king and still you could not? You left me there. Living in your shadow. Compared constantly with your beauty and your poise. To them, I am nothing but a pale imitation of you. Right down to my name: Guinevach." She cut the end of it off with a hard, sneering sound. "I thought you would be happy to see me. I thought you would explain why you never came back for me. And instead you treated me like a stranger, told me to leave. So I decided to prove to you that I am better than you, that I belong here, that the little sister you did not think was worth rescuing can be every bit the princess of that shithole Cameliard that you were. I thought if I was useful and clever and smart, if I planned your silly harvest festival, if I made your life better, that you would see I belonged. But you still did not care. So now I have been trying every-thing possible to get one of these knights to fall in love with me so I can marry and stay here."

"Guinevach, I—"

"No." Guinevach looked at Guinevere with a weary resignation that Guinevere knew all too well. This was a girl used to betrayal. Used to disappointment. A girl who had fought her way here, and would fight her way to the next thing, and the next, until finally she found a place where she could be free. "Do not try to make this better. You wanted the truth, there it is. Now tell *me* the truth. Why did you become a stranger? What did I do to make you hate me so?"

Guinevere covered her mouth with a trembling hand. The knife lay forgotten in her lap. The absolute cruelty of what she had inflicted on this poor girl took her breath away. Guinevere had stolen her real sister's place in this world, and, as if that were not enough, she had destroyed the only thing Guinevach had left of her sister: her memories of their bond. The real Guinevere might have gone back for her. Guinevere had no way of knowing. All she knew—all she could know—was that Merlin's choice for her to become Guinevere continued to ripple outward in waves of violence and pain and suffering. Just like all of Merlin's magic.

And Guinevere had done the damage herself, again. She had looked for a threat and lashed out with words and actions. She had watched a hurt, sad, scared girl try her hardest to belong, and had plotted how to destroy her.

"Oh, Lily," Guinevere said.

Guinevach startled at the name and looked up sharply, her eyes wide with pain, or hope. They were so often almost the same.

"I am so sorry. I am so very, very sorry." Guinevere stood and wrapped her arms around the sister the queen should have had. The sister the queen should have protected. Guinevere would do the same, forever, whatever it took. She had stolen the real Guinevere's place in this world, so she would accept her responsibilities, as well.

"You are never leaving," Guinevere whispered. "I will never send you back to Cameliard. I cannot excuse my behavior, or explain it other than to say that I was afraid. I was afraid that you coming here meant I would lose what I had. It was selfish and small and I am sorrier than I can say. Do not forgive me, but please trust me. You are safe here. You are home."

Guinevach collapsed against her, shaking with sobs, and Guinevere held her. The mystery of Guinevach was solved. Except the most important question: why an innocent girl who obviously loved her sister could look at a stranger and not recognize the deception.

"Do you remember anything special about these?" Guinevere gestured to the rings she had lined up on her table. She brushed and braided Guinevach's—Lily's—hair like Brangien had done for her so many times.

Lily smiled and pointed to a heavy silver ring with a pattern stamped into it. "Mother wore that one. I always tried to pull it off her finger. Sometimes she would let me. It was too big even for my thumb."

"Put it on."

Lily took the ring and slipped it onto her middle finger. "It finally fits."

"Good, because it is yours. Any of them are yours, if you want them."

"Why—why do you act like you do not remember things?" Lily asked, toying with the ring and not turning around.

Guinevere paused the brush midstroke. "Can I tell you something I have not told anyone else?"

"Of course." Lily turned at this, an eager expression on her face.

"You know when a leaf has fallen, dried and brittle? How you can crumble it in your hand and only a few bits are left, clinging to the strongest parts of the leaf?"

Lily nodded, frowning. "Yes."

"That is what my mind is like. I—something happened. At the convent. I lost who I was." Guinevere tried to feel her way through the words. She wanted to be as truthful as she could. Lily deserved as much. No. Lily deserved the truth. That her sister was dead, and she was speaking to a changeling. But that could never be said. And if Guinevere could not give Lily the truth, she would give her the most fiercely kind sister she could in exchange. "I woke up and it was as if all the pieces of my memory had crumbled and been blown away." That much was true, as well. When she had come to Camelot, she had not realized how empty her memories were and how odd that was. She had not realized that Merlin had pushed things in and other things out.

She wanted them back. She wanted them all back. And she wanted Lily to have her sister back, too. None of that would happen.

"Were you hit on the head?" Guinevach asked. "We had a stable boy who got kicked in the head by a horse and after that he could not speak anymore."

"Maybe. I—I remember looking up from a great depth, under water." Guinevere took a deep breath, trying to shake off the horror of the memory. It was her strongest one, and her most terrible one.

Lily frowned. "But you can swim. You taught me. You loved the water." At Guinevere's worried expression, Lily took her hand and patted it. Though Lily was two years younger, Guinevere could tell that she had been the stronger of the sisters. That came through in her touch. This poor girl, who came here for protection, was still determined to protect the woman she thought was her sister. Even after all of Guinevere's cruelty. "Never you mind about it. I can remind you who you were, whenever you forget. And if you get sad again, like you used to, I will be next to you until you find your way back to yourself."

"Thank you." Guinevere let Lily hug her. Brangien opened the door from the sitting room. She had peeked in a few times. She lifted an eyebrow in a silent question. Guinevere smiled.

"Well. If this is settled, I am going to retrieve Isolde." Brangien left the rooms.

"I do not think your maid likes me."

"She does not like anyone. Not at first. But she will come around."

"You know who I do like? Dindrane. She is so funny. A bit wicked, too."

"Oh, yes. That she is."

Lily's nose wrinkled. "Her husband is old, though."

Guinevere laughed. "Not so old."

"Most of the knights are too old."

"Too old for what?"

Lily blushed. She had already confessed her plan to get one of them to fall in love with her. It was mercenary of her, but Guinevere did not hold it against her.

"There is one knight who is not so old, who seems unable to form a complete sentence around you," Guinevere teased.

Lily's eyes widened as a pretty blush spread across her cheeks, beneath her freckles. What Guinevere had thought was artful before she now saw as sincerity. Lily was not good at hiding her emotions. "He is very sweet, is he not? Not so handsome as King Arthur, of course, or even Sir Tristan, but I like Sir Gawain's face."

"Ah, I did not even have to name Sir Gawain, you knew who I spoke of! Yes, he is very sweet, and good, and King Arthur values him. But you do not need to worry or rush. No one is taking you from Camelot. You can marry tomorrow or in twenty years or never."

Lily wiped under her eyes, then lifted her chin and corrected her posture. "Good. Because you need me. Your plans for the harvest festival were very boring before I got here."

"They were not!"

"Oh, they were so. Now turn around and let me do your hair."

Guinevere did as she was told. If encouraging Lily to love her was another deception, at least it was a kind one this time. For both of them.

CHAPTER THIRTY-EIGHT

"Do not say it," Guinevere growled, radiating menace.

Arthur pursed his lips, his face a picture of innocence. "Say what? That Guinevach is just a girl determined to force her sister to pay attention to her?"

Guinevere elbowed him in the side. "Yes, exactly that. And she prefers to be called Lily."

He laughed, scooting closer to her and putting his arm behind her. She leaned back to rest against it. They sat beneath a canopy, the rugs and cushions out of place in the middle of a field, but welcome. In front of them Lily was speaking with Sir Gawain, laughing more than Guinevere suspected was justified by whatever the young knight was saying. Everything was gold and blue. The fields midharvest, the cloudless sky, Lily's hair, Arthur's tunic. The entire scene was so lovely Guinevere wanted to cry for some reason she could not quite explain.

"Back to it." Arthur stood, stretching. He was wearing a simple tunic, no chain mail, no crown. All his knights wore the same. Today, they harvested alongside the people of Camelot.

Of course, there was a row of guards watching everything, and the canopy and the food and the cushions and the ladies waiting and watching, but that did not stop Arthur from threshing as skillfully as the hired men next to him and the landowner next to them. In the distance Guinevere could make out Lancelot's dark curls next to Sir Tristan's nearly shaved head. There had been no question that Lancelot should do the same work as the other knights, as opposed to staying behind with Guinevere.

It was good. It was better. Lancelot belonged with the knights.

With Sir Gawain following Arthur's lead back to the fields, Lily retired to the next canopied area and sat beside Dindrane. Their laughter was as bright as the day and just as golden. Guinevere tipped her head back and closed her eyes.

"Where is your maid?" Anna settled in next to her.

"She stayed at the castle with Isolde, my other maid." Brangien had no desire to sit outside and watch men work. Increasingly whenever possible, Brangien was staying at the castle or going on errands with Isolde. Guinevere respected their space and encouraged them to find a rhythm to their own lives. If she missed her friend, well, she was also happy for her. For both of them.

"Let me know if you need anything." Anna had a way of being present without demanding anything. It was soothing.

Snatches of conversation drifted over from Dindrane and Lily where they sat with the other knights' wives and a couple of their older daughters. Guinevere knew all of them, but the thought of walking over and making conversation was exhausting. She much preferred sitting here, feeling the breeze, enjoying being outside. The only thing that could improve it would be to be surrounded by trees instead of fields, but fields had their own sort of tempered beauty.

Eventually the section of field was cleared. Arthur, wholesomely sweaty and flushed with happiness, rejoined Guinevere to eat and drink, until, as all outings eventually did, it turned into a wrestling and sparring match between the knights. Lily laughed and shouted encouragement to Sir Gawain, who was facing off against Lancelot and therefore had not a prayer of success. Arthur and Sir Tristan were dueling with long stalks of wheat. Dindrane had Sir Bors at her side, leaning close to him and whispering something that was turning Sir Bors a deep red beneath his bushy mustache.

"Sometimes I wonder," Anna said, staring into the distance, "if I walked until I hit the forest and then kept walking and never looked back, would anything change?"

"What?" Guinevere turned toward her.

Anna sat deep in the shade, beneath the canopy's center. She kept her eyes focused on the horizon. "If I left. If I decided the trappings of this life were not for me. What would change if I removed myself from being Anna, lady's maid?"

Guinevere was confused and a little unnerved by this topic. It did not seem to fit the general mood of the day. "Do you wish to go back to Cameliard?"

"Oh, no. Wretched city. No, I would not go back to anywhere. I would just walk until I found a place that felt true to me."

"But if you left, people would miss you. Lily would miss you."

"I am replaceable. Your sister, dear thing, will love anyone who is kind to her, and is loving enough she should be able to find kindness here."

"But would you not miss her? Or your friends?" Surely Anna had friends in the castle by now. She was warm and friendly, easy to talk to. Usually. Guinevere felt this conversation like an itch between her shoulder blades that she could not reach.

Anna frowned, tilting her head in consideration. "For a while, perhaps. But when I think through the consequences, there are not many. At most, it would inconvenience a few people. At least, they would barely notice. And if I can remove myself from my life here with the merest ripple, do I truly belong? Do I have a reason for being here? Is Anna of Camelot really who I want to be for the rest of my life?"

Guinevere wanted to argue with her. Needed to, almost desperately, and she could not understand why the idea of Anna getting up and walking away from her entire life here made *Guinevere* feel panic, until she realized it was because everything Anna was saying, everything she had described . . . Guinevere realized it could apply to her, as well.

If she had followed Mordred into the trees, what would have happened?

She felt the pieces settling in her mind, the path that Arthur and Lily and Lancelot and Brangien and Camelot as a whole would have taken, and she yanked her mind from that brink before she could follow the lines of thought to their conclusion.

She stood, feeling like she did not quite fit in her own skin, like she needed to move or she would come apart at the seams.

Anna looked up at her with concern. "Can I get you something, my queen?"

Arthur was with his men. Lancelot, too. Guinevere could not interrupt Arthur, or pull Lancelot away from belonging. Dindrane and Sir Bors were slipping away, hand in hand. Lily and Sir Gawain were standing scandalously close in conversation. She did not know or love the other women and was not loved by any of them. There was nowhere for her to go, no one for her to seek refuge in.

"No, I need nothing," Guinevere said, the day still brilliant in gold and blue all around her, everything a part of that, everything belonging.

She looked down. She was wearing green.

Guinevere nodded in approval of the placement of Arthur's sun crest flag. The flags had been staked around the perimeter of the festival, a reminder of whose leadership made both this record harvest and the festival to celebrate it possible.

"You have been very involved this time," Brangien said, arm in arm with Isolde. Isolde would return to the castle before the festival began—she had no desire to be in a crowd—but she was enjoying walking around in the pre-bustle. Preparations had begun before dawn and would go until late afternoon, when the festival started. The celebration would last all night and into the next day.

"What do you mean?" Guinevere asked.

"Planning Lancelot's tournament seemed like torture for you. But I have barely seen you, you have been so busy with this. And you were willing to make the trip across the lake twice in one day to be here this morning before returning in the afternoon!"

"It has to be perfect." Guinevere squinted down the line of booths and rising tents. The air was filled with the sounds of hammers and shouting and laughter, nothing compared with how loud it would become.

"It has to have food and drink and no one will complain." Brangien eyed a cart trundling past filled with apples and dried fruit. "You should declare that we have to sample all the food before it can be approved. . . ."

Isolde laughed and Guinevere joined in, just a second too late. It was true that she had thrown herself into planning the festival, filling every hour of the past two weeks with the details, meeting with merchants and farmers, helping direct the filling of the silos and granaries, and otherwise making certain that there was never any space in her mind for quiet.

For thinking.

For doubting.

She hated to take any of Merlin's advice, but in their last conversation in that blank dreamspace where she had met him, he had told her to fight like a queen.

She had forced herself to remain as a nebulous in-between. Not queen, not *not*-queen. She could not keep standing in both worlds. Her life since returning from Maleagant and the Dark Queen had been nothing but waiting, suspecting, searching. Hurting. She had to choose what she had already chosen. It did not seem fair that a choice would demand she keep choosing it, over and over. But she would. She had to be the Guinevere she claimed to be. The Guinevere whose life she had claimed. She owed it to everyone.

She glanced back at where Lancelot stood, giving them a polite distance. No longer right at her side. It hurt. But it was for the best.

"Guinevere!" Lily rushed toward her, golden braids streaming behind her. She wore blue and pink and the ring Guinevere had given her. The ring that should always have been hers. "There will be jugglers and actors! Plays all evening! We got the same players from the theater in Camelot. Oh, they are wonderful. It will be hard to go anywhere else. But I am excited to see Sir Gawain try to catch a chicken." She giggled, wrinkling her nose. That had been one of her ideas: setting cross chickens loose in a pen with knights competing against chicken maids to see who could catch the most chickens the fastest.

A man with light hair and the thick, powerful build of someone who had labored all his life stopped near them. His hands were an angry, splotchy red, perhaps from the work he was doing spreading rushes on the ground where it was muddiest. The rushes would help, though the entire festival was hardly tidy. There was so much activity. With the harvest complete, all the extra workers who had hired themselves to landowners were here for one last job before returning to the various places they had come from or settling in Camelot for the winter.

"I am glad you are here," Guinevere said.

"Me too!" Lily embraced her, kissing her cheek. "I love having my sister back."

Guinevere could not bring herself to answer. Fortunately, Brangien saved her by tugging on her arm. "Come, we need enough time to prepare you."

Guinevere almost relished the terror of the lake crossing. It was nice to be overwhelmed by something so contained, so specific, so familiar. She understood the contours of that fear, her physical reaction to it. Brangien held one hand and Isolde the other. They were not as comforting as Lancelot or Arthur, but it was enough.

At the dock someone called Guinevere's name. She turned to see Ailith, arm in arm with a young man who had the same stocky build as Gunild. Ailith beamed and waved, and Guinevere smiled in return. She had not done *everything* wrong these past few weeks. She wondered if, somewhere, Mordred was arm in arm with Gunild. The thought made something curdle in her stomach. Which made her angry that she would feel that way.

She would focus on the festival. The festival, and then whatever came next for Queen Guinevere.

At the castle Isolde and Brangien combed and plaited her hair, weaving it with bright-yellow thread. Guinevere's dress was yellow, with Arthur's sun, gorgeously embroidered in silver by Isolde, in the center. The evenings were chilly now, so she wore a pale-blue cloak. Brangien pulled out several small pots.

"Lily taught me a few new things." Brangien frowned in concentration as she spread a reddish substance on Guinevere's cheeks and lips and then an ashy black powder along her top and bottom eyelashes. Guinevere blinked back tears of irritation, but after a few moments it passed.

Isolde gasped, putting a hand over her mouth. "Oh, my queen. You look beautiful."

Guinevere smiled ruefully. "Well, if I am anywhere near as pretty as my two lady's maids, I am pleased." She had something for Lily, as well: two smooth rocks that Guinevere had used blood magic to knot a spell of connection. Because it was Guinevere's own blood that had fed the iron knots at the doorway, this blood magic should last past the thresholds. If she had one rock and Lily the other, she would always be able to sense how close Lily was. She would not be able to explain the gift to Lily, of course, other than pretending they were pretty rocks, but it was a small protection. A way of making up for what she had done.

All that was left to do was put on the jeweled circlet Arthur had given her before Lancelot's tournament. But something about it did not feel quite right. Whether Guinevere associated it with that night and everything that had happened between Mordred kissing her and Maleagant abducting her, or whether it was simply too ornate and decorative compared with what the king wore, she could not say. She hesitated, her fingers hovering over the piece.

There was a knock at the door. Brangien opened it and then bowed. Arthur stood there with his hands behind his back, resplendent in a blue tunic over a white shirt. His cloak, pushed back from his broad shoulders, was yellow, an inversion of the colors Guinevere wore. Guinevere glanced at Brangien, and Brangien's satisfied smile was enough to prove that she had planned the coordination herself.

He really was handsome, this king of hers. Like a hand as steady and patient as the Lady of the Lake's had carved him in addition to Camelot. Every line of his face was precise, every angle strong, except his eyes, which were always kind.

"Almost ready," Guinevere said.

"I have just what you need." Arthur pulled his hands from behind his back, presenting something shiny with a flourish. Guinevere stared at the silver crown. It was a better match to his, though hers was more elegant. Instead of a simple circle, it had delicate points at precise intervals. But it was still crafted in the same spirit as his. Direct. Strong. Unadorned save the metal itself.

"May I?" he asked. She tipped her head and he slipped the crown into place. It fit perfectly on the circle of braids Brangien had plaited around Guinevere's head.

"How do I look?" Guinevere asked, surprised at how nervous she both sounded and felt. She wished she could see herself, wished she could tell whether or not the crown looked like she deserved it.

"Like my Guinevere," Arthur said, reminding her of their conversation. If she did not know who she was, at least Arthur knew who she was to him. And he saw it when he looked at her.

He offered his elbow and she took it. With the first step, the crown slipped slightly to the left. Brangien commanded them to stop and pinned it in place.

Not quite a perfect fit after all.

CHAPTER THIRTY-NINE

Guinevere shrieked, ducking as a burst of flame scorched the air around them.

Lily laughed and clapped. The man bowed, sweeping his small torch to the side with flair. How he managed to breathe fire, Guinevere did not know, but it reminded her with a pang of the dragon. She hoped it had found somewhere beautiful to rest before burrowing into the earth alone.

"Come on." She tugged Lily's arm. They passed a juggler throwing knives, minstrels singing a song about plowing and planting that Guinevere was pretty sure was actually about something else entirely, and a puppet show. That one made her pause. There had been a puppet show telling the story of Arthur's life the day she first met him. It had left out so much, in part because it tried to edit out the role of magic but also because Guinevere suspected most people did not know much of anything that had really happened. They never did.

"Come, I do not want to miss Sir Gawain!" Lily pulled her along. There were so many people at the festival that not even Guinevere's crown could cut a path for them. The noise was unrelenting, shrieks and laughter and talking. The scent of roasted meat clung to everything, along with a dozen other smells. It was even bigger than the tournament celebration had been, twice as large as any market day. Wine and food and happy faces wherever Guinevere turned.

So *many* faces. Lancelot followed closely, keeping a watchful eye. She would take no chances this time. While Maleagant was gone forever, Guinevere had had more than enough of being abducted for an entire lifetime. But she had checked the night before, pushing out and sensing for magic nearby, and had found nothing. Tonight, there was only Camelot.

And Camelot was happy. And Camelot was drunk.

Guinevere turned to look at Lancelot. "Will you participate in any of the games?"

"If my queen wishes it." Lancelot's tone was cold.

Guinevere tried to stop, but the momentum of the crowd pulled them along. She wanted to speak with Lancelot, to tell Lancelot that she missed their closeness. But she owed to it Lancelot to be strong. To give her the space to be the knight she was. The best knight in the land.

They arrived at what would have been the field for a tournament. It had been divided into sections. Nearest them was a line of cows. Women were filling buckets with such speed Guinevere could not believe it. Lily pulled her right along, though Guinevere would have liked to stay and pat the cows on their sweet noses. The sound of wood being chopped echoed around the space, along with that of a crowd cheering on various contenders.

"There he is!" Lily squealed, and rushed forward. In a fenced section a chicken was running madly, chased by Sir Gawain.

"Go for the legs!" Lily shouted. Sir Gawain dove, narrowly missing the legs and getting a face full of feathers for his efforts. He laughed and tried again, with Lily giving useless advice. Guinevere doubted Lily had ever so much as touched a chicken, but it made her happy to see the girl so involved and delighted.

Guinevere had not had a chance to give Lily her gift. It was probably better to wait until they could speak someplace calm and quiet. Guinevere turned her back on Lily and Sir Gawain and looked for Arthur. They had been separated early on when Lily wanted to explore.

Sir Tristan was watching the woodcutting competition. Guinevere waved to him, but he did not notice, all his attention on the competitors. A man in the center of the contestants had taken off his shirt. His back rippled with his efficient, powerful motions. Guinevere felt a flutter low in her stomach watching him. There was something she loved about the broad span of his shoulders and the trim point of his waist.

"Oh, that is Arthur," she said, putting a hand against her stomach and the giddy surge she had felt there. She felt almost guilty for being attracted to him *before* she had known it was him. But she did not stop watching him.

Lily turned to see what Guinevere was watching, and her cheeks pinkened as she realized what she was seeing. "He is almost naked."

"Yes." It was the most undressed Guinevere had ever seen him. And the rest of the kingdom was seeing it, as well, which felt unfair. Would she always have to share him? Her crown slipped and she reached up to push it back in place.

Anna weaved her way through the crowd, holding two cups. She handed one to Lily and the other to Guinevere. "Spiced wine!" she shouted over the noise. "I hate everything here except this."

Guinevere laughed, grateful for the distraction. She glanced at Lily, but Lily was not going to abandon Sir Gawain. It looked like he would be chasing that chicken for a long time.

"Come, I know a quieter spot where we can rest for a bit," Guinevere said. She did not want to keep watching Arthur. Or she *did,* but not in public. And she did not like the idea of being watched as she watched him. She sipped her drink as they walked. It was not hot, but something in the wine made warmth travel all the way down her throat and into her stomach. It was odd, but not unpleasant.

Behind the field and past several rows of market stalls was a space where farmers could bring extra produce for sale. Behind that was a section for showing animals for purchase or trade. Anna found a bench of rough-hewn wood and they sat. Anna, always busy, pulled some sewing out of the pouch she wore at her waist. It was a far larger pouch than the discreet one Guinevere had tucked under her belt.

Lancelot stayed several paces away, out of earshot. Guinevere drained her cup. She wished she were running through the festival, drinking and dancing and laughing, with Lancelot on one side and Arthur on the other. That their roles were not so set. She knew it was necessary, but it was also unfair.

"You seem unhappy." Anna set down her sewing and turned her full attention to Guinevere.

"No, I am very happy."

"Yes, people who are very happy always insist they are very happy with a tone that aggressive."

Guinevere tried to laugh, but ended up sighing. "I have been thinking, and—"

"My queen!" Ailith bounded toward her, happiness in every step. "I bought a chicken!" She held up the creature by its ankles. It seemed resigned to its upside-down state, staring at Guinevere with round, blank eyes.

"So you did! Congratulations!" Guinevere's whole body felt warm, as though she had bathed in the wine. But that made no sense. She would never bathe, and certainly not in wine. She cleaned herself with fire like a civilized person. Like a civilized witch. She was neither of those things. She squinted as her thoughts became as round and unblinking as the eyes of that chicken.

"Thank you! I— Oh, hello, Morgana! I did not know you were in Camelot now, too! The queen is very forgiving." Ailith beamed at Guinevere, then waved goodbye, running toward Gunild's waiting brother.

"Morgana?" Guinevere turned toward Anna. "Why did she call you—"

Anna had a knife pressed against Guinevere's side. It was hidden by the angle of their bodies so that Lancelot could not see it when she glanced at them. "I prefer it to Morgan le Fay, but I have so many names these days. I did not expect to see one of Rhoslyn's girls here. No matter. I am nearly finished with Camelot anyway."

"You are—you are bad." Guinevere's tongue felt thick and unwieldy.

"Am I? Hmm. Tell me, dear, what are you really?"

"Changeling," Guinevere said, then frowned. She wiped her mouth as though that would take away what she had said.

With her free hand, Anna patted Guinevere's knee in a comforting gesture. "I made your wine special. Mordred tells me you work mostly with knots. I prefer potions myself. What do you mean, a changeling?"

"I am not Guinevere. She died. Poor Guinevere. Do you think she would have liked it here?" Guinevere tried to be concerned about what she was saying, or about the fact that she was saying it to Morgan le Fay, but everything was so warm and sleepy in a way that made it impossible to care too much. The patch of dirt in front of them looked as inviting as her bed. She could imagine curling up in it, going to sleep.

"You are not Guinevere?"

"No. Why am I telling you this? Merlin is my father. Or he is not. It seems like he is not, but I remember that he is? Or he told me he is. I have maybe four memories of him as my father?" Guinevere held up her fingers, squinting at them, trying to count whether she was in fact holding up four. "The cabin. Sweeping. The falcon who brought us food. And . . . three? Is it only three? Lessons! That is four. Do I really remember any of them, though? I think the Lady of the Lake is my mother, though. I have dreams. About her. But I am also frightened of her. And water. Water." Guinevere shuddered.

"What has he done to you, you poor child?" Anna took Guinevere by the chin, turning her head so they were face to face and so Lancelot could not see Guinevere's expressions. "Listen to me. You are Guinevere."

"No. I lived in the forest before this. I like the forest."

"Yes, the forest is nice, but that was not your home. I searched Guinevach for any evidence of magic. No one has touched her or her mind. And she loves her sister more than anything. She would never be fooled by a changeling. Whoever else you are—whatever else you are—you are Guinevere. Or you *were*."

"I am not." Guinevere wished Morgan le Fay would stop saying that. It was mean. "I had another name. I gave it away to the fire so I would not say it. Did you send me to see Mordred on purpose? In the forest?"

Morgan le Fay smiled. "Well, I certainly pushed you in that direction. I was surprised you did not put it together. I was hardly subtle in my advice to make you visit Rhoslyn. He misses you. I thought— I hoped—it would have a different outcome. But you have changed the subject. What was your other name?"

"I do not have it anymore." Guinevere shook her head. "It is very sad. I am sad. Are you here to kill Arthur?" She should signal to Lancelot, but Lancelot was so far away and the knife was still pressed against her side and none of it felt urgent at all. Something bleated mournfully nearby. She liked things that bleated.

"Why would I kill him?" Morgan le Fay asked.

"You tried to when he was a baby."

"Ah, yes. That story. That is what happens when men tell your stories. Would you like to hear the real story?"

Guinevere shook her head. "The real stories are always worse."

"Yes. They are. I am going to tell you anyway." Morgan le Fay leaned close, her voice low and melodic as she rewrote everything Guinevere knew.

The Enchantress Morgan le Fay

Morgana was not married. It was a problem, and an increasingly hard-to-hide one, as her stomach swelled with the life inside.

Lady Igraine asked who the father was, but Morgana could not answer. Not because she did not wish to, but because she physically could not. When she thought of him—her love, her only—he was moonlight and the new green of budding leaves. He was the scent of crushed grass beneath two bodies. He was the first warm breeze after the icy grip of winter.

He was fairy, and things of fairy could not be named or explained in a way that would reassure a mother her daughter was not ruined forever.

Igraine loved her daughter as fiercely and loyally as she loved her husband. She knew what their world would do to her, to the baby. And so, out of love, she sent Morgana away. Up to the north, where no one knew her, where a baby could be born in secrecy and eventually brought back with a story of a foreign husband and fresh widowhood. It was the only way Igraine could protect her child and her grandchild, and so she wept as she watched Morgana ride away.

But Morgana did not go where she was supposed to. She went into the woods, the deepest woods, the darkest woods, the ones without men and their rules and their judgments. And her love found her there and held her. And the fairy queen who created him found them there and watched, curious, as Morgana gave birth to a beautiful baby boy who was almost human.

One mother protected Morgana until she gave birth, and the other protected her after. The Dark Queen loved this wild and determined young woman, even if she did not understand her. She had little use for humans—when she noticed them, it was usually bad for them—but Morgana and the baby amused her. And her creation, the one men would come to call the Green Knight, loved Morgana and his son in the only ways he could. Fits and starts, lavishing of attention and wonder and then forgetful stretches where they did not see or hear from him for months at a time, nearly starving in their shelter in the woods. The joy of spring and summer followed by the slow decline of autumn and the cruel indifference of winter.

Morgana could have stayed there forever but for the child. Mordred was a sweet infant who grew into a clever child. If he was going to be as smart and strong as he needed to be, he would have to learn about their enemies. About how to survive in a dangerous place filled with death and treachery. He would need to know humans.

Morgana knew her mother would take them back. And Morgana's lover would always be with her on the scent of spring, in the lazy droning of insects on infinite summer afternoons, winking at her with butterfly wings.

The Dark Queen met them at the borders of the forest.
Where are you going? *she said in her voice that was not a*
voice so much as a dream experienced while waking.

Morgana told the truth. They were returning to her mother
so that Mordred could be raised as a human.

You are too late.

Morgana had not idled away her time among the fairies.
She had given birth to a boy partly of their world, eaten their
food, sampled their wine. She had been opened to magic in a
way no human before her was. Seized with terror at the Dark
Queen's words, Morgana used her newfound power to pierce
time and distance. To see what had happened, and what was to
come. She saw it all. She wished she had not.

Merlin plotting with Uther Pendragon. Her mother, her
beautiful mother, her kind mother who loved fiercely, tricked.
Used. There would be a baby. Her own half brother. And then
she saw—

The wizard.

The wizard.

The wizard.

Morgana could not see past the wizard. Everywhere she
searched for her mother's future, for the coming baby's future,
she saw only Merlin. She screamed, unable to stop seeing him,
realizing she could not find her mother, Igraine, in the future,
because there was no future for her beyond this. Sobbing,
tearing at her face, she looked instead for the baby. For her half
brother.

And still she saw Merlin. He was like a fog, settling over
everything. She could not pierce it.

She would not allow the wizard to have that baby. Not after
everything else he had taken. Morgana ripped power from the

fairy world around her. Even the Dark Queen shied from the rage she wore like a crown as she left the forest, a child on her hip and a baby her goal.

But Morgana was too late. By the time she arrived home, her mother was dead and the baby had been stolen. She tried everything to find him, but the wizard blocked every attempt, as she had already seen that he would. He had taken her mother, and then taken everything that was left behind.

The wizard had brought Arthur into being and then made certain he had only one path to choose from. One destiny, predetermined. No family to protect him, to let him grow as he chose, to let him find his own way in the world.

Morgana looked at her own precious child and wept, holding him close, swearing to him that he could be whoever he wished. That he would be raised among both humans and fairies, live a life of whatever wonder he could find.

But even that was a lie. Because Merlin chose Arthur's path, and Arthur's path led him to Mordred. Mordred had seen how his mother mourned and suffered. How ephemeral and fickle the affections of his father and grandmother were. He wanted to know his human family, to see if there was a way for him to save Arthur from the wizard's rule, to alter his course. And so Mordred had to watch as Arthur unmade the Green Knight. He had to watch as they chased down the body of the Dark Queen and hacked it into pieces. He had to watch as Arthur systematically hunted and destroyed the magical things in the world that had led to both of their births.

And Morgana had seen it all. Had always known what was coming, and had always been unable to prevent any of it. She had not even been able to choose her own part in the story. Merlin had written it for her, creating her as a villain for her own half brother so that she could never bridge their divide and offer him what Merlin had stolen:

A family.

And that was the great tragedy of Morgana, Morgan le Fay, the sorceress. Magic and power and vision, and still she was unable to save her mother, her lover, her brother, or her son from the destinies Merlin decided they would have. Nothing she saw or did changed Merlin's plans.

Until a girl arrived in Camelot with secrets knotted into her very being.

CHAPTER FORTY

"But—but that is not—it cannot be true." Guinevere's fingers were cold and her toes beginning to tingle. Some part of her was coming back, starting to raise the alarm that should always have been there with a knife at her side and Morgana murmuring in her ear.

"Has the wizard *ever* told you the truth?"

Guinevere could not say that he had.

Morgana sighed. "I really did like helping your sister. I am glad she is out of your father's clutches and safe here. But mostly I wanted to meet you. To see for myself the girl who brought back the Dark Queen and undid Merlin's destruction. Mordred thinks you are something special. Something new." Morgana frowned, pressing her forehead against Guinevere's in an embrace. "But we are always special. We are always new. Until they manage to destroy us."

Guinevere's hands had enough sense to reach into the small pouch at her waist, pull out the rock intended for Lily, and slip it into Morgana's own pouch.

Unaware of what had happened, Morgana moved the knife from Guinevere and stood. She clasped Guinevere's hand, her grip as tight as a chain. "Poor Arthur never had another choice but to become this. I can save you still. Come, we will—" She froze, then shifted so her back was to Lancelot. Guinevere glanced in that direction. Arthur was striding toward them, smiling easily, his hand on the hilt of Excalibur. Morgana leaned down and whispered, her voice harsh with haste. "Do not let the wizard erase every other Guinevere you could have been. If you want to learn the truth, I might be able to help. The offer will be there, whenever you are ready." She turned, then paused at the sight of Guinevere's stricken expression. "My sweet, foolish boys. My stolen brother and my tragic son. You may yet be the death of them both."

With a whisper of skirts, Morgana walked away into the soft purple of evening, vanishing between tents.

Arthur was still talking to Lancelot. Guinevere wanted to call out to him. To warn him. But Morgana was heading in the other direction. And if what she had said was true—if any of it was true—did Guinevere want Arthur to catch her? He was convinced she was Morgan le Fay, the villain out of Merlin's stories. Would he listen to her?

Should he listen to her?

Dazed, Guinevere did not know how much time had passed before Arthur reached the bench and crouched in front of her. "That was the most fun I have— Guinevere? What is wrong?"

She had to tell him. This was not Mordred in a faraway forest. This was a sorceress in Camelot. "Morgana," Guinevere gasped, still not in full control of her body or her mind. "That was Morgana. She was here."

Arthur stood, his happy ease replaced with steel-like tension and resolve. "Sir Lancelot!" Arthur pointed at Guinevere and then sprinted in the direction Morgana had disappeared. Guinevere did not want him to go alone, but he had Excalibur. He was better off without her.

Lancelot rushed to Guinevere's side, hand on her sword, staring after Arthur in confusion.

"Get the other knights," Guinevere said. "Follow him. Anna is Morgan le Fay. I will light anyone on fire who touches me. Your king needs you right now."

After only a moment's hesitation, Lancelot ran. Guinevere did not know how long she stayed frozen on that bench, but night had fully settled around her before someone broke her horrified reverie.

"There you are!" Dindrane and Lily approached, arm in arm, laughing. Dindrane sat next to her. "You found the worst-smelling place in the entire festival to rest. But I am happy to see you managed to keep yourself from being captured by enemies this time."

Guinevere burst into tears.

Dindrane looked at Lily, at a loss for why Guinevere had reacted the way she did. "I—I am sorry, it was a joke. I said it in jest. I did not mean—"

"It is not that," Guinevere squeezed out, her throat tight with pain and sorrow. She imagined Arthur catching up to Morgana. Drawing his sword. Killing her. She imagined Morgana, vengeance and fire in her eyes as the sorceress Morgan le Fay, killing him.

But if Morgana had wanted Arthur dead, he already would be. They all would be. She had been living in the castle for weeks now. There was poison. A dagger in the side. A quick push off the soaring stairways. All that time Guinevere had suspected Lily when the real threat was sitting in the corner, quietly helping.

None of it made sense. Or maybe it was as simple as Morgana had told her. A woman, plagued by loss, hopeful that someone else could break the cycle created by Merlin.

She pulled her own rock out of the pouch and clutched it. If Morgana were still near, it would have been hot. Instead, it was cooling. Morgana was getting farther away, and quickly.

Lancelot rejoined them, barely out of breath. "They are all with Arthur." She did not have to say who was, or why she was not. "We should get you back to the castle."

"What is wrong?" Lily asked.

"Nothing," Guinevere said, before Lancelot could answer. "I am tired is all. I want to go to bed."

Dindrane curtsied and bade them good-night, unwilling to abandon the party, but Lily stayed.

"I will escort you." Lily grasped Guinevere's hand, helping her up and drawing her close, an arm around Guinevere's waist both for support and comfort. There was something familiar and practiced about the movement that made Guinevere think Lily had done the same thing with her sister many times before.

It was a full moon, and with the cloudless night it was bright enough to cast shadows. The revelries had not calmed down; if anything, they were ramping up. Thankfully, Lancelot skirted the edges of the festival, keeping them out of the crowds. All the things Morgana had told Guinevere spun in her mind as they walked. Could she believe any of what Morgana had said? Should she believe all of it? Where was Arthur? What was he doing? The rock continued to cool. Guinevere clutched it so hard her fingers ached.

Lily looked around crossly. "Anna was supposed to stay with you."

"She is gone. She left."

"Back to the castle?"

"I hope not." But if so, Guinevere would feel it as they got closer. She did not know how to explain it to Lily. And she was afraid this new loss would hurt her poor sister. Whatever Morgana was, Anna had been a loyal companion and protector to Lily. "Anna was not— she is not—if you see her again, tell me or a knight immediately."

"Why?"

"It is complicated. I will explain later. She is not allowed to be in Camelot."

Lily sighed. "It is the magic, right?"

"You knew she was doing magic?"

"Well, there was a bit of it, here and there." Lily shrugged. "I never told Father because I knew he would make her leave. And when we found out Camelot had banished all magic, I did not tell you because I did not want her to go. I will miss her. But she said she would have to go home sooner or later. I had hoped for later."

"Did she ever tell you about herself?"

"Only that she was a widow and had a son a few years older than me. She worried about him a lot."

Lancelot led them through the night. Even in the darkness Guinevere could feel the intensity of Lancelot's watchfulness as she scoured the night for a sorceress. But Guinevere did not think Morgana was anywhere near. Even Morgana would not want to face Excalibur.

Was it wrong that she hoped Morgana got away?

"Oh!" Lily stumbled, bouncing off a man who had appeared in their path. "Pardon me!"

The man stood there, a looming bulk in the darkness. Then he tipped his head and stepped out of their way. Lancelot spun toward him, but the man did not move or do anything threatening. Everything felt menacing now, though. They walked on toward the ferry, which was packed, mostly with families trying to get back to their homes for the evening. Children were crying or screaming in tantrums or already asleep in their parents' arms. Guinevere and Lily were pushed into the middle, Lancelot at Guinevere's side.

Guinevere leaned close, grabbing Lancelot's arm so she would bend her head. "You will have to alert the guard as soon as we arrive, and lead a search of the castle, to be safe. I think Morgana is gone, but we have to be certain she does not get back in." The rock was cold to the touch and not warming as they neared the city.

Lancelot's voice trembled with rage. "I was standing *right there.*"

"I am sorry. I could not call to you. She had a knife, and I was under—"

"I am not angry with *you.*" But her tone still made Guinevere flinch. They reached the docks at Camelot and rushed off the ferry in the midst of the press of people. Lily kept Guinevere close as they trekked up the long hill toward the castle.

Lancelot may as well have prowled in circles around them, her unease and desperation to do something about what she had learned palpable.

The rock was cold. Still, Lancelot held up one hand to keep Guinevere and Lily there until she had spoken with the guards at the gate to make certain that Morgana had not been back. Only when they confirmed it—as well as confirming that a guard was already on duty outside Guinevere's rooms—did Lancelot allow Guinevere and Lily by. She stayed at the gate, giving instructions for the castle search and waiting for pages, who would convey the message about *Anna* to every guard in the castle and run it back to the festival.

Guinevere and Lily took one of the side stairways that wound around the outside of the castle, since it was a more direct route to their floors. The moon was so bright they could see each step clearly. Everything was cold light or black shadow. They paused on the landing that led to Guinevere's and Arthur's rooms. Guinevere was not ready to be alone, though. Or to be with Brangien and Isolde, breaking up whatever private time they were having by bringing her problems with her.

Although Morgan le Fay showing up was everyone's problem, it felt personal in a way that was hard to articulate. If Morgana was to be believed, her masquerade as Anna had been about Guinevere alone. It was Guinevere she had spoken to, Guinevere she had been intending to leave with. Anna had never made an effort to speak to Arthur. Guinevere could not recall a single conversation between them, or Anna reacting oddly or intensely when Arthur was around. Her focus had always been on getting close to Guinevere.

"Guinevere?" Lily prodded. They had stopped, but Guinevere made no move toward the door.

"Can we go to your rooms?" Guinevere turned toward another set of stairs that wound behind a curve and up to the next flight. She wished she had not blocked the interior stairway between their rooms, but she would have that undone tomorrow. Though in retrospect, knowing who Anna was, it had probably been wise.

Guinevere's head pounded ferociously, probably due to an aftereffect of the potion. Lily led her up the stairs and opened the door to the sixth floor.

A man stood in the hallway. He wore the livery of a page, but it fit him poorly. Though there was only one torch lit, there was something familiar about him. His fists clenched. They were bright red and splotchy, but not from spreading rushes, as Guinevere had assumed when she saw him earlier. They were burns, not yet healed. Something about his shape made her positive he had been the one to bump into them earlier, as well.

She stepped forward, putting an arm out to block Lily. She pushed Lily back toward the door. "I think we are in the wrong place."

The man did not smile. Now that she really studied him, she knew his face. It had been obscured by a beard before, but it was familiar. "Your sister?" He nodded toward Lily.

"No, my lady's maid. Can I help you?"

He shook his head, pointing one shiny, burned finger at Lily. "Your sister. I heard. I had sister. Hild. I no longer have sister. *You* no longer have sister."

Guinevere could not catch her breath from the blow of pain his words delivered. Hild. Hild was dead. She had killed poor Hild, who had just been trying to help her brothers. Who had never done her harm. Guinevere had saved herself and flung out damage and death in her wake. "I am—I am so sorry. I never meant for her to be hurt."

The man clenched his fists again and stalked toward them.

"Run!" Guinevere pushed Lily. Lily, panicked, turned right instead of left, going farther up the stairs. Before Guinevere could correct her, Hild's brother was behind them, blocking their retreat to the fifth floor, where a guard was waiting. Just out of reach.

Lily lifted her skirts, taking the stairs two at a time. Their ascent was too swift, dangerous even during the day and doubly so in the dark. Guinevere knew they did not stand a chance if they faced him. She doubted she could even use magic fast enough to prevent him from hurting Lily.

Her choices had destroyed Hild; now they might kill Lily, too. She had taken this man's sister, and still he had not made enough of an impression on her for her to remember his name.

"Right!" she shouted. Lily pivoted toward a branching set of stairs. These floors were unguarded. Every servant in the castle was at the festival. There was no help. There was only a hope—a desperate hope—that Guinevere knew something about the castle this man did not. That even she herself did not *know,* except for the time she saw it in a dream. "Left!"

Lily was breathing hard, and so was Guinevere. She could hear the man's steady progress behind them. Hild's brother did not need to rush. There were only so many flights of stairs left, only a handful of doors they could use. There was nowhere to hide.

They passed Mordred's alcove and went around a sharp corner. This flight of stairs led only to a series of decorative columns. Guinevere glanced over her shoulder. The corner had cut them off from their pursuer's view, but not for long. The end of the delicately col-umned platform dropped off into empty air. The last column, carved like a tree, jutted over the edge.

"Behind there!" Guinevere pointed to the edge.

"What?" Lily looked at her, confused and terrified.

"There is a secret chamber. Be careful! Do not fall in!" She grabbed Lily's hand and half threw her around the column. Lily scrambled for a grip, and Guinevere had a moment of horror that she was wrong. That her dream had been wrong. That it had been just a dream after all, and there was nothing back there but more rock. Lily would die.

And then Lily disappeared. "Come on!" she whispered. "We can both fit!"

"Stay silent!" Guinevere walked back to the middle of the plat-form and stood, the wind whipping her hair and cloak. In their scramble she had lost her crown.

Hild's brother rounded the corner. He was barely out of breath. He looked at Guinevere, then leaned to see past her. "Where?" he growled.

"Not here. She took another stairway."

He glanced over his shoulder, frowning doubtfully.

"I am sorry," Guinevere said. "Truly, I am so sorry. I never wanted Hild to get hurt."

"You are a witch. You brought a demon. All our homes, gone. Hild, gone."

Guinevere felt the impulse to argue. To remind him the reason she had called the dragon was that he had decided to ignore his sister and help Ramm hold Guinevere ransom instead. But whatever the reason, whatever the justification, the result was the same. Guine-vere was alive, and Hild was dead.

"No help tonight," the man spat. "I killed your dragon."

Guinevere staggered in shock and devastation. The dragon had not escaped. She had called it, used it, and sent it away. And they had hunted it down and killed it. Everything she had done to Sir Bors to protect the dragon, undone by her own actions. A piece of true wonder, of magic, was gone from the world. Not by choice, burrowing into the earth to go to sleep. But by violence. Violence Guinevere had triggered. If she had known the dragon would die, Hild would die, she would *never* have done it. She would never have done any of it.

Merlin had always known. He had known the cost of his actions, and he had done them anyway. Morgana's story clung to her, whipping around her like her hair, obscuring her vision and making everything sting. Merlin had sown death and destruction and absolute heartbreak, and then he had simply sealed himself away from the world. Left them all to pick up his pieces. To keep moving along the paths he set for them, doing his will and suffering the consequences.

Or to watch as their loved ones suffered the consequences. Guinevere would not let Lily suffer for this.

Hild's brother took another step forward. His face was as still as stone, but his cheeks were wet. "You must pay."

Guinevere met his gaze. "I agree. But you cannot hurt my sister."

He closed the distance between them, one hand raised toward Guinevere's neck, his eyes dead save the tears streaming from them. And then he gasped as the tip of a blade appeared from the middle of his stomach. It disappeared, and Hild's brother stumbled to the side, falling off the edge of the platform and down the mountain.

"Guinevere," Lancelot breathed, bloodied sword in one hand and Guinevere's crown in the other.

CHAPTER FORTY-ONE

Lancelot's sword was black in the moonlight. Guinevere could not look away from the terrible length of it as Lancelot whirled, searching for more threats. "I saw him on the stairs. I ran as fast as I could to catch you. I should never have let you out of my sight. Did Morgan le Fay send him?"

"No. It was me."

"What?"

"I made it happen. It is my fault." Guinevere tore her eyes from the blade and stared out into the night sky pressing in around them. The night sky that had swallowed Hild's brother. She still could not remember his name. And he was another person dead because of her. Because she was queen.

"Where is Lily?" Lancelot edged toward the drop-off, her expression terrified.

Guinevere went to the last column and extended her hand. "He is gone."

Lily grasped Guinevere's hand. She clung to the column and

eased one foot around until it was on solid ground, then swung the rest of the way into Guinevere's arms. "Are we safe?" she asked.

Guinevere could not answer honestly. How could she ever tell anyone they were safe? She had destroyed King Mark's mind and thrown his kingdom into upheaval. She had killed Ramm. She had killed Hild. She had killed the dragon. She had killed Hild's brother. She had killed Maleagant and his men, and then her choices had brought the Dark Queen back to physical form. She had brought Morgan le Fay to the castle simply by being here. And who could say what the Lady of the Lake would do if she ever found her?

No one was safe around her. She was not a protector. She was a curse.

She patted Lily's back, then shifted her toward Lancelot and swung herself around the column, her foot barely reaching the other side. She scrambled inside. The space was exactly as she knew it would be. Whatever Morgana had said, whatever face Guinevere wore, Guinevere had known about things only the Lady of the Lake had. Her back to the stone wall, she shuffled around the dark circle. Far beneath her she could hear greedy, eternal water. Darkness beneath darkness. She stared into the hole and wondered.

In the dream, everything that drew her here had also pushed her in. Guinevere had been terrified when she woke up, but in the dream there had been no fear. Only assurance. Purpose. Determination.

If she jumped, would she find those things again?

"Guinevere!" A strong hand grasped her arm. One of her feet slipped over the edge and Lancelot yanked her back, pressing her against her own chest. "What are you doing?"

"I do not know," Guinevere whispered. "I do not know."

"Come on." Lancelot maneuvered both of them along the tiny ledge around the hole and then back onto the walkway. Lily was waiting, her eyes so wide the moon caught white all around her irises.

Lancelot escorted them back down. She instructed the guard outside Guinevere's rooms to take Lily and check all her rooms before standing watch outside. Then she knocked on Guinevere's door. When Brangien opened it, her expression shifted from curiosity to fear. "What happened?"

Lancelot shook her head. "Go with Lily. Stay with her tonight." She took Guinevere into Arthur's room and made her sit down. Lancelot handed her a cup of wine and watched, waiting until Guinevere drank the whole thing.

"Who was he?" Lancelot asked. "I did not see his face."

"Hild's brother. Hild died. And it was my fault."

Lancelot looked stricken at the news but also angry. "*They* took *you.* They were holding you ransom. What do you think they would have done if King Arthur had not paid? Any violence that happened was violence they brought on their own heads."

"She did not deserve to die." Guinevere was not even certain Hild's brother deserved to, either. Maybe no one ever deserved to die. Was there any greater arrogance or evil in the world than deciding life and death was a choice that could be made by a single person?

"I am sorry Hild is dead, I am, but I will not see you suffer because her people decided they would rather kidnap and steal than work."

The door burst open and Arthur entered like a summer storm, sudden and overwhelming. "We lost her." He knelt by Guinevere's chair, taking her hands. "Did she hurt you?"

It took Guinevere a few confused moments to realize he was talking about Morgana. Lancelot bowed and moved toward the door.

"No, stay," Guinevere said. "We have no secrets, we three. Or at least, no secrets that I have not kept from both of you. Hild's brother was here tonight, too. He tried to kill me. Hild died because of me."

Lancelot shook her head. "That is not your—"

"I summoned a dragon to the village so I could rescue myself. It came because it loved me, and then they hunted it down and killed it." Guinevere stared at the floor. "I might have been hunted and killed, as well, had Mordred not found me in the forest and lit the signal fire for Lancelot."

"What?" Arthur and Lancelot said at the same time and with the same amount of shocked vehemence.

"You saw him before Rhoslyn's village?" Lancelot demanded.

"You saw him *in* Rhoslyn's village?" Arthur looked at Lancelot, livid. "And you did not tell me? Or bring him back here?"

"Once before, as well," Guinevere answered. "He said he was trying to save the wolves from the Dark Queen's possession. And then he left. At Rhoslyn's village, he saved the women. He was not there for us. Though we *were* meant to meet, but not by his design. By Morgana's."

Arthur sat back. He was still on the floor, his long legs at angles. He rubbed his face, unbuckled his sword belt, and tossed it to the side. "Tell me everything."

Guinevere did, as best as she could piece it together. Morgana had gone to Cameliard right after Guinevere raised the Dark Queen and Mordred fled. She had found a place with Lily and encouraged her to come to Camelot instead of going to a convent. And then she had waited, wanting to get to know Guinevere and maybe Arthur. She had not made Mordred cross paths with Guinevere after Hild— though Mordred had been looking for an island based on Morgana's directions. Who could say how much she had seen with her power of vision? She had certainly maneuvered them at Rhoslyn's village.

"This whole time, Morgan le Fay was right here." Arthur shook his head, confusion wrinkling his strong brow. "What did she want?"

"She told me a story." Guinevere repeated it from start to finish.

It was not difficult to remember. It was seared into her mind, written as though in the flames Merlin was so adept at controlling.

"She is a liar." Arthur wrapped his arms around his legs and drew them closer. It made him look younger. "Obviously she was lying. It is all a trick. They are conspiring."

"*Was* she lying?"

"How can you wonder? She is Morgan le Fay! Everyone knows she is a sorceress. And she is Mordred's mother. Mordred, who betrayed us."

"Did he, though?"

Arthur released his legs and stood, anger propelling him. "What do you mean, 'did he'? Were we three not there in the meadow? Did he not trick you into raising the Dark Queen with your own blood?" Just as Lancelot had done, he pulled the ends of Guinevere's sleeves up, revealing the thin white lines of the scars along her forearms where the trees had cut her to make her bleed more freely. "And then he held your life between Excalibur and the Dark Queen!"

Guinevere nodded, this time not replacing her sleeves. "He did. He did all those things. But . . . you killed his father. You destroyed his grandmother. He fixed what he could. And then he left. He has not hurt us again, nor even tried to. The Dark Queen's attacks have been all her, no help from Mordred or from Morgana. Maybe they are not threats at all."

"*No.*" Arthur's voice had the same razor edge as his terrible sword. Guinevere rarely heard him speak as a king, but she was hearing it now. He was not talking *to* her; he was commanding her. "They are with her. On her side. You have seen with your own eyes what she does. The chaos. The violence. There is no room for the Dark Queen in this world if men are to survive and thrive. And there can be no forgiveness for those who help her."

Guinevere put her face in her hands. That was true. She knew it was true. But there had been so many things she knew to be true that had turned out to be lies, or something far more nebulous and complicated than true or false, good or evil.

"Merlin sent you here to—"

"We do not know why he sent me here." Guinevere looked up, certain of this, at least. "To protect me, to protect you, to protect his precious legacy. We do not know and we will never know. I do not trust him."

"You trust Morgan le Fay and Mordred over Merlin?" Arthur stared at her, incredulous.

"They have lied to me less than he did!"

"And what did Mordred say to you when he found you alone in the woods?" Arthur's voice was cold, his expression stone hard.

"Very little."

"But Morgan le Fay tells you a story and you take her side over Merlin's? Merlin, who helped raise us both? Clearly, Mordred and his mother were working together this whole time to use you. To manipulate you. They want you confused."

"It is not hard to confuse me! I do not even know who I am! I dream of the Lady of the Lake. I know secrets of Camelot that only she could reveal. But Morgana is convinced I am actually Guinevere. And Lily recognized me."

Lancelot broke in, her voice gentle. "They could have used magic on her."

"It would have broken when she came into the castle. I do not know how, or why, but Lily sees her sister when she looks at me. How can I be Guinevere? I *know* I am not. There is nothing of her in my memories. Which makes me feel like my mind is not my own." The dreams of the Lady felt more vivid than any of Guinevere's own memories. And they were real, whatever else they were, however they had come to her. Tonight had proved that.

Guinevere touched her forehead, wishing she could push into her own mind, pull apart what Merlin had put there, but she was terrified of what might happen. "I do not know what Merlin did to me, or why, and the more I try to fix things or claim who I am, to be queen or to wield magic as a protector, the more people get hurt. Where will it stop?"

Arthur walked toward her from where he had been pacing. He knelt before her and took her hands in his. For once she did not want to cling to the assurance and strength she always felt in his touch. She did not want to feel anything that was not her own.

"That is what it means to have power," he said. "You make the best choices you can, and there are consequences. There are always consequences. And usually you are not the one to suffer them. Other people do. You have to accept it, and live with it, and continue to move forward trying to do the most good for the most people."

"I did that. I did. But my actions killed *innocents,* Arthur. And I do not know how to accept it, or how to move forward, or even how to do the most good. I am not sure that being here, being queen, is the most good for the most people."

Arthur squeezed her hands. "It is. Merlin would not have sent you otherwise. We may not always understand it, but everything he has done has been for Camelot. For our people."

That was not true. Merlin did not care about people at all. He cared about Arthur, and Arthur's path to power, and about his own plans. But even if Morgana had been lying, Guinevere still knew enough to know that Merlin cared nothing for the good of individuals if they got in the way of his plans. If he wanted Guinevere here, he would not care what happened around her, or who suffered, or who died.

But she could not argue this with Arthur. He worked so hard. And he was good. He deserved to be king. In spite of everything else, she believed that. Camelot was better than anything else she had seen out in the world. Whatever consequences Arthur's choices caused, he considered them all. He weighed them all. And he did what he could, wherever he could, to make every life better. If Arthur needed to believe in Merlin to continue as king, Guinevere would not take that from him. But she could not do the same.

Guinevere gently pushed his hands away and stood. "I am tired. You should return to the festival. Keep Excalibur with you, but Morgana is gone. I will know if she gets near again."

"I can stay."

"No." Guinevere put a hand on his cheek. Who would he have been if Morgana had gotten to him first? What would have happened to Uther Pendragon? To Camelot? Would Lancelot have been allowed to kill that tyrant, setting Camelot free? Or would another tyrant have come in, someone like Maleagant? What had she done in King Mark's land when she removed him from power? Would they get their own Arthur now, or someone just as bad as King Mark?

If Arthur could go back and make every choice for himself, without interference, what would he do differently? She could not imagine him as anything other than what he was.

"Go," she said. "Be with your people. Celebrate, and let them see you celebrating. Be where you are supposed to be and who you are supposed to be."

"I do not want to leave you alone."

Guinevere turned to Lancelot. She had been so unfair to her knight. Lancelot would never be like the other knights, not truly. Guinevere had taken the choice from her, had determined what their relationship should be. She would not do that again. "I have Lancelot."

"Always," Lancelot said, her dark eyes intent, as powerful as any of her strikes, as determined as any of her fighting.

Guinevere looked back up at Arthur and caught a flicker of
something—anger, or concern, she could not say which—before he
bent over and retrieved his sword.

"Very well. We will speak more, once you have rested." Holding
his sword out to the side so it would not brush against Guinevere
even in its sheath, Arthur bent down. The kiss he pressed against her
lips felt deliberate in a way she could not quite explain. Then he left.

Lancelot and Guinevere went back to her room. Brangien had
already prepared it for sleep. Guinevere wished Brangien and Isolde
were still here to help her undress. It was difficult to unlace the
sleeves from her dress, and she could not undo the ties in the back
on her own. She did not want to sleep in the dress and risk ruining
it after all Isolde's work.

"Can you—can you help me?" Guinevere had unlaced the sleeves
but could not reach the back of her dress.

Lancelot nodded.

Guinevere turned her back and Lancelot began tugging on the
strings. "I am sorry," Guinevere whispered. "I wanted to protect you.
I wanted you to be a real knight. No different from the rest of them."

"I want to be different from the rest of them," Lancelot said, her
voice as soft as the callused fingers pulling the laces free one by one.

"But you wanted to be King Arthur's knight."

"No. I want to be Queen Guinevere's knight. But also—" She cut
herself off, then continued, hesitant. "But also your friend."

She had finished with the laces. Guinevere turned around. "You
are my friend." Lancelot knew the truth about her. Had known for
longer than anyone but Arthur. And in so many ways, Lancelot knew
her better than Arthur did. They spent more time together. Lancelot
trusted her and treated her as a queen but also did not hesitate to
disagree when she thought Guinevere was wrong. Which made her
support all the more valuable. Guinevere realized with a start that

what she missed most about Mordred was the sense that he *saw* her. In every room, in every situation, he had seen her first and foremost.

But she had not lost that when he left. She still had it in Lancelot. And perhaps it was even better, because Lancelot did not look at her with any ulterior motives or any deception. Lancelot was always herself, and she was always true. Much the way Arthur was, the difference being Lancelot was always *there*.

Lancelot smiled, something shy in her expression as she stared at the stone floor. "It is harder to find a good friend than a queen, I think."

Guinevere laughed. "It is hard to be either one. But I will try to be both the friend and the queen you deserve." She pulled off her dress, then removed her stockings and boots. Lancelot sat in a chair near the door as Guinevere climbed into bed.

Guinevere closed her eyes. But she kept seeing the sword point appearing in the stomach of Hild's brother. Watching him fall. Hearing Morgana tell a different story and rewrite the past. And, most of all, she kept seeing the terrible promise of that hole and the water beneath. Wondering what would have happened if she had jumped. Tempted in a despairing way to climb up and do just that.

"Lancelot," she whispered, keeping her eyes closed.

"Yes?"

"Please do not leave."

"I never will."

CHAPTER FORTY-TWO

Guinevere had awoken to find Lancelot standing next to the door. But instead of being formal and reserved, Lancelot had smiled at her, and they had chatted easily through breakfast. One thing repaired, at least.

Lily invited Guinevere to return to the festival grounds with her, but Guinevere declined. She was in no mood to be seen. Sir Gawain was more than happy to be permanently assigned to guard Lily when she was away from the castle, and Brangien was more than happy to return to Guinevere's rooms.

"I like Lily," Brangien said with a tone of voice at odds with her words, "but I will not be filling in anymore. We can find her another maid, and she has the young, daft one in the meantime."

Isolde clucked her tongue in reproach, but seemed relieved to be back in their own rooms. As though Brangien felt sorry she had not been there to help protect Guinevere—and shocked at the revelation of Anna's true identity—she fussed over Guinevere far more than normal. By early afternoon Guinevere's rooms, which normally felt large, were beginning to feel downright crowded. When there was another knock on the door she told Lancelot to tell them to leave, afraid it was Lily or Dindrane or someone else who would need to be invited in and chatted with.

Instead, Arthur stood there. He barely acknowledged Lancelot, holding his hand out to Guinevere. "Will you join me?"

"Of course." She took his hand, expecting him to tuck hers into the crook of his elbow. Instead, he laced their fingers together. They left through the outer door and climbed up and up the exterior stairs. Guinevere clung to his arm, terrified. She knew they were going to the hidden chamber above the drop to the black depths of the lake lurking beneath the city. She did not want to look into that circle again. Did not want to contemplate what about it called to her.

Instead, Arthur took another route. They climbed to where the top of the castle met the unformed rock of the mountain behind them. There, Arthur smiled as he stepped aside. An opening revealed a room without a roof, open to the air and filled with plants. Someone had grown a garden there. And while little was blooming this late in the season, there was a joyful amount of green life to find this high in the middle of so much gray rock.

In the center of the garden were two cushions, with a pitcher and goblets between them. Guinevere looked up at Arthur. There was something tentative and hopeful in his smile. Not the usual confidence he wore as easily as his crown.

"I did not know this was here!"

Arthur led her inside the space. "I confess, I did not, either. But I was speaking with one of the cooks and asked where she got her herbs. She brought me up here. I knew as soon as I saw it that you would love it."

"I do." Guinevere sat and Arthur did the same.

"I wanted to— We need to talk. You are right."

"About?"

"About everything. This has all been unfair to you, from the beginning. You came here under false guidance. You were lied to, or at least misled, and I supported that lie."

"You had your reasons."

"I was selfish. I was so glad when you came, because it meant I finally had a friend, a confidante. Someone I could be merely Arthur to, instead of the king. But bringing you here that way meant you always had to pretend. I did not—I hated the thought of you pretending to love me. Pretending to be my wife in more than just name only. It felt like I was tricking you, or taking advantage. I only wanted you to want to be with me in that way if it was what you wanted. I am saying the word *want* too much." He rubbed his jaw, blushing. "I am sorry. I had this better in my head. I know it has hurt you, my caution."

Guinevere was having a hard time looking at him. She stared out at the shining lake and the cleared fields beyond it. "It has been . . . difficult. Trying to navigate my feelings. Worrying that I am not what you need."

"That is just it. It is not about what I need. You did not choose to marry me. I want you to— I need you to— It has to be your choice. To love me. For us to love each other. You do not owe it to me. You do not have to choose me. We can continue like this forever, and I promise I will be happy to have you as my friend and companion, to help me rule. I wanted to prove that to you. It was not always easy. But I do not expect anything more from you and will *never* ask it."

He took her hands and she turned from the fields to look at him. Truly look at him. His face was beloved. She could not deny that. She would not give Merlin credit for the sense that she had always known him; that was *her*. There was something about Arthur that, from the moment they met, had been familiar and right. She also could not deny that she had wanted him. At least in snatches of time, breathless moments of surprise.

"I am ready," he said. "I am ready to be husband and wife. King and queen. Rule together and be together. I do not care who you were, or why Merlin sent you here. I am not saying it does not matter, because I know it matters to you. But whatever circumstances brought you into my life, I am glad they did and I would not change them. All I care about is that you are here, we are together, and I do not ever want that to be different. So. That is—those are my feelings. I am ready to be whatever you want us to be."

Guinevere searched his face, his warm brown eyes, his strong jaw, the assurance there. He was not terrified. He was ready. For whatever she said.

She opened her mouth, but he squeezed her hands. "Do not answer me now. Take your time to think about it. Maybe all this pain has been because you have been trying to be so many things to so many people. Queen and protector and witch and wife and sister. So many secrets, so many identities. It is too much for anyone. When you chose me before, in the meadow, you chose Camelot. And I love you for that, because I will always choose Camelot, as well. But now I want you to choose *me*."

Arthur was not right. She had not chosen Camelot. She had chosen Arthur. But she had chosen Arthur the *king*. What he was asking her now was far more intimate, and in a way far more dangerous. She believed him when he said he would continue as they had been. He would not lie. And when she was with him, she was happy. It was a joy to be in his company, at his side.

But she knew he was also telling the truth when he said he would always choose Camelot. Camelot would come first, before everything, every time. She would love him and he would leave, again and again and again. His love for her would not be a duty exactly. But it would be one of many things that Arthur felt and did, and on any given day, it would not be the most important.

If he had kissed her then, she would have said yes. But he was Arthur, not Mordred. He would take nothing that was not already his. Instead, he pressed his lips to her hand. "I have to go."

Her face must have fallen because he laughed. "Just to the great hall. We are having a feast tonight to celebrate being done celebrating the harvest. And I am leaving on purpose, because I want you to have time and space to make this decision. I will wait as long as you need." But his step was light as he walked away. He knew what she would choose.

Guinevere sat in the garden for a long time, wishing he had kissed her, given her an excuse to jump without looking. That was not Arthur's way, though. It never had been.

When the sun grew low, she returned to her rooms. Brangien complained at her being late and rushed to get her ready. "Do you want to wear the crown?" she asked. It was an offhand question, but it felt as though it carried all the weight in the world.

Did Guinevere want to wear the crown?

"Yes," she said.

Brangien pinned it in place, and together with Isolde and the guard who had taken Lancelot's place, they left for the great hall. When she entered, Arthur stood and smiled at her. It warmed her through. There might not be the dangerous sparks she had with Mordred, but this was a strong love. A true love, built on friendship and admiration and trust. She could not trust Merlin, or her own mind, or her past, or even her future. But she could trust Arthur.

This time she had a place at his side. Arthur had changed the seating arrangement so that the women and men were not separated. Dindrane was nearby, laughing at something Sir Bors had said. Brangien and Isolde stood ready in the corner, leaning close and sharing a whispered conversation. Brangien tucked some of Isolde's shining auburn hair into place, a simple tenderness in the movement. Lily was on Arthur's other side, Sir Gawain next to her. He had a look on his face like he could not quite believe his luck, and Lily, sweet girl, beamed and chattered, but with an ease that made Guinevere realize how desperate and scared Lily had been before. Arthur laughed at something Sir Tristan said. The sound rang through the room. Everyone had a place here, and everyone was happy with that place.

Guinevere glanced at the opposite end of the table. Even though the other unmarried knights were around Lancelot, she seemed separate. She was not speaking with anyone, or laughing. Her eyes met Guinevere's, and there was a loneliness in them that Guinevere felt and understood instinctively. She and Lancelot managed to be both a part of Camelot and apart from it.

Arthur's hand found hers beneath the table. He slipped his fingers between hers and she stared down at them. Her fingers, pale and slender. His, tanned and rough. Guinevere and Arthur. Queen and king.

"I have an answer," she whispered.

He squeezed her fingers.

The door opened and a page hurried to Arthur's side with a scroll sealed with wax. Arthur reverted to being king. He pulled his fingers free from Guinevere's and opened the scroll, glancing at it without curiosity. But then he froze, his eyes widening. It was almost the same expression Hild's brother had made when the sword went through his stomach.

"What is it?" Guinevere asked, suddenly afraid. The room continued chattering around them, the noise covering their conversation.

"My son. He is alive. He has been alive this whole time."

"*Elaine's* baby?" Guinevere leaned close to read the letter. It was from a lady's maid in a southern lord's house. She had heard of Arthur from his visit, heard that he was a good man. Now that Maleagant was dead, she felt safe enough to write.

Elaine had died in childbirth. Arthur had not been there, and Guinevere knew it was one of his deepest regrets. Even though Elaine had been Maleagant's sister, working with the evil man to manipulate and overthrow Arthur, Arthur had loved her. And he had sent her away, and then she had died giving birth to their son.

A son Arthur had been told also died at birth. A son this woman was writing to tell him was alive and well and *his*.

Arthur stood, his face frantic. "I have to get him. Right now."

"Yes. Yes, of course." Guinevere did not know what to do. Should she go with him? She could help. She knew she could.

"Brothers," Arthur said, his voice instantly quieting the room. "I have news and require men to help me on a quest. Perhaps the greatest quest I have ever—" His voice cut off. He was holding the letter so tightly, the edges were wrinkling. "It is a personal quest. I do not know what we will find on the other end, whether we will meet with a fight or not. But I want my most trusted men at my side."

Sir Tristan stood without hesitation. Sir Bors, Sir Percival, Sir Caradoc, Sir Gawain. Every knight stood.

Lancelot did not. Arthur had asked for his brothers. For his men.

"Sir Lancelot," Arthur said.

Lancelot's face went pale as she stood.

"I entrust Camelot and the queen to you in my absence. Guinevere will rule, and you will protect her and the city."

Lancelot bowed, a hand over her heart. But there was a moment of hesitation where Guinevere saw the pain of being left behind. She knew it all too well.

Arthur turned toward Guinevere. He did not ask why there were tears in her eyes, if he saw them at all. Arthur kissed her forehead and then strode from the room, followed by all his most favored knights.

Only the women were left.

Guinevere rushed out of the great hall, almost running, back to Arthur's room. She could help. And even if Arthur would not take her, she did not want to him to leave on a question. She wanted him to leave with an answer.

She burst through his door and was hit by a wall of nausea, spinning blurry terror as she felt the essence of herself being pulled apart, burning away like mist in the sun.

"Guinevere!" Arthur sheathed Excalibur and Guinevere collapsed against the wall, trying to catch her breath and unable to stand on her own. The stones held her up. It was an answer, of sorts, at least to her demand to go with him to help. She could not. She would be a problem, not an asset. And with the sickness of Excalibur still clinging to her, she could not formulate an answer, or even move to kiss Arthur, if that was what she wanted.

"Go," she said, closing her eyes. "Bring him home."

CHAPTER FORTY-THREE

The next morning she met Lancelot and Brangien in the alcove. They were supposed to discuss what needed to be done in Arthur's absence, but Guinevere had no desire to meet with officials in the great hall. She would have to do plenty of that in the days—or even weeks—to come. Arthur and his men were traveling to the southwestern end of the island, and who knew what they would find when they got there. If Maleagant had controlled the household where the child was left, there was a good chance they would not willingly give up Arthur's son. And if winter storms came early, the roads would get bad, delaying either their journey there or back. Guinevere steeled herself against the possibility that it could be as long as a month or even two before Arthur returned.

"Does this mean you are a stepmother?" Brangien asked.

Guinevere sat on the floor of the alcove. Lancelot leaned against the outer wall, looking across the city and the fields, always keeping watch.

"I suppose it does."

"But this is good. It puts less pressure on you. Arthur has an heir now. A bastard heir, but still, a son."

Guinevere had not even thought about that. Part of what she had feared about her relationship with Arthur was that it denied him heirs, which threatened the stability of his rule. When Arthur brought his son back, Camelot had an heir. Which meant it was even more Guinevere's choice what she and Arthur became. The last true outside pressure was gone.

"I will not watch him," Brangien said. "I hate children. They are messy and loud and never do as they are told."

Guinevere laughed, grateful for the respite from her thoughts. "You are a lady's maid, not a nurse."

"Sticky! They are also sticky. Always. Isolde loves them, though. Maybe she can help."

"I am certain we will find a nurse." Guinevere hoped so, at least. She was happy for Arthur—truly—but she did not want to be a mother. Not yet. And not to Elaine's child, as petty as that was. She would be kind to the boy. But she did not want to claim him as her own in any emotional way.

How would Arthur be as a father? Did that change things between them yet again? Arthur barely had enough time to be a husband. With one more demand on his attention, and a genuinely important one at that, how would things shift? Would he decide he was not ready for them to be husband and wife after all? That it was easier to remain as they were?

And what did Guinevere want? Why could she not decide?

Lancelot did not stop her watch or turn toward them, but Guinevere could hear the thoughtful frown in her voice. "Did you know he had a son?"

"Yes. Or at least, I knew what he knew, that Elaine and the baby both died in childbirth."

"I had never heard about it."

"It was a secret. Both the affair and the aftermath. Elaine was Maleagant's sister."

"Oh," Brangien said, drawing out the word.

"Yes. Precisely. The only people who knew about the baby were Arthur, Elaine, and Maleagant. It was why Arthur banished Maleagant instead of killing him." Guinevere stopped, a terrible realization gripping her. "They were not the only people." She stood, her heart racing. "They were not the only people who knew. Mordred knew."

At this, Lancelot finally turned around. Her face mirrored Guinevere's horror. "Mordred knew about the baby?"

"Yes. He told Arthur to kill Maleagant, not banish him. He knew about Elaine. Which means Mordred knows that if he sent a letter to Arthur about a son miraculously alive, hidden these past few years, Arthur would leave Camelot without hesitation. And take Excalibur, too."

Brangien whipped around to look at the fields as though expecting them to be crawling with enemies already. "But we can hold the castle, right? Even with the missing knights, we have all the soldiers and trained men."

"We can hold the castle." Lancelot had her hand around the pommel of her sword. "It will *not* fall."

They could hold the castle, yes, but at what cost? And why had Mordred waited until now to deploy this trick? Guinevere stared down at the familiar lines of the city. The houses. The arena. The church. The silos.

The *silos.*

"This timing is no accident," Guinevere said. "The castle does not have to fall for them to destroy Camelot. All the granaries and silos are full. If they can get to those, if they can destroy our food supply, we will starve this winter. People will die, or flee to try to find food elsewhere. Arthur's rule will be over."

Lancelot stepped aside. "Brangien, send out every page to find Arthur. We do not know the exact route he will take, so they will have to search widely."

"But are we certain? That this is the plan, the attack?" Brangien frowned, worried.

It was a carefully laid plan, expertly deployed. Cunning. Clever. "Yes," Guinevere said.

Brangien lifted her skirts and sprinted down the stairs.

"We cannot count on the messengers finding Arthur in time." Guinevere paced. "Mordred will not delay. Not if he is smart, and he is." How could he do this? After everything? How had she once again trusted that he did not have malicious intent? Morgana had pretended she was here to speak to Guinevere. But she had been all over the city with Lily. Between Morgana and Mordred, they knew where all the food was stored. And Mordred knew the city—and the secret passage in and out of the castle—better than anyone.

"It is up to us," Guinevere said. "Call everyone into the city. Set soldiers to guard this side of the shore. Prepare arrows and pitch to light boats on fire. I will need you with me." At least she knew no attack could come from over the mountain, thanks to her magic.

Lancelot looked torn. "I am the only knight left. I should manage the defense of the city."

"That is exactly what we will do. Once all the citizens are across the lake, we will seal it. Everything. No one will be able to get in once we are done." Not over the lake, and not through a secret passage. If Mordred wanted Camelot, he was going to be disappointed, and Guinevere was going to be the one to thwart him.

"How?"

Guinevere looked at her hands. Fight as a queen, Merlin counseled her once again in her memory. She clenched her hands into fists. She was not a queen. She was not Guinevere. She did not know who she was. But she knew what she was, and what she could do. This time, she would do something that *only* protected. No one would suffer.

"Magic."

Fortunately, most of the citizens of Camelot were already in the city proper or had been camping on the field by the lake after the end of the festival. By the end of the day they had everyone in who was coming in. It was difficult to convey urgency without communicating panic, but Guinevere issued it as a decree for protection while King Arthur was away. There were enough empty buildings in Camelot to house most of the farmers and laborers, and the rest they put in the rooms of the castle that were not full.

Soldiers gathered along the bottom of the city, ready to attack any boats that made the journey. The secret passageway had been sealed on the castle end. Guinevere had three men unsealing it at that moment, clearing the rocks and wood barriers. If they could do it, so could Mordred, and she would need the way clear for her own purposes.

Guinevere moved Lily down to her rooms. Lily sat on her bed while Guinevere searched through her trunks, looking for anything that would help with the task ahead. She had an idea of how to do it, but it was bigger and more complex than any spell she had attempted. It went far beyond knots.

"Guinevere, what is really happening? I am scared."

Guinevere stopped to look Lily in the eye. "Something is coming. With Arthur gone, Camelot is vulnerable. I am going to make sure nothing gets through. But—listen. If it comes to it, you and Brangien and Lancelot can run the city. I know you can. You are smart and capable and better at being a princess than I ever could have been."

Lily slid off the bed, joining Guinevere on the floor. "What do you think will happen?"

Guinevere shook her head. "Arthur left me in charge. I will do whatever it takes to keep Camelot safe. I need you and Brangien to take over my duties in the meantime."

"But you are not a knight or a soldier! Lancelot can do all that!"

Guinevere's hands closed around the iron dagger Arthur had given her. Rock and water and iron and blood. That was it. She knew what she needed to do. And what the cost would be. This time, she would pay it. No one else.

"You are different," Lily said. "You are—you are so much braver than you were. How did you get braver?"

She had no answers. "Lily, listen to me. You are not my shadow. You are a princess. You defied your father. You claimed the life you wanted as your own. Use that same strength for Camelot now. And trust that, whatever happens, I am glad you came and I am glad to know you."

Lily's lip trembled, but she nodded, then lifted her chin. "I will do whatever I need to."

"We all will." Guinevere pulled her into a hug. "Tell Brangien—" Her voice cracked. She waited a moment until she could sound strong. She released Lily, then stood. "Tell Brangien what I said. The three of you. And if you need help managing anything—officials or knights' wives or anyone—get Dindrane. She can handle anyone."

Brangien would never forgive Guinevere for leaving her out of this plan, but Brangien had to be here for Isolde. Guinevere would not ask her to choose between them.

Leaving Lily behind before she could change her mind, Guinevere pulled on a red cloak, stuck the dagger in her belt, and walked out of her rooms. She went through Arthur's door. His rooms did not feel empty. There was a sense of him there, like at any moment he would come in. Laugh at something she said. Pull her close in that warm comfort he radiated.

But then he would leave again.

She took off her crown and set it gently in the center of his bed.

Lancelot strode at her side as they walked down the main street. The city was crowded, the atmosphere crackling with nervous anticipation. At the dock, Guinevere climbed into a small boat and squeezed her eyes shut. Lancelot followed, doing her best not to rock it, then rowed them a safe distance from where the southern waterfall pounded with relentless strength. When they were near the shore, Lancelot jumped out of the boat and dragged it the rest of the way up onto the pebbled beach. Guinevere got out.

"What exactly are we doing?" Lancelot asked.

"We are protecting Camelot."

"Yes, I know." Lancelot looked annoyed. "You have said as much. You have not told me *how*."

"We are going to form a barrier. No one will enter or leave. A little like the magic we did over the river, only stronger." If the river magic had been an attack, this was a defense. No more deaths at her hands.

Lancelot stopped walking. "But we cannot let the people know you use magic. You would be banished, or worse."

"No one will see who does it. They will only see the result. For all they know, it is a threat, not a protection. When Arthur returns and unmakes it with Excalibur, he has once again saved the city from her."

"He will be the hero." Lancelot narrowed her eyes, troubled.

"He is always the hero. Camelot needs him to be the hero." Guinevere knew it, and Lancelot did, too. Lancelot had tried to be Camelot's hero, and the Lady of the Lake herself had stopped it.

"But it is more complicated than that."

"It always is." Guinevere kept moving. They had no time to waste. She was not entirely certain her plan would work, and if it did not, then she would have to figure something else out. The southern waterfall pounded next to them, a fine mist in the air creating rainbows where it caught the light. She could not hear their steps anymore by the time they reached the hidden entrance to the cave. Guinevere pulled aside the draping vines.

"Has this always been here?" Lancelot shouted to be heard over the waterfall's roar.

"Yes. But only a handful know about it. Merlin. Arthur. Mordred. And now you. It will take you directly to the castle, into an unused storeroom."

"We are here to block it, then?" Lancelot examined the entrance. "Maybe if we climbed up the side of the mountain and somehow diverted the waterfall?" She eyed the cliff appraisingly.

"No. We need it open." Guinevere had been right about her plans. That water—the river split at the top before falling down on either side of Camelot in the twin waterfalls and becoming the lake—and this rock of the mountain that Camelot itself was carved out of were the two borders of the city. Rock and water and iron and blood. It would work.

Instead of feeling elated, Guinevere was terrified. This was it.

Her last chance to make a different decision. To wait and see what happened. To do something vicious and dangerous like she had done at the river, or to King Mark, or to Ramm. To risk hurting innocents in the cross fire. Arthur would meet the threat head on, the way he met everything, because he knew who and what he was and how to fight for what he believed in.

Lancelot looked at her, face open and expectant. Behind Lancelot, through the tunnel, was the castle that held almost everyone Guinevere cared about. And out there, somewhere, was Arthur, riding after certain heartbreak. Guinevere did not think he had a son. It was a cruel trick, the cruelest imaginable.

Guinevere had sworn to protect Camelot. She would not break that promise, whatever else she broke today.

"Give me your hand," Guinevere said.

Lancelot held her hand out, unquestioning even when Guinevere pulled out the knife. She sliced a line down Lancelot's palm and one down her own. Then she clasped their hands together. The blood pooled and dripped down the sides of their joined hands.

She walked, Lancelot following, connected to her. From the other side of the cave opening, with Lancelot's back to the mountain and Guinevere's back to the open land behind them, Guinevere let their blood fall on the rock, pressing their hands against it. Then she guided Lancelot, drawing an unbroken line of blood from the face of the mountain beyond the passageway, down the pebbles of the beach, and, finally, to the water just beyond the waterfall.

Guinevere moved their hands together, keeping the line continuous and dripping a single knot. A knot she knew in her soul, though she had never used it before. A knot of binding. It was complex, intricate, a knot that could not be undone by any means she had access to. And then, to finish it, she extended the line of blood to the edge of the water. When it hit, it spread, fast—faster than it should have. A flash of blue rose between Guinevere and Lancelot like a line of flames. Guinevere released Lancelot's hand, jumping back just in time. They watched the blue burn up, racing across the surface of the lake and the mountain behind them, until the two lines met in the sky and formed a shimmering dome nearly invisible to the naked eye. They had connected the stone to the water and everything between them was unreachable now.

"What is it?" Lancelot shouted.

Arthur had a sword for Camelot's protection. Guinevere had given them a shield.

A black moth fluttered from the sky, landing on Guinevere's sleeve like a smudge of ash. She brushed it away. Lancelot took a step toward Guinevere, but Guinevere held up her hands. "No! You cannot cross the line. The magic is anchored to our blood. If you cross the threshold, it will break. Go back through the passageway."

"Come on." Lancelot held out one hand, careful not to extend it past the line of the magic.

Guinevere took a step back. It hurt far more than slicing her palm had. It hurt more than anything she had ever done, and the look in Lancelot's eyes was the deepest cut of all. "I am the other anchor. If I cross, it breaks. I have to be on this side."

Arthur had asked her to make a decision. And she had just sealed herself off from Camelot.

Lancelot shook her head, trying to reason away what Guinevere was doing. To fix it. "So you are going to camp here until Arthur returns?"

Guinevere's heart was racing, the full reality of what she had done, what she was going to do, shimmering around her like the magic. Sealing her off from who she had tried to be. What she had tried to be. "I promised I would protect Camelot. And I have. But I cannot—I cannot stay. I keep hurting people. I keep hurting myself.

And until I know who I truly am, I do not think I can be Guinevere anymore. Not the Guinevere Lily needs, or Arthur needs, or Camelot needs."

"What about the Guinevere *I* need?" Lancelot's dark eyes were filled with tears. Guinevere had never seen her cry, had never seen her anything other than strong or brave or supportive. Nothing had ever broken Lancelot. Not the loss and tragedies of her childhood, not the battles she had to fight every day of her life to attain her place, not the constant work she had to do to maintain it. Nothing until Guinevere.

"You are my knight. I am commanding you to protect Camelot until King Arthur returns."

"Where will you go?" Lancelot paced along the edge of their magic. She ran her hands through her wild curls. Guinevere could see how much it was costing her not to cross the barrier. She prayed that she had not overestimated Lancelot's devotion to Camelot.

"I am going to free Merlin. To get the truth. To reclaim my past so I can choose my future." She put the dagger back in her bag, alongside her thread and supplies and the warm rock connecting her to Morgana.

The *warm* rock. Another black moth alighted on her arm. And then another. And another. She looked up. Lancelot met her eyes. Lancelot had been in the meadow that night. She had seen the cloud of black moths that erupted from the ground, that heralded the Dark Queen's return.

Lancelot unsheathed her sword. "I am—"

"If you love me, you will stay on that side." Guinevere took a step backward, her own words ringing in her ears. Had Merlin said almost the same thing to Lancelot, before being sealed in the cave by the Lady of the Lake? Would she never be free of Merlin's influence?

She heard a horse in the distance, getting closer. She was paying the price of this magic, yes, but so was Lancelot. Guinevere's heart felt as though it would break from the pain.

"Please do not ask this of me." Lancelot dropped to her knees, her head hanging. "Please."

"I love you, too. I am sorry," Guinevere whispered, knowing the waterfall, the treacherous water all around them, would steal her words, so that Lancelot never heard them. She turned away and walked toward the sound of the horse. She was unsurprised to see Mordred. He was riding fast, but pulled up short when he noticed her. A look of genuine shock flitted across his face, followed by panic.

"What are you doing out here?" he demanded, dismounting and glancing over his shoulder.

Guinevere lifted her chin. "I am here to stop you."

"Stop me from what?"

"From taking Camelot. I know that is the plan. You lured Arthur out so you could attack the city without fear of Excalibur. But it will not work. I have sealed it. You cannot get in. No one can."

Mordred looked toward the secret passageway; then he closed his eyes and hung his head in the same devastated posture as Lancelot. "Oh, Guinevere. What have you done?"

"Exactly what I told you."

"They are not coming for Camelot! They are coming for *you*!"

Another black moth alighted on Guinevere's arm. "No, you—you tricked Arthur. You were going to use the secret passage."

"I was going to use it to warn you. My mother sent me ahead so I could reach you first. I did not trick Arthur. Maleagant knew about Elaine and the baby, and he told his men, and his men are loyal to others now. They are the ones who sent the letter. They wanted Arthur gone so you were vulnerable. We have to—" Mordred froze, then looked over his shoulder once more. In the distance there was a fast-approaching cloud of dust that obscured whatever was there. The rock was so warm now Guinevere could feel it through her bag.

Mordred glanced desperately around, anguish on his face. "Can you go back through the passage?"

"No," Guinevere whispered. It was not true. She could. But if she did, Camelot was at risk.

"We cannot outrun them." He put his hands on Guinevere's cheeks, his gaze hotter than the magic burning through the rock that connected Guinevere to Morgana. "I know I do not deserve it, but please. Please trust me. Do not lose faith in me, whatever happens."

She did not have time to answer. He grabbed her by the waist and lifted her onto his horse, then mounted behind her and rode toward the approaching dust cloud.

The Pictish king, Nechtan, a bulk of fur and menace, stopped, surrounded by at least two hundred men. The black fur mantle around his shoulders shifted in the light, and Guinevere realized it was covered in moths. One crawled up the side of his face, lingering at his ear.

The attacks from the Dark Queen were never meant to succeed. Only to keep them watching for magical threats while she manipulated human threats to the north. The Picts had not gone silent out of peace. They had gone silent to prepare for war. And Guinevere and Arthur had been exactly what the Dark Queen hoped: distracted.

"I did not know you would be here," Nechtan said, looking at Mordred.

"I sent for him." Morgana rode closer, barely glancing at Guinevere.

Mordred laughed, his tone light. No longer the Mordred who had fixed her shoulder, or given her a flower beneath the shelter of trees, or even begged her, desperately, to leave with him. This was the eel, the man everyone warned her about, who slipped and slid through the cold darkness to get what he wanted. "Hello, Mother. King Nechtan. I got her out of the city for you. A queen for a queen."

King Nechtan glanced toward Camelot, narrowing his eyes.

"Not yet," Morgana said, her voice curt.

"I can take it."

"Look closer." Mordred jerked his head toward the shimmering blue dome over the city.

The king grunted in agreement, but reluctance kept Nechtan's face turned toward the city even as he swung his horse back around in the direction they had come from. North. He shouted, and every horse began to gallop. Guinevere looked over her shoulder, but she could not see Lancelot. She could not even see Camelot. Everything was swallowed in a cloud of dust as she was taken from the city and the king and her knight and the Guinevere she might have been.

She was surrounded by enemies, held by a man she did not know if she could trust, aimed at a land where they served a queen both dark and wondrous.

So be it, she thought. Let the Guinevere who might have been be left behind. They had no idea what she was capable of, but she was finally ready to find out.

ACKNOWLEDGMENTS

I'm supported by my own veritable round table of champions.

From the Kingdom of Delacorte and Random House Children's Books, aka the greatest kingdom and one I'm continually honored to be a part of, Wendy Loggia, Beverly Horowitz, Ali Romig, Kristopher Kam, Regina Flath, Alex Dos Diaz, Heather Hughes, Adrienne Waintraub, Kristin Schulz, and the entire Get Underlined team.

From the Kingdom of Tiny Business Warriors, my agent, Michelle Wolfson.

From the Kingdom of Far-Flung Friends I Couldn't Survive Without, Stephanie Perkins and Natalie Whipple.

From the Kingdom of My House, Noah—handsomest champion; sorry, everyone else—and my three young pages, Elena, Jonah, and Ezra. Though Elena and Jonah would probably prefer to be categorized as witches, and Ezra would rather be a skeleton, so I guess that's fine, too, since this is just an acknowledgments section most people won't read. We can be flexible on the theme.

From the Kingdom of Big Families, Patrick and Cindy White, as well as Erin and Todd, Lindsey and Keegan, Lauren and Devin, and Matthew and Tyler. Also Kit and Jim Brazier, and Tim and Carrie, Seth and Shayne, Eliza, Christina and Josh, Emma and Brad, Beverly and Nick, Colton and Cassie, and Thomas. And while we're at it, knights-in-training Joseph, Audrey, Will, Lucas, Asher, Ruby, Milo, Luca, Graham, Lilah, June, Lydia, Rachel, Abram, Georgie, Peter, Rocky, Boston, Chase, Charlie, Grant, Nigel, Sienna, Henri, Eli, Beverly, Eden, Miles, James, and whoever managed to be born between when I wrote this and when the book actually came out. I'll never remember any of your birthdays, so please accept as a disappointing consolation prize your name in the acknowledgments section of a book only a couple of you are old enough to read yet. Best! Aunt! Ever!

Sir Jim gets his own second mention for making so much of my travel possible with his willingness to steer his silver Honda steed where it needs to be to get kids to and from school in my absence.

And hello, reader! Not only did you continue on Guinevere's adventures with me, you also stuck around for the credits, which is wild and generous. So tell people I thanked you, *personally*, and drafted you for my round table. Write your name right here:

DON'T MISS THE GRIPPING CONCLUSION
TO THE ACCLAIMED ARTHURIAN FANTASY
TRILOGY FROM *NEW YORK TIMES*
BESTSELLING AUTHOR KIERSTEN WHITE.

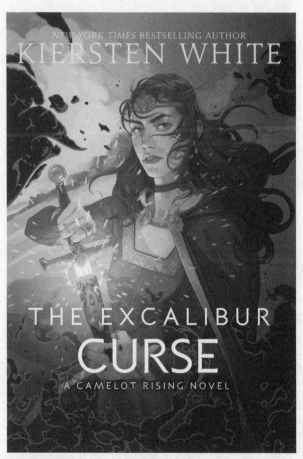

Once, not so long ago, Guinevere had ridden surrounded by armed soldiers and marveled at her power. Now she rode surrounded by armed soldiers and marveled at her smallness. She tried to hold on to both thoughts at once: her power *and* her smallness, each a comfort in its own way. She was only one girl, after all, in a world full of them.

Unfortunately, the armed soldiers around her at this precise moment were enemies of Arthur: Picts, led by their king, Nechtan; the sorceress Morgana, Arthur's half sister; and his nephew, Mordred the betrayer.

Guinevere had thought herself triumphant in sealing the city just before they arrived. But they had never been coming for the city. They had been coming for *her*. It was enough to drive her mad, but she was too tired for it. Guinevere half suspected the reason they had not dismounted and rested for the past twelve hours was to ensure that her nether regions were so painful that she would not try to escape. She had lost feeling in her toes, and her spine ached from sitting as straight as possible so as not to lean back against Mordred.

The least they could have done is give her a horse instead of forcing her to ride with him.

She had no idea how many leagues they had covered, but it was certainly more than she had ever traveled in a single stretch. Their pace was hurried without being frantic. The Picts were practiced soldiers. They were not going to risk their horses' health, but their horses had been trained to do exactly this.

Camelot falling farther and farther behind them as they rode into the night worried Guinevere less than the fact that they were galloping in the opposite direction of her goal. Merlin's cave would take her so much longer to reach now. She had planned on walking straight there, figuring out a way to free him from the Lady of the Lake's trap, and demanding answers about who she was. So she could finally know. If she could only know that, everything else would make sense. Would be easier. She was certain of it.

She focused on the cave, because that was less painful to think about than Camelot. About how she had left it. About who she had left.

The image of Lancelot on her knees behind the magical barrier they had created to keep armies out—but Lancelot in—lingered in Guinevere's mind like a wound. Guinevere knew what it meant to be denied crucial information. To be manipulated into a course of action without the freedom to decide. And she had done exactly that to Lancelot, not telling her brave knight until it was too late that Lancelot would be inside the city's shield, and Guinevere outside it.

It had been cruel, and unfair, and a betrayal of the trust Lancelot had always given her.

So she tried her best to not think about it. Fortunately, between the enemy soldiers and Mordred and this wretched, endless ride adding to the already long walk between her and Merlin's cave, she had an abundance of distractions.

At last, with dawn stretching pink and terrible across the sky, Mordred called out, "The horses need to rest."

It was the first time he had spoken the entire journey. The first time he had spoken since he had arrived at Camelot, begged her not to lose faith in him, and then announced he had successfully kidnapped the queen. Other than his chest at her back and his arms around her holding the reins, their only interaction was when he periodically passed her a canteen to drink from.

As soon as Mordred declared the horses needed to rest, word spread along the traveling party. Guinevere estimated there were two or three hundred soldiers. She slipped a hand into her pouch. All this long journey, she had tied knot after knot in her mind, from the most innocuous to the most vicious. It was time to choose.

A shudder rippled through her. She knew what she had to do. She would need her iron thread, and she would need blood, and it would be the worst knot she had ever tied. Worse than the protection she had placed in the river above Camelot that would kill anyone who ventured past it with intent to do her harm. Worse even than what she had done to Sir Bors, reaching into his mind and manipulating his memories. Perhaps not worse than what she had done to King Mark, destroying his mind but leaving his body, but certainly an evil enough magic that it would haunt her the rest of her days.

She was going to tie a death knot, loop it around herself so that any living creature that touched her would immediately die. And then she would walk out of the camp. It would not matter if they followed her all the way to Merlin's cave, because no one could touch her. The knot would mean she could not take a horse, but after twelve hours on one, that was almost a blessing.

She had to get away from Mordred first, though. Someone would touch her, doubtless, before they believed her threat. But it could not be Mordred. Not Mordred. It had to be someone whose name and face she did not know. A soldier sacrificed to a conflict Guinevere had not started.

A person, both small and infinite, ended because Guinevere valued herself more.

How did Arthur do this? How did he make these decisions? Her stomach churned, gnawing at its own emptiness. She squeezed her eyes closed. She could do this. She would do this.

Mordred's fingers circled her wrist, his grip gentle but insistent as he pulled her hand out of the pouch. He detached the pouch from her belt and tossed it to a tall, elegantly cloaked woman. His mother, Morgana. She caught it neatly and tucked it into her own bag.

Guinevere did not know whether she was about to cry out of frustration and disappointment or relief. Mordred had taken the choice from her. No one would die at her hand today. She would figure out another means of escape, hopefully one with a less desperate cost.

Feeling blurry with exhaustion, she watched as a camp appeared around them with practiced efficiency. Soldiers laughed and called to each other while they worked. Then everyone stilled as King Nechtan rode past them. He slowed, fixing eyes that had possibly once been wide and kind on Guinevere. Whatever they had been was hidden beneath bushy eyebrows and a permanent glower. He would have been intimidating even without the fur mantle he wore around his shoulders that shuddered with black moths. Guinevere knew that each moth carried a bit of the Dark Queen inside it. A constant reminder of whom King Nechtan was working with, or for. It was hard to say which with the Dark Queen.

One moth rode on his earlobe like an ornament. Nechtan bent his head toward it, his gaze turning distant and unfocused, before snapping back to Guinevere with an almost physical force. She sighed with relief when he turned to Mordred. It was not only the presence of King Nechtan but also the knowledge that anything he did or said was not him alone. The Pict king and the Dark Queen were each a formidable enemy on their own, and now Guinevere had to contend with them both.

Nechtan said something in his language. Guinevere did not understand, but she did not need to. The way he spoke made it clear that Mordred was in trouble. If she were in higher spirits, she would tease him. As it was, she was grateful that King Nechtan continued riding past, his head bent once more toward the whispering wings of his passengers and the queen they were part of.

Mordred dismounted, then held up his hands to help Guinevere down. She deliberately threw her leg over the opposite side of the horse and slid off. But she had not accounted for how numb her legs would be after a ride that long. As soon as her feet hit the ground, her knees buckled and she fell gracelessly on her sore backside.

A woman laughed nearby. Guinevere looked up to see one of the Pictish soldiers—they were all dressed alike in leather and fur—hold out a hand. The woman who laughed was a *soldier*.

Guinevere took the offered hand and was pulled swiftly and unceremoniously to her feet.

"Your king should ride you more often." The woman winked. A bold blue cloth was wrapped around her head, and her face had freckles that put Guinevere's to shame. Her pale blue eyes were framed by nearly white eyelashes and eyebrows that were tinged with orange. She had two axes strapped to her back, and a belt full of knives.

"*Fina.* Enough." Another woman, taller than the first by a few inches with almost the same face and even more weapons, shoved Fina's shoulder. She looked down at Guinevere without curiosity, her expression cooler than even the icy blue of her eyes. "I am Nectudad. Most of the soldiers do not speak your language, so trying to speak to them will be a waste of energy."

"I learned your language to marry your husband." Fina grinned. She had a gap between her front teeth that made her smile seem even larger and happier. Guinevere did not know whether she was expected to apologize for marrying Arthur, but Fina smiled even bigger. "Lucky for him I did not. I do not think he would have survived me."

Guinevere's eyes narrowed. "Arthur is the strongest man I have ever known."

"I did not mean in combat. I meant in bed. Not if he prefers delicate morsels like you."

Mordred appeared next to Guinevere. "Oh, good, you have met the princesses." He bowed deeply. "They make princesses very differently in the north."

Even Nectudad smiled at that, a more reserved reaction than Fina's brash laugh, which was so loud the horse next to Guinevere startled, stamping its hooves. Mordred reached out a hand and put it on the horse's neck. The animal calmed immediately.

"My father wants to see you, fairyson," Nectudad said. "He has questions about how you came to join our party."

Morgana appeared again with a sweep of her black cloak. She looked none the worse for wear, even after such a grueling journey. Her hair, black with streaks of silver like metal woven through it, was perfectly plaited, and her eyes, a darker and older green than Mordred's, betrayed no weariness. "Of course. We have much to discuss with him."

Morgana held the two stones—the ones with which Guinevere had done blood magic, the ones that had failed to give her enough warning of Morgana's return to be of any use—in her hand. So she had discovered the stone hidden in Guinevere's pouch, and its mate.

How long ago had Morgana discovered the secret stone? Had she only realized what it was when she saw the same rock in Guinevere's bag, or had she kept it to warn Guinevere of the approaching army? Guinevere could ask, but how could she ever trust an answer from the woman who had disguised herself as Lily's maid, infiltrated Camelot, and tried to make Guinevere leave with her?

But then again, Morgana had had ample time to hurt Guinevere, or Lily, or even Arthur. None of them had suspected her. Even after Morgana had given Guinevere a potion to make her tell the truth, Guinevere had not feared her. She had felt compassion, sorrow for her losses, and confusion about what Morgana really wanted.

None of those feelings were likely to change soon. Particularly the confusion.

"Come, Mordred," Morgana said, her face inscrutable. "Fina, Nectudad, will you see our guest fed and settled? And watch her hands."

Fina raised a dubious eyebrow. "I should be afraid of this slip?"

"Make sure she does not sew or tie knots in anything. Bind her hands before she goes to sleep."

"Southerners," Fina muttered, shaking her head. "I do not understand you. Well, come along, Slip." She put her arm around Guinevere, forcefully guiding her. Guinevere looked over her shoulder. Mordred was watching, concern shaping his brows, but then he turned and followed his mother.

Mordred and Morgana were not her allies. She could not trust anything they did or said. But at least they were familiar. Nothing else here was. All around her, soldiers—men and women both—were bustling about. She could not understand anything they said. Even the scents of the meals being cooked over fires were unfamiliar.

Her despair must have shown on her face. Nectudad patted her shoulder roughly as they stopped outside a hide-covered tent in the center of camp. "We have no quarrel with you. Only with your king."

"And with our new queen," Fina grumbled.

Nectudad shot her a narrow-eyed warning, hissing softly.

Fina straightened, grinning once more. "And you have no need to worry about your virtue. Unless you want me to relieve you of some of it, in which case you can tell your king exactly what he missed. But you will never want to go back to him after tasting me, so be certain before you ask."

"Fina." Nectudad said the name like an exasperated sigh.

"What? She looks too tense. I am offering solutions, being a good caretaker."

"Go get food." Nectudad shoved Fina in the direction of the nearest campfire and then turned back to Guinevere. She lowered her voice so only Guinevere could hear. It was clear and calm as a lake on a windless afternoon. "I will protect you because I need you. But if you do anything that threatens my father or if you try to escape, I will break both your legs and all your fingers. Do you understand? Nod if you understand."

Guinevere nodded, her throat tight. She understood perfectly well. She had left Camelot to figure out who she was. She had left Arthur, Lancelot, Brangien and Dindrane and Lily, everyone who loved her. She had left behind the castle and the crown. Now she was surrounded by enemies. She had no allies, no one she could truly trust. Only herself. But that would have to be enough for now. With or without Merlin, she *would* discover her past.

Preferably with all her limbs intact.